BROWN GIRLS

John Wesley Ireland

*To my beautiful daughter Brooke
All my love
Dad*

John W Ireland

PublishAmerica
Baltimore

© 2004 by John Wesley Ireland.
All rights reserved. No part of this book may be reproduced, stored in a retrieval system or transmitted in any form or by any means without the prior written permission of the publishers, except by a reviewer who may quote brief passages in a review to be printed in a newspaper, magazine or journal.

First printing

Cover photo by Hinoi Henry, courtesy of Elijah Communications Ltd. Back cover photo by Katrina E. Scott.

ISBN: 1-4137-3231-3
PUBLISHED BY PUBLISHAMERICA, LLLP
www.publishamerica.com
Baltimore

Printed in the United States of America

For my wife Heather.
Without her love and inspiration, this book would not have been possible.

My heartfelt thanks to George Pitt and Jeane Matenga, Glen Mills and Kim Holland, Brenda Anderson, Jackie Davis, Moana Vaevae, Tetini Pekepo, Pasha Carruthers, Alicia Ika, and my special muses: Maeva Arnold, Lena Wong, Tina Kae, Helani Kapi, Michelle Chaloner, Maryanne Short and Kriszara Hoff.

This book is a work of fiction. Names, characters, places and incidents are either the product of the author's imagination or are used fictitiously, and any resemblance to actual persons, living or dead, events, or locales is entirely coincidental.

Things happen on islands.
— NICK SMITH

WEDNESDAY

ONE

They say that three types of people wash up in the Cook Islands: missionaries, mercenaries and misfits. As Jack Nolan adjusted his digital camera, he idly speculated which category would best describe the naked man floating face down in the swimming pool of the Rarotonga Outrigger Villas.

Jack nodded to the young policeman standing on the pool deck. Jimmy Tauranga's uniform—white shirt with epaulettes that matched the navy blue of his shorts—was crisp and pressed despite the mid-afternoon heat. The tattooed arms protruding from the shirt's short sleeves were cabled with muscles.

"Hey, Jimmy."

"Kia orana, Jack." Jimmy made a show of looking at his watch. "That didn't take long."

Jack smiled. "Someone from the Outrigger phoned the paper," he said.

"Lloyd Dempster hoping to make the *Tribune's* next edition, eh?"

"That's the idea." Jack knelt by the pool, lifted the camera to his eye, and began snapping images. The body drifted. Jimmy hooked his black uniform shoe around the corpse's arm, toeing it back into position.

"Thanks, mate," Jack said. "Any idea who he is?"

Jimmy shrugged. "He's papa'a," he said. "A white man. No clothes, so no ID. The maintenance man found him when he came back to clean the pool. The manager's calling in all his registration clerks to see if anyone recognizes him as a guest."

Jack switched his camera to playback mode. Using the LCD display screen, he scrolled through the images he'd just captured. Satisfied that he had something Lloyd Dempster, the editor of the *Island Tribune,* could use, Jack turned his attention back to the dead man.

He'd grown fatalistic about death during the five years since he had arrived from Canada. Perhaps it was the island way rubbing off on him, how the locals wasted little time contemplating the vagaries of existence. You're born, you die. To worry about what fell in between was to introduce needless complications into the equation. A loving companion, a healthy sex life, and friends to buy you the occasional drink; anything else bordered on excess.

Jack looked away from the pool, away from the body. He gazed instead at Rarotonga's interior mountains. It had rained that morning and steam still rose from their jungle-clad flanks like thin smoke. In the distance he could hear the surf hurling itself against the coral reef's protective battlement.

This is why people come to the Cook Islands, he thought. To sample paradise, South Pacific-style. To shed the scaly corporate skin of civilization.

What they didn't come here to do was die.

Jack's eyes returned to the pool.

And if they did end up flying home in a box, it was seldom as a result of drowning.

There was, in fact, an almost systematic predictability to death on the island. When it happened to tourists—especially those who could be slotted into the overweight, overage, over-indulgent categories—it was inevitably due to the lethal combination of too many umbrella drinks and too much heat. The locals died mainly on the road—drunk, driving with a drunk, hit by a drunk—or due to the inherent ravages of a poor diet. As it passed through the Cook Islands, the road to eternity was paved with salted grease.

Murders were rare and, when they did occur, were often committed by a woman who had grown weary of being her partner's punching bag.

And then there was Willie Laofia. The local man had been found sprawled in a taro patch one gun-metal-hot afternoon. Cause of death was sudden loss of penis. The severed member had been rammed down his throat.

He'd been caught diddling kids. Or so the coconut wireless said. Tried, convicted and summarily dealt with by island justice during the dark of the moon. Or so the coconut wireless said.

Jack still shuddered at the image. That had been some nasty business indeed.

"This one still got his pane?" he asked.

Jimmy shrugged again. "I haven't turned him over, but I'm guessing there would be blood in the water if he'd been cut up. Only marks I can see from here are some sort of bruising on the top of his shoulders."

Jack nodded and lifted his camera again. "One for the locker room?"

The constable squatted on his haunches, gingerly pulled the body closer to the edge, and put on his best professional face. Jack focused.

"Kia matakite!" a man bellowed from behind him. "Be careful!"

"Hello, Karl," Jack said without turning.

"It's Chief Inspector Lamu to you." A large uniformed man brushed past Jack. Rum and garlic followed in his wake.

Lamu grunted as he slowly lowered to one knee at the pool edge. A Cook Islander of mixed and dubious heritage, the man was obviously physically unfit for the exertions of the job. But a blast-furnace demeanor and family connections in government circles allowed Lamu to graze in peace at the Ocean Beach Resort's buffet tables.

Fortunately for the country's reputation, and the hordes of visitors whose spending habits fueled the economy, Lamu was a dutiful cop. What he lacked in imagination, he made up for with an obstinate determination. You did not want to mess up in the Cook Islands, unless of course you somehow relished the idea of Chief Inspector Karl Lamu's considerable weight descending on your imprudent head.

Lamu pulled a pen from his pocket and used it to poke the corpse. "What do we have here?"

Jimmy Tauranga consulted a notebook. "White male, approximately 45 to 50 years old. Found at 13:20 by the maintenance man. Manager rang the police at 13:23. I arrived on the scene at 13:31."

Lamu tried to stand. Failing on his first attempt, he waved an impatient hand at Jimmy. Lamu leaned heavily on his constable; their faces bulged purple with the strain. For one terrible second, Jack actually thought the two of them might tumble into the pool. On top of the corpse. He raised his camera in anticipation.

But Lamu managed to regain his balance, then quickly shook off Jimmy's hand. The effort had caused more sweat to smear his sweeping forehead. Jack noted that Lamu's uniform shirt, although sorely in need of a pressing, was still relatively dry. The Chief Inspector had obviously been indoors most of the day.

"Are there any other bruises or wounds, other than those I can see on his shoulders?" Lamu asked Jimmy. "Any distinguishing marks at all?"

"I haven't turned him over—"

"I guessed as much," Lamu snapped.

Jack winced at the growling. He knew Jimmy from the paddling crowd at Muri Lagoon. He was a good man and a fearsome competitor in the vaka. Jack felt embarrassed at having to watch Jimmy flinch under the brutish glare of his superior.

Lamu continued to snarl. "Ambulance been called?"

Jimmy cleared his throat and checked his notebook again. "At 13:39, sir."

"When the doctor arrives, have him officially pronounce." Lamu grunted again. "Then get the body out of the pool before it attracts the dogs."

Jack placed his camera in its bag. "Aren't you just a little bit curious who this guy is?"

Lamu strode away from the pool. "Probably just another drunk tourist who thought he was a fish." Lamu scowled at Jack as he passed. "And tell Dempster that if he prints that, I'll burn his house down."

"You think this was an accident?" Jack said to the broad expanse of Lamu's back. "What about those bruises?"

Lamu stopped. Turned slowly. His scowl deepened. His considerable brows gathered into a horizontal storm cloud as he stared at Jack.

"You've been watching too much *CSI*, my friend," Lamu said. "You should go back to writing books and leave police work to the professionals."

Jack bit off an angry retort. He had no desire to have Lamu's fury unleashed on him. He would be patient. Lamu had enemies in high places. He would stumble one day and Jack would be right there to record it.

Lamu waved a finger at Jimmy. "Take care of this, constable," he said. "I've got paperwork to attend to."

Yeah, right, Jack thought. The cardboard coasters at the Ocean Beach Resort were all the paper the Chief Inspector was likely to be shuffling this afternoon.

TWO

Jack's Toyota truck idled in the driveway of the Rarotonga Outrigger Villas. He looked left, then right along the Ara Tapu, the coastal road that circled the island's perimeter.

The Villas sat on the southwest edge of the island, between the districts of Vaimaanga and Arorangi. The *Tribune* office was in the principal town of Avarua, located almost dead centre of the north coast.

The advantage of going left and into Avarua was that Jack could download his camera to an office computer while passing along what information he had gleaned about the dead man directly to Lloyd Dempster. He could also pick up a few groceries for tea before he went home.

A right turn would take him to his house in Matavera, sitting on the coastline where it dropped its shoulder to the northeast. He could use his own equipment to empty the camera and then e-mail a photo and his notes to the newspaper.

He absently tapped the radio on while contemplating how much he really needed to endure both Lloyd Dempster and Karl Lamu in the same afternoon.

"—*listening to the Great and Wonderful Johno on Radio Raro. This is Teen Scene, the show where you tell us what to play. Hip-hop, rap, boy bands, ballads, techno: we've got 'em all."*

Perfect, Jack thought, *every genre of music that I detest.* He really did need to invest in a CD deck.

"You know the number, so ring us and request a song," the DJ babbled.

Jack was surprised to hear a familiar accent. The Great and Wonderful Johno was obviously a fellow Canadian. What the hell was he doing in the broadcast booth of the Cook Islands' national radio station?

"I can send it out to your best friends, your teammates, your school buddies, or even someone you looooove," Johno continued.

Jack groaned at the exaggerated way that final word was drawn out. Somebody had been a keen student at DJ school.

"Kia orana, Johno," a young girl said, her voice reedy from being filtered through the studio phone. *"It's Shaggy."*

"Hey, Shaggy. How's my special shop girl?"

"I'm doing fine, thanks. I'd like to make the next dedication to you

because you're da bomb."

Nice gig if you can get it, Jack thought. Play their music, let them talk on the radio, and the girlies will fall all over you. He wondered how old Johno really was; he didn't sound like a teenager.

"Ah, Shaggy, I bet you say that to all the boys. What would you like to hear?"

"I'm requesting your favorite song, Johno. You're My Mate by Right Said Fred."

"Thanks, Shaggy, I'll get that right on. And, speaking of mates, in the studio today is my lovely co-host Michelle Cha—"

A horn honked. Jack snapped out of his reverie, reached for the dash, and flicked the radio off.

"Jack, my friend!" A broad brown face garnished with a hedge of beard protruded from the driver's window of a converted all-terrain vehicle. "Are you sleeping at the wheel again?"

Jack smiled and waved. It was Captain Tai, the senior driver for Mountain Motor Tours. The company was a prime attraction for tourists who enjoyed the 4x4 excursions into the island's rugged interior, an area otherwise inaccessible unless you were in the mood for a good tramp.

Captain Tai was not only a wealth of information ("My only problem," he had once told Jack over a Cook's Lager in the Rocket Bar, "is that I know everything.") but he was also fearless when it came to challenging the rutted trails that twisted up from the coast into the rocky wilds.

Jack hopped out of his truck and crossed the road to clasp Captain Tai's hand. The tour driver was one of the most colorful characters in the country, a significant accomplishment considering the motley collection you'd find most nights exchanging lies at the Rocket Bar. His features were a deeper brown than most of the locals, his nose large and flat, and eyes so dark that the pupils were barely visible. His hair was wiry and jet-black, even after 60 years of being exposed to the South Pacific sun.

"I am a pureblood Cook Islander," he had bragged to Jack over that same beer at the Rocket Bar.

"Really?"

"Yes, Mr. Papa'a." Captain Tai's tone grew serious. "Between your bloody European missionaries, the US soldier boys on Aitutaki during the war, the Asian fishermen, the Kiwis and Aussies and all those other Pacific Islanders chasing our women around, the local blood has been sadly corrupted. They aren't too many of us true Cook Islanders left anymore."

"Other than close your borders, what can you do about it?"

"Exactly what I've been doing all along." Captain Tai winked at Jack over the mouth of his bottle. "I seek out purebred Cook Islands women."

"And?"

"And I have sex with as many of them as I can. It's my sworn duty to keep the gene pool pure and unpolluted."

"You really are a courageous captain."

"And a thirsty one. You want another beer?"

Captain Tai nodded past Jack in the direction of the Villas.

"Did you see the body?" he whispered, cutting a quick sideways glance at the passenger area in the back of his vehicle.

Jack didn't bother asking how Captain Tai could have learned so quickly about the dead man. News travels fast when your island is only 67 square kilometres in area. If you cheated on your wife before going home, odds were she had already burned all of your worldly belongings by the time you pulled into the driveway.

Jack looked into the back of the vehicle. A small group of tourists perched on the rows of seats attached to both sides of the truck's box. They were all papa'a, decked out in hiking shorts and lightweight shirts of varying hues and designs.

Their appearance didn't surprise Jack. What he did find unusual was that they were all middle-aged men. Not a wife or girlfriend to be seen. He turned back to Captain Tai.

"What's the deal with this bunch?"

Captain Tai shrugged. "Tourists," he said, and Jack detected the depth of weary resignation encapsulated by that single word.

"I'm not even sure how much English they speak," Captain Tai said, "because they haven't made a whole lot of noise. The good news is that they're all staying at the Breaker Point Lodges, so I only had to make one pickup."

He wiped a hairy forearm over his crinkled brow. A small shred of coconut peeked out from the rat's nest that clung to his chin. "The bad news is that I'm not really saving any petrol money."

"How's that?"

Captain Tai jabbed a thumb towards the back. "The big guy who does the talking said they're all here for some kind of a conference on worldwide education. So they had me drive by Avarua College before we left town.

That's not on the tour route, and it was slow going because the students were just being let out for the day. But I suppose that's all part of keeping the customers happy."

"The college, eh?" Jack glanced again at the passengers. They conversed in hushed tones, but fingers stabbing at wristwatches indicated that they were starting to question the delay. Jack easily picked out the bloke Captain Tai had mentioned. He was an imposing broad-shouldered man with short blond hair. A ragged scrap of bleached epidermis under one eye marred his flat Slavic face. It looked as if the drippings from a melting skin candle had splashed onto his cheek and hardened there.

"Mariko had a group from the same conference out this morning, and he said they asked him to drive by Titikaveka College," said Captain Tai. "I'm guessing part of the reason they're here is to inspect our school system."

He laughed. "Not that it taught me anything because I was born smart. That's the sign of a true Cook Islander."

He shook Jack's hand again, then coaxed the 4x4 into gear and rumbled off. Jack watched as the truck pulled away. Some of the men in the back stared at him blankly. For tourists in paradise, they didn't seem particularly happy. Must be a boring conference.

Jack pulled left out of the driveway. He would go into Avarua after all. It wasn't that much out of his way. Besides, it was a beautiful day for driving.

The November heat was intense, but Jack enjoyed its caress. It was January and February that he disliked, when the sun's scorching fingers were intensified by a soggy sheath of humidity. All you could do was drink plenty of fluids and try not to tackle anything strenuous. The locals had a saying for it: no hurries, no worries. It was advice best heeded.

But this was one of those designer days that postcards were invented for. The breeze funneling into the truck's cab brought with it the heady scents of gardenia, jasmine, plumeria and frangipani. Through gaps in the groves of coconut palms and casuarina to his left, Jack caught glimpses of the sun sparkling off the teal waters of the lagoon. The blossoms of the flamboyant trees added a crimson explosion to the visual palette.

Traffic was light and Jack took advantage of this to absorb the many wonders that never ceased to tantalize his senses. Rarotonga was a living, breathing kaleidoscope of sights, sounds and smells. You could look at the same scene a hundred times and think nothing of it. Then one day—maybe it was a trick of the light, or because a particularly good long black from

Sparky's Café had sharpened your brain—you suddenly noticed something that you'd never seen before.

It was one of the reasons why he would be quite content to live the rest of his life on this island.

He passed a dairy. Further on, a group of local girls huddled by the side of the road. There were five of them, all in their mid-teens, dressed in identical school uniforms of white blouses and chocolate-brown skirts. Two were barefoot; the others sported well-worn jandals. They were eating vanilla ice cream out of sugar cones as they talked. The contrast of the frozen white treat against their dark complexions twigged a professional reflex in Jack.

He applied the brakes and glided to the shoulder. He dug out his camera and screwed on a telephoto lens. Twisting in his seat, he leaned out the window, worked the camera's focus ring.

Too absorbed with their conversation to notice him, the girls continued to chatter animatedly, their words punctuated by frequent exclamation marks of laughter.

There were five girls in the group; Jack recognized two of them. The short, pretty one was Maeva Benning. Her grandfather, a rugged granite block of a Scotsman named Alex, had arrived on Rarotonga a middle-aged widower. Enraptured by the island's many attractions, he'd married a local woman and started a second family in his new home.

An ardent train enthusiast, Alex Benning used his connections in Europe to purchase a small steam locomotive and a flatbed car and had them shipped to the island. Not content to merely tinker with his new toy, Alex constructed a track. The line of metal rails and wooden sleepers eventually stretched for a kilometre across the family property. Every Saturday, tourists could ride the Raro Railroad and have their pictures taken aboard an honest-to-goodness, steam-belching train in the middle of a South Pacific jungle.

During his early days on the island, Jack had interviewed Alex Benning and sold stories about the Mad Engineer of Rarotonga to several travel magazines. In the process, he had watched Maeva grow up around the attraction, earning herself a lolly allowance by taking admissions and serving cold juice and train-shaped cookies to appreciative tourists after their ride.

Jack had heard that Alex was still hard at work on his pet project, even though he was now well past 70. Something about a track extension, according to the coconut wireless. He made a mental note to stop by and have a chat with the old man one of these days. Alex Benning was good company on a slow, lazy afternoon. Better yet, he shared Jack's proclivity for well-aged malt whiskey. There might even be some of Maeva's fresh-baked cookies available, if he was really lucky.

The second girl he knew only as Helani. He had seen her at the Catholic cathedral in Avarua where she helped Father Conlan conduct mass each Sunday morning. His appearances at the cathedral were rare—only Mother's Day and Christmas—and were really only a long-distance nod to his parents, who'd raised Jack and his brother Porter in an Irish Catholic household.

In an effort to become familiar with his neighbors in Matavera, he had initially attended the village's Cook Islands Christian Church. Now he was a member of the Rev. Albert Smail's flock at the Church of Christ's Blood.

It was the hymns that prompted Jack to endure long pants and a real shirt once a week. Cook Islanders have magnificent voices, and their harmony-laden hymnal singing is famous throughout the world. Even if you didn't understand a single word, the rich interweaving of voices raised to the Almighty, reverberating off the thick coral walls of the old churches, could still invigorate the spirit. Even one as dog-eared as Jack's.

Pink tongues darted as he stabbed at the shutter. Tiny eels emerged from moist caves and licked at the sticky sweet flow of melting ice cream as it dripped down the cones to pool on fingers. The girls had their thick black hair pulled into braids or buns on the back of their heads, revealing high, smooth foreheads. Their noses, some broad, others aquiline—revealing a European branch in the family tree—wrinkled and flared as they breathed in the hot air. White teeth flashed between full lips. Hibiscus blossoms were tucked jauntily behind ears.

Jack peered intently through the viewfinder. He felt a pang of guilt at invading the girls' privacy, but he was too intrigued by the non-verbal aspects of their conversation to put the camera away just yet. He had always been fascinated by how the locals could communicate with only a minimal use of words.

Instead they substituted fluttered eyelids or hoisted eyebrows. A flick of the head could convey an entire sentence; a nod was as good as a paragraph. A jut of the chin spoke volumes. It was a form of oral shorthand that Jack had dubbed 'face-talking.'

He fired off several more shots, then lowered the camera. He took one last look at the girls as he steered the truck back onto the road.

Polynesian women had never crossed Jack's radar before he arrived on Rarotonga. Then, it seemed, he was literally surrounded by tawny-skinned beauties. Like the kid locked overnight in the candy store, he found it impossible not to sample.

He loved the promise of mischief flickering about the edges of a coy grin. The glint of wickedness that occasionally rose to the surface from the luminous depths of huge dark eyes. He was intrigued by the kindness that was instantly bestowed upon strangers, himself included, and flattered by the attention he received everywhere he went. He found this affability just as attractive as the gleam of eager teeth or the fierce seductiveness implicit in the frenzied motions of the traditional dances.

Jack was considered somewhat of a prize in the early days—a papa'a with money—and he seldom lacked for company.

What Jack encountered in dim bedrooms, or on starlit beaches, were genies of desire waiting only for his touch to unleash them from tattooed vessels of savage sinew and ancient bone. He watched, mute with febrile appreciation, as hair, finally emancipated from the confinements of the cooling braid, gleamed like black oil in the candlelight. How coffee-colored nipples quivered into hard knots of pleasure as his tongue danced over them. The way taut bellies shivered under the whisper of his fingertips. The sex was frequent and unfettered and very, very loud.

And, for a couple hours at least—as his cheek rested lightly on the shapely swell of a thigh, and the sweat of exertion dried in the furnace of the night—Jack was allowed to forget that he no longer possessed the gift that had once defined him as a man.

THREE

WALNUT GROVE, 1996

"This is the best fuckin' book I've read in years!"

"I—"

"You're a genius, kid. Fuckin' A-1 grade genius."

"I—"

"I'm going to make both of us very rich, my fine young cannibal."

The words were coming in machine gun bursts. Jack could only press the phone to his ear and attempt to keep up. He had no idea who the man was, or what the hell he was talking about.

"Filthy rich. You hearing me? Hello? You still there?"

"Yes," Jack squeaked.

His younger brother Porter, who had brought the cordless phone down to his bedroom, stood in the doorway with a 'What's happening?' expression on his face. Jack shrugged and turned back to the verbal tornado whistling from the receiver.

"Excuse me," he finally managed to interject.

"—all the way to the top. What?"

"I'm sorry, but I didn't catch your name."

"I'm Ray Chimera. What, you nuts? Aren't you Jack Nolan?"

"Yes."

"And didn't you send your book—hang on, here it is—*Resurrection Waters*, to the Chimera Literary Agency?"

"Yes."

Jack was starting to understand. He turned to Porter, mimed a typing action and then flashed a thumbs-up. Porter whooped and sprinted upstairs.

"What was that?" Ray asked. "You livin' with Indians or something?"

"No, that was—"

"Where do you live, anyway? I got your cover letter around here somewhere."

"I'm in Walnut Grove."

"Walnut what? Where in the hell is that?"

"We're in British Columbia. Canada? Just outside Vancouver."

"Oh, OK, that I heard of," Ray said. "Now listen, buckaroo, you haven't sent your manuscript out to anybody else, have you?"

Jack gulped. "Yeah," he said, then quickly added, "a few."

"Judas priest!" Ray thundered down the line. "Rank amateurs, the fuckin' lot of them. Listen, kid. Kid?"

"I'm still here." Jack backed up until he felt the edge of his bed against his legs. He sat down, suddenly feeling very dizzy.

"OK, this is what you do," Ray Chimera continued. "I'm going to wire you a ticket to Los Angeles. Soon as it arrives, you fly straight down here, understand? Someone will pick you up at LAX. I'll get all the paperwork ready to sign. Let's make a shitload of money, shall we?"

Jack held the phone at arm's length and stared at it for a minute. He could still hear Ray's excited chirping, but his brain felt carbonated, unable to focus.

He heard a commotion in the doorway and looked up to see Porter and his mother hugging and grinning into each other's faces. *Oh my God*, Jack thought, *is this what I think it is?*

Had all those years of hard work and research and typing and rewriting and editing and doubting and abandoning hope and picking up his deflated writer's ego and dusting it off—of still living in his parents' basement even though he was 25 years old, for chrissakes—had all that finally paid off?

Oh. My. God.

"Mister?" His voice cracked as he returned to the phone.

"Yeah?"

"Do you really like my book?"

"Fuckin' A, kiddo. Fuckin' A."

And so the nightmare began.

FOUR

Lloyd Dempster was contemplating the motivation for Miss December to have her labia pierced when his office phone rang.

"Are you choking the moko again?"

"Hello, Sofia."

How is it that wives can be so goddamn psychic at times, Dempster wondered as Sofia began to drone into his ear. With his free hand, he refolded the magazine's centre pages, opened the top drawer of his desk, and carefully placed the magazine on top of last month's issue. He touched his forefinger to his lips, then placed it over the cover model's face.

"Yes, dear," he said absently as Sofia stopped to catch a breath.

Psychic, yes. All-seeing? Hardly. Sofia, it seemed, had never picked up on all those little birds that Dempster played with when he was supposed to be working late at the *Tribune* office. But, then again, maybe she didn't much care where his dick was, just as long as it wasn't anywhere near her. Bitch.

"Are you writing this down, Lloyd?" Shit, now he was in trouble.

"Uh, just grabbing a pen, dear."

"I know exactly what you're grabbing, you pervert," Sofia growled him. "Now get your hand out of your shorts and start taking notes. The French ambassador is going to be here and I want this party to be perfect."

"OK," Dempster said, casting his gaze to the ceiling as if to seek divine intervention. "I'm ready."

"Good. We'll start with some fresh tuna. Get some from that Roger fellow at the Rocket Bar. He seems to have good contacts with the local fishermen. And—"

Dempster looked out his office window and smiled. Divine intervention had arrived after all. A little late, but soon enough.

"Sofia? Darling? I have to go. Bye." Lloyd Dempster slammed the phone down and launched himself out of his chair.

"Do you have the first idea what a deadline is!"

If Jack had hoped to sneak quietly into the *Tribune* office, download his camera and be off without actually having to talk to Lloyd Dempster, he had sadly miscalculated. He had barely entered the office and nodded to the receptionist stationed at the front desk when an inner door flew open and Dempster was bellowing in his direction.

In Jack's opinion, Lloyd Dempster was an arsehole. Plain and simple. And a loud, bullying arsehole at that. Which explained why Jack had steadfastly refused to join *The Tribune's* permanent staff. He was quite content to snap off the occasional spot news photo whenever Jordan Baxter, the paper's full-time reporter, didn't have the time, and then e-mail it from the safety of his Matavera house. That way, Jack managed to darken Dempster's doorstep only when it was absolutely necessary.

Dempster was an Englishman, and his florid, fleshy face and stubby body spoke of ale-soaked evenings spent in neighborhood pubs with curious names. A librarian from Dorset, Dempster had always fancied himself something of a journalist. He was certainly more talented, in his estimation, than those hacks whose swill was printed in the newspapers that he filed each day.

Twenty years earlier, during a trip to Rarotonga with Sofia, Dempster had been in the right place at the right time when a political power struggle put the government-funded newspaper, a twice-weekly disaster called the *Cook Islands Guardian*, in jeopardy of folding.

Dempster had boldly marched into the *Guardian* office, spewed an outrageous fabrication about having just sold his chain of community newspapers at home, and how he would be the perfect man to take over the floundering publication and turn it around. The government agency in charge of printing *The Guardian* hadn't even bothered checking Dempster's references. It had even agreed to provide a subsidy for the first five years of operation.

And just like that, Lloyd Dempster—Dorset librarian, frustrated journalist—owned his own newspaper, complete with printing press and an established circulation infrastructure.

He was now the emperor of hyphenates: owner-publisher-editor-writer-salesman. There had even been mornings when he had driven the circular coastal road to deliver the damn thing.

Jack did have to give Dempster credit for not only possessing balls but for having the audacity to place them on the chopping block. And he begrudgingly noted that the new daily publication, now christened the *Island Tribune*, had consistently made money. Of course it could hardly not turn a profit, considering that it was the only newspaper in the country. Dempster could charge outrageous prices for ads and not have to worry that business owners would simply march across the street to a cheaper competitor.

He further increased his profit margins by keeping the *Tribune's* size to a minimum. Local news dominated the first three pages, and sports occupied the final two. The pages in-between were crammed with as many ads as Dempster and his two-man sales team could sell. Whatever editorial space survived was filled with press releases, international news downloaded from Internet wire services, and a trio of columnists, only one of whom, a local mama who called herself Aunty Pati, actually lived in the Cook Islands.

But, if you wanted to read about Rarotonga, as opposed to listening to Radio Raro or watching the country's only TV station, you slapped down a dollar at your favorite dairy and took home the *Island Tribune*. It was the sort of all-powerful media empire that a Hearst or a Murdoch would have appreciated. Too bad, then, that Lloyd Dempster was such a pernicious prick.

Dempster waved Jack over.

"I—" Jack began.

"Yeah, yeah, whatever," Dempster interrupted Jack's attempt at covering his arse. "What are you doing tomorrow night?"

"I—"

"Good, then you can take pictures at a party I'm throwing for the French ambassador," Dempster charged on. "There's going to be a great assortment of high-and-mighty wankers there and I want a photo page of them eating my famous barbecued tuna."

"Fine," Jack said. "I'll be there."

It wasn't a tough decision to make: party equaled free booze. And the Dempsters did own a spa pool. Nothing like a good hot soak at the end of a long workday.

"Now let's go see what you've got for me." Dempster led Jack down a short hallway and through a door that opened into a huge area dominated by an ancient printing press. Two local men tended the clanking device as it spat out color flyers advertising a supermarket's weekend sale of tomato sauce and fresh taro. Jack winced at the deafening noise.

Sitting to one side of the metal monstrosity, a man and a woman worked at computers perched on decrepit wooden desks.

The man glanced up from his monitor and smiled. Jordan Baxter looked as smarmy as ever. The unventilated room was an oven, but Baxter seemed unperturbed by the intense heat. He wore a white, long-sleeved shirt and a conservative tie tucked tight under his chin. His dress pants were woollen and his feet were clad in brown leather shoes, carefully polished each morning before breakfast.

His hair was thinning and his narrow features culminated in a fading chin. His face was oddly wan for someone who had grown up in the tropics, and was only redeemed by a pencil-thin mustache. This carefully groomed slash of hair always gave Jack pause. He marveled at the patience it must take to shave so precisely. Jack hated shaving. His hack-and-whack approach often left ghastly cuts, to be covered by even ghastlier pieces of tissue to staunch the bleeding.

Jack knew that Jordan Baxter fancied himself rather the cultured gentleman. A dandy of sorts who, in another time and place, would be attired in an ice cream suit and drinking rum punches while discussing great literature and stars of the silent screen.

Jack also knew that Baxter wouldn't recognize good journalism if it reared up and bit him. While he did demonstrate a talent for typing, Baxter had a noxious habit of manipulating the various aspects of a story. A scoundrel with a tape recorder, he was infamous throughout the country's 15 islands for the mismanagement of direct quotes. When he wasn't making them up entirely, that is.

"Why let the facts get in the way of a good story?" was his retort whenever Jack complained about an article that bore no resemblance whatsoever to the event Baxter had been assigned to. The scary thing was that he wasn't being flippant; he actually believed the nonsense he was spouting. It was painfully obvious that Jordan Baxter and integrity had yet to be formally introduced.

Under any other circumstance—in other words, had he worked for a real newspaper—Jordan Baxter wouldn't have survived his first day on the job. But this was the *Island Tribune*, after all. And this was the Cook Islands, where locals often considered it impolite to complain. Instead, to avoid having their reputations blemished by Baxter's dubious prose, politicians had resorted to submitting their own press releases, or insisted on talking directly to Lloyd Dempster.

Some, knowing Jack's literary background, implored him to put his camera away and show the country what a real wordsmith looked like. But he had consistently turned a deaf ear to these pleas. He, of all people, knew the power of the pen, of how it could destroy as well as create.

No, he would leave the scribbling to the likes of Jordan Baxter who, at the very least, possessed the one quality that endeared him most to Lloyd Dempster: he worked cheap. It was all bottom line at the *Island Tribune*,

Baxter's journalistic misadventures be damned. No consideration was given as to how badly this reflected on the newspaper's other employees, Jack Nolan included.

Dempster gestured at the men operating the press and the machine shuddered into silence.

"The prodigal photographer returns," Baxter said. "Did you get a picture for us?"

"Shut your pie hole, Jordan," Dempster snarled, "and let me ask the questions around here." He turned to Jack. "Did you get a picture for us?"

Jack glanced at the woman. Mona Vaevae rolled her eyes at Dempster's performance. Mona was an absolute genius when it came to newspaper layout. If *The Tribune* had one saving grace, it was that it looked good on the page, thanks to Mona's considerable skills with a computer.

She was arguably the sanest person in the entire operation and certainly the only one in the building whom Jack would admit to liking.

"There's a couple you can choose from," Jack said, handing his camera to Mona. She plugged it into a USB cable snaking from the back of her computer's tower. "All horizontal, however."

Dempster fluttered his hand derisively and Jack wondered, not for the first time, if the man actually knew the difference between horizontal and vertical. There had been more times than Jack cared to remember where his photos had been cropped to hell so they would fit a hole on the page they were not originally framed for. It was times like those when he was secretly pleased that Dempster refused to print photo credits.

It took several minutes for the images to be transferred from Jack's camera to Mona's computer. Jack used the time to relate what little information he had been able to gather at the Rarotonga Outrigger Villas.

"I'm way ahead of you, bro," Baxter announced with an imperious smile. "My sources have already called me with details."

Jordan Baxter's contacts. That was another bone of contention with those who had to endure having their names dragged through the mud of *The Tribune's* front page. Baxter insisted that he had at least one informant in every village on the island, and several scattered throughout the various government agencies. He referred to them as 'unnamed sources.'

He said it was to protect the identity of those who desired to see justice done, democracy protected and evildoers punished. As far as Jack was concerned, these anonymous do-gooders were as fictional as everything else the man wrote.

Baxter waved his notebook and read from it with artificial inflection. "The deceased is one Gert Junger, a German national staying at the Breaker Point Lodges."

"Breaker Point Lodges? Then what was he doing in the Outrigger's pool?" Jack asked.

Baxter gave Jack a look reserved for slow children. "How would I know? Does it matter?"

Not to a hack like you, Jack thought.

"Anything else?" asked Dempster.

Baxter returned to his notes. "Not much. Only that he was here for some sort of educational conference."

Jack's eyebrow flinched. Educational conference? He made a mental note to ask Captain Tai if any of the passengers on his tour had mentioned a missing colleague.

"Here we go," Mona announced. She pointed at her monitor.

Jack leaned in to look at the row of images. He had already viewed them on his camera's screen, but the photos were now displayed in a larger format and he could pick out more details.

"Jesus Christ!" Dempster huffed over Jack's shoulder. "That all you got? Jimmy Tauranga and a big pink blob floating in the water?"

"No Pulitzer this time," Jack muttered. "Sorry."

"Don't be sorry," Dempster said. "Just try to do a better job."

"What do you want?" Jack said, his tone dangerously close to exasperation. "Karl Lamu hadn't shown up yet so we couldn't touch anything. And that pink blob, as you call it, is some poor bugger's mortal remains."

"I can't see his face," Dempster whined. "And there isn't any blood."

Jack turned slowly and indicated the printing press. "You make a lot of money off those flyers, Lloyd?"

"They're my bread and butter some weeks. Why?"

"Do you really want blood and gore on page one?" Jack spoke in measured tones as if it were he who now conversed with a slow learner. "I see that staring out at me on the dairy counter, I'm thinking, 'I don't want to look at that while I'm having breakfast.' So I don't buy it, I don't see the flyer, Food Village doesn't get my business, and next time they think twice about advertising in *The Tribune*. Are you getting any of this?"

"Don't patronize me," Dempster snapped, his ruddy cheeks glowing darker as the fuse of his temper danced perilously close to the flame. Jack saw Mona's head hunker tighter into her shoulders. She was making herself a smaller target.

"I was merely inquiring," Dempster continued in a forced cadence, "if, experienced professional that I pay you to be, you might have thought to take another photo from a different angle."

Dempster looked back at the screen, reached in past Mona, and tapped a fingernail on the second photo from the left. "This one appears to be in focus," he said, not bothering to cloak the insult in subtlety. "Blow the shit out of it and," he glanced at his watch, "make it fast. I got a paper to put out tonight."

He stomped away as Mona worked her keyboard. Baxter returned to his desk and began rooting through the deadfall covering its surface. Ignoring him, Jack watched as his photo grew larger on the screen.

Mona made one final adjustment and sat back to admire her handiwork. "Any bigger and the pixels will blow out," she said.

Jack didn't answer. He was staring closely at the screen.

"You see that?" he pointed.

"It's a scratch," Mona said. "I tell you to replace that old skylight filter every time you're in here."

"I can see the scratch," he said. "But that's not what I'm talking about."

"You've lost me."

"Look. There, on the ankle."

"It's a blotch of some kind," Mona said. "A birthmark maybe. Didn't you notice that when you were there?"

Jack straightened up. "Hurricane Lamu blew in almost as soon as I arrived. Dempster won't want to hear it, but I was lucky to get the shots I did. I was probably contaminating the crime scene being that close."

"Crime scene?" Mona looked up, her forehead made jagged by puzzlement. "I thought this was an accident. I'm surprised Lloyd's even bothering with this photo."

"What? Right," Jack said, momentarily flustered by Mona's eager questions. "I was just thinking out loud. Listen, can you enhance that area a bit more?"

"I'll try." Mona attacked her keyboard again. A black outline appeared on the screen and she used the arrow keys to move it onto the section of the photo that Jack had indicated. She began tapping a key. The image inside the black lines grew larger. By the time it filled the screen, however, it was little more than a blur of color. Mona worked another key and the image became progressively smaller.

She stopped. "That's as big as I can make it before it becomes pixilated."

"Sweet as." Jack studied the image: a man's leg, covered in coarse hair. Just above the anklebone, made fuzzy by magnification, was an illustration done in black and red.

"It's not a birthmark," he said. "It's a tattoo."

"You're right," said Mona. "Good eye, for a photographer. What do you make of it?"

Jack stepped back and contemplated the image from a distance. "It's an animal of some kind. A dog maybe."

"That's one ugly—"

"Got it!" Jordan Baxter announced loudly. "What do you think?"

Jack reluctantly took his eyes off the monitor and looked over. Baxter waved a magazine he had just exhumed from his desk and thrust it into Jack's hand.

It was the latest edition of *Surfie Chicks*. The cover featured a young Polynesian woman, her fluorescent green swimsuit accentuating a body that was seal-sleek. She clutched a yellow surfboard tightly to one hip. A gentle surf swirled around her ankles. Behind her, small white clouds tacked across a sky that was painfully blue. Her dark hair hung in wet curls, framing a face that was nearly expressionless as she stared into the camera. A slight uplifting of her chin was the only indication that there was some attitude behind the frozen exterior.

Jack waved the magazine. "Yes? And?"

"Take another look," Baxter urged.

Jack shook his head and turned back to the surfer. She was undeniably attractive. And she was definitely a disciple of the three T's of cover art: teeth, tits, thong.

"The photo's been airbrushed," was all Jack could think to say. Seeing the look of exasperation on Baxter's face, he read the cover copy. "'Chaka Tane: Rapa Nui's Surfing Siren.' Am I supposed to be impressed?"

Baxter snatched the magazine back and held it up with two hands, as if displaying a priceless family heirloom. "What do you think of her?"

Jack looked at Mona. "Maybe this is a test to see if you're gay or not," she chuckled.

"What?" Baxter frowned as he processed her words. "No, no, no," he finally said. "What I'm trying to do here is introduce you to my latest girlfriend."

Jack's laugh was harsher than he'd meant it to be, but Baxter's announcement had caught him by surprise. The idea of the reporter having anything to do with a woman the likes of Chaka Tane was just too absurd to even contemplate.

Baxter dropped the magazine on his desk in disgust. "Sure, laugh at me now, Jackie boy. But we'll see who's laughing tomorrow night when I bring her to Mr. Dempster's party."

"She's surfing here?" Mona frowned.

"She's doing more than surfing." Baxter grinned. Jack saw the smug bastard's chest swell under his shirt. "She's hosting a documentary on the best surfing spots in the South Pacific. She's brought a film crew with her from Tahiti."

"But the surfing here isn't that great," Mona said. "You have to be careful that the reef doesn't cut you to shreds."

"Well, it's no Banzai Pipeline, but Chaka says she's still getting some sweet footage."

Baxter slammed down into his chair to signal that the conversation was over.

"Now the only thing I want to hear is the sound of fingers typing," he said to Mona. "We've got a paper to publish and I just happen to have the perfect story for the front page."

He made a dismissive gesture. "Goodbye, Jack."

FIVE

LOS ANGELES, 1997

"Hello, Jack!"

Disco was dead and buried. Someone had forgotten to tell Ray Chimera.

Jack stood just inside the doorway of the Revelation Room in L.A.'s ubertrendy Magellan Royale Hotel. He watched as Ray scurried towards him. Even if I was to invent such a character, Jack thought, no one would believe it.

His agent's leisure suit was a powder-blue horror. Under the jacket, a wide-collared paisley shirt screamed. A multitude of gold chains glittered amidst the matted hair on Ray's chest. Clunky rings flashed in the light as the agent's soft, damp hands fluttered. His hair was too black and had been slicked back with industrial-strength gel. Brown-tinted sunglasses perched on the tip of his long, thin nose.

A pair of cream-colored platform shoes completed the image, but they still managed to only elevate the top of Ray's lubed head to the level of Jack's chin.

Ray intercepted a waitress bearing a silver tray filled with champagne glasses. The woman was dressed in a toga and very little else. Ray grabbed two glasses and handed one to Jack. Ray took a long swallow, smacked his lips loudly in appreciation, and waved an arm around the interior of the room.

"Whaddya think, kiddo? Pretty smooth, huh?"

Jack stared into the Revelation Room. It was ostentatious. It was gaudy. It was definitely not smooth.

It certainly wasn't what he'd expected when Ray announced that he was throwing a book launch party for *Resurrection Waters* and insisted that Jack return to California immediately.

During his initial visit with Ray in Los Angeles, Jack had been cloistered in a hotel room for several weeks while a professional editor doctored his novel. Later, while Jack ploughed through several drafts, Ray shopped the manuscript to every publishing house where he had a connection. Even after Ray convinced a senior editor at William Burch & Sons that *Resurrection Waters* had bestseller written all over it, there still had been three more flights south.

Jack was barely home from his fourth trip to the US when the call came. Ray had organized a book launch. Jack was being summoned.

"The book's not even printed yet," Jack said, as the soup his mother had made him for lunch grew cold on the table. "How can you launch something that doesn't exist?"

"Details, details." Ray was speaking on the car phone in his BMW. "Trust me, kid, most of the people who'll be there will never read the book anyway. I'm not even sure if they can read. They're professional schmoozers. All they're interested in is the free food and booze. But they know people who know people who can do great things for us. Anyone interested in actually reading the book will see it at the galley stage."

Ray adjusted his car's air conditioning. "We don't actually need a book to host a book-launching party. It's all in the marketing, bucko, which is why I'm constantly reminding you how lucky you are to have Ray Chimera on your side."

"I understand," Jack said. "It's just that I've been talking to other writers—"

"Whoa, whoa, whoa. You did *what*?" Ray was pissed.

Jack winced. "I was just looking for a little advice from other people in the business. I thought it might help."

Ray vented his frustration by thumping on the Beamer's horn.

"You *thought*?" Ray said. "You don't think, Jack. That's my job. All you have to do, now that I've weaned you off that armpit of a bookstore, is write. And then write some more. Are we clear on this?"

Ray's voice was frost. Jack shivered despite the heat of the kitchen.

His agent was right, of course. Jack had won the literary equivalent of the lottery. It did seem impudent to gnaw at the one hand that had agreed to feed him. As a rule, first-time novelists did not meet the likes of Ray Chimera, unless it was during a meaningless conversation at a writers' conference.

Ray's comment about Jack's job had been cruel, but only because it contained the sting of truth. Jack had started working at The Last Page bookstore while he was still in high school. Six years later, he was the oldest employee—the manager was a mere lad of 23—at the outlet.

In an ordered world, he would not be at the store. He would not be wearing the same blue formless, unisex shirt. He would not be serving clueless shoppers who could never seem to remember a title or an author but only that the book they so desperately needed was about a dog, or had a green cover.

In an ordered world, he would have moved on to another job, one that paid a decent wage, with a good pension plan and a benefits package. Or, if he insisted on remaining loyal to the Last Page chain, he would have at least worked his way up the food chain to management.

But Jack had done none of those things.

Instead, he used those six years to indulge the one true passion that had engulfed him since he had first picked up a pencil. Jack Nolan wanted to be a writer. Jack Nolan wanted to be a *published* writer.

Jack regarded his job as an opportunity to conduct his own research while still earning a paycheque. The Last Page had a staff lending library and he was its most devoted partaker.

While his fellow employees flipped mindlessly through magazines dedicated to fashion or entertainment or sports, Jack would pull up a chair at the Planet Bean coffee shop tucked against the store's back wall, crack open the latest bestseller, and devour it page by page.

He kept a notebook at his elbow and scribbled down observations as he read. How the writer introduced characters: were they were believable; did they inspire emotion in the reader? Did the dialogue sound realistic? Was the story plausible or at least digestible? Were descriptions so dense that the reader tuned out? Or so lightweight and inadequate that the reader failed to grasp any sense of time or place? At what point did the book become so absorbing that it became impossible to put it down?

What made a book demand to be read?

These were all minute details and manipulations that a casual reader wouldn't necessarily recognize. But Jack gradually came to grasp what made up the unconscious, subtle differences that separated a good read from the rest of the junk on the shelves. And, by extension, what constituted a manuscript that would appeal to a publisher.

He studied the reference books, consulted experts, absorbed the knowledge of how scenes should unfold, how characters should interact, and how chapters should flow effortlessly into each other like a river into the sea: turbulent at times, but always with a final, inevitable purpose in mind.

When his notebooks were full, he sat down and wrote his novel. And when he was finished writing, he sent an inquiry letter and three sample chapters to ten literary agents.

One of them was Ray Chimera.

The Revelation Room wasn't huge to begin with, and the bolts of white cloth draped in folds along its walls made it appear even smaller. Jack sensed that the room hunched under the heft of the decorations, as if hugging itself in embarrassment at the tackiness of its new look.

Massive pillars constructed of lightweight wood and covered with plaster—carved and painted to resemble marble—stood in each corner. A large buffet table straddling the centre of the room was the focal point for a crowd of strangers industriously filling plates with roast beef, fried chicken, baked vegetables, salads and desserts.

On one side of the room, inflatable plastic coconut palms surrounded a portable hot tub. Lounging around the tub was a comely collection of young women dressed in one-piece bathing suits cut low and high.

There was an excited buzz to the conversation that nearly drowned out the music wafting from the room's sound system: a society of freeloading bees attracted to the honey of a free meal.

Jack took another look at the decor—the faux marble, the palm trees, the togas—and finally realized that they were meant to represent the small Greek village that was the setting for the final third of his book. The hot tub would be the Tear Pool, which figured so prominently in the book's dénouement. Jack was torn between bemusement and disgust. This was bullshit raised to an art form.

It took him three years to write *Resurrection Waters*. He'd ride the 10 p.m. bus home after the store closed, fire up the family computer, and start typing. His father would droop into the house from the graveyard shift at the mill to find Jack sitting at the computer desk, face pale, eyes too bright with exhaustion.

Ordered to bed, Jack's brain would refuse to shut down. It was as if the novel had a life of its own; it wouldn't stop percolating. A few hours of restless sleep and then it was back to the store.

It was a grueling timetable and one that inevitably took its toll. His friends wandered away. A pinched nerve in his neck that sent shivers of pain down his right arm forced him to type with one hand.

But he refused to quit. His desire to finish the book burned too incandescently to be interrupted.

Strangely enough, it was his shifts at The Last Page that kept his motivational fires stoked. He merely had to enter the store and be greeted by the thousands of books that nestled there to know that the opportunity to become a published writer actually existed. Someone, somewhere, had believed in each and every one of these writers.

He just needed someone to believe in him.

Ray clapped Jack on the back. Champagne sloshed dangerously.
"I almost forgot to tell you the good news." Ray smiled widely, his teeth too white, too perfect, too straight to be real. "See that fat guy over there?" Ray pointed with his glass. "By the pool?"

Jack bobbed his head until he picked out the man Ray was indicating. The fellow was indeed grossly overweight, but his suit was tasteful and impeccably cut. It conveyed an image of wealth and an attention to detail that deflected attention from the man's considerable girth and fleshy collection of chins.

"That's Paul Stengler, head of Citation Films," Ray said, his words bursting with importance.

"OK."

"We're way beyond OK, kiddo." Ray turned to Jack and fixed him with a look that was intense even through the smoked lenses of the sunglasses. "Paul Stengler is interested in buying the movie rights to your book. Are you hearing me?"

Jack stared. "You're shitting me," he finally said.

"I shit you not," Ray said. "Not only that, he wants me on board as a producer. He's scheduled an interview for tomorrow with *Silver Screen Weekly* so he can announce his plans for the movie."

Jack fumbled for words. His life had become a speedway of possibilities and Jack could only hope that he possessed the skills to drive there.

First the book launch, now this talk of movie rights. When Ray had originally announced, with his typical flare, that he'd found a publisher, Jack had visions of selling only as many copies of the book as his family and close friends could afford to buy. But a movie? His grip tightened on the glass in his hand. He needed the cool contact of its curved stem to assure himself that this was not a dream.

Ray leaned in close and gave Jack a light punch in the chest. "There's even rumors on the street," he whispered in a conspiratorial tone, "that Russell and both Toms are interested in playing the lead."

Jack knew he was grinning like the village idiot. He didn't care. His head was filled with helium; he couldn't vouch that his legs still worked. White noise filled his ears. The people moving around them were little more than blurs.

Jack tore his eyes away from Ray's smug face and scanned the room again for Paul Stengler. Found him. Found more.

Stengler was deep in conversation with a young woman. Even from across the room, she was stunningly attractive: blonde hair fell past her shoulders; her black dress, dipping dangerously low in front, clung tightly to contours. Even her posture was perfect.

Ray was talking again; Jack ignored him. Ray stopped in mid-sentence, looked up at Jack, and followed his gaze across the room.

"Oh good," Ray said. "Nile's here."

"You know her?"

"That's Nile Ramsay, Paul Stengler's personal assistant at Citation."

Ray waved his arm and Nile, glancing away from Stengler for an instant, caught the movement. She raised her glass in salute. Ray motioned her over. Nile touched Stengler on the sleeve, said something, then moved away.

"What are you doing?" Jack grimaced at the terror he heard in his voice.

"I want you two to meet," Ray said, sipping at his drink. "Don't worry, she won't bite." Ray leered over his glasses. "Unless you want her to."

Jack watched, mesmerized, as Nile threaded her way through the crowd. Her movements were cat-like, fluid; there was confidence in every gesture.

"She's pretty."

Ray snorted. "Christ, you really are from the sticks."

Jack's experience with women had been limited to one befuddled relationship with Karen Norton, a fellow bookstore employee.

It had been a clumsy affair and Karen soon grew weary of his awkward fumbling. The same night she gave her notice at the bookstore, effective immediately, she announced in the staff room that she didn't care if she ever saw Jack Nolan or his limp dick ever again.

To the best of Jack's knowledge, she had been true to her word.

The sex scenes in *Resurrection Waters* were obviously not drawn from his own limited experiences. He relied instead on a fertile imagination and the unlimited resources of the Internet, cloaking his characters' physical encounters in delicate subtleties, trusting that his readers' imaginations would fill in the blanks.

Ray read these passages. Ray went ape-shit.

"What are you, Jane fuckin' Austen?" Ray raged. "'Cause if you are, then you'll be needing another agent. Me? I know only one thing, and you might want to write this down: sex sells. You need to have some serious push-push in the bush here. Know what I mean?"

"Nile, my dear, you look good enough to eat." Ray stood on tiptoe to peck at her cheek. Nile threw air kisses at Ray, but her eyes never left Jack's face.

"Who's this yummy young fellow?" she asked. Her voice was husky. It issued from deep in her throat. Something stirred in Jack's pants.

"This is Jack Nolan," Ray said, stepping sideways so Nile could move closer. "The guest of honor."

The slit down the front of her dress gaped even wider as she stepped forward, revealing flesh that was round and pink and enticing. Jack clenched his fists and willed himself to stare into Nile's eyes. They were hazel; green lines radiated from the iris. Jack wondered if she wore contacts.

He held out his hand; Nile ignored it. She embraced him and brushed her lips against his ear.

"Pleased to meet you," she whispered and the hairs on the back of his neck snapped to attention.

Ray held up his glass. "Oh my," he said a little too eagerly. "Look at me, fresh out. Can I trust you two kids alone for a minute?"

"Take your time." Nile smiled.

Nile Ramsay was even more devastating up close. She was tall, willowy, and plush. Her skin was smooth and clear, her hair channeled sunshine. Her lipstick was filled with sparkles. Tiny fireworks exploded when she spoke.

Jack blushed. His face was a red beacon of embarrassed silence. *What do I say?*

Nile was accustomed to having this effect on weak men. "Ray sure knows how to throw a party, doesn't he?" she said.

Jack could only nod.

"He spent some serious coin here, Jack," she said. "He must really believe in you."

Nile's eyes navigated the room. "I'm guessing it's a celebration of both your success and the end of his dry spell."

Jack found his voice at last. "Dry spell?"

Nile turned back to him. "Yeah. Poor Ray. It's been nearly three years between home runs for him. You came along just in time." She smiled; her lips were mirror balls. "We were beginning to think the poor man was done."

This was disconcerting. Ray had never mentioned any dry spells; he had only ever given Jack and his family the impression that he was a player of the highest calibre. That Jack was fortunate indeed that Ray Chimera was finding time in his busy schedule to tutor a novice in the ways of the publishing world.

Were there flaws in the portrait Ray had so gloriously painted of himself as a well-connected literary agent with a finger in every lucrative pie? Pies that, for a measly 15 percent, he was quite willing to share with Jack Nolan.

Jack pondered this new development. Silence slipped in like an uninvited guest. Nile was suddenly very interested in her nails.

"What kind of name is Nile?" Jack blurted.

She cocked an eyebrow. "You might want to ask the Egyptians." She smiled thinly. "I believe it's the name of a big river in their backyard."

Jack reddened again. His face was cooking. "I'm sorry," he stammered. "I wasn't making fun of you. It's a pretty name, actually. An unusual name."

The eyebrow hovered for a second longer, then slowly unfurled. "It was my parents' idea of being creative," she said. "Or cute. I'm not sure which. Apparently their second choice was Catillion."

"Ouch."

"Oh, yeah." Nile smiled, once again wrapping those spangled lips around the edge of her glass. "I may purr like a kitten, but no way do I want anyone calling me Cat." She pointed her glass at him. "What kind of accent is that?"

A welcome rinse of coolant coursed through his body. The early awkwardness appeared to be fading. "I always say Vancouver, because that's the closest major city that everyone's heard of."

"Right." Nile nodded. "I was in Seattle once myself."

Jack shook his head. "Actually," he said, "it's Vancouver, British Columbia."

No reaction.

"Canada?" Jack said. Somewhere in his brain a warning light started to glow into life. She's kidding me. *Isn't she?*

Her face remained blank for a second longer and then she laughed, sharp and high-pitched. She swallowed the last of her champagne in a hurried gulp. Scanned the room for a refill.

The warning light was flashing now.

"Canada," Jack ventured again. "That big land mass to the north. The one with all the igloos and polar bears."

Nile looked back at him and her mouth moved as if she were chewing a stray thought.

Jack tried another angle. "We breed ice hockey players."

Her face brightened. *OK*, Jack thought, *maybe that gorgeous head does have a brain cell or two rattling around in it.*

"I know hockey," she said. "I like the fighting."

Jack's shoulders slumped; Nile didn't notice. She'd spotted a waiter with a full tray of glasses. She patted Jack's hand. "I'll be right back," she said. And was gone.

Ray materialized. "So?" He nudged Jack's ribs with a bony elbow. "Whaddya think?"

Jack hung his head.

"What's with the long face?" Ray was confused. "Tits not big enough for ya?"

"Ray." Jack fought the urge to sprint from the Revelation Room.

"She can always have them enlarged."

"*Ray*." Jack's voice was sharp. It cut through Ray's crap.

Jack lowered his head until he was speaking directly into his agent's face. "She doesn't know where Canada is, Ray," he said.

"Yeah? So what?" Ray seemed genuinely confused. "Nobody knows where the hell Canada is. And you know what? Nobody fuckin' cares."

Jack flattened against the wall. "If these people are going to pretend to be my friends, they should at least know something about me."

"Listen, kid, piece of advice." Ray exhaled champagne fumes. "And this is free, so you might want to write it down. These people don't give a shit about you. They're here to eat and get pissed. Nile? She's only looking to get laid. And she ain't that particular, believe you me."

Ray stabbed a finger into Jack's chest. "So that just leaves me and you. And that's all that really matters, understand? Now lighten up, will ya? You only sell your first novel once, Jack. So shut up and have some fun."

SIX

Hungry chickens occupied Jack's thoughts as he parked his Toyota on the forecourt of the Matavera Beach Store. His house was next door, separated by a hedge. He could have parked in his own yard and walked over, but he was feeling lazy. Dealing with Lloyd Dempster and Jordan Baxter tended to sap his energy.

Daylight was fading but it remained hot. Jack knew from experience that it would be several hours of restless, sweaty sleep later before the air would cool.

It was hotter still inside the shop, as the thick air hung motionless, a ponderous, steaming mantle of heat begging for the touch of a fan blade.

The shop served but one purpose in the community: convenience. If you wanted selection and competitive prices, you drove the ten minutes into town. If it was after normal business hours or all you needed was a can of corned beef or a litre of milk or a roll of toilet paper, you visited the Matavera Beach Store.

The bread shelves were to his left as Jack waded into the blast furnace of the shop's interior. Farther along the same wall were two low freezers, where reefer units gurgled and clanked in a Herculean effort to prevent frozen goods from melting. Against the back wall sat a pair of upright, glass-doored chillers, where the various drink containers were stored. A long counter on the right separated customers from a three-tiered row of shelves filled with sundries. A small collection of video movies, their cardboard display cases faded and dusty, stood in a forlorn row on a top shelf.

An electronic cash register squatted on the end of the counter nearest the doorway. Beside it, several copies of the *Island Tribune* sat in a neat pile. Lloyd Dempster paid extra for this prime location, but it seemed to work; there were seldom any returns.

Jack reached to his left and grabbed three unsliced loaves. When the bakery truck had made its delivery before dawn that morning, the bread had been soft and still warm from the oven. Now the crusts were hard; they crumbled in Jack's hands. Freshness wasn't a factor in his shopping, however. There would be no complaints about his offering.

He placed the loaves on the counter while he rooted through the various compartments of his hiking shorts for any spare change that might still lurk there. He came up empty, as he'd anticipated. Jack hated the weighty feel of coins in his pockets and made an effort to empty them every day into a glass jar that sat on a shelf in his kitchen. But sometimes he could be too thorough: he never had a coin when he needed it.

"Chicken bread again, eh Jacko?"

Mama Rosie was at her customary station, perched on a high, wooden stool behind the cash register. Jack had lived beside the shop for five years and the only reason he knew the old woman actually stirred off that stool was because he had seen her shuffling down the road to attend Sunday morning services at the Matavera CICC church.

The woman's face was as brown and worn as a saddle. The skin slumped in slack sheets from her cheekbones. If she owned more than five of her original teeth, Jack had yet to see them. The flesh drooped in wrinkled flaps from her stick arms where they poked out of her pareu; her hands were a madman's puzzle of liver spots. She wore a kerchief over her head and what hair straggled out from underneath it was a dull ivory. There was an opaque quality to her eyes, as if they had been soaked in milk.

Because of her permanent station in the store, it was not beyond reason that she would draw her final breath while still perched on that stool. Jack could picture her body fluttering to the wooden floorboards. Exploding into dust motes on impact. Disintegrating like an Egyptian mummy under an archeologist's probing fingers.

It would be a sad day for Matavera because Mama Rosie knew everything that happened in the village: who was cheating on their partner, who was the real father of that girl's baby, who had just mortgaged their land for a new 4WD.

She was also an excellent reference for anyone who wanted to know the history or the legends of the Cook Islands. She'd been an invaluable resource for Jack when he was still doing travel pieces. Before his creative juices had dried up completely, forcing him to turn to photography to stimulate his imagination.

Mama Rosie's favorite stories were of Rarotonga's pre-Christian cannibal days, when eating one's slain enemy was still an accepted practice. Clacking her gums together, she would delight in telling Jack of the time before the missionaries intruded on the natural order. Before the islanders were forced to relocate from their villages in the central valleys to the coastline, the better for the ocean-going papa'a to reach out to the newly-converted brown children of Christ. Before the wooden gods were incinerated in the bonfires of the white man's piety.

Before the time of clothes.

"When I was a tamaine, I would attend church with my great-uncle Maara," she told Jack. "I was too young to understand what the preacher was saying, so I would watch my great-uncle as he prayed. I noticed that, no matter how fervently he talked to God, he would never close his eyes."

In contrast to Uncle Maara's ever-vigilant eyes, the two sets of doors—the main ones located at the back and a second, smaller set in the church's west wall that led to a small cemetery—remained tightly closed.

One Sunday morning, young Rosie finally screwed up the courage to ask her great-uncle why, unlike the other worshipers hunkered in the wooden pews around them, he alone never closed his eyes nor bent his head in prayer.

Maara reached down to pat the top of Rosie's head then pointed his chin at the thick growth of Polynesian Chestnuts and Homalium that stretched down from the sloping hillside nearly to the stained white coral walls of the church.

"I was no older than you are," he said, his voice rustling like dried coconut husks as he cast his thoughts back. "It was a hot Sunday, much like today, and the elders had propped the doors open to let in the sea breeze."

The minister was in the middle of his service, Maara explained, the congregation's heads were lowered in prayer. Suddenly a small group of cannibals burst out of the tree line and charged into the building.

"Papa Noo was sitting nearest the door and they just clubbed him over the head and dragged him away to cook in their umu," Maara said, chuckling at how wide his grandniece's eyes had grown. "It left a terrible mess on the floor."

"And that's why," Mama Rosie told Jack, "to this day, the church doors are always kept closed, no matter how hot and stuffy it gets. And my great-uncle always kept his eyes open in case the cannibals ever tried to sneak in again and snatch him up."

Jack laughed at the tale, charmed by Mama Rosie's talent for storytelling. He was silenced by the expression on her face.

"You're serious?" he said. "You didn't just make that up?"

"Do you want to see the bloodstains for yourself, Jacko?" she asked, leaning so far forward on her stool that Jack thought he might have to reach out to prevent her from crashing onto the counter.

"Uh, no," he said quickly. "I'll take your word for it."

Jack finally gave up on his search for coins and plucked a note from his wallet. Mama Rosie looked closely at the bill for a long second, then punched at the cash register's buttons.

"You spoil those chooks," she admonished. "Once you have chickens in your yard, you'll never sleep."

Jack nodded, thinking of the eight roosters who strutted across his lawns, making life miserable for the hens and crowing at all hours of the day and night, rising sun be damned.

"You should spend your money on children instead." Mama Rosie reached over and gently patted Jack's hand before placing his change in it.

"Before I have children, there might actually have to be a woman in my life." Jack tucked the bread under one arm. "Funny how that works."

"You want Mama Rosie to introduce you to someone?" the old woman asked, a wide smile revealing every one of her surviving teeth. "I know lots of nice local girls in Matavera who'd love to have children with a handsome papa'a man like you."

Jack blushed and started his retreat. "Thanks anyway, Mama Rosie, but I think I'll stick with the chooks. At least they eat the centipedes."

Jack shook his head as he threw the bread on the Toyota's seat and climbed in. He wasn't sure which frightened him more: the idea of Mama Rosie playing matchmaker or the thought of centipedes.

There were many reasons why Jack embraced Rarotonga. Near the top of the list was the fact that the island was relatively free of creatures that bit or stung. There were no land snakes. The protective reef stopped sharks and jellyfish from entering the lagoon. It can be extremely painful to step on a stonefish, but wearing reef walkers or jandals in the tidal pools could prevent this.

Insects, however, were another matter. Mosquitoes were a constant nuisance, especially during the rainy season. They had ravaged Jack when he first arrived. He'd been fortunate not to fall victim to the outbreaks of dengue fever that occasionally swept across the island.

Ants tended to mind their own business unless Jack was careless enough to leave food uncovered or dirty dishes in the sink. He spotted the occasional wasp in his yard but a regular sweep under the rafters with a kikau broom discouraged nests.

It was really only the centipedes that scared the shit out of Jack. There was a good reason for that: one had nearly killed him.

Centipedes can grow to a length of 15 centimetres or more. They are aggressive. They are nasty. And, as Jack had the misfortune to discover one night, they bite.

He was fumbling behind the couch for the remote control. His groping fingers grabbed onto a centipede in the dark and the creature reacted by clamping its jaws into the meat of his right thumb.

Jack shook the insect off and crushed it with his boot. He ran cold water over his bleeding thumb, applied antibiotic ointment and a plaster to the puncture marks, then went back to the TV.

It took less than an hour for Jack to realize he was in trouble. The discomfort in his thumb grew progressively worse until it was throbbing with pain. His hand swelled until he could barely move it. He could feel his heart racing as a wave of nausea swept over his body.

"What the—" he muttered as he fought the urge to vomit. He swayed up from the couch, his head spinning. His tongue was thick in his mouth.

Jack's first thought was to go next door to the dairy. Mama Rosie would know how to treat a centipede bite. By the time he staggered through the shop door, he was wheezing for breath and his complexion was flushed and burning. Mama Rosie's fingers flew to the telephone.

Dr. Rangi met the ambulance at the Emergency Room entrance. He took a quick look at Jack's ballooning hand, noted his tortured breathing, and knew that Jack had gone into anaphylactic shock. Dr. Rangi quickly administered an injection of epinephrine and then placed an oxygen mask, complete with a Ventolin nebulizer, over Jack's face. Once Jack had stabilized and his breathing returned to normal, the doctor started him on a program of Hydrocortisone and Benadryl, with fluids to counteract the insect venom's effect on his system.

"You suffered an allergic reaction to the centipede bite," Dr. Rangi told him later. "What's known as an IgE antibody response. With some people, a sting from a bee or a hornet causes this response. With you, it was a centipede."

"How much danger was I in?" Jack said.

"If you'd waited much longer to get help, your throat could have closed up completely," Dr. Rangi said. "Within minutes you would have suffocated and—"

"And what?"

"And died."

Jack's breathing stuttered. "So what's your professional advice?"

"If I were you," Dr. Rangi peered over his glasses, "I'd make damn sure not to get bitten again."

Jack returned to his house with trepidation. He imagined centipedes lurking in every corner, slithering under every pillow, every cushion. It was Captain Tai who solved his dilemma.

"Chooks love centipedes," the bearded tour operator told him. "They consider them a delicacy. If you have chooks, you won't have centipedes."

Jack immediately commenced buying bread from the shop and scattering it around his backyard. He initially attracted only a small handful of the chickens that roamed freely through the neighborhood. But word must have spread because his poultry population now stood at close to 30. Some days that number could easily grow to 40 or more if a mother hen suddenly showed up trailing a scramble of fluffy chicks.

"You're stuffing those chooks while they're still alive," Mama Rosie scolded Jack one day after several members of his flock followed him through the hedge. They stood just outside the shop, impatiently pecking at the packed dirt while he purchased their breakfast. Jack smiled and continued with his shopping, secure in the knowledge that not a single centipede could be found on his property.

Jack glanced to his right as he pulled away from the front of the shop. He drove down the shoulder for five metres and made a hard left through a wide gap in the hedge that enclosed his property on three sides. The driveway ran down the right side of the house.

The house itself was nothing flash, simply a rectangular bungalow made of concrete blocks into which several rows of louvered windows had been set. The exterior was painted a vibrant orange, the roof tiles were a matte red, while the teal of the wooden door and window frames reflected the ocean, whose restless roar could be heard through the thicket of pawpaw plants, banana palms, Norfolk pines and casuarina trees that separated the house from a narrow tract of beach.

Jack drove to the back of the house, then swung the Toyota in a big arc to the left, careful not to clip the wire clothesline. He peered up through the windscreen to ensure that he was well clear of the coconut palms. Coconuts have a nasty habit of dropping without warning, causing considerable damage to anything they happen to connect with in the process.

Jack killed the engine, then reached for the bread loaves and his camera bag. Already he could see several of the chooks speed-wobbling in his direction. Soon he would be surrounded by a clucking, clamoring horde demanding to be fed for their labors.

Jack turned to the house. He had a visitor. A teenage girl sat on the steps that led to the back deck. She was a Cook Islander, but he didn't know her. She was dressed in typical island fashion: T-shirt, shorts, jandals. A battered duffel bag sat in a slumped heap on the steps beside her.

Jack nodded. The girl didn't acknowledge the greeting.

He saw that her skin was darker than most of the locals, more of a cinnamon than milk chocolate. She was pretty enough, but not striking. Her face was a bit too long, the almond-shaped eyes a fraction too far apart under thick eyebrows. It was if she was still in the process of growing into her own face.

Jack's gaze was drawn to a small dribble of pale scar tissue that originated at the left corner of her mouth and ran down her chin.

She had full lips and a wide, slightly flattened nose. Her cheekbones sat high and tight. Her hair had been swept back from a prominent forehead and fashioned into a long braid that lay draped over her left shoulder like a black snake. Tiny flowers had been plaited into it.

The girl maintained her silence as he approached, her expression that of concerned contemplation.

"Can I help you?" Jack asked as hungry chooks swirled impatiently around his legs.

The girl spoke for the first time.

"This is my house," she said.

SEVEN

LOS ANGELES, 1999

"This is your house!"

Jack didn't know who had made the joyous announcement. In fact, he wasn't even sure he could pinpoint his exact location at that moment. He felt disjointed, confused; his senses scrambled.

It didn't help that his eardrums were slow to adjust to the altitude after the interminable, winding ascent through the canyons and up into the hills above LA. His brain still sloshed around the interior of his skull from the snake-spined switchbacks that Ray Chimera's Cadillac had taken at speeds that far exceeded the posted limit.

In woozy hindsight, he regretted his activities of the previous night. The frantic and ultimately vain quest for inspiration that had propelled him endlessly through the neon-clad Los Angeles night was haunting him now, churning his stomach in the process.

Ray had treated them to the seafood lunch buffet at the Net Worth, but Jack had been forced to gulp down the contents of his plate because they were running late for their appointment with Monica Flanders.

Apparently Monica, who specialized in exclusive properties for exclusive clients, did not take kindly to tardiness.

"If you hadn't dicked around so long getting out of bed, we wouldn't be in such a hurry," Ray said as he gunned the Caddy around another sharp bend. Hunched in the back, Jack grimaced and gnawed on a knuckle while Nile smirked at him from the front seat.

"Did the lobster taste alright to you?" Jack burped, tasting bile.

The Caddy made a final charge up a steep lane and braked sharply. Jack was flung forward, then back. He felt a clenching down the entire length of his digestive tract.

"This is it," Ray said.

Jack staggered gratefully from the car, flung his head back, and sucked in huge gulps of fresh air. He swallowed the urge to vomit as he watched Monica Flanders, the electric pink of her outfit working to scorch his aching eyeballs, disengage herself from the interior of her candy-apple red Corvette. Jack was reminded of a spider unkinking its legs upon sensing a vibration in its web.

Air kisses exchanged, Monica led them into the house, babbling on about how the place was originally built by some 1940s movie star whose name Jack did not recognize.

What followed was a blur of polished wood and gleaming chrome. Of Italian tile floors and ankle-deep pile. Of soaring ceiling beams imported from New Zealand, and yawning brick fireplaces that were exact duplicates of those found in some French chateau.

None of this registered on Jack, who studiously concentrated on the placement of his feet to avoid pitching unceremoniously onto his face. Nile and Ray made appreciative noises. That was a good sign: Jack understood that theirs would be the only opinions that would matter anyway.

He made it all the way to the top floor before his legs gave out. He slumped heavily onto a sectional sofa. Dropped his head into his hands while the others twirled around the room in front of him: stimulated to dance by architecture. There was a flash of color as Monica Flanders darted past him. With the dramatic flare of a circus ringmaster, she swept aside the heavy brocaded curtains to reveal a massive expanse of glass.

"Just look at this view," she squealed to Ray and Nile, who cooed in rapture as they pressed close to the window. Jack peered from between the protective bars of spread fingers. He was blinded by a dominion of radiance. It was a portal of pain. He quickly averted his eyes before his brain exploded.

He turned his gaze instead to the real estate agent's clothes, amazed that someone would actually spend money on something so effulgent as to turn stomachs. Monica's pantsuit was beyond pink. It actually screamed through the color spectrum all the way to chartreuse. Matching shoes and purse in the same gut-churning shade completed the carnage.

"Miss Flanders, this is wonderful," Ray drooled. "Kid, you gotta take a look. I think you can see all the way to the studio from here."

Jack waved a hand, his mouth too dry to function.

"Wait until you see the master bedroom," Monica said, grabbing Nile's hand and leading her away. Jack could feel the castanet clacking of their heels in every nerve ending.

Ray turned from the window and saw Jack slouched on the sofa, windbreaker unzipped, one side of his golf shirt pulled sloppily out of his jeans. His head was bowed. Ray could see where the sweat had soaked the edges of his hair.

Ray sat beside Jack and touched his shoulder. Jack flinched at the contact.

"I don't even want to know what the fuck you're up to," Ray said.

"Good plan."

"Your wife is pissing herself over this house, Jack. The least you can do is pretend you're interested."

Jack could hear the excited voices of the women from along the hall. Or maybe they were downstairs again. Sound does weird things in big houses. Sound does weird things when your brain is on fire.

"Can I afford this?" he asked, turning bloodshot eyes on Ray.

"Oh, you're not buying, kiddo," Ray chuckled. "Winning movies buy. Nominated movies can only afford to rent. Maybe next time. If we're lucky."

It wasn't just today that seemed fuzzy to Jack. It had been three years since Porter handed him the phone in their parents' basement and he'd first heard Ray cursing in his ear. More than 1,200 days had passed and Jack could put a mental page marker on very few of them.

Somewhere in all the confusion, one thing became painfully clear: twentysomething novelists aren't supposed to win the publishing lottery the first time they buy a ticket.

Logically, his writing career should have started with baby steps. First prize in a local writing contest, for instance, before graduating to having a short story published in some elitist literary magazine that six people actually read. Maybe sell a couple of feature pieces to a daily newspaper.

The rejection slips should have piled up, from agents and publishing houses alike, until he could paper the downstairs bathroom with them. He should have tucked *Resurrection Waters*, and probably his next three books as well, into a shoe box and shoved it so far under his bed that only the dust bunnies would ever find it.

That's how it played out for everyone else, it seemed. Except for those cherished few who managed to beat the odds. Except for those blessed with the luck and the talent of Jack Nolan.

That luck included hooking up with an agent as well connected as Ray Chimera. That was another thing that never happened to rookies. Ray was vulgar, he was rude, he was obstinate. But he was also a born huckster and the written word was the snake oil he specialized in.

Resurrection Waters was published a month after the book launch party. Ray sent a comp copy to every media outlet in North America. He flew Jack across the continent to meet the influential book reviewers. Ray pulled strings, called in favors, even bullied when he had to. But he managed to place Jack on several daytime talk shows, watched by the housewives who make up the majority of book buyers.

There were times when Jack only appeared on air for a fleeting moment or two, and he was frequently scheduled last so he would be the first one bumped if the show ran too long for its time slot. But Ray insisted that any air time, no matter how minuscule, would pay off in additional sales of his book.

"This is a face made for TV," Ray said, grabbing a blushing Jack by the cheek. "First the ladies will get wet and then, once they've changed their knickers, they'll head straight for the nearest mall and snap up your book. I guaran-fucking-tee it, kiddo."

Jack was a natural. His boyish enthusiasm endeared him to interviewers and readers alike. He appeared so genuinely surprised to be in the limelight, so aw-shucks humble, that people shunted aside the usual feelings of envy and jealousy and instead embraced him as The Next Great Thing, Literary Division. Time Limit: 15 Minutes.

It helped that the book itself was an entertaining read. That fact, more than any prodding that Ray Chimera did, was the deciding factor in *Today* naming the debut novel by wunderkind author Jack Nolan as one of the initial selections to its new book club.

Sales, which had been pleasantly steady to that point, skyrocketed overnight. When Ray's official announcement about a movie deal with Citation Films followed soon after, William Burch & Sons was forced to issue a second printing.

These were good times for Jack, times he would later look back on with a mixture of wonder and disbelief, as if they had happened to someone else and he was just fortunate enough to be in the same room to watch. He flew his family to Anaheim for a book signing at The Last Page's flagship store. His parents, unaccustomed to such grand gestures, reverted to the smile-and-nod mode of defense when the media pressed them for comments.

His brother Porter, who was dating an accountant and so knew about such things, wanted to talk finances. Who was paying his taxes and was it being done on time? Who was organizing his bill payments and ensuring that his agent received his commission?

Jack assured his younger sibling that Ray himself was taking care of everything.

"Can you trust him?"

"He's the only one I do trust."

The money Jack did see from his publishing contract and the sale of the movie rights gave him a warm tingle of accomplishment. He had only a rudimentary idea about how much the contracts were worth, but his share was certainly more than a bookstore clerk, the son of a career millwright, had ever expected to earn from the performance of a single task.

Ray set him up in a three-bedroom condo in a neighborhood safe enough for his mother to stop worrying. He arranged for the lease of a late model 4WD with enough bells and whistles to keep Jack amused during those rare times when he decided to match wits with the California traffic.

It was Christmas every day for Jack. No one cared that he was overwhelmed and stunned by how quickly his life had been turned on its ear. No one inquired as to how he was coping with the instant adulation. He had made it to The Show; he was the luckiest bastard in the world.

Jack could only blink at the spinning carousel of talking heads and cameras and microphones and extended hands and the badgering for his attention. "This is the gravy train, kiddo," Ray laughed up into Jack's bewildered face. "All ya gotta do is hang on and enjoy the ride."

But the one memory Jack could never seem to pin down in the twister that was now his existence was when the hell he'd made the decision to marry Nile Ramsay.

"Monica wants to show us the pool area."

The women were back. Ray stood up to greet them. Jack didn't.

"Is he going to make it?" asked Monica, her voice an arctic wasteland. "We can reschedule the rest of the tour for another day if that's more convenient."

Ray grabbed Jack by the elbow and hauled him off the sofa. Jack put on a brave face but kept his back to the glass wall.

"He'll be just fine." Ray smiled grimly. "Just as long as he remembers that you're not allowed to soil the furniture until after you've signed the contract."

The rocket scientists in the marketing department at Citation Films—people with fluorescent tans and caffeine in their veins—convinced Paul Stengler that while a title like *Resurrection Waters* might sell books to romance-starved housewives, it would never draw the Almighty Demographic of 18 to 24-year-old males into theatres. You might as well subtitle it *Gigli 2,* the marketing gurus nodded solemnly over their venti soy lattes, before resuming the debate over which was better, Coke or Pepsi.

However, the rocket scientists said, if Citation was interested in making some serious greenbacks, here was a short list of alternate titles, each one guaranteed to put bums in seats.

In his capacity as a producer, Ray Chimera was privy to the list. As the person whose only contribution to the movie was its source material, Jack was not entitled to see the list. Ray was kind enough to surreptitiously e-mail it to him.

"Are you serious?" Jack screamed into his phone. "Please tell me you're kidding."

"I would never joke about shit like this." Ray was surprisingly calm considering his prize client was chewing nails and spitting the shrapnel at him.

"Shit is right," Jack fumed. "Please tell me that English is not the first language of the moron who excreted this mess."

"Calm down, Jack." Ray lifted his mouth from the receiver and grinned across his office at where Paul Stengler and his assistant, Nile Ramsay, sat stone-faced. He gave them a wink that was more bravado than confidence.

"Pay attention here, kiddo," he said. "Believe it or not, these guys actually do know what they're doing. Citation had four movies top 100 mill last year alone. It's been my experience that it's imprudent to argue with success."

Jack's breathing was still strained, but Ray could hear it slowing. That was a good sign. He quickly took advantage of it.

"They're leaning towards *Blood and Ruins*, Jack," Ray said, closing his eyes and steeling himself for the next outburst. When Jack remained silent, he flashed another wink at Stengler and Nile.

"Hey, buddy," Ray said, "how's about we pretend this whole thing's a game, huh? We don't fight them on this one, maybe we can pull a few fast ones down the road. Get you unrestricted access to the set, make you a script consultant or something. That way you still have some sort of creative control. Whaddya say?"

The fight had drained out of Jack. "OK, Ray," he sighed. "But the next time you see Stengler, you tell him that I'm not a happy camper."

"Will do," Ray said. "It's nothing personal, kid. It's just show biz."

Ray hung up and flashed a victory smile at Paul Stengler. "Jack loves the new title," Ray announced. "He won't be a problem at all."

Stengler nodded at Nile. "Oh, we already know that," he said.

Citation head-hunted a young music video whiz to take the helm. Paris, AKA Graham Dundicker, sported a shaved head, several body piercings, and a number of garish tattoos, one of which said *Grand Motherfucker*. His taste for pain aside, Paris was both talented and ambitious. *Blood and Ruins* would mark his feature film debut and he was determined that this would be the first step in a long and illustrious career.

Paris was in no position to demand much in the way of salary, which suited Citation's budget constraints just fine. That penny-pinching fiscal attitude extended to the cast as well. Several character actors with low price tags were hired for the secondary roles, while somebody's mistress played the love interest. The male lead, Billy Apollo, fell to an actor named Payne Laidlaw.

The contents of Payne's C.V. were sparse—bit parts in several relatively unsuccessful movies, a couple of guest spots on TV sitcoms—but they did include a hugely successful ad campaign for a burger company. Those commercials, featuring the bare-chested actor biting into a sesame-seed bun while juice dripped seductively down the chiseled contours of his chin, were enough to earn him the No. 48 slot on a weekly magazine's list of the Top 50 People We'd Like to Boink. It was also enough for Payne Laidlaw to become Billy Apollo.

Sets were built on a Hollywood sound stage, but, just when the closest Jack thought the production would get to the book's Aegean Sea setting was when the finished product played in an Athens, Georgia, multiplex, the entire operation packed up and flew to Greece for a week of location shooting.

It was on the set that Jack met Nile again. Caught up in the mechanics of the film making process, he was at first unaware of how much time they were spending together. It was only much later that he discovered how Paul Stengler had given his assistant specific, and graphic, instructions to ensure Jack didn't interfere with the project.

"I don't care if you have to treat his johnson like an all-day sucker," Stengler told Nile. "Just make sure he doesn't do anything stupid that is going to cost me money."

By the time Nile told him that story, Jack was in too deep to care. There was a part of him that cried out that Nile Ramsay was all flash and no substance: a pretty, empty façade. But another part of him—the lonely part, the sleeping dragon that Karen Norton had barely prodded when they'd worked together at The Last Page—that part didn't care that Nile knew nothing about Canada.

That part, where the blood pumped and the muscles hardened and the skin was soft, that part loved the way this woman smelled when she leaned in close. How this woman sounded when she laughed in his ear. How this woman felt when she took his hand and brushed it against her breasts.

It was that part of Jack Nolan that fell in love with Nile Ramsay. That part that worked to blank Jack's mind so the rest of their relationship was one long dark corridor down which he blundered blind. All the way to the altar.

They were married the same week *Blood and Ruins* was released on 3,000 screens across North America. They were occupied in yet another robust bout of sweaty sex when Ray Chimera called to say that box office estimates for the opening weekend were close to $70 million. They were sitting in the biggest bathtub he'd ever seen, giddily toasting their success with an expensive vintage courtesy of Citation Films, when Jack decided that he was the happiest man in the world. That everything was perfect.

Too bad it didn't stay that way.

Jack's ears had stopped working. As he trudged back downstairs, he could clearly see that Ray and Monica were engaged in a discussion. He turned to Nile. She threw her head back and laughed. But their voices sounded muted, as if Jack was listening to them through water.

Jesus, he thought, *what if it wasn't undercooked lobster?* Maybe he was going down with something. It didn't matter if it was just the flu; Jack hated being sick.

He looked again at Ray. It struck him that all he could recall of recent conversations with his agent was snippets of dialogue.

For instance:

"Paul Stengler is creaming his shorts, that's how excited he is, kiddo. You and me, we got it fuckin' made."

"Nominated for three awards, Jack, including best picture. Can you believe that?"

"We was robbed, what can I say. But we'll take the award for best sound editing. Better than nothing, eh kiddo?"

"Warm up your computer, Jack, my son. Stengler's talking sequel, maybe even franchise. And this time, cross my heart, you'll get a percentage. I would not shit you about such matters."

And finally: "I think we're in trouble."

This is what he meant:

Paris took the money and ran. After the box office success of *Blood and Ruins*—a domestic gross of $130 million US and the lucrative overseas markets yet to be tapped—he had his pick of the project litter and eventually priced himself out of the sequel's budget.

"Fuck him," Ray spat. "An ape could direct the sequel and it'll still crack $100 mill."

Payne Laidlaw was another story. In the eyes of his adoring fans—who ate his burgers in the billions, according to the ads—he *was* Billy Apollo. His contract for *Blood and Ruins* contained the standard sequel clause and Payne was quite happy to return to what had now become his defining role. But...

But there was this small part in a micro-budget indie production that he'd promised to do for an old film school buddy as soon as he had a break in his schedule. He'd only be in Ottumwa, Iowa, for a week, max. Staying at the Birdsong Bed and Breakfast Lodge if anyone needed to contact him.

And that's exactly where Mrs. Edna Birdsong found him. In the Bullfinch Room of the Birdsong Bed and Breakfast Lodge, hanging from his belt in the shower. Naked.

Coroner ruled his death accidental, yet another case of a celebrity succumbing to the temptations of autoerotic asphyxiation.

"I think we're in trouble," said Ray Chimera.

More than he knew, actually.

It was the bubbles gurgling in the hot tub that finally did him in. Monica Flanders had led them back downstairs and onto the pool deck, a concrete tile and wood construction that jutted from one side of the house and extended over the three-car garage. There were plastic chairs and glass-topped tables and wooden lounges scattered around the edge of the swimming pool, which was designed to look as if it ran right off the deck and into the valley below. The hot tub was built into the deck, near the end of the pool that featured the swim-in bar.

Monica bent over to push a white button set into the side of the tub. There was a mechanical hum and then the spa's surface started to churn. Jack looked at the bubbling action, then collapsed on one knee beside the hot tub as his mouth suddenly filled with saliva. It felt like he was gargling motor oil. His stomach spasmed; he emitted a low moan.

"Mr. Nolan?" Monica leaned over him as Nile fluttered in the background. "Are you alright?"

His hand latched onto her arm for support. Caught off-balance, a surprised Monica Flanders staggered, her purse windmilling off her shoulder to thump into Ray's chest. Her designer shoes scrabbled for purchase on the wet tiles.

For an awful second time was suspended, as the combined weight of their bodies hovered between two spheres of gravity.

And then physics took over.

Monica's feet slipped out from under her. Jack's hand was knocked aside and the real estate agent tumbled headfirst into the hot tub.

Monica righted herself immediately, legs kicking, arms flailing as she splashed upright. She pawed wet hair off her face, then stood, spluttering, as mascara streamed in black runnels down her cheeks as if she wept coal dust.

Her three companions reacted true to character. Nile yelped in dismay. Ray cursed in embarrassment.

Jack gagged once, then deposited the partially digested remains of six lobster tails down the front of that magnificently garish pantsuit.

EIGHT

Jack stopped in front of the girl sitting on the steps.

"I'm sorry," he said, cocking his head. "What did you say?"

The girl shot him a dark glare. "You heard me," she said, her top lip curling in defiance. "This house belongs to my family."

The commotion of chooks around Jack's legs grew louder. He looked down, tore a piece off one of the bread loaves, and tossed it. A mad dash ensued, accompanied by much squawking. Several loosened feathers lay scattered on the grass.

He turned back to his visitor. "What's your name?"

"Maina Rima."

"Well, Maina," Jack said. "I rent this house from a man named Nga Rima. Is he related to you?"

Maina nodded. "My uncle."

"Right." Jack idly ripped off another chunk of bread and flipped it towards the flapping host that pecked at the ground beside his truck. "Listen, I'm sorry but your uncle doesn't live here anymore. He left for New Zealand when I moved in five years ago. I haven't spoken to him since then."

"So how do you pay your rent?"

The next piece of bread froze in Jack's hand. "Not that it's any of your business, but I deposit a cheque each week into a bank account in town." Jack flung aside the remnants of the loaves and moved towards the steps. "Now you'll have to excuse me, I'm meeting someone for tea. It was nice meeting you."

Maina remained still. "Look, Mr.—"

"Jack Nolan."

Maina held out her hand. Jack regarded it for a second, then slowly reached out to shake it. Her hand was small and warm, but its grip was firm.

"Look, Mr. Nolan," she said. "I've just spent two days on a boat traveling from Pukapuka. I'm tired, and I really do need a place to stay."

Jack disengaged his hand. "And this has what to do with me, exactly?"

Maina tilted her head at the house behind her. "You may be living here now, but this is still my family's land."

"And your point is?"

"My point, Mr. Nolan," Maina stood up; the step's elevation brought her level with Jack's face, "is that I'm exhausted and stinky and I'd like to take advantage of my family's hospitality. Whether or not there is any family here to offer it."

"You've got to be joking," Jack chortled in disbelief.

"Listen, I'd love to sit and chat, but I really do need a shower." Maina's mouth formed a smile, but her eyes grew chillier with each word.

Jack was taken aback by the girl's boldness. Then, with the blood already stirred up by the afternoon's events having reached the boiling point, he grabbed Maina's bare arm and hauled her down off the step.

"Ow!" she protested, squirming in an attempt to break his grip. "What are you doing?"

Jack was silent as he dragged Maina around the corner of the house, marched her through the gap in the hedge, up a short dirt path and through the entrance of the Matavera Beach Store. His grasp lessened once they were inside. Maina shook his hand off and backed away. She made a face as she rubbed her arm where the skin had reddened under the pressure of Jack's fingers.

"You arsehole," she spluttered. "That hurt."

"Good," Jack shot back.

Mama Rosie's gummy mouth gaped pinkly as she watched the exchange. Jack glanced at the shopkeeper, then made a wild swipe to grab Maina again. She twisted out of his reach.

"Good on you, Jacko," Mama Rosie cackled. "You've finally found yourself a brown girl. She's a little young, but she's definitely feisty."

Jack jerked a thumb at Maina, who had backed up against one of the upright chillers and seemed poised to bolt from the shop.

"Do you know this girl?" Jack asked.

"Eh?"

Jack gritted his teeth. "I found her hanging around my house. She says she's Nga Rima's niece, but I think she may have been trying to rob me."

"Hah!" Maina yelled, her face flushed. "I've already been inside, toe rag. Believe me, you got nothing worth stealing."

Jack scowled at the girl. He knew that gaining access to his house was as simple as removing two or three of the louvre slats on any of the windows. The knowledge that someone had actually done this brought a bitter taste of violation to his throat.

Mama Rosie squinted at where Maina hunkered against the chiller.

"Come closer, girl," she said. "What's your name?"
"Maina Rima. My mother was Repeta Tavera."
"The dancer?"
Maina nodded.

Mama Rosie reached out to touch Maina's face. She ran her prune fingers in gentle strokes over the girl's brow, down the bridge of her nose, and across the full lips. Hesitated on the scar.

"Of course," she said. "You look just like she did at your age. I used to love to watch her perform at the National Auditorium during Te Maeva Nui. How is she these days?"

The breath hitched in Maina's throat, her eyes dropped. "She's dead. My papa too. I was living with my Uncle Ben until he got sick."

Mama Rosie gasped. "Oh my, how terrible."

The old woman's eyes were glowing coals as she turned them on Jack. "You would deny an orphan's right to her family home?"

"But it's my house," Jack said, suddenly put on the defensive.

Mama Rosie raised an index finger to quiet him. "You are only renting, Jacko, never forget that. The house, the land, it belongs to the Rima family. Now and forever. That is the Cook Islands way."

Jack spread his hands. He knew when he was beaten. "I know how the ownership of land works here, Mama Rosie," he said. "And you're right, it's not really my place. But," he pointed at Maina, who drew up to her full height at the gesture, "she is not my problem."

"You're absolutely right, Jacko," Mama Rosie said.

"Sweet as," Jack said, rubbing his hands together. "Then I'll leave you two here to reminisce about old times. Cheers."

"Not so fast, Jacko." Mama Rosie smiled. "I meant it when I said that Maina's not your problem. But she is your new flatmate."

"I don't have a spare bedroom," Jack said as he led Maina through the back door and into the kitchen area.

"You do now." She waved her hand at the other side of the room.

Jack put his camera case on the floor and saw the cardboard boxes stacked around the kitchen table.

"You've been a busy girl," he sighed.

He looked through the doorway to his left, into the lounge that marked the centre of the house. On the far side of the lounge, a short hallway separated a pair of bedrooms. To the right, a closed door led to his room. To the left, a length of material formed a makeshift curtain over the entrance to his office. Or what used to be his office.

"I didn't look at anything," Maina assured him. "I just moved it all out here."

"I guess you can put your things in that old vanity I was using as a desk," Jack said. "But I'm not sure what you're going to sleep on."

"I saw a foldaway bed on a shelf in the bathroom. I can use that."

"If you were in the bathroom," Jack said, "why didn't you use the shower?"

"Without asking?" Maina appeared genuinely surprised. "That wouldn't have been very polite."

"But it is polite to break into my house and sort through my stuff?"

"I didn't sort," she said. "I just moved."

Jack rubbed his eyes. His brain was starting to hurt. "You know that there's no door on that room, right?"

Maina nodded. "The curtain is fine."

"Just be gentle with it," Jack said. "The track at the top is warped and you've got to give the curtain a good tug to close it completely. But if you pull too hard, the whole thing might just come down on your head."

"I'll be careful," Maina said. "Promise."

Jack walked onto the back deck and turned left to enter the bathroom. He had never understood why the bathroom was located outside the house, but assumed it had something to do with the ancient mysteries of plumbing. He was just glad for the hedges around the yard that provided a natural shield for those mornings when he couldn't be bothered with clothes. You can do things like that when you live alone. He heard Maina moving about the kitchen and reminded himself that those days were over.

The large bathroom space accommodated a washing machine and a dryer as well as the sink, toilet and shower stall. There were storage shelves built into the back wall and it was here that Maina had spotted the bed left behind by her uncle.

Jack pulled it down, carried it outside, and set it up on the grass to air out. He looked at the stained mattress and the rusted frame and was glad it wasn't him who had to sleep on it. It appeared to be some sort of military issue and Jack remembered Captain Tai talking about the American servicemen who were stationed in the Cook Islands during the Second World War.

Maina was sitting on the couch in the lounge when he returned to the house. Jack grabbed the big chair from in front of the TV, spun it around to face her, and plunked himself down.

"We need to talk," he said.

"Does it have to be now? I really am feeling a bit crook."

"This won't take long."

"Alright."

Jack rubbed his chin in thought; he'd have to shave before he went out.

"Let's get a few things straight from early days," he said. "Starting with the fact that I don't want you here. I'm only doing this because Mama Rosie asked me to, and out of respect for Cook Islands' family values."

"How very noble of you," she said, hugging a couch cushion to her chest.

"Right." Jack quickly formulated a plan of attack. He needed to be firm without being an egg. "Ground rules."

"Yeah?"

"We don't touch each other's things."

"No problem."

"We knock on closed doors, especially the bathroom."

"Fine."

This is going well, Jack thought. He continued: "You're welcome to share any of the food in the house, but just remember that we only have one income and two mouths."

"I'm way ahead of you on that one," Maina said. "While I was waiting for the bus in town, I went to Sparky's Café. The owner knows my Uncle Ben and he offered me a job."

"What about school?"

"I'm a school leaver," she said. "So I can work all day."

"Is this where I give you the speech about the importance of a good education?"

"Not unless you're trying to bore me to death."

"OK," Jack said. "Then maybe you can help out with the rent as well."

Maina nodded in agreement. "I'm trying to save up enough money to fly to New Zealand so I can stay with relatives, but I'll give you as much as I can."

"That sounds good." Jack stood up. "Then I guess we're done here."

"Uh, wait a minute." Maina held up her hand. "What about my rules?"

"Excuse me?" Jack returned to the chair. "Your rules?"

"Yeah. If I'm paying rent, then I should have a say in the rules."

Jack chewed the inside of his cheek as he looked at her. He had a bad feeling about this, but she had a point. And best to get everything out in the open now so they both understood the parameters of their forced treaty.

"You're right," he finally said. "What would you like?"

"First of all," Maina said, ticking off her fingers, "you put the toilet seat down when you're finished."

Jack sat back hard. "But I'm a man," he protested.

"Exactly," Maina said. "Next: I get the shower first each day."

"Fine," Jack said. "Just remember the hot water tank here is very small. Get in, get out, and save some for me."

She narrowed her eyes. She face-talked: *Are you done yet?*

"And, most importantly," she continued, "no perving. I hate guys who stare at me."

What? Jack's jaw dropped. *Perving?* OK, so he needed a shave, maybe even a haircut, but surely he didn't look that depraved.

Did he?

"Look, Maina," he sputtered, the words tumbling over each other in the haste of his protest. "I'm 32 years old. And you're what? Fourteen?"

"Sixteen!"

"My point," Jack said, ignoring her indignant reply, "is that you're a baby. Let me assure you right now that there will be no perving in this house. You don't have to worry about that."

"I'm not trying to wind you up," she said, clutching the cushion tighter. "You're the one who wanted to have rules. If you don't like mine, we can always go next door and discuss this with Mama Rosie."

Jack put his hands up in a gesture of surrender. "No," he said firmly. "We don't need to do that. I think the two of us can live together just fine as long as we're polite and civil and have respect for each other's privacy and belongings. Agreed?"

She gave a quick flick of her chin. "Agreed."

"Choice." Jack smiled. "Hey, look, I'm sorry for grabbing you. It's just that I'm not used to having people in my space. Especially ones who just drop in out of the blue."

"Yeah," Maina said. "I guess that was a bit of a shock."

"So you're from Pukapuka?"

She shook her head. "Not originally. That's my mom's home island but my father grew up in New Zealand. I was born in Auckland. We moved to Raro when I was five, and then to Pukapuka when I was 11."

"Now your parents are both dead and . . ."

"And my Uncle Ben is sick, so I'm trying to get to New Zealand to be with my father's family," she said. "Can I ask you something that's been picking at my brain, Mr. Nolan?"

"Please call me Jack."

"OK, Jack," she said. "I'm trying to figure out why your name sounds so familiar. Have you ever been to Pukapuka?"

"Never been there," he said. "Aitutaki is the only other island I've visited. But I did write a book once. Maybe you saw it in a library or something."

Maina's face it up. "Of course! *Resurrection Waters*. I loved that book!"

Jack's eyebrows jitterbugged. "You've *read* it?"

"Don't sound so surprised," Maina said. "I can write too."

Jack flapped his hands. "No, no, I didn't mean that. It's just that the book's been out of print for three years or so. I'm amazed that you were able to find a copy."

"Before my Uncle Ben's diabetes got real bad, he owned a café where he trained me to help him," Maina said. "He had a small library in the place that customers and tourists were welcome to use. You know: take a book, leave a book. That sort of deal."

Jack nodded.

"I was dusting one day when I found a copy of *Resurrection Waters* that someone had left behind," she continued. "It had a neat cover, so I decided to read it."

It had a neat cover?

"And?"

"And I already told you. I enjoyed it," she said.

She tilted her head as she talked to Jack. Took in his eyes, saw that they were more grey than blue. Took in the head of unkempt hair, thinning at the temples, that was mostly brown but streaked with blond and red highlights from the sun. The three days' worth of stubble somehow gave his face a dangerous bent, as if it had known trouble and could very well make its acquaintance again. He wasn't particularly tall, but appeared to be well-proportioned. He was, she decided, a decent enough looking bloke. For his age.

"You don't much look like your picture," she said.

"That was five long years ago," Jack laughed. "I'm betting even you look different than you did then."

"I've only grown more beautiful," Maina said, playfully batting her eyelashes.

Jack frowned. "But there wasn't a picture of me printed on the book's jacket. Where did you see a photo?"

"On the Internet. I did a search for your name because I was hoping to find a list of other books you'd written," she said. "But that was the only title listed. In fact, other than *Resurrection Waters* being made into a movie, there's not a whole lot of information about you. Nothing at all about you living in my uncle's house in Matavera."

"Except for my family," Jack said, "I don't think too many people know that I'm here."

"So what happened? Why haven't you written more books?"

"It's a long story," Jack said, "and you really do need a shower."

"I'm starting to like the way I smell," Maina said. "It's kinda funky, don't you think?"

Jack started to reply. She cut him off. "Are you still writing?"

"I did a few travel pieces during the first year I was here," he said. "But nothing much since."

"But you're much too talented to stop."

Jack grinned, and ducked his head "You're going to make me blush."

Maina pressed on. "Please tell me that you're working on another book."

Jack glanced through the doorway, at the laptop on the kitchen table. "I have been fiddling around with a couple of ideas. It's been a struggle getting the words out, and I can't say that I'm completely happy with any of it, but it's a start."

"Maybe you just need some inspiration."

He shrugged.

Maina playfully tossed the cushion into his lap. "Maybe that's why I'm here," she said. "Maybe I'm supposed to be that—what do you call it?—that thing that makes you write?"

"My muse?"

"Exactly." She blessed him with a wide smile. "Just call me Maina Rima, your very own personal muse. No charge, just as long as you feed me."

Jack coughed out a humorless laugh. "Where were you five years ago when Ray Chimera was chewing on my arse?"

Maina crossed her arms. "I was in the Cook Islands. Where were you?"

NINE

Jack derived no pleasure from discussing his past. He'd been adamant about that point from his first day on the island. Lloyd Dempster recognized his name, of course, as did a few others who'd either read *Resurrection Waters* or saw *Blood and Ruins* when a bootleg DVD, taped by someone using a camcorder in a Malaysian movie theatre, showed up for rental at the Avarua Video Emporium.

He was delighted to encounter a general feeling of apathy from the locals about anything he had done before he moved to Rarotonga. They were content to accept him as a man with a strange accent who came for a visit, discovered that he possessed some talent with a camera, fell under the siren spell of the South Pacific, and eventually became a permanent resident.

It was only the time he'd spent in the Cook Islands that most people cared about. What had passed before he arrived seemed irrelevant, best left behind in that other place. On the beach, where life flowed at a languid pace, everyone started with a clean slate, missionary, mercenary and misfit alike.

Pondering the answer to Maina's query about what had brought him to this place, Jack was forced to dredge up memories that had lain undisturbed for five years. Where to start, and what to include? He wasn't even sure why he was doing this at all, except the girl seemed genuinely interested.

Despite her initial cheeky attitude, Maina proved a good listener, and so Jack simply drew a deep breath and waded in. And there, in the still air of the lounge, as his young listener sat motionless and intent, while traffic rumbled its way to and back from town on the road in front of the house, Jack proceeded to tramp through the sludge of his past. And while he revisited this once-familiar terrain, he filtered the events through mental fingers, carefully examining each clod for a possible clue as to where, and how, it all went wrong.

It wasn't a pleasant tale he spun, but he hoped it could somehow prove a cautionary one. Later, when the words had ended, and he remained sitting while Maina drifted off to the shower to wash away the grit that will accumulate when you spend two days sitting on the crowded deck of a small boat, he felt a sense of emptiness. He'd dusted off the buried layers of his past to reveal them to a 16-year-old stranger and found nothing had changed with the passage of time. No hidden meanings were revealed, no forgotten revelations flooded back. No great truths stripped naked.

The exquisite and painful drama of his former existence seemed laughable—trite even—now that the quiet pulse of island time had become his new reality.

The book, the movie, the marriage—these seemed little more than ludicrous plot points in a fairy tale about some kid who dared to dream of the bright lights and then, against insurmountable odds, had his wish granted. He had lapped it all up, splashed in it, while remaining oblivious to the reality that, on the other side of those wondrous, blinding lights—on the other side of that voluptuous curtain in the Emerald City—was a dark and brutal path indeed.

LOS ANGELES, 2000

He craved drugs. Crack, horse, E, uppers, downers: he didn't care. He wanted an addiction; he needed to be hooked. He wanted to be slipping wadded hundred-dollar bills to the pimply-faced kid who delivered the mail each day to his office on the Citation Films lot.

In return, he'd be handed an envelope, a vial, a syringe, a handful of pills: salvation in chemicals.

He craved alcohol. Great flagons of red wine, magnums of champagne whose bubbles would twitch his nose and send him into thunderous fits of sneezing. Cardboard boxes of beer clawed to shreds in his haste to get at their contents. Dead soldiers on every available surface, leaving sticky rings because he was too busy getting pissed to give a shit about coasters.

He sweated for a virus. A diabolical confederation of coded evil that would lurk, unseen, in the bowels of his computer. Upon the mere touch of a solitary pad on the keyboard, the mere presence of a single letter, flashing like a tiny lighthouse beacon on the great grey ocean of his screen, this virus, this collection of ruthless binary buccaneers, would launch forth, seize that unfortunate character and eradicate the bastard.

It all came down to this: he was searching for a crutch, an excuse, a logical reason he could point to and say, there, that's why I'm not writing. It couldn't possibly be my fault, he would carefully explain, that the part of my brain that had once tumbled out *Resurrection Waters* in such a freshet of words that my fingers could barely keep pace, is now a tattered and empty bag of tricks.

Jack saw Maina's eyebrows arch as he told of meetings during which Ray Chimera had practically dropped to his knees and begged him to write something. *To write anything.*

"You're killing me here," Ray whined. "I, uh, *we* need another book."

Resurrection Waters went to a third printing, timed to the release of *Blood and Ruins.* Everyone was happy.

For a time. Before things changed.

Before an industry that constantly required fresh blood to fuel its momentum became demanding. Before the Beast, the Machine, having chewed up Jack's first book and finding the flavor to its liking, commanded a second helping.

Only that second helping needed to be soon, before the Beast, the Machine lost its taste for Jack Nolan and moved on to its next meal.

"Please, *please* do not be a one-hit wonder," Ray implored. Jack thought the little weasel was actually going to cry. "That would be a fuck-up of Biblical proportions. Jack, my son, you need to start typing and you need to start typing right fucking now."

Jack looked blankly across the desk at Ray, just as, in the evenings high in the hills, he looked blankly across the dining room table at Nile. How could he possibly explain to these people that the well had run dry?

They could wave contracts under his nose, or cite rapidly dwindling bank accounts, or exchange the costly 4WD for a more modest sedan. None of it could alter the stark awful truth: Jack Nolan was empty.

Was it writer's block? Sophomore slump? Mind cramp? Jack didn't know. He knew only this: something had caused the right side of his brain to clench into a tight fist.

Jack stared at himself in the shaving mirror. Stared at the haggard ghoul he saw in the reflection. Stared into the abyss of reality: that he had within him the talent, the desire, *the burning*, to write one book, and one only.

Now that he'd accomplished that feat, the magic had simply evaporated.

He was convinced that he could sit at his desk in front of his computer terminal in his air-conditioned office on the lot of Citation Films until the length of his beard set some sort of world record, and he would never again be able to write another thing worth reading.

Ray could cajole and bluster and curse. Nile could heave expensive crockery and slam doors and eventually demand that he sleep in the guest bedroom. Paul Stengler could fume and brandish papers and spout his lawyer's name. All those people who had once supported him and loved him and stroked him could finally, irrefutably, show their true colors, and it would matter not one bit.

Jack Nolan, the writer, was no more. He was smoke.

He spoke rapidly as he related all of this to Maina, as if the pain could be prevented from penetrating as deeply this time if he were to only tread lightly on the details, like a man on ice, not knowing which step will cause that terrible rippling crack of doom.

He told of the day his agent arrived at his office with the mail boy, both of them juggling empty cardboard boxes.

"Stengler wants you out," Ray said simply, then left.

When Jack carried out the first load, he discovered that the lot maintenance crew had somehow moved his car and were busy painting out his name on his parking stall.

There were two messages on the answering machine when he returned to his dark house in the hills. One was from his brother, saying hello. The other was from his wife, saying goodbye.

"Porter wants to talk to you," Jack told Ray when he finally tracked his agent down.

"I talked to Ray," Porter told him later after introducing him to his new wife, Maryanne, who had once been his girlfriend and was still an accountant. "He's fucked you, bro. Do you understand me?"

Porter related how it took several loud outbursts and much pounding on desks before Ray agreed to let Maryanne and him have Jack's financial records.

"He'd make a great chef, because he's been cooking the books since the day he met you," Porter said, while Jack stood looking out that impossibly huge picture window and wondered which pair of those millions of headlights belonged to Nile.

"He didn't steal from you directly, but the dodgy bastard charged a lot of his personal expenses against your share of the royalties."

Jack didn't move.

"Are you even listening?"

Jack turned then, his face a vacant mask of resignation. He looked at Porter and Maryanne and saw how their discovery of Ray's dubious accounting practices had brought a flush of excitement to their cheeks. Two hounds licking the fox's salty blood from their teeth.

"Oh, I'm listening alright," he said. "It's just that I'm not as surprised as you seem to be."

"Your agent's a crook and you don't give a damn?" Maryanne was stunned by his lack of emotion.

"You're not seeing the big picture here." Jack's smile was a sad smear across his face.

"You're absolutely right, big brother," Porter said. "So why don't you explain it to us."

"It's simple, really," Jack said. "I used to think those stories about the small-town schmuck who struck it rich were pure crap, thought up by some hack who'd never entertained an original thought in his life. But you know what? I'm living proof that crazy things do happen."

"Is this going somewhere?" asked Porter.

Jack held up his hand. "My point is that these last two years have been a bad movie for whatever reason—maybe I pissed off the God of Good Literature or something—and I was the star. And now it's merely heading to its logical conclusion. If you were watching this at the Walnut Grove Twin Cinemas, you would have predicted the same thing I have."

"And that is?"

"Because I had everything, now I have to lose everything. So, of course, Nile buggers off at the first sign of trouble. And, of course, Ray is ripping me off."

"You're talking crazy," Porter said.

"Maybe. And maybe not. But it makes sense to me, and that's all that matters. I even know how this ends."

"Oh, this should be good," said Porter. "Do tell."

"The small-town schmuck, his life now a tattered mess, goes crazy and drives off a cliff."

"How very *Thelma and Louise* of him."

Jack shrugged. "I told you it was a bad movie. Now what do you want me to do about Ray?"

"You really should sue the bastard," Maryanne said. "But—"

"But what?"

"But that could get expensive," Porter interjected.

"Am I correct in assuming that there is a Plan B here?"

The look on Porter's and Maryanne's faces confirmed that they were indeed way ahead of him. When had his baby brother become so smart?

"We, uh, worked out a deal with Ray, on the threat of going to the press," said Porter. "He's in enough trouble as it is, what with Citation Films pulling the plug on his production deal."

"The plot sickens," Jack said, dropping into a chair. "This is all because of me, isn't it? It's my fault."

"It doesn't much matter whose fault it is now," said Porter. "The thing is, Ray Chimera was taking you up the ass from the second you signed on as a client."

"Squeal like a pig," Jack murmured to himself while Porter and Maryanne exchanged concerned glances.

Maryanne had also found discrepancies in the way Jack's taxes were paid, with money owed to both the US and Canadian governments. After agreeing to straighten that mess out, Ray reluctantly signed an agreement allowing all future transactions involving Jack's royalties to be handled by Maryanne's firm. In return, Porter assured Ray that no one in his family would take any further action.

"We done here?" Ray asked as he watched Porter and Maryanne snap close their briefcases.

"You're the one who's done, Mr. Chimera," Maryanne smiled, baring her canines. "Have a nice day."

"Yeah, well fuck you," Ray growled. "And fuck your brother."

Now it was Porter's turn to smile. "You already did."

"What do I do now?" Jack asked, even though he already knew the answer.

After Porter and Maryanne left, he packed up the few belongings he actually cared about and drove down through the canyons and away from the house. He left behind everything he associated with Nile. In the process, he managed not to drive off a single cliff.

"Well, that sucked," Maina said when he had finished his story.

Jack laughed. "My thoughts exactly."

Maina's eyebrows drew together. "But you still haven't told me how you ended up here."

It was, Jack told her, Porter who'd suggested that he take a short holiday while his finances were put in order. If he decided to stop somewhere for any length of time, Maryanne's firm could always wire cash to his new address.

His mother drove him to the travel agency, located in the same strip mall as The Last Page bookstore where this had all started what now seemed like centuries ago.

"I had absolutely no idea where I wanted to go," Jack told Maina. "All I really wanted was some place hot and quiet."

And there, taped to the window of the travel agent's office, was a four-color poster of Muri Beach. Rarotonga. The Cook Islands.

"I didn't even bother asking about any other place," he said. "That was five years ago."

"And you've been here ever since?" asked Maina.

"Yup."

"But you will go home again sometime, right? Back to Canada?"

"I don't think so."

"Why not?"

"Because," he said, waving his arm, "this is my home now. My demons can't touch me here."

"Oh," said Maina. "Lucky you."

TEN

"I want only old, ugly women in my church!" Rev. Albert Smail thundered, causing a great roar to erupt from the group of men sitting around his table on the Rocket Bar's outdoor deck.

"Why is that?" someone asked, right on cue.

"Because then I will never be tempted to seduce anyone from my own congregation!"

Another roar of laughter followed. It was an old line, one that Jack and the others had heard the reverend use on numerous occasions, but they still found the humor in it. Maybe it was because they knew the close rein that Albert's wife Apii kept on the holy man. Maybe it was because they knew Albert had six children, with number seven on the way, and therefore had neither the time nor the energy to stray.

Other than these weekly Wednesday evening meetings with his close friends, which Apii only grudgingly agreed to let him attend, the Rev. Albert Smail rarely had time for matters that didn't pertain to home or church.

There were three other men at the table with Jack and Albert: a local artist named Tini Katu; Ford Nelson, owner of the Deep Blue Sea Diving Company; and Tommy Niomare, the man in charge of media relations for the prime minister's office. In their own way, Jack's four companions were among the most influential men on the island, and he felt privileged to be invited to share in their weekly gatherings.

"Tell us about the body." Albert raised his glass of beer at Jack.

The reverend was an interesting mix. His mother was a Kiwi, but his father's blood was equal parts Cook Islands Maori, Tahitian and Niuean. The result of all this blending showed in the color of Albert's skin—which was lighter in tone than most of his fellow islanders—and eyes that were more hazel than deep brown.

He was below average in height and had somehow managed to maintain a trim waist despite the fattening temptations of the numerous umukais his parishioners invited him to every month. But what the Rev. Smail lacked in stature or bulk, he made up for with character. He was a born leader, a man who could talk to anyone on nearly any subject and had the good sense to simply listen if he had nothing meaningful to contribute. Men admired him because he both understood and forgave their weaknesses. Women respected him because they could gush at his charm and cheeky wit without feeling that their virtue was in any danger.

A friend to those in need, a shoulder to lean on in tough times, a calming influence when a marriage seemed about to implode into violence, the Rev. Albert Smail was a genuine island hero, beloved of all.

Well, almost all.

Albert was a second-generation rebel. Thirty years earlier, his father, the Rev. Isaiah Smail, unhappy with the political squabbling among the rank and file of the Cook Islands Christian Church, had joined forces with the equally dissatisfied Rev. Dante Akimo to break away. The two of them formed the Sonrise Christian Church of the Holy Spirit. Albert had followed his father into the ministry, just as Rev. Akimo's son, Moses, had emulated his own father.

But, five years ago, Albert and Moses had a falling out over dubious bookkeeping practices and, once again, a Smail opened a new house of worship. The Church of Christ's Blood had moved into an abandoned shop just down the road from Jack's house in Matavera.

Albert spent two eternally hot weeks striding through the neighborhood, knocking on doors, talking to shoppers at the Matavera Beach Store, joining the parents who waited in the shade for their children to emerge from classes at the Matavera Primary School.

He'd stand there, suit jacket slung over an arm, straw hat clutched in one hand while he wiped the moisture from his brow and his crown of bristling hair with a white handkerchief, and simply visit with the people. He wanted to know what their concerns were, what made them happy, what scared them, how their life in the village could be improved.

He walked for miles, a tiny man with a huge smile, a firm handshake, and an uncanny ability to know when a wide-eyed child needed a cooling ice block. Leaders from the other churches on the island, including Moses Akimo, scoffed at his street-level approach to spreading the Good Word. They said he was maki maki, that he was sick in the head.

Jack met Albert several times during the reverend's walking tour, had even taken photos of him for *The Tribune*. Had been impressed by the man's views and opinions.

"I'll be honest with you," Albert had told him. "You come into my church and I promise not to shove Christ down your throat. You don't want that, I don't want that. I intend to show by example how a man of the Lord lives his life, and then maybe you and the other villagers might want to come listen to me talk every Sunday morning at 10:30."

Jack wasn't the only one who saw something different in the Church of Christ's Blood. That first service, during which the Rev. Albert Smail announced that he wasn't interested in offering last chances, but rather the 50th chance or the 100th, attracted a standing-room-only crowd to the converted shop. One that was quite happy to leave behind nearly $3,000 in the collection plate.

Jack drained his beer, waved to Roger Henderson at the bar, and turned back to Albert.

"Not much to report, actually," he said. "And I certainly wouldn't want to scoop tomorrow's *Tribune*. You'll just have to spend a dollar each to find out all the juicy details."

Ford Nelson snorted. "As if we read that piece of shit. C'mon, spill the beans."

Jack shrugged. "All I heard was that the fellow's a German who was staying at the Breaker Point. He was part of a group of visitors here for some kind of seminar on education."

Albert clapped his hands. "Perfect!" he exclaimed. "Where are they from? America? Europe? It doesn't matter. All those currencies are strong against the Kiwi dollar. We must make a point of inviting them out to Sunday's service."

Tommy Niomare's eyebrows arched in puzzlement. "Seminar? What seminar?"

Jack leaned forward. "You don't know about a seminar being held at Breaker Point?"

"First I heard of it."

"For a spin doctor, bro, you are seriously out of the loop," Tini Katu said, shaking his great shaggy head.

Ford chuckled. "Tommy's too busy deciding where his services are required the most. Between the Tahitian film crew shooting their surfie doco, or holding the French ambassador's hand during that fine, gift-bearing gentleman's annual visit, he hasn't got the time to worry about some lousy teachers trying to shovel more maths into our kids' brains."

Albert finished his beer and smacked his lips. "My policy is to always go where the cameras are."

"But there'll be cameras at both events," Tommy pointed out.

Roger Henderson leaned into the table, depositing a bottle of Lion Red in front of each of the men.

"In that case," Albert said, raising his fresh beer, "my advice to you is to go where the women are."

"Surfies!" the men sang out in an enthusiastic chorus, joining in the reverend's toast.

"Everyone seen that superyacht in the Avatiu Harbor?" asked Ford.

Jack frowned. "I drove right past there today and didn't even notice."

"That's because there's always a couple dozen of them moored there at any one time," said Tommy.

"I guess I've just stopped looking at them," Jack said. "It only depresses me that I can't afford one."

"She's been here a week and I still haven't figured out where those pricks get the money to buy one of those beauties," said Ford.

"They'll be crying in their caviar if they don't push off before hurricane season starts next month," Tini piped up.

Jack hitched his chin at Ford. "What nationality is she?"

"Don't know," Ford said. "I don't recognize her flag."

"The harbormaster says it's Belgian," Albert interjected. "Says she's doing some kind of cruise around the South Pacific."

His companions turned to him.

"Do you know everything, or does it just seem that way?" asked Ford.

Albert grinned. "I know everything," he said, then turned his gaze on each of his companions in turn. "Now what else is new since last Wednesday?"

With Albert acting as the conductor, conversation swept around the table. It started with Ford, who expressed concern that his head instructor at Deep Blue might have done one too many dives. Apparently the poor bugger could no longer remember what day of the week it was.

"How terrible," said Albert. "Ford, you've definitely got to help this unfortunate. At the very least, inform him when it's Sunday so he can attend my service."

As for Tini Katu, he returned to a favorite rant, the one about how visiting artists are allowed to sell their work on the island.

"Don't you go rolling your eyes at me," he said, wagging his finger at his drinking partners. "I don't care if you have heard this all before. The point is, it has to be stopped. These people come here, use our land and our people as subject matter, then turn around and make a profit from their work while the local art community—and yes, that does include me—struggles to survive."

Tini's finger stopped under Tommy's nose. "And it's all the fault of your bloody government."

"My government?" Tommy's eyes widened at the accusation. "And which government would that be? I've had this job for four years and I've already had to deal with three prime ministers." He turned to Jack. "Maybe if the local newspaper kept its nose out of other people's business, we could actually retain a government long enough to make some worthwhile changes."

Jack took a big gulp of beer then shook his bottle. "Oh, look," he said, "I'm empty."

He pushed back his chair and hurried towards the bar.

Roger Henderson was busy serving a pair of women tourists. Jack hung back to watch the bar owner at work.

Roger was in his 60s, but he was still a charming rogue. He wore his blond hair long and tied back in a ponytail so it wouldn't obscure the perfectly chiseled cheekbones that had at once incited fits of hysteria among teenage girls. His teeth still gleamed, as capped teeth will. His tan, a deep oak, only served to make the metallic blue glint of his eyes all the more startling. The two girlies who giggled at his naughty double entendres while he mixed their umbrella drinks didn't know it, but they were talking to rock' n' roll royalty in the flesh.

Jack's eyes were drawn once again to the framed photograph hanging over the bar. The colors had faded in the 40 years since the image was first captured on film, and the inked autographs were barely legible, but the bold confidence on the faces of the young men in the picture was unmistakable.

There were five of them in the photo, all dressed in matching white shirts and crisply pressed tan chinos, their shaggy moptops symbolic of a new generation that was eagerly rattling the cages of the old world order to the jangling accompaniment of electric guitars.

The young men formed a rough circle around a Ludwig drum kit. The band's name was emblazoned across the stretched skin of the bass drum: Roger and The Rockets. During the '60s, anyone who dug songs about surfing and cars and girls bought records by three groups: the Beach Boys, Jan and Dean, and Roger and the Rockets.

Roger Henderson and his bandmates scored six No.1 hits during a four-year run at the surf-rock throne, and played at sold-out concert halls across North America, Europe and Japan. But that was before it all turned to custard.

As Roger grinned and winked broadly at his customers, Jack mentally ticked off each member's fate as his gaze circled the photo.

Chip Foster, 25, bass guitar, collector of exotic pets, crushed to death on August 12, 1965, by a ravenous Burmese python who mistook him for the biggest rat in God's wide kingdom. Eric Crozier, 30, rhythm guitar, left the Rockets to form Muney Shot, playing guitar in bathtub on Oct. 25, 1969, when his girlfriend, confusing the power cords while vacuuming, accidentally plugged in his amp. Dunc Ritchie, 32, drummer, stoned on acid, decided to play golf in the nude during an electrical storm, hit by lightning on July 6, 1974, outside Baton Rouge, Louisiana.

Dennis Cooper, 59, co-founder and lead guitarist, popularized the wearing of Ben Franklin-style sunglasses. Car found crushed amidst the rubble of a parking garage near the World Trade Centre on Sept. 11, 2001. Missing and presumed dead.

Roger Henderson, co-founder, keyboardist, singer/songwriter. Farm boy from Wisconsin who was 18 before he ever saw the ocean. Fell madly in love with its salty seductiveness during an outing to Huntington Beach while his family was in California to visit Disneyland. Went back to the heartland, formed a band, wrote songs about a lifestyle he could only imagine, and rode those dream waves to wealth and fame.

Watched helplessly as the group disintegrated in a squall of drugs and alcohol and clashing egos. Lost his recording contract. Put his first million up his nose and his last million into a yacht.

Caught in a hurricane near Fiji, limped into Avatiu Harbor and never left. Invested in a seaside bar, christened it after his group so the name would live on, and embarked on a new career of flirting with female tourists. Living and breathing at 62.

The girls scooped up their drinks and turned away, laughing to themselves. Roger watched their shapely retreat, nodding his head in appreciation.

"Hey, Jack," he finally said. "What for can I do ya?"

"One more for the road." Jack handed over his empty bottle. Roger reached into the cooler behind him for a replacement.

Jack looked back at the photo. "Where does it all go?"

Roger placed the new bottle on the bar. "I sell it to you, you piss it out, and then I sell you another one. It's called commerce."

Jack shook his head. "I mean talent, Roger. What happens to the talent? What causes someone to go from being a creative genius one day to where you can't string two ideas together the next?"

"Ouch," Roger winced, drying his hands on a towel. "You sure know how to hurt a guy."

Jack tugged at the beer. "Sorry, Rog. I didn't mean you specifically. Hell, the Rockets were the greatest," he said. "My dad loved you guys. Used to sing your songs around the house all the time. He wasn't a great singer, mind you, but he sure was enthusiastic."

"Your dad? Oh shit, man." Roger's expression grew pained. "First I'm a washed-up, no-talent has-been and now I'm *old*? You're Suzy Flippin' Sunshine tonight, my friend, let me tell you."

"I wasn't picking on you, Roger," Jack said. "I was just thinking out loud."

Roger used the towel to wipe moisture rings off the bar. "I'd love to still be making records," he said. "Only I guess it would be CDs these days. I can feel all these songs just rattling around inside my head, but I can't seem to get them out."

Captain Tai saluted as he headed for the door. Roger waved back. "And even if I did, who'd want to listen to them anyway? I could never write that shit the kids are listening to these days."

"Do you ever think that maybe talent is a finite gift?" Jack asked, straddling a barstool. "That it's somehow pre-packaged in these fragile boxes of words or notes or drawings or speeches, and that each person only gets so much. A ration. But once you use up that talent, once that box is emptied out, that's it, you're done. I think that's what happened to me, Roger, and probably to you as well."

Roger looked at Jack for a long moment in silence, then reached over and scooped up Jack's bottle. "OK, cowboy, I think you've had enough for one night. Why don't you go back and talk to your friends."

"Did I touch a nerve, Rog?"

"Not really, Jack," Roger said. The lines on his forehead crunched. His eyes narrowed. "I just don't happen to agree with you, is all. Your theory of limited talent sounds like a copout to me. A sorry excuse to stop trying. To just give up. There are a million reasons why I'm behind this bar right now and not in a recording studio, and it's very important to me that I believe that it has more to do with me falling out of favor with the paying customers than running out of talent. But you don't see my crying about it. I turned the page, Jack, I moved on. So I'm not Roger Henderson, Teen Idol, anymore. Who cares? The important thing is that I still think the rascal I see in the mirror every morning is a good guy."

"Holy shit," Jack said. "You bartenders really do know all the answers."

"Not really." Roger shook his head. "But I'm at peace with myself, and I don't think you are."

"No?"

"No," Roger said. "You hit a dry spell. So what? It happens to all creative people. The key is to get over it and get on with it. You've moped around this island for years, hiding behind some lame-ass excuse about writer's block when all you need is to stop screwing around and just sit down and start typing."

"It's that simple?"

"Damn straight," Roger said.

Jack leaned across the bar. "What if I told you that I've actually started another book?"

"I'd say good on ya, mate," Roger smiled. "Now take your goddamn talent boxes and get out of my face. Some of us have to work for a living."

"Ready for another beer?" said Albert when Jack returned to the table. "I'm shouting the next round."

"I've had enough, thanks," Jack said. "I'm meeting Heather in a couple minutes and I need to be sober."

"I'll drink to that," said Tini Katu.

Jack looked around the table. "I might have a problem," he said.

"Yeah," chortled Ford Nelson. "You're missing a beer."

The other men started to laugh. Albert waved them to silence. "Shush," he said. "Jack's trying to be serious here. What sort of problem, my friend?"

"There's a girl at my house."

"That's my kind of problem," Tommy Niomare piped up before a withering glance from Albert closed his mouth.

"Who is she?" Albert asked.

"Her name is Maina Rima," Jack said. "She says that her uncle Nga owns the house I'm renting."

"Isn't Nga dead?" asked Ford.

"He's in New Zealand," Jack said.

"Same thing."

"Give it a rest, Ford," snapped Albert. "What does the girl want?"

"She thinks she can stay in the house because it's on her family's land. Moved herself right in today while I was out."

"Oh dear," Albert shook his head. "There goes the neighborhood."

"Great." Jack threw up his hands. "Now everyone's a comedian."

Albert laughed and the others followed his example. "I'm sorry, Jack, but I wish you could see the look on your face. You'd think your dog died, or at least one of your precious chooks."

"So what's the problem?" asked Ford.

"I would think it's obvious," Jack said, his exasperation building. "I can't have a sixteen-year-old girl living with me. People are going to think I'm some kind of creep."

"Can she cook?" asked Tommy.

"What the hell does that have to do with anything?"

"If she can cook, send her to my place," Tommy grinned. "My partner burns raw fish."

Jack pushed away from the table. "You guys are starting to piss me off."

Albert placed his hand on Jack's shoulder and pushed him back into his chair. "We're just winding you up," Albert said. "All this beer has given us the Rocket's red glare."

Albert removed his hand and leaned in close. "But I'm serious now. What would you like us to do?"

Jack glowered at his tablemates, almost daring them to be cheeky. "I'd like you clowns to help me find someone on the island who's related to Maina, someone else she can move in with."

"No problem, Jack," Albert said. "I'll even mention it at Sunday's service, if you like."

"That would be great," said Jack. A movement on the other side of the room caught his attention. "Gotta go," he announced, getting to his feet. "My date's here."

ELEVEN

"So I'm wiping this guy's arse—"

Nurse Heather paused to spear another juicy chunk of ika mata.

Jack sighed, downed his fork, and nudged aside his own plate of raw fish marinated in coconut sauce. Normally he would be eating his favorite local dish with as much gusto as Heather was displaying, but the image of some stranger's soiled bottom had curtailed his appetite. He glanced around at the other diners in the restaurant, but no one was looking their way. That was a good thing.

Heather and Jack had walked from the Rocket Bar around the gentle curve of Avarua Harbor to the Seabreeze Café. It was only a short distance away and the soft wind off the water felt refreshing, drying the sweaty residue of another scorching day. The restaurant was crowded with tourists, but the hostess, a middle-aged local woman named Ina, found them a quiet table on the outside deck where they could see the stars reflected in the ocean's inky surface.

Heather had been Jack's ward nurse when he was hospitalized with the centipede bite, and they had gradually forged a comfortable relationship based on conversation. Jack had a writer's natural ability for listening and Heather never lacked for a good story.

Heather's surname was Flynn, but no one on the island bothered to use it. Everyone who knew her—her friends and co-workers, her patients and the members of their extended families who camped out in the hospital rooms until the healing process was complete—referred to her simply as Nurse Heather.

She was a Kiwi, raised in Gisborne, where she attended Campion College before earning a degree in Nursing from Massey University.

Her hair was cropped short—"I don't want it dangling into open wounds," she said—and indoors it reflected the color of fine whiskey. Outside, where the tropical sun worked to bring out the brilliance in everything, her head bore a crown of burnished copper.

Her eyes, large and green and flecked with fissures of gold, also demanded attention. Jack knew from experience that those orbs contained a life force of their own. They were twin emerald drill bits possessed of an uncanny ability to bore out even the most deeply buried of truths. You lied at your own peril in the presence of Heather Flynn.

She was in her mid-40s, tall and still attractive despite carrying the extra kilos that, over the years, had rounded her face and flared her hips. "There's just more of me to hug," she'd roar, before quickly placing the blame where it rightly belonged: on the twin evils of Cook Islands doughnuts and New Zealand ice cream.

Heather's history, for anyone who cared about such things, included two husbands—one buried, one divorced—and a desire to do more than be a glorified maid to the hypochondriacs who took up valuable beds at the St. Paul the Healer Hospital in Wellington. Nursing in Rarotonga—while oftentimes a struggle due to a shortage of supplies and trained personnel—provided the challenge she'd needed to revive the spirit and skills of a natural healer.

She enjoyed the enthusiasm of the local nurses and doctors, the way everyone pitched in to work as a team when dealing with the problems associated with small countries and even smaller health budgets. She loved the way meal breaks were considered a communal event, where everyone packed enough kai to share with the rest of the on-duty staff.

But if her professional life had risen anew from the ashes, her personal life remained a smoking ruin. By the time Jack met her, Heather had sworn off men entirely, in large part due to the influence of one Poto Rao.

She told the story to Jack one night, while they were drinking their way through the Stupor Tour.

The name of the tour personified truth in advertising: it consisted of a busload of tourists, hell-bent on destroying kidneys and brain cells, being driven around the island for one drink at as many bars as they could manage. The Stupor Tour ended when the hired driver was too off his face to steer properly. Passengers could only hope to be within walking distance of their accommodation before the driver passed out on the side of the road.

They'd started at the Rocket, then hit The Hole, Terry's, and the Boiler Room. They were now at the Mango House, with the Balcony Bar still ahead.

According to Heather, Poto had trouble written all over him, but it was in Cook Islands Maori, so she hadn't recognized the signs until it was too late.

Poto put on a beach show for tourists twice a week. Visitors paid handsomely to be entertained by a local troupe of musicians and dancers before tucking into a meal of island food prepared in an umu, or underground oven. The highlight of the show, however, was Poto Rao himself, who delighted audiences with his uncanny ability to snatch live fish from the lagoon with his bare hands. The catch would then be added to the menu as the main course. The fact that no one ever went away hungry from one of his shows only served to add another chapter to the burgeoning legend of the amazing Poto, God of the Sea.

Heather attended one of his shows shortly after arriving on the island, and had been impressed enough with his showmanship to linger afterwards to compliment him. Poto was pushing 50 but he was still attractive—tall, well-muscled, with a swimmer's sleekness topped by a great expanse of chest. Heather, lonely and vulnerable, soon fell under his warrior spell. They became lovers and co-workers.

She wrangled tourists, showed them how to weave plates out of palm fronds, and helped with the preparation and serving of the meal. What she didn't do was reveal Poto's secret: that the fish he supposedly plucked from the ocean's depths were actually held captive in a wooden cage wedged unseen beneath rocks at the edge of the lagoon. While the entertainers distracted the punters, Poto would simply swim down to the cage, open the trap door, reach in, and grab one of the fish he had placed there that morning. It was all sleight-of-hand, easily detectable by anyone who cared to take a close look. No one ever did.

Heather discovered that the people skills she used at the hospital were just as valuable on the beach. The coconut wireless spread the word, tourists heard it, and the business flourished. The show became so popular, in fact, that they added a lunch matinee on Saturdays. It was a little trickier for Poto to pull off his chicanery in the full light of day, but Heather solved that problem by hiring younger dancers. Beguiled by the delightful efforts of small children, no attention was paid to what Poto was up to in the lagoon until he emerged, blinking salt water out of his eyes, triumphantly holding his catch over his head.

Heather and Poto worked so well together, in fact, that marriage was inevitable.

"It was quite the wedding," Heather told Jack. "To this day, people still talk about that party, maybe because it was the first time they could remember Poto actually shouting anyone a beer."

"So what happened?" Jack asked. "Why aren't you still married?"

"He pissed me off."

"He pissed you off?"

Heather shrugged. "The party lasted all night, with bonfires on the beach and everyone dancing and singing and playing ukuleles and drums. It was great fun."

"And then?"

"And then we got back to our place, Poto sat down, put his feet up and demanded I fetch him a beer," Heather said. "When I opened the fridge door and that little light went on, it seemed to set off a light in my head at the same time. I closed the fridge, packed my things and left."

Jack stared. "And so the marriage lasted—"

"Less than a day."

"Shit."

"Exactly." Heather nodded emphatically.

"But it's a small island," Jack said. "Didn't you two keep running into each other?"

"We did for awhile," she said. "And he was always whining about me coming back to him. Finally I told him that if he didn't stop bothering me, I'd tell everyone that the real reason I left was because he had a small pane."

"Remind me not to piss you off."

"Then just behave yourself," she said, then added, "Now I steer well clear of men."

"What about sex?" Jack asked, swallowing a belch.

"Who needs sex when I have Roland?"

The burp died in Jack's throat. "And just who is Roland?"

"He's big and he's black and he's hard," Heather purred. "And he sits quietly in the drawer by my bed until I need him. Sometimes I even take him to work if I'm on the night shift."

Jack grimaced. "OK, now you're starting to gross me out."

Heather ignored the remark. "I don't have to cook for him," she continued. "Or clean up after him, or wait up for him when he's, you know, 'working late.' And, best of all, he doesn't make me sleep on the wet spot."

"The perfect love machine," Jack said. "But I am disappointed in one thing."

"Only one?" Heather's right eyebrow arched. "I must be losing my touch. Alright, what is it?"

"You're still perpetuating the myth about how bigger is better."

Heather laughed evilly. "I hate to shatter your illusion, Jack, but size really does matter," she said. "For centuries, women have protected the fragile male ego by telling our partners that we didn't care if they were hung like a mozzie. But we were lying because we wanted to get laid."

Heather pointed to the pained expression on Jack's face. "What's the matter, you don't like to think that maybe we can be the aggressor as well?" she asked. "That we might have fantasies of our own?"

Jack squirmed in his chair as Heather explained how women long to be taken by a passionate lover skilled in the art of seduction.

"And what do we get instead?" she said, waving a finger under Jack's crinkled nose. "A couple seconds of tongue that's supposed to pass as foreplay, a few frantic pokes, and then it's 'where's the remote, love, the game's on.' That's about as romantic as having a rabid dog hump your leg."

"You say that like it's a bad thing," Jack said.

Heather shook her head in disappointment "So what do we do about it? Zilch. We play the dutiful lover. We moan and wriggle around and sometimes let out a scream or two of rapture, then sigh and snuggle into our hero's arms. We bat our eyes and whisper about what a wonderfully skilled cocksman he is. Pure bullshit, let me assure you."

Jack frowned. "I'm still confused," he said. "How is it that, if you're so busy acting, that you still have time to make observations about size?"

"Are you saying that the truth hurts, little boy?" Heather wet her lips with a quick dart of her tongue.

"OK, here's a real news flash for you," Jack scowled. "Men hate it when women use 'little' when describing anything about them."

"What is it about men and their meat?" Heather gave her head a weary shake. "Poor sad creatures, thinking that having a dick somehow makes a difference. Frankly, I'm tired of the whole subject matter. I've seen so much pane over the years at the hospital that I don't even think about them anymore."

"Do you ever think about mine?"

"Only if it's shouting my next beer."

They'd abandoned the Stupor Tour soon after, staggering arm-in-arm back to her place. They were probably singing, but neither could remember later. But there were things they never forgot.

She'd said something. He leaned in closer to hear it. She opened her mouth and placed her lips on his. Then their clothes were on the floor.

They were going hard on the bed, with Jack still in his long, slow strokes, when Heather put her hands on his shoulders to stop him.

"What are we doing?"

He thought about her question. The more he thought, the softer he grew. When the answer hadn't occurred to him by the time he fell out of her, he dressed and drove home, suddenly and terribly sober.

They never talked about that night again. Instead they became best mates, slipping comfortably into a platonic relationship. She returned to Roland. He continued his pursuit of brown girls.

"Are you going to finish that?" Heather pointed her fork at the remains of Jack's ika mata.

Jack pushed the plate towards her. "Be my guest."

Heather used a paper napkin to swipe coconut milk off her chin. "This is so good," she said around a mouthful of fish. "Now where was I?"

"I was asking you about autopsies and then you started in on some story about cleaning up a patient," he said. "Then I felt crook, you ate my entrée, and I'm sitting here wondering where your story is going."

Heather's fork clattered to the table. She sat up straighter. "It's been a long time since breakfast," she said.

"What are you talking about?"

"If someone shit in your Ricies, you really should be over it by now," she said. "There's more bothering you than some dead tourist, isn't there?"

Jack rubbed at his eyes. A busy day was catching up to him. He was suddenly very tired.

"Through no fault of my own, I've somehow acquired a flatmate," he said, explaining how Maina came to be occupying his second bedroom.

"Now I understand why you seem a bit preoccupied," she said. "So you're forgiven for not giving me the 100 percent attention that I demand. But this girl, she hasn't got any other place to go?"

"So she says," Jack sighed, his head drooping.

Heather reached across the table, took hold of his chin, and lifted his face so she could see his eyes. "She can always stay with me, you know."

Jack nodded. "I appreciate the offer, I really do," he said. "But this has somehow become my problem and I'll just have to deal with it."

Heather shrugged, and returned to her meal. "Personally, I think the company will do you good. I worry about you rattling around that house all by yourself."

"Excuse me," Jack said. "But I do not 'rattle.' I have lots of things to keep me busy."

"Name one."

"I freelance for *The Tribune*, for one."

"And then you take your camera home, plug it into your home computer, and e-mail it by using your home phone line." Heather laughed. "Oh yeah, that sounds terribly exciting to me."

Jack reached for his wineglass. "Anytime you're finished ripping apart my personal life, you can always continue with your story."

Heather chewed thoughtfully on the final piece of raw fish. "I just thought you might be interested in that particular patient," she said. "The silly bugger had the incredibly poor timing to be walking under a palm tree when a coconut decided to fall. The impact cracked his shoulder and knocked him to the ground. He landed the wrong way and broke his other arm. So now he's basically helpless."

"Hence the wiping of arse." Jack nodded. "Now I understand. But why would I be interested in that particular patient?"

"Because," Heather leaned over the table, "he was attending the same seminar as the man who died. I just thought it was such a terrible coincidence that two men, both here for the same reason, would have such terrible luck."

Jack perked up. Now Heather had his attention. "Are you sure your Coconut Man has something to do with the seminar?"

Heather sipped at her wine. "Well, he does have a thick European accent, but I'm certain that he said something about that being the reason he came to Raro. What's going on, Jack? You usually don't get this excited about my stories, especially the ones that concern men's butts."

Jack stroked his chin in thought. "It just seems strange that Tommy Niomare wouldn't know anything about this educational seminar. There might be a story idea in there somewhere."

Ina stopped by their table to collect their empty dishes. Jack smiled and thanked her.

Heather watched as Ina maneuvered an armful of dirty plates to the kitchen. Then she returned her attention to Jack. "A story idea? You mean for *The Tribune*?"

Jack flashed a secretive grin. "Maybe," he said. "Or maybe it's for me."

Heather took his hand. "You're writing again? Jack, that's wonderful news."

Jack pulled his hand away. "Don't get too excited just yet," he said, a note of caution creeping into his voice. "I'm only mulling over some plot points at this stage. But, over the past week or so, it just seems that my brain and my fingers are connected again."

"I'm going to assume that has something to do with the writing process."

"You'll have to excuse my overactive imagination," Jack said. "Roger Henderson just gave me hell for sitting on my arse and feeling sorry for myself. He's got a point. Maybe the words are still here," he tapped his forehead, "and I just have to try harder to get them out."

"So what do you think has caused this sudden reappearance of your muse?"

Jack flashed to Maina's reaction at meeting the author of *Resurrection Waters*. He smiled to himself.

"I couldn't tell you," he said. "Maybe the heat here has suddenly melted away whatever brain freeze I was suffering from."

He held up a finger. "But don't get too excited just yet. There's a big difference between my brain cells starting to crackle again and anything actually appearing on the shelves of Vonnia's Bookstore."

"I'll be patient," Heather assured him. "But I want a signed copy and I want it free."

"Done," Jack said. "Now indulge a curious writer and tell me more about this dead tourist before the main course arrives."

"You probably know more than I do because you work for the newspaper," Heather said. "The ambo boys fished him out of the pool and brought him to the hospital. Dr. Rangi did a quick examination on site, took a closer look at the hospital, and then someone collected the body. It was all over probably within two hours of you being at the scene."

"Did Dr. Rangi determine cause of death?"

Heather regarded him for a beat. "I'm no expert, but unless this fellow discovered how to inhale water, I think it's safe to assume that he drowned. C'mon, Jack, you were there. You saw him."

Jack picked up his table knife and began to tap it. "I saw a body in a pool. What if he had a heart attack or a brain aneurysm?"

Heather grabbed the knife out of his hand. "Maybe he was just a bad swimmer."

"I saw bruises on the man's shoulders?"

"And?"

"And those might have been the sign of a struggle."

"Or maybe he was hit by a coconut too," she said. "But, yeah, you're right about one thing."

"I am? Which part?"

"The part," Heather said, "about your overactive imagination."

Jack slumped in his chair. "Gee, thanks."

"Sometimes you just think too much."

Jack's eyebrows flinched. "I only asked about the possibility of an autopsy. Just to be absolutely certain."

Heather sighed. "An autopsy costs $900. Who's going to pay for that? You?" Jack shook his head. "I didn't think so. If the police are satisfied that it was an accident, then that's good enough for me. And it should be good enough for you as well."

"And the body has already been released?"

"Yes. One of the seminar organizers collected it."

"That was fast."

"Have you seen our morgue? It's about the size of this table," Heather said. "There's just enough room for two gurneys. After that, it's strictly standing room only. You want someone's dearly departed grandfather propped up in the corner just because some dead tourist tripped and hurt his shoulder?"

"Of course not," Jack said. "Did you see who picked up the body?"

"I just caught a quick glimpse," she said. "But I can tell you he was massive. Like a footy player or something. Big and blond."

Jack flashed back to Captain Tai's tour group: the big man who appeared to be in charge of the other passengers.

Heather reached across the table again and gave his ear lobe a gentle squeeze. "Let it go, Jack. You know what they say about places like Raro."

"That things happen on islands?"

She nodded. "Exactly. Sorry, but you'll just have to look someplace else for your next story." She looked up. "Oh good, here comes Ina with our meals. You didn't happen to see what was on the dessert tray when we came in, did you?"

TWELVE

Her eyes snap open in the dark. *There is someone in the room with her.*

She holds her breath, struggling not to generate a single sound. Hears, at first, only the bass notes of her own heart thudding behind her ribs.

There, near the doorway. The sibilation of ragged breathing, of air being sucked between teeth in quick, excited bursts.

Oh, God, he's back.

She strains her eyes until she makes out his form, a lighter shadow in a well of darkness. He moves towards the bed and she wills herself to be still. If he thinks she's asleep, maybe he'll go away. It has worked before. *Just don't turn your back to him*, she reminds herself. *Whatever you do, do not turn away.*

He moves again. Closer now. His agitated breathing grows louder, his outline more distinct as he looms over the end of her bed.

"Hey," he whispers, hoping to stir her. "Don't be afraid. It's only me."

He reaches out to touch her and the motion spurs her to action. She kicks frantically to disengage herself from the bed's lone sheet. Digs her heels into the thin mattress for traction. Her legs pedal madly to get away, far away, from him. She stops only when her back slams hard up against the cold concrete blocks of the wall. She cracks her head.

Through a prism of hot tears, she sees the singlet and panties she'd stripped down to in an effort to escape the smothering clutches of the hot night. She stretches out trembling fingers, touches the crumpled sheet, and yards the thin material up to cover her body. Clutches it tightly under her chin, a shroud for those whose spirits have died.

"You're awake," he breathes huskily. "Good."

There comes the soft whisper of cloth hitting the lino floor. He sits on her bed. The springs protest with tiny, metallic squeals. Movement now—up, down—as he hunches into himself. The bedsprings mark time: coiled metronomes measuring the rhythm of depravity. He sucks in labored gasps.

He grunts once, heaves to his feet, and shuffles to stand beside her. She strains back against the cinder blocks, eyes welded shut. Wills her body to squeeze between the blocks, to ooze her molecules through the mortar of coral dust and tiny pebbles retrieved from the beach in rusting wheelbarrows trundled by old men with thick hands. She won't stop until she is outside the house, until she is where the air is cooler and there are no monsters saying: "Give me your hand."

She doesn't move.

"Give me your goddamn hand, you little bitch," he hisses and she can smell his breath now. It's a putrid dragon's lair of corned beef, taro, coconut milk, cheap beer and hand-rolled smokos. She swallows hard, and wills her stomach not to buck at the stench.

He swears again, his voice as hard-knuckled as the back of his hand, as sharp as his belt.

"Have it your way, cunt." He's holding something, forcing it at her. "Now you're going to have to use your mouth," he says.

Trapped, unable to move, she does as she is told. Spreads her lips, unclenches her teeth, tilts her head back. Opens wide.

And screams.

Jack sat bolt upright in bed. *What the hell?*

The noise came again. A high-pitched scream that ripped through the walls to seize his throat in a raw vise. Jack frantically ground the heels of his hands into his eyes, forcing himself awake. The night air had cooled in the darkness, but he felt himself starting to sweat.

Jack's mind reeled as he fumbled at the lamp sitting on the small bedside table. Blinking in its sudden glare, he glanced at his watch: three-thirty. He focused on the glowing numbers. *Was he dreaming?*

Another scream, this one louder. Definitely not a dream.

He hopped out of bed and danced from foot to foot as he yanked a pair of sweatpants over his boxers. Ripped open the bedroom door. His movements were decisive; there was only one room that the screams could be coming from.

He veered right in the cramped hallway, then grabbed for the curtain. It stopped short in his hand as the hooks bunched up in the kinked section of the track. Jack swore silently as he roughly pushed the curtain aside and stepped into the room. His fingers scrabbled along the wall for the light switch and flicked it.

Instinctively assuming a defensive crouch, he gave the room a quick scan, cursing himself for not grabbing up his vaka paddle from the corner of his bedroom. But he didn't see anything that needed clubbing. No rats, no centipedes. Nothing at all.

His gaze turned to the bed. The blood skidded in his veins.

Maina crouched against the far wall, the sheet wound tightly around her body so Jack could see only her face and the top of her head.

Her eyes, huge and unblinking, were locked on the end of the bed.

Jack crossed the room, tore the bottom of the sheet loose from the mattress, and lifted it. Nothing. He dropped to his knees to peer under the cot. A small green moko, suckered toes spread wide as it clung to the far wall, froze at his sudden intrusion. Surely the harmless gecko could not be the source of Maina's distress.

Jack was still craning his neck in a frantic search for any other nocturnal intruders when Maina shrieked again. The suddenness startled him. The sheer terror in its tone lifted the hair on the nape of his neck. He jerked his head up, and saw that she was now staring at the doorway. He spun on his heel: nothing but the curtain, hanging motionless.

He turned back to her and saw the horror carved into her face. She didn't move when he sat beside her, her eyes still wide and concentrated on something he was unable to perceive.

"Maina," Jack said softly, brushing a loose strand of hair from her face. She remained motionless, knees drawn up and planted firmly under her chin. A ball of fear.

He said her name again, moving closer. Her eyes were glassy, straining out of her face. She breathed through her mouth in rapid bursts. Her body shuddered under the sheet's thin covering.

Jack's mind scampered. *What do I do?*

The room was cold, as if an icy presence had passed through it. Jack stood and closed the louvers. He retrieved a T-shirt from his room, turning on the hallway light as he passed. He yanked aside the curtain to allow the illumination to spill in, then turned off the light in Maina's bedroom.

Her breathing slowed, her eyes became less fixed. *This is good*, he thought. She'd simply had a nightmare and now it was wilting, shredded by the fury of her screams.

Jack gave the sheet a cautious tug. There was resistance at first, then Maina's fingers opened and he was able to pull back the covering. She shivered and Jack could see the goosebumps that had formed on her bare skin.

He straightened her legs, moving slowly, carefully. Understood that she wasn't fully conscious yet despite her open eyes, that she was somehow sleepwalking without leaving the bed. He mustn't wake her.

Moving gingerly, he eased Maina out of the corner until she lay on her back. Her eyelids fluttered, heavy, weary. Her features relaxed as sleep rose to claim her.

Jack was rearranging the sheet when Maina rolled towards him and flung an arm across him. Her fingers tangled in the material of his T-shirt; she buried her face in his chest.

Maina appeared to be dropping back to sleep. He didn't want to disturb her, but he didn't feel comfortable sharing her bed. What would happen if she woke and found him there? Would she remember the nightmare and the part he was playing to soothe her? Or would she scream again at his intrusion?

And, most importantly, no perving, she'd said. *I hate guys who stare at me.*

Squeezing himself onto the small cot, Jack decided to take his chances, to stay where he was, at least until Maina drifted into a deeper slumber. That had been genuine terror he had heard in her screams. If his presence now brought her peace, then he had no choice but to remain.

He laid on his back and, with Maina's head rising and falling with his breathing, stared at the ceiling in the faint light that leaked in from the hallway.

He was fully awake now, the adrenaline that Maina's outburst had triggered still surging through his system like high-octane caffeine. He looked down at the top of Maina's head, and felt her breath warm on his chest. Her hair, clean from the shower, smelled of flowers: frangipani, bougainvillea. It was a comforting fragrance.

Somehow, in a way he was unable to describe, he felt at ease: Maina tucked warmly up against him in this narrow bed in this small room in this cinder block house in the dead of night, with the sound of crashing waves rushing up through the trees from the beach.

While he waited for her breathing to slow, his thoughts wandered. It was bleak territory where they chose to go.

This close contact with the girl, no matter how innocent, seemed foreign to him. Intimacy had become a stranger in Jack's house. There was intermittent sex, but no love. There was the physical act, but no pleasure. No hugs were offered or expected.

In his darkest core, tiny circuits were powering up. Why? Was it because he had recklessly charged into a darkened room, not knowing what he would find there? Knowing only that he was needed?

That he had, for the first time in years, thought about the well-being of someone other than himself?

The bitter fruits of his fame, and the fiery aftermath of their ingestion, had left him hollow, bobbing on the tides of society like a coconut husk in the lagoon. His ability to write—his one true skill—was only now beginning to manifest itself again. But through all those years when that spark of creativity had, for some inexplicable reason, refused to ignite, he had existed in a vacuum, making no effort to exert himself beyond the elementary motions it took to exist.

Where empathy and sympathy and desire had once flourished, nothing remained but apathy.

He had tucked himself away here. Away from the memories, away from pain or love or anything else that might be considered a genuine emotion.

Jack Nolan had simply stopped caring. He had rolled up his feelings like a dirty carpet and shoved them inside the shallow cave that was now his life. He had enough money to live comfortably, if somewhat frugally. He had his health. He had the most magnificent lagoon in the entire world to play in. Nothing else mattered.

And then Maina barged in—could it really have been mere hours ago?—and suddenly something did matter.

This is my house.

He carefully disengaged himself from Maina, and rolled out of the bed in one smooth motion. She snuffled, then turned to face the wall, safe at last.

Jack stood looking down at the sleeping girl for a long moment. His fingers tingled. He needed release. He needed to write.

** THURSDAY **

THIRTEEN

Shel Freeburg was on the phone in his office when Bobby Turner appeared in his doorway.

"Do you kiss your mother with that mouth?" Shel's voice was playful. He had his back turned and the receiver tucked into the crook of his shoulder so Bobby had to strain to hear.

"Of course I enjoyed myself, Ta'wanka," Shel said. "I had no idea that you were an actor, singer, dancer *and* a gymnast. Now that's what I called multi-talented. Let me tell ya, baby, you are going to go far in this business."

Bobby slapped a hand over his mouth to smother the embarrassed giggle that threatened to burst out. He ducked back into the hallway but didn't leave; he was curious to know what other mischief *Silver Screen Weekly's* associate entertainment editor might be up to.

"No problem, love," Bobby heard Shel say. "The story's done and Patterson has promised that you'll be on the cover. Now tell me again how you're going to thank me."

Bobby swallowed hard and popped his head back into the doorway. This time Shel caught a reflection in his monitor. "Listen, I've got to go. Thanks for the tip," he said, lying badly. "I'll follow that up this afternoon."

Shel cleared his throat and swivelled his chair around to face Bobby. The intern tried desperately to appear as if he'd arrived just this very moment and had overheard absolutely nothing about a starlet named Tonka (or some such thing), whose many talents apparently included swallowing anything Shel Freeburg cared to feed her. Was Bobby going to be the gossip star of the lunchroom or what?

"Correct me if I'm wrong, Mr. Turner," Shel said coldly. "But did I miss the memo mentioning that an intern's job description now includes spying on senior staff?"

Bobby's mouth flapped opened, and his lips writhed silently like a beached fish. Incapable of speech, Bobby instead stepped into Shel's office and shoved a Tampax box under his nose.

Shel's face clenched into a fist of disgust. He used his toes to backpedal his chair away from the young intern. "What the fuck?"

Bobby looked at Shel, then down at the box in his hand. His face glowed redly. He lowered the box, laughing nervously.

"What are you doing?" Shel's confusion turned to anger. "If this is your idea of a joke, I'll make sure you're laughing all the way out of the building. You'll spend the rest of your worthless, miserable existence toiling for some lower entity, like a newspaper or something."

The thought of being turfed from the offices of the world's No. 1-selling weekly entertainment publication worked to loosen Bobby's vocal chords.

"Mr. Patterson sent me to see you," he said. He shook the Tampax box; Shel could hear something rustling in its cardboard depths. "He wants you to pull from here."

"That better not be what I think it is," Shel said, still keeping his distance.

Bobby giggled again. "Oh, no. Miss Schwarmer emptied the box before Mr. Patterson put the pieces of paper in it."

Linda Schwarmer, Shel fumed. This would be that fema-Nazi's idea of a joke. Har-de-fucking-har.

"You're losing me, Bobby," Shel said, puzzlement knitting his eyebrows. "What pieces of paper?"

Bobby shook the box again. "Mr. Patterson says it's for the next cover story."

"Cover story?" Shel said, glancing at his telephone. "But that's already been typeset. The—"

"Mr. Patterson changed his mind," Bobby said. "Said that's why he's the editor-in-chief. To make tough decisions at the last minute, he said."

"Oh for Christ's sake." Shel spun his back on Bobby, then reached for his phone. "I'll straighten that old knob-licker out."

"Sorry." Bobby smiled weakly. "But he's already gone for lunch."

Shel thumped the receiver against his forehead—once, then again—his eyes squeezed tight. He pictured Ta'wanka. It was a moist image. This could not be happening. Not now. Not after they had both bent over backwards to put her on next week's cover. He lowered the receiver carefully, fighting the temptation to smash it into plastic molecules on his desk. He turned back to Bobby.

"Please explain," he said, his smile thin as a razor and just as sharp.

"You've heard of Bengt-Ake Dumbrovsky?"

"The director?"

Bobby nodded. "According to CNN, he died this morning in Sweden."

"OK?" Shel could feel his body coiling. One more second and he would launch from his chair, clamp his hands around the intern's skinny neck and choke the ever-loving life out of the little fucker.

"So Mr. Patterson initially decided to do a special column on Dumbrovsky because of how well *Sweaty Cheese* performed in—"

"Get to the point, you pathetic shit!" Shel roared, the veins on his neck knotting into cables of fury.

The outburst caused Bobby to lose his grip on the Tampax box. He juggled it for several terrifying seconds before his fingers found purchase again. The words flowed out of his mouth in one breathless gush.

It seemed that Garnet Patterson had just excreted another of his Great Ideas. This one concerned the now deceased Bengt-Ake Dumbrovsky and how, as an award-winning director, he deserved more than just an obit column. Because the Swede's most successful film, *Sweaty Cheese*, had been released in 1998, wouldn't it be absolutely brilliant if *Silver Screen Weekly* took a look back at the top five box office movies of that year? Do one of those Where Are They Now stories on all the major players for each of those films.

To eliminate any temptation his senior writers might have to cherry-pick, Patterson had one of his assistants write the film titles and contact numbers on slips of paper. He was looking for a container to draw out of when Linda Schwarmer earned brownie points by hastily filling the bottom drawer of her desk with tampons and dropping the empty box on his desk.

Shel reached out a tentative hand as Bobby pushed the box towards him. "Please tell me that *Saving Private Ryan* is still in there."

"Sorry," Bobby said. "Ormond Glutermein already drew that."

"It figures!" Shel snarled. "That officious little fag."

Bobby found his admiration for Shel Freeburg growing, despite his abject fear of the foul-tempered writer. He had never heard anyone use the word *officious* before. This guy really must be brilliant.

"*Armageddon?*"

"Miss Schwarmer."

"Mickey-licking bitch!" Shel shook his head, then plunged his hand into the box. He shuddered as if he were dipping his precious digits into a steaming pile of dog shit. Bobby drew some satisfaction from that image.

Shel's fingers scrabbled around the bottom of the box then emerged, delicately clutching a slip of white paper between index finger and thumb. He unfolded the paper, read the first line.

"Fuck me sideways with a lawnmower! Not this rubbish!"

Bobby took a long step back towards the door. He still had two more writers to deal with and he was growing rather weary of being the proverbial shot messenger. "Bad news?" He tried to sound more sympathetic than he felt.

Shel waved the paper in the air. "*Blood and Ruins.* I don't fucking believe it. Who got *Sweaty Cheese?*"

"No one yet," Bobby said, giving the box a quick shake. "It's still in here."

"Let me know who draws it, will you?" Shel said. "I'll offer them a blowjob to trade."

Bobby blushed again. "Mr. Patterson said absolutely no trading," he said. "He was very firm on that point."

"Perfect." Shel slammed the paper down on his desk. He gave it a quick scan. The only good news was that he wouldn't have to worry about interviewing Payne Laidlaw. One of the entries read "Based on the Book by Jack Nolan" and was followed by Porter Nolan's name and a phone number with a Canadian area code.

"I'm sure you'll do your usual wonderful job, Mr. Freeburg," Bobby said, looking over his shoulder and mentally estimating the number of steps to the door.

"Hey, Bobby, will you do me a favor?"

Bobby Turner smiled broadly. It didn't get much better than being asked to help a member of the editorial staff. This could be the big break he'd been waiting for. The great Shel Freeburg asking an intern for help. Wow.

"Sure thing" he said. "What would you like?"

Shel Freeburg smiled. "What I'd like," he said, "is for you to fuck off and die."

FOURTEEN

Jack nudged aside the shower curtain and stepped out of the tiled stall. He grabbed a towel from a wooden rack beside the toilet and worked vigorously at drying himself. The mirror over the sink had steamed over. He gave it a wipe, then cracked open the bathroom door to allow the moist air to escape. He sprayed shave gel into one palm, rubbed his hands together, and applied the white foam to his whiskers. In the mirror, his eyes were drawn to the reflection of the tattoo on his left forearm.

It had been nearly three years since he'd collaborated on the pattern with Andrew Tuara, a local carver who also dabbled in tattoos, but he still marveled at the intricacies of its design.

He had played with the idea of a tattoo for several years, but the thought of sporting a flaming skull or some other similarly trashy North American image for the rest of his life had always stopped him short.

It wasn't until he arrived in the Cook Islands and saw the exotic Polynesian symbols adorning the local men and women that the thought of acquiring one himself returned. Even then, it took two years and much coaxing from his Saturday morning paddling mates before he overcame his terror of needles long enough to allow Andrew to sit him down in his Avarua Harbor studio.

The final impetus came one evening on Muri Beach when Heather hooked a thumb in one corner of her shorts and tugged the material down to reveal a small moko etched over her hip bone.

"If a tender young lady like me can put up with the pain, so can a big, strong man like you," she teased. Jack phoned Andrew the next day to book an appointment.

The design they ultimately decided on also featured a moko. It would be larger than Heather's version, of course, and incorporated into an armband that would include several other symbols relevant to the Cook Islands. Jack insisted that it be situated just above the sleeve line so that it wasn't readily visible.

He had his doubts right up to the very last minute. Had lingered over his coffee at Sparky's Café longer than he usually did and then discovered, much to his distress, that the combination of caffeine and anxiety had made his legs wobbly and nearly useless.

He finally stumbled across the road to the studio. Andrew had his back to him as Jack parted the beaded curtain over the doorway and entered the wood-paneled room. A large black leather chair dominated the space, reminding Jack of the barbershops his father had dragged him into as a boy. Andrew sat on a stool to one side, working on something at the bench in front of him. Jack stood silently, taking the opportunity to once again examine the tattoos that adorned the stocky local's arms and legs.

Andrew had done most of the work himself. The bands and symbols and figures represented either aspects of his family history or significant events in his life. The ink had faded in some places, settling deep into the darkened crevasses of Andrew's skin, but there was no mistaking the complexity of the art form, or the talent that had guided the needle.

Andrew glanced over his shoulder, his broad features splitting into a wide grin at the horror that flickered across Jack's face.

"Kia orana bro, are you ready for this?" he asked as his fingers adjusted a small battery.

"Not really," Jack said, contemplating the cost of laser removal surgery.

"If you're afraid of fainting, don't be." Andrew picked up a nozzle-like apparatus and attached one end of it to the battery. "I've had bigger men than you keel over when they hear this."

Andrew inserted a short needle into the apparatus and depressed a small button. The panic-inducing vibration of attacking bees suddenly filled the room, a sound that bore an unfortunate resemblance to that other form of torture most hated by humans, that of the dentist's drill.

Jack swallowed hard, then stripped off his T-shirt and threw himself into the leather chair. "Let's get this over with," he said.

Andrew laughed. "That's the spirit, my friend. Just listen to the sound of my voice and forget about everything else."

Andrew slipped on a pair of latex gloves, then daubed a deodorant stick over the upper area of Jack's left arm.

"Tourists think tattooing originated in the South Pacific," Andrew said. He spoke in a calming tone as he pressed the thin piece of tracing paper bearing the hand-drawn moko motif against the sticky smear. When he pulled the paper away, the ink outline was clearly visible on Jack's skin.

"But they're wrong," Andrew continued, pulling his stool closer and revving up the inking needle. "My ancestors actually brought the art with them when they migrated across the ocean."

Head bent close, he began to trace along the outline. Jack's breathing became hard and sharp in anticipation of the pain, but he was relieved when the buzzing needle caused little more than a tingling sensation on the surface of his skin.

Andrew continued to talk as he worked, pausing only to give the emerging tattoo a quick wipe with a tissue or dip the needle into an ink receptacle.

"Tattooing actually started at the beginning of mankind," he explained as the moko began to take shape on Jack's arm. "It was well-known throughout Europe. The Romans did it, the Egyptians did it. It was a form of identification, to show whether you were a witch doctor or a soldier in the army."

The moko completed to his satisfaction, Andrew moved on to the armband itself, his voice soothing to Jack's ear as the needle flickered in and out of his skin, leaving behind lines and dots and swirls of black ink.

"The moko is the guardian," Andrew said. "Inside the outline of his body I've drawn spearheads, to add positive attitude." Andrew indicated the nearly completed band with the thumb of his working hand. "These images are of people joined together, for unity. The waves symbolize voyaging; the bird is travel. And these," pointing to three small triangles positioned inside a larger triangle, "represent the blending of past, present and future."

Jack was impressed with the detail, but Andrew wasn't finished yet. He'd purposely saved the most painful for the last. Jack winced as his arm was twisted over and Andrew began working on its tender underside.

What emerged was another set of triangles, arranged in the shape of a pyramid.

"These are shark's teeth," Andrew said. "They denote courage. The shark, to us, isn't something to be afraid of, but to respect."

He sat back, the job finished. Using a pair of pliers, he removed the needle and placed it in a homemade sterilizing tank. He applied antibiotic ointment to the tattooed area, bound it tightly in plastic wrap, and patted Jack on the shoulder.

"Today you became a real man," Andrew smiled.

"Will this help me attract a brown woman?"

Andrew's eyebrows arched in an expression of mock dismay. "You didn't tell me that was your goal, my friend. I gave you a lizard crawling up your arm. You should have asked for a dolphin."

"Nice tatt."

The razor skidded to a stop on his cheek. Jack instinctively grabbed at the towel around his waist. Maina was standing in the bathroom doorway. Turtles and brightly colored fish swam across her aquamarine pareu. Her hair was plaited into a pair of thick braids.

"The bathroom's occupied," he said curtly, reaching for the door handle.

She pulled the door open even farther. "I know it is. You've been in here forever. Worse than a vaine."

She stepped past him. "I've got to mimi. Go pee."

"I know what that means," Jack said, watching in the mirror as she turned her back on the toilet, hoisted her pareu and sat down. "I've picked up a little Cook Islands Maori over the years, you know."

"Good for you," Maina said. "Now would you mind just carrying on with what you're doing? I can't perform in front of an audience."

"I know the feeling," Jack mumbled. He leaned closer to the mirror and continued his shaving.

He'd been apprehensive about the morning, curious to gauge Maina's state of mind. He wondered if she would remember the nightmare or its aftermath.

Would she remember holding onto him as she fell back to sleep?

Judging by the way she had bulled into the bathroom and was now carrying on with her business, she seemed fine. On the surface, at least, there appeared to be no lingering damage.

Maina wiped herself and flushed the toilet. She leaned against Jack's shoulder until he stepped aside and she was able to reach the sink to wash her hands. She dried them on the edge of Jack's towel, then patted his tummy.

"Pito could use a bit of a workout there, mate," she said, then walked out of the bathroom and into the house.

Jack stood in front of the sink, razor frozen in midair, listening to Maina fill the jug from the kitchen tap. He looked at his face, still lathered in white foam, then down to where Maina's drying actions had caused the towel to settle across his hips. Was she right, was he actually growing flabby in his old age? Nah.

He leaned out the bathroom door. "I'm a paddler, you know."

Her only answer was a derisive snort.

Bloody cheeky girl.

The kitchen was filled with the aroma of hot grease when he came back into the house. Maina stood in front of the stove, carefully monitoring the progress of several rashers of bacon and two eggs as they sputtered in a frying pan.

"That smells good," Jack said, stopping by the stove to admire Maina's handiwork.

She smiled. Her teeth were white and even and perfect. "I thought the least I could do for invading your house was make breakfast," she said. "The fruit is already on the table and this will be ready by the time you're dressed."

When Jack emerged again from his room, a plate of bacon and eggs was waiting for him on the kitchen table. A smaller plate contained a sliced nita. The papaya's seeds had been scooped out and the hollow filled with cottage cheese cold from the refrigerator.

"I hope you didn't spend too much on breakfast," Jack said, reaching for a slice of toasted multigrain bread.

"It didn't cost me anything," Maina said over her shoulder as she cracked an egg into the pan. It sizzled angrily as it made contact with the hot oil.

"Oh?"

"Yeah," Maina said, pointing the spatula at the shelf where the phone sat. "There was a jar of coins there, so I just used those. Mama Rosie says kia orana, by the way."

Jack shook his head as he tore off a corner of toast and jabbed it into a yolk. "First you kick me out my office, now you spend all my change."

"I didn't use all of it," she said. "But I will if you want me to."

Jack dug a spoon into the pawpaw's orange meat. "No thanks. I use that to buy bread for the chooks."

"I start work at the café today, so I'll replace your precious change next week."

"Thank you," Jack said, wiping his mouth with a napkin.

Maina angled her body so she could watch Jack while she cooked. She'd just been teasing him about his tummy, of course. The singlet he was wearing actually served to accentuate how the hundreds of hours he had spent paddling vakas around the lagoon had sculpted his upper body into a nicely-toned mass of muscle and sinew. The moko tattoo rippled on his left bicep as he worked at emptying his plate.

She turned her attention again to his face. Except for the grey eyes that tended to flash whenever he grew passionate about a subject, there wasn't a single outstanding feature that would make a woman instantly drop her defenses. But it was a kind face, an open face. It was a face you could trust. Jack glanced up, caught her staring and smiled around a mouthful of bacon. Maina quickly turned back to the frying pan.

It was a face you could love.

Maina licked grease off her fingers as she joined him at the table with her own plate in hand. She picked up a single rasher of bacon, blew on it, and took a bite.

"You're not eating much," Jack said.

"I'm feeling a bit crook this morning."

"Might be Raro belly," he said. "It took my digestive system a month to adjust to the different foods I was eating. Do you need a ride to town?"

Maina nodded. "Yes, please," she said. "Is there any chance we can go in a bit early? There's a Te Maire Maeva Nui rehearsal at the National Auditorium this morning and I'd like to stop by and see some of the girls that I know."

"No problem," Jack said, pushing away from the table. "We'll leave as soon as you've cleaned up the kitchen."

Maina's head snapped up. "I don't think so," she said. "The cook doesn't do dishes."

Jack looked at her. "I don't remember that being on our list of rules."

She lasered him with her eyes. A defiant scowl creased her face. The scar glowed on her chin. "It's a universal rule," she said. "It's like a law or something."

Jack looked at her, then over to where a mess of broken eggshells and pawpaw pulp sat on the counter. Grease coagulated into white lard in the cooling frying pan. He took a playful swipe at her head. She giggled, easily ducked away.

"You're just lucky you can cook, young lady," Jack said as he reached for the rubbish bin. "Or your arse would be out the door."

Maeva Benning broke away from a large group of teenagers and ran towards Jack's truck as he pulled into the parking lot of the National Auditorium.

Maina bounded from the cab and embraced Maeva. They chattered excitedly for a couple of minutes, then Maina walked over to talk to several of the other girls. Maeva came up to Jack's window, stuck her head in, and kissed him on the cheek in a traditional Cook Islands greeting.

"Wassup, Jack?" she smiled.

"Not much." Jack grinned back. "Did the school burn down?"

"I wish," she laughed. "Most of the colleges are putting on a sports day, so anyone who is competing in the Constitution Celebration was allowed to come here instead."

"How is the Takitumu team looking this year?"

"Great," Maeva said. "Our ura pa'u, the drum dance, is awesome. I'm in the front row with Helani, Lee and Teina. You have to come out and watch us. OK?"

"You bet," he said. "I'm looking forward to it."

Jack watched as Maina hugged Helani and several of the other girls. "So how do you know Maina?"

Maeva looked back over her shoulder. "Maina's sweet as," she said. "We met at last year's competition when she came to Raro with the Pukapuka team. She's a really good dancer. If we'd known she was going to be here, she could have joined our team."

She nodded at his watch. "What is your time?"

Jack told her. "I've got to go," she said, leaning into the truck to peck his cheek again. She started to walk towards the auditorium, then stopped and turned back. "Papa Alex wants you to come over and see him."

"Great," Jack said. "Is he home this morning?"

"Yup."

"I'll go over right now then." Jack waved. "Have a good rehearsal."

The wind was starting to pick up as Jack drove clockwise around the island to Alex Benning's property in Vaimaanga. He ducked his head to take a quick look out the passenger window. The agitated wave action gave the lagoon a lumpy appearance. Jack eyed the whitecaps and imagined plowing through them in a vaka. That would be a challenge. He hoped the wind kept up until Saturday morning when his paddling team met at Muri Beach for its weekly practice session.

The breeze grew stronger as he drove along the western side of the island. He could feel the gusts buffeting the truck, especially in those places where the road ran adjacent to the beach and there were no trees to act as a windbreak. He watched the locals as they went about their errands on their bikes and marveled again at their ability to ride the small-engined machines under any weather condition.

Not even the fierce tropical rainstorms could deter the riders. They simply slipped on huge nylon jackets, many of them bearing the logos of NFL teams. The coats were worn backwards to prevent water from sneaking through the gaps between buttons.

Ahead to his left, Jack spied the crumbling walls of the Endeavor Hotel through gaps in the foliage. He used the unfinished accommodation project as a guide, as it sprawled adjacent to Alex's house. Both were situated on land owned by the Matenga family into which Alex had married.

He slowed down as he drew abreast of the Endeavor site, and shook his head in dismay. It was a gesture common to those who encountered the crumbling monolith. Two hundred metres further on, a colorful wooden sign, jigsawed into the shape of a steam engine, indicated the entrance to the home of the Raro Railroad. Jack turned inland.

"Jack! You should have rung to say you were coming for a visit. That way I could have hidden my whiskey."

Jack laughed loudly, then hopped out of the Toyota to clasp Alex Benning's hand.

The Scotsman could have stepped off the set of *The Lord of the Rings*. He was short and stocky and walked with a swinging gait, as if, in his younger days, he had once dragged a heavy sword and shield from adventure to adventure. He was older now, and slower, but the humor still danced a jig in his blue eyes. Red blotches sat high on his gristly cheeks, ruddy souvenirs of the many glasses of Glenfiddich that he had emptied in good company and bad. A wart, home to several white hairs, loomed from the left side of his thickly veined nose.

His hands were thick and gnarled. Jack had never seen them clean. Not surprising, considering Alex could inevitably be found tinkering on his steam engine and its track, or tending to either his taro patch or pawpaw orchard. What you rarely found was Alex Benning sitting still for any length of time.

"How are you my friend?" Jack asked as he clapped Alex on the back of his stained T-shirt.

"Better now that you're here," Alex grinned, revealing teeth stained yellow and black from years of smoking and neglect. "I thought you'd forgotten this island had a west coast."

"Sorry, mate," Jack said. "The newspaper job has kept me busy lately and I guess I just lost track of time."

"I know the feeling," Alex said, then halted and squinted up at Jack. "You haven't been chasing brown girls again, have you?"

"I don't remember stopping."

Alex roared with laughter. "Good on you, mate" he chortled. "Glad to know some things never change. How's the writing going?"

Jack's smile tightened. "It's slow," he said. "But I'm still trying."

"Atta boy."

They walked around the cinder block house where Alex and his wife, Miimetua, lived. A pair of scrawny mutts lolled in the shade of a coconut palm. They flopped their tails expectantly, but made no effort to move from their shelter.

"Just don't give up," Alex said. "Hell, if I'd listened to my critics, I'd never have finished this."

They stopped in front of the steam locomotive. The sleek black machine huffed like some mythical beast at rest. Alex explained that he was just about to take the train out on its first run of the day and insisted that Jack join him.

Beyond the locomotive Jack could see the stand where Maeva sold tickets and souvenirs. To one side of that wooden structure was the exhibition area where Alex had assembled a pictorial history of his favorite mode of transport, including a painting of Englishman George Stephenson testing his first steam locomotive on July 25, 1814. And another of the unfortunate British MP who, on Sept. 15, 1830, became the first railway fatality. *Not exactly the way I'd want to be remembered*, Jack thought.

Included in the display was the story of Alex's particular locomotive and its memorable journey from the river valleys and mountain passes of Europe to the South Pacific jungles.

Alex uncoupled the passenger car—"For paying customers only," he winked—and clambered into the cab. Jack heaved himself up the metal ladder and joined him. The wind had lessened, the sun was regaining its heat. It was the perfect day for a train ride.

"Maeva said you wanted to show me something," Jack yelled into Alex's ear as the morning air was filled with a great roaring thrush of released steam. The locomotive lurched forward.

"That's right," Alex hollered back. "While you were busy getting laid, I've been doing honest work." He pointed down the track ahead of them. "I've added another kilometre," he explained. "Even hired some local lads to help, and what a blessing they turned out to be. Hard-working, eager to learn. I tell you, they were a pleasure to work with."

Jack nodded, then stepped to the edge of the cab, leaned out, and closed his eyes. The sun on his face and the throb of the metal leviathan beneath his boots were comforting. He wanted to throw his arms wide and shout into the rush of air that tugged at his hair, but he worried that his antics might distract Alex from his engineering duties.

The track was not originally part of the display, but so many tourists had commented to Alex about how encountering a train in the Cook Islands was very interesting and all, but to actually ride on it would truly be the ultimate experience. It would also earn more money for his family, and that was always a good thing.

And so two kilometres of family land were cleared of vegetation. Bedding material was trucked in from a quarry in Black Rock, sleepers were cut from casuarina trees, and metal tracks purchased from Tranz Rail and shipped from Auckland.

For $5 you could sit in the open-air passenger car behind the engine and enjoy a four-kilometre round trip through the Rarotonga countryside, followed by cookies and juice served up by Maeva.

Alex reached over to tap Jack on the shoulder. His reverie interrupted, Jack's eyes snapped open, then widened in fright. Ahead of them loomed a solid wall of concrete. The locomotive was headed straight towards a section of the Endeavor Hotel.

"You're going to stop this thing, right?" he screamed at Alex. The Scotsman's smile was meant to be reassuring, but Jack saw the fright in Alex's eyes. His mouth was suddenly dry.

With the noise of the engine thundering in his bones, Jack gaped over the side of the cab. His throat tightened in fear at the green blur of trees and bushes that rushed past them. How fast were they going? And how much damage would he do if he jumped?

Knees flexed in anticipation, Jack peered anxiously ahead for something forgiving to land on.

The shrieking of brakes was a welcome sound. Jack sucked in a great gasp of relief, then stepped back inside the cab as a fantail of golden sparks showered the wooden sleepers behind them. Alex, his fists wrapped tightly around the brake switch, chuckled at the look of panic on his passenger's face. The engine finally shuddered to a halt, its cowcatcher positioned at the very end of the track and a mere five metres from the wall.

"I may have waited a bit too long to stop," Alex said, smiling sheepishly.

Jack looked at the wall directly ahead of them and saw how its concrete face was cracked and chipped and partially covered with creepers. He made a quick mental inventory of his sphincters to ensure that they were all still intact, then turned to the Scotsman.

"You think?"

Alex patted the instrument panel in front of him. "Not that I'm worried about denting the old gal," he said. "But this place is so rotten that we probably would have plowed right through it and not stopped until we were halfway to town."

Jack regarded the remains of the Endeavor. From where he stood in the locomotive's cab, he couldn't see much more than the section of eastern perimeter wall in front of them, and a two-storey building that stretched up the incline to the right.

He knew from driving past the site a thousand times that it was actually quite a huge complex, covering several acres. If everything had gone as planned, the Endeavor would easily have been the largest resort in the country. Instead it was an eyesore, a reminder, if one was needed, of how quickly things can turn to custard under the flaming fury of the South Pacific sun.

FIFTEEN

It was Alex Benning who first told Jack the history of the doomed Endeavor Hotel, during one of their early interviews about the Raro Railroad. They were sitting on the back deck of Alex's house, cheerfully toasting William Grant, founder of the Glenfiddich Distillery, when Jack asked about the abandoned pile that loomed out of the jungle like some ancient temple to the folly of man.

"Like most of the major projects in this country, it started with foreign money," Alex said, jabbing his cold pipe in the direction of the ill-fated resort. "This time it was Italian, $80 million US of it all told. A low-interest loan it was, from some Internet company eager to make inroads in this area of the world. Only what our government of the day didn't know was that the money was dirty. That we were being used as a money laundering service."

The Tribune's eventual unearthing of that pertinent detail resulted in much furious debate and finger-pointing in parliament. The demand that heads should roll over what was considered an international embarrassment was not enough to stop the hotel's construction, however.

It took the death of two local tradesmen—killed when faulty scaffolding collapsed—to halt work.

"After that, someone started spreading rumors that the site was haunted," Alex said, using a thumb stained the color of ancient ivory to tamp shredded tobacco into the bowl of his pipe. "It was a ridiculous notion, of course, but it worked to cast even more doubt on a project that was rocky to begin with."

"Any idea who would have done that?" Jack asked.

Alex applied a match to his pipe and puffed deeply to ignite it.

"I have my suspicions," he said, the words accompanied by an aromatic cloud of blue smoke. "There was never any concrete evidence at the time, but there was no shortage of people who took pleasure in harassing the politicians who were so eager to accept the money in the first place. In particular, it was pointed out how careless it had been not to conduct a more thorough background check on anyone who would invest in a project that isn't even located on the beach."

"What did your wife's family do during all this bloodletting?"

"Nothing," Alex laughed. "There was no risk on their part because, as you know, foreigners are prohibited from actually buying property in the Cook Islands. So if the silly buggers wanted to pay big money for a long-term lease, plus," Alex jabbed his pipe in the air for emphasis, "*plus* fork over a percentage of the hotel's annual net income, then the Matenga family was quite happy to provide the land."

"So why was it never finished?"

Alex shook his head. "After the stories about evil spirits started circulating, the locals refused to go back to work. It didn't matter that almost all of them were Christians and weren't supposed to believe in such shite. The construction company had to import laborers from around the South Pacific, Fijians mainly, but they had never worked on a project of this magnitude and were hopelessly out of their league."

The contractors, Alex said, had little choice but to halt construction while they negotiated with the local workmen to return. Those discussions were barely underway when it came to light that some $50 million of the money earmarked for the Endeavor Hotel had somehow gone missing. The fact that the lawyer hired by the government to act as its liaison with the Italians also disappeared at the same time could hardly be considered a coincidence.

"Then it became a simple matter of maths," Alex said. "Subtract the money and all you're left with is a big fat zero of a project. The foreign workers went home, the contractors went away. The only thing that didn't go away was the debt the country still owes to the Italians. Dirty money or not, it was a legitimate transaction. That was nearly a decade ago and we're still paying that loan off, and will be for many years to come, I'm afraid."

"So who owns the Endeavor now?" Jack asked.

"The land, and everything built on it, reverted back to the Matenga family when the deal collapsed," Alex said. "Every few years or so, we hear that someone has arrived on the island with the grand intention of reviving the project. But no one has ever knocked on my door carrying a suitcase filled with cash. It's all big dreams and small talk."

"I'm going to let the brakes cool down before we head back," Alex said, hopping down from the cab and digging his pipe and a worn leather pouch out of the pockets of his shorts. He pulled hanks of torn tobacco out of the pouch and jammed them into the pipe.

Jack climbed from the locomotive and walked to the wall in front of them. Ran his hand over the rough finish. The surface was hot to the touch. Faded chips of paint crumbled under his fingers.

"What color was this originally?"

Alex used a cracked thumbnail to ignite a wooden match, then lit his pipe. He spat on the match and tucked it carefully into a pocket. The undergrowth was too dry to take any chances with fire.

"The designer called it Dawn Rose," Alex said. "But it was pink to the rest of us. In fact, the locals used to refer to the Endeavor as the Pink Palace. More like Stink Palace now."

"What an incredible waste," Jack whispered.

"Would you like to take a look around while we wait?"

"I'd love to."

Alex pulled the pipe from his mouth and pointed to the right. "That's the convention hall we nearly flattened. There's a gap between the buildings over there that I used to keep clear. It's been awhile since I've bothered coming over here, but we should still be able to get through."

Stepping through a gaping crack in the concrete wall that encircled the hotel grounds, the two men passed between the convention hall and the two-storey building next to it and entered the huge centre courtyard.

Nature had been busy in the interval since construction had ceased. Small trees and bushes grew everywhere in a riot of green. In some places the grass reached above the men's knees and they were forced to move slowly to avoid stepping into holes hidden by the tangled ground cover.

The site itself was in the shape of a giant 'U,' with the open end facing the main road. The convention hall was the first structure on the south leg; immediately adjacent to it were the buildings containing the guestrooms. These began as two-storey configurations then, as the hotel arced northeast, segued to three storeys and finally four, before merging into the upper curve. The top of the curve was obviously designed to be the main entrance and reception area, as a partially-completed brick porte-cochere extended over a large opening in the wall where a set of front doors had once been planned.

A driveway, now little more than a gravel clearing through which an assortment of vegetation sprouted, wound around the interior of the complex. A number of kitset maintenance sheds, abandoned when the contractor vacated the premises, dotted the inner courtyard. Their open doors allowed Jack to glance inside as they passed.

In the dim light he could make out tools rusting on makeshift benches, as well as what looked like metal presses and table saws. One shed contained several sets of large rubber tires, meant as replacements for the trucks and graders and diggers used for excavating the grounds.

The men walked in silence, stopping occasionally to peer through vacant doorways or empty window frames. The only sounds were the scolding cries of disturbed mynah birds and the lazy hum of insects on their tours of duty. Skinks, iridescent as spilled petrol, darted away from their feet.

A pallid aura of decay hung over the wreckage. Many of the rooms Jack looked into contained crates of furniture that had never been opened; their contents rotted in the heat and humidity. Stacks of marble and slate tiles, indicators of the grandeur that might have been, sat disconsolately under thick layers of dust.

Some of the rooms were nothing more than skeleton outlines of studs and wiring and pipes, with no interior walls to speak of. Through the gaps, the men saw porcelain toilets and sinks, sunken spa tubs that would never know the caress of hot bubbles or hear the satisfied sigh of a tired body being lowered into them. Mattresses, clad in their protective plastic sheaths, slumped against walls. Bed frames were stacked carelessly, as if abandoned by a bored child.

An open wooden box filled with solar panels nestled beside a pallet of windows, their surfaces now dusty and flyspecked.

A large depression dominated the core of the complex. Concrete curbing surrounded and connected an arrangement of hollows. Alex explained how this was meant to be a series of manmade lakes. A massive collection of bricks, once stacked neatly, now lying in scattered heaps in the grass, hinted at a walk bridge over the water system. At the top end a small landing was attached to what appeared to be a restaurant/bar area.

To one side an in-ground pool was already installed, its tiled walls green with mold, its swamp of murky rainwater providing a breeding ground for colonies of mosquitoes. A circle of metal barstools was bolted to the bottom of the shallow end, intended to allow swimmers the luxury of drinking themselves silly at a pool side bar without having to venture onto the deck. Jack flashed to the image of Gert Junger floating face down in the pool at the Outrigger Villas. Maybe Heather was right about that being nothing more than an accident.

Alex touched Jack's sleeve. "Ready to go?"

Jack's eyes circled the ruins. "It's as if time has stopped here," he said softly. "Like a dead child's bedroom left untouched by its parents."

"You've the soul of a poet, mate," Alex smirked. "But I prefer to think of the Endeavor as a graveyard because a lot of my hard-earned tax money is buried here. Now you know why I seldom come over anymore. I've got better things to do than have my nose rubbed in the ignorance of idiots."

They were walking past the convention hall. Jack noted that this building alone appeared to have been completed, including the hanging of a set of double doors.

"What's the deal here?" he asked as he pulled a door open. A rush of hot, dusty air assaulted him.

Alex squinted into the darkness. "I should have brought the torch from the train," he said, stepping inside.

"This is the only building that was ever finished," he said. "The idea was to construct a showroom in here so that those in the travel business, as well as visiting dignitaries or tourists, or anyone who was just plain curious, could see what the future of Rarotonga was going to look like. The showroom never did open, but I've talked to people who saw the original plans and, apparently, they were quite impressive."

"It had 80 million reasons to be impressive," Jack said, pulling open the second door to allow more light to enter the building.

They stood in a lobby, facing another set of doors. Jack presumed that these led into the actual hall itself. To their left, a staircase climbed into darkness. The carpeted floor was spongy under their feet. The still air stank of rot.

A collection of Polynesian carvings and paintings hung on the walls. Jack's fingers traced a familiar moko pattern carved into a wooden paddle. "This is one of Andrew Tuara's works," he said, noticing the similarities to his own tattoo.

"Paid for and long forgotten, I'm guessing," said Alex as he made his own tour of the walls. "Maybe I should put a lock on those doors before this artwork grows legs and walks away."

"There's no security here?"

"We did have a local fellow living on site in one of the worker's huts in exchange for acting as a sort of unpaid caretaker," Alex said. "But he was married about two months ago and moved into a bigger house closer to town. The family hasn't bothered to replace him."

"Can you see the hotel from your place?" Jack asked as he turned slowly in an attempt to get his bearings.

"Just the taller sections, over the trees."

"Aren't you worried about strangers hanging around the grounds?"

"Not really," said Alex. "We're in the middle of nowhere out here. If the kids are looking for some secluded spot for shagging, they tend to stay closer to civilization. Besides, the place is supposed to be haunted, remember?"

"What about tourists?"

"You've noticed the two horses that graze in the front section?"

"Sure," said Jack. "You don't see a lot of horses on the island, so they tend to catch your attention."

"Which is why a lot of tourists stop to pet them," nodded Alex. "What they discover rather quickly is that those two nags aren't exactly domesticated. You ever been bitten by a horse, Jack?"

"Nope."

"Trust me, it is very painful," said Alex. "Those horses are mean and nasty, so visitors seldom stay around for long."

Jack tested the stairway's lower steps, found them solid, and kept going. At the top was a door partially hidden in the shadows.

"What are you doing?"

"Just exploring a bit," Jack said, reaching for the door handle.

"Maybe I should go fetch that torch," Alex said, but Jack was already out of sight. Alex sighed, took another look around the lobby, and climbed the stairs. He stopped in the doorway. Squinted into a black void.

"Jack!"

"Yo!"

Alex jumped at the closeness of Jack's voice. He sounded less than two metres away but was invisible in the inky gloom.

"Got any more of those matches?" Jack asked.

Alex fumbled a wooden match out of a pocket and struck it to life on the wall. He advanced in the direction of Jack's voice, the lit match extended in front of him.

"Where are ya, lad?"

"Over here."

Alex turned slowly to his right, cautious not to make any sudden movements that would extinguish his match. The back of Jack's torso loomed out of the murk, next to what appeared to be a low wall. His shoulders and head were invisible beyond the match's tiny circle of light.

"What the hell are you doing?" Alex said. "We really shouldn't be fumbling around in the dark. We have no idea what might be up here."

Jack's voice was muffled. "This appears to be some kind of balcony or viewing area."

He straightened up and Alex could see a line of dust across the front of his singlet where he had leaned over the wall.

The match burned Alex's fingers and he instinctively dropped it. The small flame bounced once and quickly flared out, but not before Alex caught a glimpse of the floor next to Jack's feet.

"Jack?"

"Yes?"

"Please don't move."

Jack didn't like the sound of that. "Why, Alex? What is it?"

"I'm not sure," Alex said, then cursed as his fumbling fingers scrambled frantically through pockets for another match.

"Alex?"

"Got it!" Alex announced as he pulled out his final match. "Steady on, Jack."

Alex ignited the match, then edged closer to Jack. He could see his friend's eyes in the light: big, white, scared. "Step towards me, Jack. Nice and slow."

Jack swallowed hard and looked down. He felt a hot flood of panic and, for a sharp, piercing second, thought his knees might give out and send him sprawling to the dirty floor.

It would be the last thing he would ever do.

SIXTEEN

Sparky's Café perched on the eastern edges of Avarua, just past Avarua Harbor. Its concrete exterior was painted a fire-engine red set off by white trim. The building featured the inside-outside design of most restaurants on the island, with large front windows and double doors that opened to allow easy access to any cooling sea breeze that happened by.

A patio of intersecting stone pavers dominated the forecourt, running the width of the building and extending nearly to the road. Several chunky tables and chairs had been set up on the patio, giving customers the option of enjoying their drinks and meals in the open air where they could observe the passing traffic. Large red umbrellas emblazoned with the distinctive Sparky's lightning bolt logo provided welcome relief from the blazing afternoon sun.

James "Sparky" Muldoon, the café's owner, was a skinny scarecrow. At more than two metres tall, the Irishman was one long stretch of skin: Ichobod Crane with an apron.

It had been several years since Muldoon had subjected the wiry grey bush on his head to a barber's attention, preferring to just pull the various tangled strands into a rough ponytail secured by a brightly-colored elastic. His beard had also been left to its own devices so that a wooly bramble engulfed his lower face.

A lifetime of hand-rolled cigarettes had produced a sickly yellow stain on the sections of Muldoon's mustache and beard surrounding his lips, as if someone had urinated into a snow bank.

If Muldoon's grooming habits were nonexistent, his expertise with an espresso machine was legend. The machine itself was a wheezing amalgamation of chrome siding, black plastic knobs, glass-faced gauges and protruding metal bits. But, under the expert touch of the lanky Irishman's bony fingers, what flowed from its porta filters was pure crema nectar.

Muldoon bought the espresso machine from a desperate yachtie who had been forced to strip his boat of its superfluous toys in a frantic effort to raise enough cash to sail back to San Diego. At the time, Muldoon had cursed himself for a fool at the price he'd let himself pay, but it was his competitors who were soon heard to damn the shrewdness of his investment.

For Muldoon had wasted little time installing the machine in his café, knowing that his would be the first establishment in the country to offer more than hot water and a jar of freeze-dried granules whenever an unsuspecting customer ordered coffee. A bit of research put him in touch with a number of prominent South American bean suppliers and the resulting product proved so popular that he was forced to add more tables to accommodate the flocks of tourists who merely followed their noses along the Ara Tapu, past the roundabout, and into the crimson building.

A former electrician from County Cork, Muldoon presented quite the spectacle as he hunched, raptor-like in concentration, over his beloved machine on the café's back counter. He was usually clad in a grease-stained apron tied over a ripped singlet and raggedy shorts, his feet bare and grimy, the ever-present cigarette nodding over lattes and cappuccinos, tall blacks and flat whites, its burning nub of ash in constant danger of flaking off into the drinks. Muldoon's unique blends gained him new converts every day and, because of his ability to feed their caffeine addiction, he had become a very wealthy man.

He had enough business sense to remain at his station, well away from the patrons who stopped by for their fix. Instead, he made it a policy to hire attractive local women to work as servers. In a more uptight society, this practice might have branded Muldoon as sexist, but he understood that this South Seas paradise was a different world. Each week saw the arrival of hundreds of male tourists who quickly learned to appreciate the exotic beauty of Rarotonga and its people, whether it was on display at the market, on the beach, or in what soon became their favorite oasis for a quiet cup of jolt.

While physical beauty was important, Muldoon insisted that good service be paramount at Sparky's Café. That's why he was all smiles this morning as he watched his newest employee moving effortlessly between the tables and the bar where both the drinks and meals were placed for the servers to retrieve. Maina Rima had obviously been trained well on Pukapuka and Muldoon could thank Ben Tavera for that.

He lifted his head from surfing the milk and followed Maina as she approached a table, pen and order pad in hand.

Maina was uncomfortable and embarrassed, but the friendly smile she bestowed on her customers never wavered. Her problem was with the official Sparky's Café T-shirt that Muldoon had handed her when she arrived for her first shift after walking over from the National Auditorium.

The shirt was a medium, according to its label, but its last owner must have shrunk it in the wash because Maina had struggled to squeeze into it. The extended breadth of her shoulders, honed by a childhood spent swimming in the ocean, only complicated matters.

As a result, the shirt's pale yellow material, lightning bolt logo adorning the left sleeve, was stretched tightly across her breasts. It was also rode up out of her surfer shorts, exposing a narrow slash of brown tummy and a gauzy layer of baby hair that glowed bronze whenever the midday sun caught it.

She needed another shirt, one that actually fit properly, but a steady stream of customers kept the other staff members too busy to help her. She finally resigned herself to the discomfort; she would ask Muldoon for a replacement when her shift was over.

That decision didn't stop Maina from feeling self-conscious as she made the rounds of her assigned section. Now, approaching the two men who had just pulled up chairs at the lone available table, she was distressed to see that they were both staring intently at her chest.

"Kia orana," she said, speaking louder than she needed to, hoping her voice would raise their eyes. It worked.

The man closest to her was a local, although his skin was quite light. He was squat and solidly built, his shaved head in stark contrast to the thick, black mustache bristling above his full lips.

He wore a navy blue suit that had collapsed around him in the heat, over a white shirt and a tie stripped in blue and red. His black shoes were cheap but clean. He appeared to be some kind of businessman, an image reinforced by the brown leather briefcase he'd placed on the floor between his feet.

His companion was much larger, a European with a broad, weathered face topped by close-cropped blond hair that had sun-bleached until it was nearly white. A patch of scar tissue roosted on one cheek. Fighting off the urge to touch her own scar, Maina forced herself to look instead at the man's hands where they clutched the lunch menu. Judging by his huge, battered mitts of flesh, she pegged him as someone who had spent most of his life at sea.

"What can I get for you two fine gentlemen today?" she asked, the hand holding her pen unconsciously tugging at the back of her T-shirt.

"Beautiful *and* well-mannered," stated the local. "I am impressed. What's your name, my little lamb?"

Maina doodled the word 'loser' on her pad even as she bestowed her best smile on the man. "Maina, sir. Now, have you decided what you'd like for lunch?"

The local looked at the papa'a, who only shook his head. Looking past his scar, Maina saw that the man's eyes were as cold as the belly of an iceberg. Those eyes locked on hers, and flickered for a brief second. She shivered.

The local caught the interaction and hesitated. Then: "Nothing to eat right now, my dear Maina," he said. "But we will partake of your lovely coffee. Let's see." He smacked his lips wetly. "I'll have a double-shot, no-foam, soy latte. Super, super hot. Tor?" He eyed his companion; the man answered with a shrug. "My loquacious friend here will have a long black. OK, Maina?"

"Coming right up," Maina said, scratching out 'loser' and writing down the drink order.

"Thanks so much," said the first man. "Say," he added, pawing at her sleeve, "is that the new Sparky's logo?"

Maina twisted away from the table. The bald man smacked his lips again as he watched her return to the bar. He leaned towards his silent companion. "That looks tastier than anything on the menu," he chuckled lewdly.

Maina's fingers fumbled at her order pad as she tore off the top sheet and handed to Muldoon. He raised an eyebrow.

"You see those two men who just ordered?" she asked, keeping her voice steadier than she felt.

Muldoon glanced past her and nodded.

"They were totally perving my titties," she said, clearly annoyed.

Muldoon nodded again, causing his cigarette to bob in the midst of his bird's-nest beard. "Don't know who the big bugger is, but the other one is the Rev. Moses Akimo. Preacher for the Sonrise Christian Church of the Holy Spirit. Be nice to him, lass, and he'll save your soul."

"I get the feeling it's not my soul he's interested in," Maina said, casting a quick look over her shoulder. Rev. Akimo caught her eye and waggled a chubby bouquet of fingers at her. She nodded and smiled: all teeth.

"Arsehole," she muttered without moving her lips.

"Better get used to him," Muldoon said. "The good reverend's a regular. He's an oily bastard but basically harmless. But I'll warn you right now that he's persistent. He's formed a youth group at his church and he'll keep pestering you to join until you finally give in. He's already recruited three of my staff."

"I don't think I'll have any problems resisting his charms," Maina said. "But if he calls me his little lamb one more time I may have to chunder right in his lap."

Muldoon chuckled, then reached under the counter. He held out a piece of folded cloth. "Put this on, girl. Might help keep the ogling to a minimum."

She shook out the cloth and saw that it was a full-length apron. It had originally been red but had faded dramatically over the years. A chorus line of lobsters danced across its front.

Maina smiled as she slipped the loop over her head and tied the strings behind her back. The apron reached nearly to her ankles; it completely covered her T-shirt.

"Thanks, Mr. Muldoon."

Muldoon nodded an acknowledgment, then leaned down to read the reverend's order. "What the hell," he growled. "This is a pussy drink."

Rev. Moses Akimo squeezed behind the steering wheel of his white Holden, waited until Tor had folded himself into the passenger seat, then slowly glided out of the café's parking lot. Akimo scanned both sides of the main street as they passed through the centre of Avarua, nodding and waving at pedestrians and the other drivers. He seemed to know almost everyone they passed. Tor picked at his teeth with a wooden match and ignored Akimo's antics.

The reverend turned to his silent companion. "You don't talk much, my friend," he said.

Tor stared straight ahead. "And you talk too much," he growled in a thick Scandinavian accent.

Akimo nodded. At least he'd managed to start a conversation. That was encouraging. "What do you think?"

"Of what?"

"Our waitress," Akimo said as he tooted his horn at an oncoming bus. The driver smiled and saluted.

"She was OK."

"But nothing special?"

"No."

Akimo sighed. "Except for that unfortunate scar, I thought she was rather pretty," he said. "An almost perfect example of the local delicacies, as you should know by now."

"Too skinny."

Akimo glanced at his passenger, caught a glimpse of the man's facial deformity, and turned his attention back to the road.

"You mean she doesn't have the biggest titties you've ever seen," he said. "You'd better get used to it. These aren't your burger-fed, big-chested

American farm girls or Danube River frauleins, my friend. We tend not to inject our animals with growth hormones in this backward corner of the civilized world, so the only big breasts you're going to find here come with the arse and tummy to match. And I don't think that's what your employer has in mind."

Tor swiveled his head; Akimo flinched at the icy glare in the big man's eyes.

"Don't presume to know what my employer wants, holy man," Tor said. "You just do your job and keep your mouth shut. That way we won't have to find out how well *you* can swim."

Akimo pulled out a handkerchief and patted at his head.

"I'm doing my best," he said. "I'm the one, you'll recall, who suggested that using Mountain Motor Tours to check out the colleges would be the best way to avoid drawing attention to yourself."

"Good boy." Tor stared blankly at the storefronts as they drove through town.

Encouraged, Akimo pressed his advantage. "I thought your boss might appreciate the fact that our girls tend not to be that well-developed," he said. "It makes them look younger and that's what everyone wants."

"Yourself included, don't forget."

Something black and vile shivered in the pit of Akimo's guts. He smiled at the unexpected buzz.

"Where are we going?" Tor asked.

"To the National Auditorium," Akimo said. "To check out the dance rehearsals. And this evening I've organized a meeting of my church's youth group. Between the two, we're guaranteed to find something interesting."

Tor grunted yet again, excavating his molars with the splintered remains of the match. "We'd better," he said. "Because I'm losing patience with your silly little country."

SEVENTEEN

"Jesus Christ," Jack hissed as a dozen centipedes—fat, black, evil—scuttled across the toes of his boots. He became a statue in the tiny domain of light shed by Alex Benning's burning match.

"Steady, lad," Alex said, fighting to mask his own panic. Jack was already spooked enough for the both of them.

Jack gritted his teeth as he fought to control the red-eyed bat of panic that fluttered up from the pit of his stomach. Dr. Rangi spoke in his head: *You would have suffocated and died. If I were you, I'd make damn sure not to get bitten again.*

Jack guessed that the centipedes had a nest nearby because there appeared to be a purpose to their movements. For the moment at least, the insects seemed too absorbed with their particular duties to pay him much attention. But Jack feared that if he stayed in that position much longer, they just might decide to explore this new intrusion into their world.

He lifted his left boot. Slowly. Cautiously.

"Easy does it, lad," Alex whispered.

Jack's action caused a minor commotion among the centipedes. Several of them suddenly grew agitated, unsure of what had changed in their environment, but knowing instinctively that it had. Jack tried to swallow, found he couldn't. He squeezed his eyes shut, silently cursed himself for being so bloody curious. It was the writer in him. It would be the death of him yet.

He willed himself to breathe slower. In. Now out. And again. That's better. They're just bugs, after all. Nothing to be afraid of. One stomp of your boot and they're grease spots. No worry. No hurry. Alex and I are going to walk out of this room, and then we're going to laugh very loudly about this later. Over a nice bottle of Glenfiddich.

He extended his left leg and placed his foot down well away from any of the centipedes. Started to shift his weight from his back leg. As he did, the largest of the centipedes hesitated on the toe of his right boot. It shifted direction suddenly and began to crawl upwards. As its middle legs scrabbled in the material of Jack's sock, the insect arched its thorax, as if contemplating its route. Several sets of front legs began to churn their way towards the bare skin of Jack's leg.

Keep breathing, dammit! I can't! Oh fuck! Oh fuck!

Alex leaped forward, jammed the burning match into the centipede, grabbed Jack by the arm, and jerked him towards the dull outline of the doorway. Jack gave his back foot a violent shake, then bounded out of the room and down the stairs. He spun frantically, like a dog chasing its tail, in a desperate effort to see the back of his boots and legs.

Is it gone? Jesus, is it gone?

Jack's heartbeat thundered in his ears as he madly swatted his hands over his body. Nothing. He cupped a hand over his dry mouth. *Shit, that had been scary.*

Jack rubbed at his temples. Now that he was out of danger, he realized what an utter fool he'd made of himself. Faced with a test of his manhood, his first instinct had been to freeze. He'd stood there like a bloody idiot when all he needed to do was knock the one aggressive centipede off his boot and get the hell out of the room. Instead his fear of being bitten again—*You would have suffocated and died*—had robbed him of any lucid thought.

The realization hit him like a slap in the face: presented with the opportunity to display courage under fire, he had failed miserably. If not for the actions of an old man, Jack might still be upstairs. At the mercy of an insect.

Where bravery was concerned, all Jack Nolan could do was write about it.

Beside him, Alex hunched over, hands on his thighs, breathing noisily through his mouth.

"If I'm going to participate in any more of these adventures," he wheezed, "I'm going to have to quit smoking."

Alex straightened and made a slow circle around Jack. "All clear," he said.

Jack smiled weakly and put a hand on Alex's shoulder. "Thanks for that, mate," he said. "You may have saved my life."

"Then you owe me one," Alex grinned. "Now what the hell were you doing up there?"

"I saw something," Jack said. "Below the balcony, in the convention hall."

"What was it?"

"Just shapes, really, but there seemed to be some order to them," Jack said. "Not just randomly scattered around like everything else we've seen here. We need to go in there."

"We?"

Jack gave Alex's arm a playful squeeze. "C'mon, bro. Where's your sense of adventure?"

Alex nodded at the stairs. "I think I left it up there when I nearly had a heart attack saving your sorry arse."

"One quick look," Jack said. "And then we can go."

Alex gave his forehead a rub as he pondered Jack's proposition. "Just a quick look?"

"That's all."

"OK," Alex said. "But you stay right here until I fetch my torch."

"I'll be goddamned." Alex's eyes widened as he played the beam of his torch around the interior of the convention hall. The light wasn't powerful enough to fully penetrate the pit of blackness at the far end of the room, but it didn't matter. It was the objects directly in front of them that had prompted Alex's outburst.

Jack ran his hand over a stack of folding metal chairs. He nudged a toe against a pair of canvas cots sitting on top of each other. He squatted down in front of a portable diesel generator, sniffing at its guts.

"You sure this place has never been used?"

"Not as far as I know."

Jack rubbed a finger along the top of the generator and held it out to Alex. "No dust," he said. "And this thing smells new."

"What are you thinking?"

"I'm thinking the Endeavor has had visitors, my friend."

"But what would they be doing here?" Alex waved the torch. Its narrow beam etched across blank walls. "It's just a big empty room."

"I don't know." Jack patted the generator. "If this was fired up, would you hear it from your house?"

"I doubt it. The hall was built to be soundproof so they could hold wedding receptions or concerts here and not disturb the other guests. That's why it doesn't have windows. You'd have to be practically right outside the walls to hear anything."

Jack gazed into the darkness beyond the torch's reach and chewed on his lower lip.

"Maybe we should call the police," Alex said.

Jack shook his head. "And tell them what? That someone has been dusting in here? It's not against the law to clean. Although you'd never know it from my place."

"But this is private property," Alex insisted. "If someone was in here, that would be trespassing."

"Do you want to explain that to Karl Lamu?"

Alex's eyes dropped. "No."

Jack headed for the entrance. "You keep waiting until the last second to brake that train of yours, and you'll have no problem sorting out your trespassing problems," he said. "You might even frighten off the ghosts."

EIGHTEEN

"The usual, Jack?" Moe asked from behind the counter at Sunset Takeaways, her pencil poised.

"The usual?" Heather cocked an eyebrow in his direction.

"What?" Jack spread in hands in a gesture of innocent denial. "So Moe has a good memory. Is that my fault?"

Heather shook her head. "I'm beginning to think that your so-called homecooking skills consist of leaving home and going to wherever someone else is cooking."

"Yeah, whatever." Jack dug his wallet out of a pocket. "Good thing my new flatmate knows her way around a kitchen. Now what do you want? I'm shouting lunch today."

Heather brightened noticeably. "Oh, in that case," she turned to Moe, "I'll have my usual as well, please."

"Two fish burgers and two chips coming right up." Moe scribbled on a pad, ripped off the page, amd pinned it above the deep fryer.

"Excuse me?" Jack leaned in close to Heather. "Mrs. I'm A Wonderful Cook also has a regular order at the Sunset? And you're growling me?"

Heather pulled away. "Shut up, Jack, and pay the lady."

Jack's tattered self-esteem was starting to mend now that he was back in town and away from the desolation of the Endeavor. He'd needed something more than Alex's company and whiskey to assuage his wounded manhood. He needed his best friend.

Leaving Alex Benning to puzzle over their discovery at the hotel, Jack had continued north along the coast before turning inland and up the steep hill to the hospital. Had announced to Heather that she was now on her lunch break. Drove her to Sunset Takeaways on the edge of Avatiu Harbor.

As Moe turned her attention to the deep fryer, Heather and Jack plunked down at a picnic table beside the clapboard building. Heather, sitting nearest the water, leaned back to get a better view of the harbor.

"Jesus," she said. "That's a big one."

Jack looked down at his crotch. "Why thank you, madam," he said. "How kind of you to notice."

Heather made a face. "You're such an egg," she said. "I was talking about the boat."

Jack walked around the table to stand beside Heather. He whistled appreciatively. "Hello, Beautiful," he said.

The giant craft looming in white splendor on the far side of the harbor had to be the superyacht Ford Nelson had mentioned last night. Jack's mind boggled at its immensity.

He counted the five storeys, noted the helipad, satellite dishes, and a bristle of antennas. The quartet of motor launches suspended around the vessel's exterior were the same size as the local fishing boats that floated in the superyacht's shadow like tick-birds trailing a rhino. The sun's rays sparkled off the surface of a swimming pool on one of the decks.

The Belgian flag, with its vertical stripes of black, yellow and red, fluttered lazily in a light breeze. The vessel's name was painted in large black letters across the bow in a calligraphic font: *Chacal*.

"What do you think?" Heather asked.

Jack stared at the floating palace. He was woefully inept when it came to all things nautical, but he knew money when he saw it.

"I'm hoping that whomever owns that goddess has a daughter I can marry."

"You really are quite delusional. You know that, right?"

"It's a trait shared by all great writers."

"Oh?" Heather said. "And are you all conceited arseholes as well?"

"Your order's ready," Moe called out from behind them. Jack eagerly retrieved a plastic tray laden with food.

"This looks yummy," he said. He surveyed the bulging fish burgers and the plates of steaming chips. Frowned. "Wait a minute."

"Something wrong with the usual?" Heather asked as she took a large bite of her burger. An ooze of coleslaw flowed from its edges.

"No ketchup."

"You mean no tomato sauce."

Jack stood up. "Whatever you want to call it, I can't eat my chips without it."

He fetched a handful of small plastic packages and tumbled them onto the table between them.

"I'm going to start bringing my own supply from home." He carefully squeezed the condiment over his chips.

Heather worked on another mouthful of fish. "Speaking of home," she said.

Jack glanced up from his efforts. "Yeah?"

Heather put her burger down, then turned her head to watch a lone kakaia skim the wave tops seeking its own lunch. *Careful, girl*, she thought, *you need to tread lightly here.*

She looked back at Jack. "They're talking," she finally said.

"Who's talking?" The expert application of the tomato sauce now complete, Jack was practically inhaling his meal. "What about?"

"The other nurses at the hospital," Heather said. "They're talking about you and Maina. How it's not right that you have a young girl—a local girl—living with you."

Jack barked a laugh. "Goss at the hospital. My, that is hard to believe. Shall I call Lloyd and tell him to stop the presses?"

Heather's eyes sparked. "I'm serious here, Jack. Having Maina staying in your house just looks bad. I know the situation, that it's perfectly innocent, but other people are starting to whisper about you being a perv or something."

Jack stopped chewing. "I don't understand," he said. "Yesterday you were fine with this whole flatting thing. Now you think I'm a child molester?"

Heather shook her head. "I told you, it's not me. It's other people at the hospital."

"Just the hospital?"

"And the supermarket. And the post office."

Jack pushed his plate away. "And the Rocket Bar and the laundromat and anywhere that people with nothing better to do will sit around and talk about other people's private matters. We both know that's a fact of life here."

"Down, boy." Heather saw a vein throbbing in Jack's forehead. Experience told her that this was an early warning sign of an outburst beginning to simmer.

"I will admit to being mildly amazed at how quickly this particular news item has traveled," Jack said. "But I'm not surprised, and you shouldn't be either."

Heather nudged at her half-eaten fish burger with a fingertip. "I'm not trying to upset you, Jack," she said. "I'm only telling you what I've heard."

She was being careful not to tip Jack over the edge, but his sudden flare had set her radar to plinking.

"And I'm telling you that it's all bullshit," Jack shot back. "I can't believe it. I'm doing this girl a favor by taking her in and this is the thanks I get? Innuendo and ugly rumors?"

He picked up his fish burger, peered over it. "It's you, isn't it?"

"What are you talking about?"

"*You're* jealous of Maina."

A harsh noise broke from her throat. She shook her head vigorously. "You'd better start wearing a hat, Jack, because the sun's frying your brain cells."

Jack's chest tightened. His nostrils flared with the deep breaths he needed to douse his anger. He knew that he'd stung Heather with his accusation. Now it was best to just let the conversation die before they both said something they'd regret.

Jack returned to his meal, took a savage bite, and chewed hard. Jaw muscles clamped with the effort.

Heather also opted for silence. She propped her chin on her hands and concentrated on the road while her lunch grew cold on the scarred wooden table between them. Jack took another bite, dropped the rest of the burger onto the plate, and wiped his hands on his shorts.

"I'll take you back to work now," was all he said.

Heather followed him to his truck, her mind scrambling to comprehend why things had so swiftly gone pear-shaped between them. She'd struck a nerve, that much was certain. She sensed that Jack's aggressive reaction was hiding something. Something that he was still trying to fathom.

Poor dull, thick boy, she thought. *This could get messy.*

NINETEEN

"You look like shit."

Roger Henderson struggled to lift his head from where it rested on the bar. His eyes, what little of them Jack could actually see, were webbed with red.

"Thanks a lot," Roger croaked.

Jack flipped open a hinged section of the counter, pulled open a chiller, and helped himself to a Lion Red. "Late night?" he asked as he flipped off the bottle's cap.

Roger straightened up on his stool and held out his hand. "Don't ask."

Jack gave him the open bottle, then grabbed another for himself. "You're not fighting with Gracie again, are you?"

Roger shook his head once, wincing at the pain. "Ancient history, bro."

The scraps between Roger and his partner had always provided abundant fodder for the coconut wireless. He would become angry over the bookkeeping or the stocktaking; she would retaliate by accusing him of sniffing around this or that coconut princess. The shouting would begin: Roger in English, Gracie in her native Maori. Followed shortly thereafter by the flight of projectiles.

If the Rocket Bar wasn't full when the fight erupted, it soon would be, as workers eagerly piled out of the nearby government offices at the sound of rising voices and breaking glass. No one wanted to miss out on one of Gracie Henderson's tantrums, even if it meant risking a full bottle between the eyes.

Jack had been a reluctant witness to several of the combat sessions. While he felt embarrassed for both Roger and Gracie that they were airing their disagreements in public, what really upset him was how often the couple's 13-year-old daughter Lindsay was caught in the crossfire. More than once his heart had clenched in sympathy at the sight of the sobbing girl fleeing downstairs to the sanctuary of the family living quarters.

"Ancient history," Roger repeated, reaching up to where the sound system's tuner sat on a shelf. The opening notes of "Charging the Pipe" issued from the speakers. Roger brightened noticeably as he cranked up the volume.

"Shit, man, this is more like it." He grinned, jerking his head to the infectious beat. He began singing softly in harmony with a song he and the

Rockets had taken to No. 1. His eyes squeezed tight as he reached for the high notes. His voice was still sweet and strong. It belied his age.

The vocals gave way to a jangling guitar solo. Roger opened his eyes and smiled.

"Sorry, mate," he said. "But I can't stop myself from joining in, even if I am feeling crook." He shook his head as memories returned with each note. "Those were the days, man."

"No problem," Jack said. "I'm just surprised you're wasting your Rocket CDs on a quiet afternoon. Don't you usually save the classics for the dinner crowd?"

"That's the radio."

"You're kidding."

Jack sought out the framed photograph of the band as he worked on his beer. He concentrated on the figure of Dennis Cooper. The lead guitarist's expression was one of mild bemusement that not even the rectangular sunglasses could disguise.

Roger followed his gaze. "You thinking about Denny?"

"How did you know?"

"Because I do the same thing every time I look at that damn photo," Roger said. "You know, it's still strange for me to see him dressed like that. You wouldn't believe the effort it took to convince him that everyone needed to look the same for that photo. Matching outfits were all the rage at the time, but Denny refused to wear anything but Hawaiian shirts, what we call pareu shirts here. The brighter, the better, as far as he was concerned. Jesus, you would have thought we were skinning him alive when our manager asked him to change for ten measly minutes. We never did get those glasses off him, as you can see."

"He was quite the character, eh?"

"He was more than that," Roger said. "He was a crazy man. He had so much energy. So much *life*. It's hard to think that it's all gone now. That Denny's gone now."

Roger lowered the volume on the radio.

"You think of all the shit we survived as a rock band, and then he stops in at the World Trade Centre to take his daughter for breakfast and he never comes back. That's not how old rockers are supposed to die."

"And they never found his body?"

"Not a trace," Roger said. "His daughter said they were walking into the restaurant one minute and the next minute the first plane hit and Denny was gone."

Jack contemplated the photo. "So no real closure?"

"That's the bitch," Roger said. "That and this niggling I get in the pit of my stomach whenever I look at that photo."

"Niggling?"

"This feeling that maybe Denny survived 9/11."

"But if he is still alive, why hasn't he contacted anyone?"

"I don't know," Roger said, reaching up to lightly brush away a cobweb from the edge of the photo's frame. "I heard stories about money problems, someone suing someone over royalties. That sort of thing. Maybe he just needed to disappear for awhile."

"I thought that *Eddie and the Cruisers* stuff only happened in the movies."

Roger turned to Jack. "Maybe you thought wrong, my friend."

The music faded out, replaced by the radio announcer's voice: *"This is Teen Scene and you're with the Great and Wonderful Johno and my guest co-host Taraani right through to five. That was an oldie but a goldie, dedicated to our very own Roger Henderson who, apparently, was once a teen himself. We're just not sure which century that was."*

"Prick!" Roger laughed, tipping his bottle in a salute.

"I can't believe you listen to that show."

"It's the only station in the country," Roger said, "so I don't have much choice. Besides that Johno fellow is actually quite popular with all the kids. Linds and her friends love him. Some of them have actually been on his show."

"Really? So what the hell does this guy look like?"

Roger shrugged. "I have no idea. The kids will only say that he's sweet as. Apparently there's a waiting list to be on the show as a co-host."

Hearing one of his former hits had momentarily energized Roger. Jack watched in amusement as the bar owner swayed energetically to the beat of the next song, the frenzied motion of his impromptu dance causing his ponytail to flap wildly between his shoulder blades.

"You're going to hurt yourself," Jack laughed as Roger hammered out a drum riff on the bar.

Roger stopped, hands suspended in midair. He looked up at Jack, down at his beer, squinted into the dimness of the room where a handful of patrons nursed their drinks and pretended to ignore the madman in their midst. Roger grabbed at his head, and slumped back onto his stool.

"God hates me," he moaned.

"So what is it that's making you feel so crook today?" Jack said. "It's got to be more than just sad memories of Dennis Cooper."

"Screwing."

"Screwing what?" Jack asked.

"Not what," Roger said. "Who."

Jack pushed his empty bottle aside. "Excuse me?"

Roger chugged the last of his beer, slammed the bottle down on the counter, belched loudly, and flashed a lopsided grin "Sorry, mate," he said, wiping his mouth with the back of his hand. "But it's low tide and you know what that means."

"Oh, right," Jack nodded, finally cluing in.

The forward section of the Rocket Bar was built atop concrete piles so that its deck and most of the eating area actually jutted out over a section of the harbor. When the tide was low, the area of beach under the building made an ideal location for lovers seeking to elude prying eyes or suspicious spouses. Once darkness fell, it was almost impossible to discern what manner of activity was being performed amidst the supports.

Unless it was the dead of night and the bar owner's bedroom happened to be on the ground floor directly above the action.

"There must be an influx of English backpackers on the island because there were girlies screaming all night," Roger said, digging knuckles into his bleary eyes. "Those Pommy sheilas are as noisy as mating cats."

"Don't tell me you spent the night playing sex police," Jack laughed.

Roger nodded sorrowfully. "You know Gracie's cold feet?" He turned his back on Jack and pointed to the area just above the waistband of his shorts. "Right there," Roger said. "Every time she thought she heard someone moaning, she brought those icy dogs up and shoved me out of bed. I think I wore out the batteries in my torch."

"Jesus," Jack said. "How many of the island boys know about the Rocket rendezvous?"

"Too bloody many! I bet I had to chase away six or seven of those bastards," Roger said. "Standing there, waving their dicks in the wind while their new girlfriends scrabbled for their knickers in the sand. It was really quite disgusting."

"You must really get an eyeful sometimes."

"It's not my eyes I'm worried about," Roger said. "I'm seriously afraid that this perfect nose is going to take a beating one night. And I can't afford to have it fixed again."

"The local sex machines getting tired of you putting interruptus to their coitus?"

"I think it's more those mongrels who come over from New Zealand," Roger said. "Whoever they are, they're becoming more and more aggressive in their actions. And it's not just when I'm rousting them out from under my house."

"How so?"

"I heard this morning that a couple of the local boys beat the living shit out of a backpacker in front of The Hole last night," Roger said. "We're talking mucho stitches here. Maybe even a broken cheekbone."

Jack whistled.

"Yeah," Roger said. "And that sort of violence is becoming more commonplace, especially among the young people."

"I must be blind," Jack said, "because I'm not seeing any of that."

"That's because you've become a boring homebody in your old age," Roger said. "If you were still hanging around bars trying to convince brown girls that you're hung like a horse, instead of going home early to watch *Shortland Street*, you'd see for yourself how trouble is starting to brew."

"Are you saying that my life is boring?"

"When was the last time you went out?"

Jack was stumped for a moment. Christ, maybe he was getting old. No, not quite yet. "As a matter of fact, I'm heading to Lloyd Dempster's party right from here."

"Really?" Roger grinned. "Excuse me while I yawn."

Jack's shoulders slumped. Roger was right: the only reason he was attending the party in honor of the French ambassador was because Lloyd was paying him to take photos.

"You should stay here instead," Roger said. "See for yourself what I'm talking about."

Jack shook his head. "If word gets out that Cook Islanders are smashing visitors, it's going to turn Rarotonga into another Bali. And we can't afford to have our tourism industry suffer."

Roger nodded. "Remember how ugly it was in 2001 with 9/11 and then Canada 3000 folding? And then SARS and Iraq in 2003? If the tourists stop coming here again, I might as well burn the Rocket to the waterline because this island is going to be a ghost town."

"Are you seeing any problems in here?"

A server approached and handed Roger a drink order. He placed it on the bar in front of him, then started reaching for bottles and glasses. He talked as he poured.

"Unfortunately, I am. And I can thank that wanker Moses Akimo for it."

"The good reverend?"

"Good my arse." Roger lifted two full glasses from behind the counter and carefully placed them on the server's tray. She smiled at the men and moved away to deliver the drinks to a corner table.

"What's a man of God doing in a bar anyway?" Jack asked.

"Man of God?" Roger snorted derisively. "That bald bastard is the biggest horndog on the island."

"Really? Jesus, the coconut wireless really has lost my number, because this is all news to me."

"I told you that you go home too early," Roger said. "Otherwise you'd see Akimo and his cronies show up here almost every night at the stroke of 10. They come swaggering in here hooting and hollering at the top of their lungs. The papa'as take one look at that sorry bunch and they can't head for the exits fast enough. I call it the White Flight. It would be hilarious if it wasn't so damn pathetic."

"But what about the Viagra Club?" Jack asked. "All those old white guys who claim to be the movers and shakers on the island? They're practically part of the furniture here. Surely they're not intimidated by someone like Akimo."

Roger laughed. "Those pricks are the first ones out the door."

"That's got to be hurting your business."

Roger nodded ruefully. "Big time," he said. "But that's not what concerns me the most." He looked over Jack's shoulder, checked out the faces at the tables, then leaned in close.

"I'll tell you what really scares me," he said.

"What's that?"

Roger's eyes darkened. "I'm awful goddamn afraid that the Cook Islands is eventually going to become another Zimbabwe."

"What?"

"Shocking, eh?" Roger said. "I'm not saying the PM's another Mugabe, far from it. And you know how much I love this country, but there is a definite undercurrent of anti-white sentiment brewing and it's getting worse by the day. Every time some rich European shows up and starts making promises that involve Cook Islanders working their arses off while someone else makes the real money, the animosity only grows."

Roger sighed; it was a troubled sound. "This island's a power keg, Jack, and Akimo likes to play with matches. All it needs is one incident—one little spark—and the whole thing is going to explode in our faces. And, when it does, it's going to get very, very ugly. For all of us."

TWENTY

Jack framed. He focused. He shot.
Flash! Lloyd Dempster/his wife Sofia/the French ambassador/the ambassador's wife.
Smile nicely and keep your damn eyes open. Teeth and eyes. Teeth and eyes.
Flash! Karl Lamu/Maddy Owensby/Rev. Albert Smail. Rev. Moses Akimo hovering in the background, careful not to get too close to Albert.
Flash! Tommy Niomare thoughtfully adjusting a dancer's coconut bra. That one was going to pay for Jack's beer at the Rocket Bar for several Wednesdays to come.

Jack, tucked out of sight near the back of the property, hunkered amidst a grove of palm trees. Empty champagne flutes lay discarded in the sand around him. Some of them were his. He peered at the display screen on the back of his camera. He studied faces immobilized by a white strobe. He eyeballed the rich and famous.

Flash!
The prime minister, Sir Edward Pitt, conferring with his Minister of Health, Donald Amahu. Pitt's wife, Nanie, tucked tightly into the PM's chest, huddled nearly out of sight against the contours of his black suit jacket. Nanie was 20 years younger than her husband and a constant source of gossip on the island. Her look, as she stared into the camera, was one of plaintive vulnerability. She knew things—secret things, *dark* things—and that both excited and scared her.

Flash!
Maddy Owensby again, this time accompanied by a cultured gentleman. Greying, tanned, athletic. An unmistakable air of dignity: he has money. Lots of it. A goatee framed the man's thin, bloodless lips.
"Jack, my dear, allow me to introduce you to Andre Larouche."
Handshake: too tight. A challenge? Held a beat too long.
"Jack's a writer."

"Really?" European accent. Raised eyebrow. An affectation more than genuine interest. *He doesn't give a shit*, Jack thought.

"Monsieur Larouche is from Belgium. Isn't that exciting? What a terribly long way to travel! Oh, did I mention that he owns that rather impressive yacht that's been moored in Avatiu Harbor for the past week?"

"Madame flatters me," Larouche said. "The ship, she actually belongs to my company. I'm just lucky enough to be permitted to use it on occasion. Such as to visit your beautiful country."

"Good for you," Jack said.

"What part of America are you from?" Larouche asked.

"The Canadian part."

"Excusez-moi," Larouche said. "It's just that the accent—"

"Yeah," Jack said. "It fools a lot of people." He started to turn away.

"Oh, Jack, dear." He raised an eyebrow at Maddy. "I hope you don't mind ever so much, but I've taken the liberty of inviting Monsieur Larouche to join us for tennis tomorrow morning. Apparently that ship of his has all the amenities you'd ever want, except for a tennis court. Imagine that."

Jack's smile was forced. He hoped it showed. "How utterly barbaric."

"I understand that the young Rima girl is staying with you," said Maddy.

"Yes she is."

"I knew her mother," Maddy said. "What a wonderful dancer! And just the most darling person you'd ever want to meet. I was actually introduced to the daughter once, but that was many years ago. She was quite young at the time and I'm sure she's forgotten all about me by now. Or maybe she hasn't. Who knows. Funny things, our memories. Don't you agree, Jack?"

"Oh, yes. Treacherous creatures at the best of times."

"Oh, I can see that you're busy with your little camera, so I won't keep you. But please tell dear, sweet Maina that Mrs. Owensby says hello, and that she is always welcome to come round for tea and bickies."

"I'll be sure to tell her. Thank you."

Flash!

Karl Lamu and Jordan Baxter. Nose-to-nose.

"Your story was rubbish, as usual! Nothing but speculation and innuendo! How can you put your name to such malicious lies?"

"You're just upset that the media knows more than the police do."

"You know nothing!"

"My sources tell me that this was no accident."

"Your sources are shit!"

"OK, tell me right now, in front of Jack here, what your version of the incident is."

"I'll tell you nothing!"

"And how is that different from any other day?"

Flash! Dancers on the portable stage—coconut-shell bras, swiveling hips—backed by enthusiastic drummers and singers with ukuleles.

Flash! Tables laden with the offerings of the umukai, being picked clean by jostling guests with sharp elbows. Too hungry to be polite.

Flash! Hangers-on in the spa pool. Bikini tops stretched valiantly over round flesh, hardened nipples pressed tightly against sheer material. These would go into Lloyd Dempster's private electronic file.

Jack worked the camera's controls. Photos flicked past; a miniature slideshow. Sofia had slipped him the guest list when he arrived. Names were circled, those whose egos could be stroked by appearing in *The Tribune*. Jack mentally checked off the list as he scanned his pictures. He was done.

He stood up, stretched out kinks, and brushed off sand. He glanced at his watch and winced at the time. He needed to go home. Matavara was a safe village, but he still didn't like the idea of Maina being alone in the house at night. Being alone with her dreams. He slung his camera case over his shoulder and stepped back onto the lawn.

He swayed, he staggered, he propped himself against a tree. The camera case slipped down his arm and thudded onto the grass. Jack's head hung low, his eyes drifted, his knees were gone.

His world fractured. It became staccato. It became his own private slideshow. *Flash, flash, flash.*

He stared at the overturned wineglasses at his feet. How much had he drunk during his photo shoot? Roger had nailed it perfectly: He *was* out of shape. Of course it didn't help that he was already well-oiled by the time he'd arrived at the party. He'd stopped at the Rocket Bar to flush Heather's concerns out of his head, but once he'd started chatting with Roger, he had simply continued to drink.

He pawed at his eyes. He hadn't realized how completely wreaked he was until he'd tried to move again. He shouldn't drive; he probably *couldn't* drive. Not on a narrow road, one with too few streetlights and too many curves. He needed to sober up. Was there coffee in the kitchen? And could he even make it there?

The sounds of splashing and laughter came from the direction of the spa pool. That was closer than the house. There was a wooden deck there. Chairs and lounges. Jack could sit for a moment, collect his senses, let the hot night sweat the alcohol out of his system.

The spa pool was located near the back of the Dempster property, tucked behind a flowering hedge. Jack carefully manoeuvred his way across the width of the yard, guided by the flickering flames of tiki torches.

Flash! A mental image to bank for future reference: Moses Akimo deep in conversation with Maddy's new friend, Larouche. And something else: Police Chief Inspector Karl Lamu urinating against a tree. Was he listening?

Whoever had been using the spa pool had since moved on. The Fiberglass tub and its surrounding wooden deck were both empty when Jack rounded the hedge. He sprawled into a canvas wing chair, swallowed a juicy burp. His stomach heaved; reflux burned the entire length of his esophagus. The pain in his chest reminded him again why he had toned down his late-night carousing. Tonight's stupidity was a one-off. Never again. Full stop.

He eyed the pool. The flames from the tiki torches were reflected in its azure surface. Would the jets serve to invigorate his weary body? Or would the heat of the water lull him to sleep? And how idiotic would it be to pass out in a spa? Lamu would blow a heart valve if he had to deal with two drownings in one week.

Too bad for him.

Jack stood on tiptoe and peered over the hedge. No one moved in his direction. Good. He fumbled open the buttons of his pareu shirt. Kicked off his sandals. Slid out of his pants. No togs: no problem. His boxers would suffice for a quick dip.

The water in the spa was heated to at least 40 degrees. Jack's breath clutched. He moved gingerly. He eased—*hello scrotum!*—into the tub's depths. Goose bumps puckered—blood rushing to the surface of his skin, his body instinctively compensating for the sudden change in temperature.

It took only seconds to adjust to the heat. He tapped the switch to activate the water jets. His head still spun, but he could feel his muscles relaxing under the pulsing ministrations. His eyes closed. Just a few minutes of this and he'd be good as gold. Sweet as. He hoped Maina wasn't waiting up for him.

A soft footstep. His eyes fluttered open.

He'd died. He'd gone to heaven. He'd met an angel.

A young woman stood at the side of the spa. She torpedoed Jack with her beauty. She hammered him. She crushed him.

Her face was smooth. It was flawless. It was the color of milky lattes, except where darker freckles were drizzled across her cheekbones. A brilliant yellow pareu only served to draw attention to the thick mane of black hair that cascaded past her shoulders.

She looked familiar but Jack couldn't quite place her. He hadn't taken her photo tonight. His fizzy brain knew that much. But how could he possibly forget a face like that?

She saw Jack watching. She blushed. He liked what it did to her freckles. He liked what it did to him.

"I'm sorry to disturb you," she said in a Polynesian accent. "I'm Chaka."

Her name completed the circuit. The cover of *Surfie Chicks*. Jordan Baxter's woman.

"Jack Nolan."

"The photographer? Jordan has talked about you."

Chaka dipped a toe into the spa. Jack's eyes skittered up her bare leg. "Mind if I join you?"

"Please do."

Jack slid away from the steps. His boxers crawled up his butt. He shifted again to liberate them. When he turned back, the yellow pareu was a crumpled heap on the deck. Chaka stood naked on the edge of the spa, her hair swept back over her shoulders.

Except for the ebony circles of her nipples, stationed high on firm breasts, the rest of her body—supple, round, *magnificent*—was the same café au lait tint as her face.

The light from the tiki torches caressed her moist highlights, draping her body in gold. Her pubic hair had been carefully shaved into a thin vertical line. Her pierced navel sported a silver band. It held a small jewel that sent off green sparkles from the centre of her smooth tummy.

Jack blinked. He gasped. He drooled.

Biology betrayed him. Abandoning its work as a coolant, his blood surged to another, lower, part of his anatomy. Panic constricted his chest. He snapped his eyes down. He felt immense relief that the bubbles churned up by the spa's jets made it impossible to see below the surface.

Chaka slipped into the spa. She stooped. She bowed. She was a cat. She was a goddess entering a vessel brimming with the blood of virgins. She balanced on her hands, holding herself on the edge of the spa for a second, half-immersed. She teased the water.

Jack marveled. He stared. He gawked.

Poised like that only served to magnify the definition in the taut muscles of Chaka's arms, her shoulders, abs. It arched her breasts even higher. Jack's throat closed. He couldn't swallow. He couldn't breathe.

Chaka slid into the spa. The bubbles swallowed her. Jack raised his head. He looked at the night sky. He saw planets. He saw stars. He saw constellations. None of them matched the splendor of the creature beside him.

He exhaled. He inhaled. He pondered how the hell a loser like Jordan Baxter could ever hook up with a beauty of this magnitude.

She rested the back of her head against the side of the spa. She sighed deeply. She closed her eyes.

"Is it me, or does this party blow?"

"It is rather dull," Jack admitted.

"Why are we here, then?"

Jack studied her. He appreciated. He categorized. He memorized.

"I don't know about you," he said, "but this is what I call staying in the loop."

"How so?"

"Lloyd only invites the most influential personalities in the country to these little soirees. I make a point of interacting with these people because, some day, I may have to call in a favor from someone I met here."

"Are you and I interacting right now?" she purred.

"Oh, I sure hope so."

A tiny smile skipped across her mouth. Jack noted it. He charted it. He filed it away for future reference.

"Are you important?" she whispered.

"I used to be."

Jack squinted up again. What was it about the South Pacific that made the night sky appear so thickly populated? Start with the lack of pollution and go from there.

"What did you do? Please tell me you were a bad boy."

"I wish," he said. "Actually I wrote a book that sold a few copies. It made me very popular for a couple of minutes. But that was years ago."

She turned slightly in his direction. Her eyes remained shut. Her face was smooth. It was calm. It was untroubled by thought.

"And now you take pictures, yes?"

"It's Lloyd's way of humoring me, I suppose, of keeping me close." Jack lifted his hands out of the water. He waggled his fingers. "Just in case I ever rediscover the magic in these babies."

Chaka opened her eyes. She looked at his fingers. She measured his hands. She nodded.

"So you're a surfer?" It was an idiot's question. It was a pathetic attempt at small talk. Chaka didn't seem to mind. She laughed. The sound came from somewhere dark. It chilled him.

"Surfer?" She tossed her head. Her hair slapped the water. It caused splashes. It caused ripples. The ripples broke against Jack's chest.

"I'm surprised Jordan didn't tell you," she said. "I'm much more than that. Because I'm one of the few female surfers in my country, that apparently makes me important. A shining example for my people, they tell me."

"Like a Miss Rapa Nui, or something?"

"Or something."

She smiled. Her teeth gleamed: white framed by pink. "I've also made a couple of documentaries with a production company based out of Tahiti. We're filming here right now, as a matter of fact."

"I'm impressed."

"Don't be. We set the camera up on the beach, aim it at the ocean, press play and then I go surf. Monkeys could do it."

"It still sounds like fun."

Her lips spread again, different this time. This was the smile of someone who has just been very, very wicked. Or is about to be.

"Not as much fun as getting naked with pretty white boys like you," she said throatily.

Jack's mouth gaped. It flopped. It chewed air.

Chaka eyed the far wall. "Is that the thermometer? How hot is it in here anyway?"

Africa hot. Volcano hot. Magma hot.

She stretched out for the thermometer's bobbing plastic casing. Jack moved. He tilted. He *leaned*. Her shoulder brushed against him. Her breasts nippled across his skin.

She lost balance. She flapped. She sought purchase. She found it. She steadied herself. She popped her eyes.

"Oh my."

"I'm sorry," Jack stuttered. He ground his teeth. He *stiffened*.

"Don't be," she laughed. "I'm from Easter Island, remember. I'm used to large, hard heads."

"Oh God."

"Hey you two."

Jordan Baxter stood by the side of the spa, hands on his hips. Chaka straightened. Jack didn't need to.

"Did bad Chaka forget her togs again?" Mock reproach and champagne diluted Jordan's growling tone. "C'mon, girlfriend, I want you to meet some people."

Chaka stood. She leaned forward. She glided towards Jack. Her nipples—hard, dark buttons—trailed just beneath the surface of the foaming water. "Later," she whispered in Jack's ear. The heat of her breath tingled. His toes curled. His fists clenched. His blood surged. Again.

Jack played the gentleman. He didn't want Jordan to catch him perving his girlfriend. He averted his eyes as Chaka turned to step out of the spa. But something caught his eye as she lifted her leg. A flash of color. His head snapped around. His eyes focussed.

He only glimpsed it for an instant, and even that was through the water streaming down her shiny flanks. Then Chaka stepped into the yellow pareu Jordan held open for her and expertly tied if off at the shoulder.

But Jack had no doubt what he had seen: a tattoo. Tiny yet distinctive, situated low on her left cheek where her swimming togs would normally cover it.

Black and red and dog-like. The same design he had seen in his photograph of Gert Junger. But this time Jack recognized the creature.

A jackal.

TWENTY-ONE

Stench: salt/rotting vegetation/dead things. *He's here again.*

He slumps onto the end of her bed, dripping filthy green water on the sheets Jack is always so diligent about washing.

"Look at me."

No.

"What are you afraid of?"

Not you. Not anymore.

She shuts her eyes, places both hands over them. Doubly blind now, yet she still sees him. The blood is a thick, crusty mat in his hair. It has dried in crimson rivulets down the bony outcroppings of his cheeks. His mustache is a slash of gore. His grey skin has been nibbled at. Fish have sampled him, assuming he was submerged for their dining pleasure.

"Why did you do this?"

You know. Oh, God, you know.

"You can't possibly think that I deserved it."

That and so much more. You did not suffer nearly enough.

"You won't get away with it."

I already have.

"Look at me."

Never again.

"See how the ropes are already sloughing off? You really should have used a better knot. You never were any good with knots."

Unlike you.

"Soon I will be free again."

I don't care.

"Soon they will find me."

I don't care.

"Soon they will know what evil you have committed."

I don't care.

"Give me a kiss."

No.

"Just one more. Please. Here, on my lips. And here."

No.

"GIVE! ME! A! KISS!"

"Jack!"

A disturbance in the atmosphere. Jack stirred, grunted, lifted his head, and let it thud back on the pillow.

"Jack! Wake up!"

He rolled over, sat up, flicked on his lamp, and recoiled at its brightness. His eyes were puffy slits, his hair poked up in greasy spikes. The room smelled of second-hand booze. Jack tasted crud.

What army had camped overnight in his mouth?

Maina stood by his bed. She was shivering. He looked at her. His eyes focussed. His eyes grew wider. He was awake now.

"What's wrong?" he asked. He cleared his throat with a wet hack. "Are you OK?"

"He's back."

Jack looked past her, to the bedroom door. "Who's back, Maina?"

"The boogey man."

Shit, fuck, damn. It had happened again. "Here, sit down. You're safe now."

He disengaged himself from the sheet and swung his legs over the side. He stood up, rocked unsteadily, and regained his balance. So much for sobering up.

"Where are you going?"

Jack touched her shoulder. "To brush my teeth," he said. "Believe me, you'll thank me."

Maina watched him stagger through the lounge and into the kitchen, switching on lights as he went through the rooms. He veered right and opened the back door. She heard him pee, then run water in the sink.

In the bathroom, Jack put his toothbrush down and looked at the haggard, unshaven beast in the mirror. God, what a mess. He didn't look much like a hero right now.

He pictured Maina sitting on his bed: eyes flared, dark pupils circled by white. How they darted around his room, into corners, into shadows. Seeking what?

He's back. The boogey man.

So she had remembered the earlier nightmare. But what could possibly haunt the dreams of a 16-year-old?

"Maina?"

Her eyes jittered across his face, encountered the wall, then returned to him.

He sat down beside her. This was different from last night. She was awake this time. She was aware.

"You've had a bad dream," he said. "Can you tell me about it?"

She was trembling. Her T-shirt was drenched with sweat. It was plastered to her chest. Jack tried not to look.

She shook her head, as if to dislodge visions. "He scares me," she said.

"Who? Who scares you, Maina?"

"I don't know," she said. "A man. A bad man."

"And you don't recognize him?"

"No."

There was a hesitation in her answers that Jack's mushy brain told him he should question. But his mind was still foggy from too much alcohol and not enough sleep. He was in no shape to concentrate on anything.

He stroked her hair. It was soft, smooth. He put his arm around her and pulled her close. He tried to *squeeze* the fright out of her. Physical contact: it was all he could think of to do in his condition.

"I love you."

The words skidded across his brain, smacked into the other side of his skull, tumbled and crashed into each other. An icy spear pierced his guts.

What did she say?

He held her at arm's length, trying to see her eyes. She bent, she squirmed, she avoided the interrogation of his gaze. Was she still half-asleep? *Was he?*

She reddened, embarrassed. Jack watched the flush spread across her cheeks and work its way down her throat. His heart sank. How could he possibly respond?

"Maina," he said, fighting to keep his voice level. To keep his voice calm, neutral. All while his heart hurled itself against his ribs. "You're tired. You're worn out. And I'm guessing you're still freaked by whatever it was you were dreaming about. I think you need to go back to your bed and try to get some sleep."

She finally raised his eyes to meet his. They were wet. She was going to cry. That was going to break his heart. He drew her back to him, her head tucked into his sternum, her face registering every bass note of his heart.

"Don't you like me?" she said, her voice muffled by his singlet.

Jack's eyes traveled around his room. He needed answers. He needed guidance. He needed Heather here to help him find the words. To help him not hurt this young girl's feelings. Something told him she had been subjected to enough abuse already.

He pulled them apart. He slid away from her on the bed so that they could face each other. The tears had come, as he knew they would. Glistening on her cheeks in the light from the bedside lamp. Plump, salty droplets of despair. Staining his shirt.

"Of course, I *like* you," he said. "You're a cheeky pain in the arse, but that doesn't mean I don't like you."

"Then what's the problem?" she sniffled.

"The problem," he said, speaking slowly, deliberately, "is that we met each other yesterday. You don't even know me."

"You have a kind face."

"And I have a tattoo on my arm and I used to drive my brother barking mad by curling my toes whenever I watched TV," he said. "All of which does nothing to lessen the fact that we are still virtual strangers. I could be a serial killer. Hell, *you* could be a serial killer."

The levity helped. She smiled. She pulled up the neck of her T-shirt and used it to wipe the snot from her upper lip.

"You took me in and let me stay here," she said. "I don't think serial killers do that sort of thing."

"I didn't have any choice about letting you stay," he said. "And just how many serial killers have you known in all your 16 years, young lady?"

"None."

"See?"

"I feel safe here," she insisted. "I feel like I belong here."

Jack ran a hand through his hair, gunking it even more. "That's because this is your family's house. You feel connected to it, or something. Cook Islanders have this spiritual side that is all quite wonderful and fascinating, but it's not exactly what I want to discuss with you in the middle of the friggin' night."

"Don't you want me?" Her eyebrows jigged. She face-talked: *Don't you want me?*

"Want you? *Want* you?" His eyes widened. "You mean sexually?"

She nodded.

OK, now this was getting scary. Jack stood up and started to pace the narrow confines of his room. His legs were still unsteady. His drinking spree wasn't finished with him quite yet. He started to sweat. It wasn't from the heat.

He stopped. Ran a hand over his face, scratched at the stubble. He was shaking. Steady on mate; here there be dragons.

"First of all," he said, crossing his arms to control the shuddering, "you're way too young for me. Understand? And, secondly, even if I was interested, I'm pretty sure there are laws against that sort of thing. I'm not a serial killer, but I'm also not a pedophile."

"I already know you like younger women," she said, jutting out a defiant jaw.

"Says who?"

"Says everyone who saw you with Dani Reka."

Jack thudded back against the wall and slid down it until he was perched on his haunches. Dani Reka. Now there was a blast from the past.

Dani was 22 when they met on Muri Beach. He was suntanning, blissfully tuned out to the world. Then her dog ran up and buried its nose in his crotch. Dani was nearly apoplectic with embarrassment. Jack laughed it off.

The dog was disengaged from his nether regions. They introduced each other. They talked. Dinner followed. They became a couple. The dog grew bored with his crotch. Dani never did.

It was perfect timing for both of them. Jack had been on the island for a year. In that time, he'd been very diligent in his pursuit of island women. He liked them brown. Liked them exotic. Liked them screaming beneath him.

He would buy drinks for an entire table of local ladies in the hopes of bedding at least one of them. His was a sexual crusade, fueled by a raging libido that had roared into fully engorged life under the blazing ministrations of the tropical sun.

And then had come the e-mail from Porter. His sensible, boring, brutally honest baby brother.

Keep up the carousing, the message said. Keep it up and you'll be broke before the end of the calendar year. Book sales have slowed, just as we knew they would. The studio is still negotiating the finer details of the director's cut DVD; it could be 18 months or more before it's in stores. You have to tone down your wild lifestyle. Tone down, slow down, or you will—and this is where Porter was most adamant—you will run out of money. Plain and simple. Cheers. Your devoted brother. PS: Maryanne sends her love. PPS: Nile is engaged to Ray Chimera. Just thought you'd like to know.

Jack printed the message. Burnt it in the rubbish pile behind his house. Kicked the ashes into the bush.

Dani was the eldest daughter of Paul Reka, chief executive officer for the

Cook Islands Tourism Corporation. She had been in university in Auckland. Then came the World Trade Centre. 9/11. The same shit that claimed Dennis Cooper.

People thought twice about boarding a plane. People cancelled holidays that involved flying. People *drove*. You can't drive to the Cook Islands. Tourism was threatened. The country's very lifeblood was threatened. The government panicked. The government went to Plan B. The government demanded that each of its ministries trim 20 percent from its budget. The hospital lost a perfectly good Canadian nurse. Paul Reka took a pay cut.

The Rekas made sacrifices. One of those was Dani's tuition. So she left university at the end of the term. She returned to Rarotonga. She found a job in the Mills Gallery of Indigenous Art. She saved up her own money for tertiary education. She took the family dog for walks on Muri Beach.

They were partners for two years and, if pressed, Jack might admit that a residue of love existed above and beyond the simple act of lovemaking. But not enough to prevent them from drifting apart. Dani wanted a commitment before she left for New Zealand to continue with university. Jack, still bearing the scars from his marriage to Nile Ramsay, preferred the good-time-not-a-long-time approach. It was never going to work out.

Night. Phone ringing. "Hello?"

"Hello, Jack."

"Dani? Where are you? I thought you were coming over here."

"Hear that noise in the background, Jack?"

"Course I do. What is it?"

"That's the jet that's taking me back to New Zealand. Good bye."

That was three years ago. He hadn't seen her since.

"That was different," Jack said to Maina. "And, if you were paying attention to the story, you'd know that Dani was still older than you are."

"I love you."

There, she'd said it again. It dangled in the still air between them, a bulbous, palpable thing. Jack's mouth was sour. The brushing hadn't helped.

"How can you possibly know how love feels?"

She came right back at him. "I know what hate is. And this feels exactly the opposite of that."

She was determined. She was beating him down. She was chipping away.

Jack felt crook. His stomach heaved. His face burned with fever. His saliva glands switched to overdrive.

"Look," he said. "I don't mean to hurt your feelings, Maina. You're a wonderful person. You're beautiful and funny and sweet."

"But—"

"But you've just been jarred awake by a nightmare," he said. "And I've had a rough day followed by too much alcohol. So what we really need is to just go back to bed for a couple of hours and try to sleep a bit more. We'll talk all about this over breakfast, how about that? I'll even cook."

She looked at him warily and saw the purple swelling under his eyes, the slackness of his mouth. He was dead on his feet.

"Walk me to my room?"

"Sure."

He pulled aside the curtain and Maina ducked under his arm. She sat down in front of the vanity, his old desk, and caught his eye in the mirror. "Thanks, Jack."

He made himself smile. "Don't mention it. What are flatmates for, eh? Now try to get some sleep."

She returned his smile. It looked good on her. The tears were gone. He'd done something right after all.

"And, hey?"

"Yes?"

"Change out of that top first. That one's kinda gross."

"Sure thing."

Jack dragged the curtain across the doorway and turned in the hallway. He shuffled; he was knackered. What time *was* it? And what time had he told Maddy that he'd show up for tennis in the morning? Maddy…

He turned back. "Hey, do remember a Mrs. Owens—"

The curtain was jammed on the bent rail. It hadn't closed properly. It never did.

He saw her through the gap between the stalled curtain and the doorframe. He watched as she crossed her arms in front of her. Grabbed the bottom edges of her T-shirt. Lifted it over her head.

She was topless. She was half-naked. He stared. He swallowed hard. He saw that she was watching him watching her. In the mirror.

She turned on the seat. She stood up. She approached the curtain, pulled it aside, took his hand, and led him to the bed. *Her* bed.

They sat down. She took his hand and placed it over her breast. The nipple hardened under his touch. His penis twitched.

"Make love to me."

Time slowed. Time clicked into Frame Advance mode. His brain thudded with each individual beat of his heart.

Beat.

He was on top. His hands were underneath her, hooked into the firm flesh there. She was tight, oh God, she was *tight*. Her knees were high and wide, her feet dangled clear of the mattress. Her fingertips played keyboard on his shoulder blades.

They bucked, heaved, shuddered.

Beat.

A sharp knock on the door. Jimmy Tauranga: grim-faced, handcuffs. What *was* the age of consent in the Cook Islands? Jack in the backseat of a police car. Mama Rosie tsk-tsking in the doorway of the Matavera Beach Store. He'd always seemed like such a nice man.

Beat.

Jack in court. Jack sentenced. Jack about to find out if the joke was based in reality. The one about how the sign that read Prison—Keep Out actually read Prison—Keep In on its flip side.

Beat.

Jack deported. Jack escorted back to Canada. Porter and Maryanne at the Arrivals gate at Vancouver International Airport. Porter shaking his head; Maryanne weeping. Porter and Maryanne and the Mounties.

Beat.

He pulled his hand away. He took Maina by the shoulders. She sighed and leaned towards him. He spun her. He turned her around. Something made a noise deep in her throat.

He ran his hands over what he had seen there. The scar tissue was white and lumpy and incomprehensible. Criss-crosses in jagged patterns. There were layers of them. There were *years* of them.

He whispered into her ear. "Who did this to you?"

"The bad man," she whispered back. "The boogey man."

"Where is he now?"

"A place where he can't hurt me anymore."

"Did you go to the police? Did you report this?"

"Yes."

"And?"

"And they asked me what I did to deserve such a good hiding."

"Is he the one who marked your face?"

"Yes."

"What monster would do this to a child?"
"I told you."
"Tell me his name."
"Some people call him Piri," she said. "I called him 'Father.'"

Jack pressed his forehead against the devastation. He squeezed his eyes tight. The tears would not come. Nile Ramsay had taken those with her as well.

He stood. Maina looked up hopefully. She moved her legs. She spread them slightly. She was waiting. Eager. *Slickery.*

Jack moved. He went back to his room. He pounded his fist into the concrete wall and bled on the sheet. He pursued sleep. It eluded him.

And so he did the one thing that always worked to calm him in the juddery graveyard hours of the night.

He turned on his computer and he wrote. Typed with one hand while the other one seeped red in his lap.

FRIDAY

TWENTY-TWO

Jack loved mornings. It was his favorite time of the day, when the hours still stretched out in front of him like a lazy cat in a pool of sun. When it still felt as if he had all the time in the world to be creative and productive. Maybe even a little adventuresome, if he was up for it.

He stood in the front doorway and watched as the sun, rising out of the sea behind his house, licked at the tops of the interior mountains. The widening band of light glinted off the craggy rock faces and painted the jungle vegetation with gold fire.

Wearing a silk kimono over his boxers and singlet, he sipped coffee—Starbucks' Arabian Mocha Java; thank you, Porter, you saint—out of the largest mug he owned. He'd wrapped a strip of cloth around the abrasions on his knuckles. It hurt, but it was a good hurt, an earned hurt.

He should have been bagged after the train wreck that was his night. But, instead, he felt a curious buzz that had nothing to do with the coffee. Maybe it was because he was writing again; that alone was enough to rejuvenate his spirit. Maybe it was the promise of another glorious day.

Maybe he would feel differently when Maina woke up.

Jack didn't have enough caffeine in his system to think about that right now. Instead, he allowed his mind to flutter back to the Dempsters' party. Back to Chaka and the spa pool. Something pinged in his lower gut, a pleasure point. Jack shifted his stance, took another slurp of the steaming coffee, and forced himself to concentrate on motor muscles instead of blood and soft tissue.

He mentally scanned Chaka's body, zoomed in on her tattoo. It was an unusual design and yet he'd now seen it twice in the span of two days. Pure coincidence or was there a link between a dead German tourist and the Rapa Nui surfer? Jack had no idea what possible connection these two disparate people, living in different parts of the world, could have with each other. Except for a strange fascination with African scavengers.

Cloth rustled. He swallowed quickly. He had dreaded this moment from the second he had given up on sleep.

Maina bumped her head against his arm until he lifted it, then snuggled against his side, splaying her fingers across his chest.

"Good morning," she said in a sleepy voice. "I smelled the coffee."

Jack held his cup away from her.

"I hope smelling is all you plan to do, young lady, because this brew is from my secret stash," he said playfully. "When it comes to Starbucks, I do not play well with others."

Maina squeezed in tighter, wrapping him in her arms so that he was trapped in the doorway.

"Don't worry, Mr. Coffee Hog. I don't touch the stuff. It stunts your growth."

"Yeah, right," Jack sniffed. "Which is why I'm nearly six feet tall?"

Maina grinned up into his face. "I wasn't talking about height."

"You little—" Jack tried to wriggle out of her grasp, but Maina only clutched tighter, fingers locked in the folds of his kimono. Jack stopped resisting. He relaxed the space between them. She let go. He placed a hand on the back of her head.

"My hair is a bush," she said, laughing self-consciously.

"Did you get back to sleep?" he asked.

Maina yawned. "Yes."

Jack savored the final mouthful of coffee. He gazed back at the mountains, his fingers absently combing through the jet tumble of Maina's hair. *Get this over with. Now.*

"Listen," he said. "About last night—"

She pulled away and walked into the kitchen. Her baggy shorts had settled precariously low on her hips.

"Forget it," she called back. "What can I make you for breakfast?"

Jack followed her. She looked at the table, saw the stack of paper sitting by the laser printer.

"Jack's been doing the hard yards," she said. "I'm impressed."

"I'm reverting to habit," he said. "When I wrote my first book, I did some of my best work in the middle of the night."

"So I am your muse after all."

"You just might be."

"Choice," she chirped.

"How's your job going?" Jack asked casually, following her lead into neutral territory. *Keep it safe*, he told himself, *but keep talking.* Silence would not be a good thing this morning. The dissection of the night's events could wait until they both felt more comfortable.

"It's OK," Maina shrugged. "But I'd like it better if tipping was part of our culture. I could be in New Zealand, and out of your face, a whole lot faster if customers would leave a few coins behind. Preferably gold ones."

"Speaking of customers."

"Have I met any jerks?"

"You took the words right out of my mouth." Jack smiled.

"And I wasn't even kissing you." Maina grinned back. "No real arseholes yet, touch wood. Oh, except for that Rev. Akimo. He's a bit of a perv, eh."

"I didn't even know Akimo drank coffee," Jack said.

"I think he must spend half his life sitting in that café," Maina said. "I'm surprised he gets any work done at all because he's continually hogging one of our tables."

Jack frowned. "What does he do, just sit there and watch the traffic go by?"

"When he's not staring at my arse," Maina said. "Actually, he meets another man there and the two of them huddle together and make notes of some kind."

"What other man?"

"I've heard his name, but I forget what it is," she said. "He hardly ever speaks, but he's quite tall and very muscular. Looks like he works outside a lot. On a boat or something."

"So is Akimo trying to convert this guy? Talk him into joining his church?"

"I have no idea," Maina said. "I try to stay as far away from their table as I can."

Jack refilled his cup. Breathed deeply. The coffee smelled good. He could feel brain cells widening, like pores responding to warm water.

Maina yanked the fridge open and squatted down to stare into the battered appliance's chilled guts. Her shorts hitched even lower. Jack pictured Rev. Akimo staring. Just like he was right now. He quickly turned his attention to the window. Several of his chooks were industriously pecking through the hedge on their way to the shop's backyard. Mama Rosie often tossed scraps out there. Chooks have evolved digestive systems. Their stomachs remember where the food is.

"Maina."

"I can probably put an omelet together," she said, craning her neck to examine all the shelves. "But we really need to go shopping soon."

"*Maina!*"

She popped her head up over the door, saw the look on his face, straightened, and closed the fridge.

"Yeah?"

Jack leaned back against the sink. "I've got to go play tennis in about 40 minutes," he said. "It's sort of my Friday morning ritual. But I'm not leaving this house until we talk about last night. I need—*we* need—to get a few things out in the open and deal with them."

"This isn't about house rules?"

"No," Jack sighed. "It's a little more important than that, I'm afraid."

She adjusted her face. She took a deep breath. She smiled as wide as she could. She flashed teeth. She raised her eyebrows. Her face—her body—talked: *I'm OK. I'm ready. Nothing can hurt me.*

Jack read the signs. He noted the posture, and watched her face ripple as it sought the correct expression for the occasion. She was summoning up false courage. He knew it.

"First of all, let's talk about the nightmares," he said. "How can I help stop them?"

"You can tell me that you love me."

Jack put his mug down and shook his head. "I can't do that, Maina," he said. "And that's got nothing to do with you. My wife left me. Dani left me. I think by now it's pretty much a scientific fact that I'm incapable of giving a woman the love she needs."

"Maybe you just haven't met the right woman yet."

Jack locked on Maina. He narrowed his eyes. "You just don't give up, do you?"

"I've learned to be persistent," she said. "You quit, you die."

Jack lifted himself onto the counter. "Can you tell me about him?"

Maina dropped her eyes to the floor. Her toes were dirty. She rocked from one foot to the other.

"There's nothing to tell," she said softly. "Not anymore."

"Your father beat you?"

"Yes," Maina said. "For a long time. And then he stopped. And he stopped making me touch him. He stopped putting things in my mouth. And he stopped raping me."

"Jesus Christ!"

"I don't think my father will be seeing *him* any time soon."

"What made him finally stop abusing you?"

"He died," she said. "And that's when all the pain went away."

Jack squirmed. Her tone of voice was defiant. It scared him.

"What happened to him?"

Maina played with her hair. She twirled the edges. She avoided looking at Jack.

"He went fishing. He never came back," she said. "They found his boat washed up on one of the beaches."

"And his body?"

"It didn't wash up," she said. "There's an empty coffin buried in my Uncle Ben's yard."

Jack bored deeper. He pressed her. "So there's no real proof that he is, in fact, dead?" he said. "In reality, he's just missing."

"Oh, he's dead alright."

Jack cocked his head. "How can you be so sure?"

Maina brought her eyes up. They shone. They crackled. "Call it intuition," she said bluntly.

Jack nodded. "I didn't realize how rough your life has been," he said. "And I'm sorry if I've made it even more miserable by being pig-headed."

"Not a problem," she said. "Now, how about that omelet?" She reached again for the fridge handle.

"I'm not finished yet."

Maina turned back. A cloud passed over her face. They both knew what was coming next.

Jack drew a deep breath.

"I think you're a wonderful person," he started. "And I like you a lot; I really do. We get along well and, even though it's still early days, we seem to very compatible living in the same house. But," he voice became louder, firmer, "that's all there can ever be between us. We're mates. Nothing more. Full stop."

Maina's fists clenched at her side. She blinked rapidly, but no tears came. Jack was impressed.

"OK," she said. Her voice quavered but refused to break.

She walked to Jack. He hopped down from the counter. She took his hands, peeled off the piece of bloody cloth, brought the wounded knuckles to her lips, and kissed them lightly.

His knees quaked. His breath quickened. *We're mates and nothing more.* But he couldn't deny that he liked it when she touched him.

Be strong.

"Promise me one thing, Jack Nolan."

"Anything, Maina Rima."

"Promise that you'll always protect me from the bad men."
"I promise."
She let his hands go, stretched up, kissed him on the cheek, turned away, walked out of the house, and closed the bathroom door behind her. Cried until she was empty.

Jack returned to his computer. His fingers worked the keyboard. He typed. He created. He wasn't sure what it was exactly he was writing, what direction this new plot was taking. It was little more than random thoughts for the moment. He'd link them together later. That's how it worked for him, this alchemy of turning the motion of fingers into words. He didn't attempt to understand the process; he merely channeled it.

The Starbucks coffee sat, cold and ignored. Normally that would be a crime. Today, on this bright and brilliant morning in Matavera, it didn't matter. Jack Nolan: author. He was starting to remember how that felt. He was starting to remember how much he *liked* how that felt.

"You got any spare condoms?"

Jack's fingers became stationary; they dangled, motionless, over the keyboard. He stared at the flashing cursor.

"What?"

"Condoms?" Maina: leaning in the back doorway, voice calm, measured, as if she had just asked where he kept the spare soap. "Durex?"

"I know what you're talking about," he said, frowning. "Why would you need one?"

Maina pulled on her lower lip. She looked mischievous. She looked devious.

"I met this boy at the café..." Her voice trailed off into silence.

Jack's guts churned. His stomach stuttered. His frown deepened.

She caught his reaction. She ate it up. "He asked me out, and since you and I are just mates, I thought, hey, why not give him a go."

Jack was silent. Words jammed in his throat.

She was right, of course. He had just finished preaching how whatever vibes there were between them were strictly of the friendship variety. She was as free to date other people as he was. Other than his vow to act as her guardian against the evils of the world, they had no obligations to each other. So this request was no big deal. He'd tell her where he kept his box of condoms—bedroom, dresser, sock drawer—and go back to his book. No problem.

No problem whatsoever.

He didn't speak. He replayed the sensation of her lips on his hands. He blinked the image away.

Maina waited a full minute. She tortured him and made it two. Then her face cracked. She laughed. She howled. Giggles galloped around the kitchen. Jack's eyebrows zipped skywards.

Maina ran to him. She threw her arms around him, hugging him. "I'm just winding you up," she said, still laughing. "Oh man, you should see your expression."

Jack played it cool. "I have no idea what you're talking about," he said, stone-faced. "Now, if you're finished being a hoon, I've got a book to write."

She poked his ribs. She pinched his cheek.

"Stop it," he said, flinching like a schoolboy. And then he started to laugh. He didn't stop until the hiccups came, and then he had to stop just so he could breathe.

"I think Little Jackie was a bit jealous there," Maina teased.

"Get real."

"Just for a minute?"

"Not even for a second."

"Right." Maina nodded. "Now, about those condoms."

Jack stopped smiling. "I thought you were just joking."

"I was," she said. "About me needing them, that is. They're for someone else."

"Who someone else?"

"Her name is Teina," Maina said. "She dances with Maeva. I met her at the auditorium yesterday."

Maina pulled out a kitchen chair, coiled onto it, and sat on her legs. Jack pushed his own chair back, his laptop and the early seeds of his new novel now forgotten.

Maina continued. "She's met someone and she thinks it might get serious. She *hopes* it gets serious. I told her she'd better use protection or I'd give her a good hiding."

"Always the diplomat," Jack noted. "But why didn't she ask her own family for condoms?"

Maina snorted. "Yeah, right," she said. "Her mom's really strict. Teina's not even allowed to go out with boys. So she can't very well announce during tea that she wants to have sex. Besides, there are complications."

Jack nodded. There were always complications. "And those are?"

"This guy's older than she is," Maina said.
"And?"
"And he doesn't live here."
"So he's a tourist?"
Maina shook her head. "I think Teina said he's some kind of sailor."
"*Another* sailor?" First Akimo's café mate and now Teina's boyfriend. "He wouldn't also happen to be papa'a, would he?"
"Yup."

Jack shook his head. Bloody white men. Swordsmen, the lot of them. He should know. They had been his toughest competition in the bad old days. Before Porter demanded that he stop thinking with his dick.

"So how much older is he?"

Maina's brows congregated. "He's way too old for her."

"So that makes him what? Nineteen? Twenty?"

Maina shook her head. "Way older than that," she said. "He must be at least 25."

Jack's eyes widened. "That old, eh? I'm amazed he can still get it up."

TWENTY-THREE

Maddy Owensby dinked her volley. The ball, lacking juice, barely limped over the net.

Andre Larouche, patrolling the front of the court, made a half-hearted stab at the ball. Jack, the deep partner, could only watch in frustration.

Maddy whooped in delight and high-fived her husband, Trevor. Larouche winked at Jack. I could have played that shot, the wink said, but I let it go. I let the olds have the point.

Larouche was humoring Maddy. He thought he was being the good guest. He was making a mistake.

Maddy Owensby was 77 years old. She looked it. Her legs were sticks. Mottled skin sagged and drooped. Her face was a road map. Her dentures were too big for her mouth. She was much too frail to be playing doubles tennis.

But Jack had learned the hard way not to take Maddy Owensby for granted. The top-ranked female player in the Cook Islands in her prime, and the holder of several New Zealand tennis titles as well, Maddy now compensated for a lack of strength and agility by exhibiting a fierce competitive streak. That and an uncanny knack for placing the ball in the exact spot her opponents would never think to be. Take her lightly, show mercy, and she would pick your game to the bone. Jack's head had been handed to him on more than one occasion. Now he didn't care how old she was: he battled her to the final point.

Maddy was unofficial royalty on the island, the grande dame of its society circles. Held in high esteem by locals and papa'a alike, she'd been respectfully courted as an unofficial consultant by nearly every government voted into power during her time in the country. Her prowess with a tennis racquet was matched only by her reputation for integrity and foresight.

Her paternal family, the Casenbys, had once been among Great Britain's elite. But, riddled by gout and clogged arteries, they had grown fat on their estates, complacent in their hunting lodges. A younger generation, intrigued by the promises of the New Zealand Company, had sewn their fortunes into the linings of steamer trunks and set sail to forge a new life in the Southern Hemisphere.

Through a combination of hard work, hard currency, and some fruitful investments, the Casenby fortune had multiplied in the family's new homeland. They once again became wealthy landowners blessed with privileged lives. The subsequent generations of children, including Maddy, attended exclusive private schools to be instructed in the ways of the rich and the powerful.

While the rest of her clan attended to their financial portfolios from within their gated Wellington sanctuaries, Maddy nurtured other, wilder enterprises, provoked by a rebellious streak. And so she used her share of the family fortune to support the arts. It was while immersing herself in this dubious pursuit that she met Trevor Owensby.

A struggling novelist attempting to survive in Napier, Trevor was dashingly handsome. A rakish young fellow in possession of an active imagination and empty pockets. Of course Maddy fell voraciously in love with him.

Her family attempted to dissuade her from associating with this gypsy, this rogue, this *writer*. But the more the Casenby women denigrated poor Master Owensby for his lack of breeding, the stronger Maddy's love grew. With her trust fund secure, she simply eloped with the fellow.

They traveled extensively: Europe, Asia, the Americas. They lived at various times in Provence, New England, Punta del Este, the Gold Coast, before finally settling in Rarotonga.

Her family swore the marriage would never last. To their dying days, her mother and sisters predicted that Maddy—the superior partner in every way—would grow bored of the common boy. Fifty-five years of marriage had since proven how wrong all those dire forecasts had been.

Trevor Owensby never published a single word. It didn't matter. Maddy had more than enough money for the both of them.

These days the couple lived in an elegantly simple house on the beach, swam in the lagoon every day, and enjoyed each other's company in a lovingly tended garden scented by frangipani and bougainvillea. They threw lavish dinner parties and, in return, were always at the top of the guest list whenever anyone else entertained. They were close personal friends with at least a dozen of the ambassadors currently assigned to New Zealand and were influential in helping Cook Islanders raise the standards of their educational programs and health system.

And every Friday morning they could be found on the tennis courts at the Ocean Beach Resort, taking on all challengers. It was Maddy herself who had dubbed the weekly sessions Nearly Dead Fridays, taking a good-natured jab at her own advancing years.

Jack, who had spent his youthful summers practically living at the courts adjacent to the Walnut Grove high school, was a regular at these matches. His partners varied, depending on who happened to be visiting the island at the time, or which residents were feeling the urge to curry favor with the Owensbys. Lloyd Dempster could be counted on to show up at least once a month, pretending to be only casually interested in the answers to the many questions he insisted on asking.

Today it was Belgian yachtie Andre Larouche who was being taught a lesson about age and ability.

The two men took up their defensive positions. Jack unconsciously twirled his racquet in the palm of his hand, shifted his weight from foot to foot, and waited for Trevor to serve to him. They needed to break the Owensby serve now or the match was a lost cause.

Trevor took his time setting up, carefully noting where each of his opponents was located. He and Maddy were immaculate as always in matching whites. Larouche had also dressed for the occasion: a cream polo shirt, freshly pressed shorts, knee socks and shoes that appeared to have been taken out of the box for the very first time that morning. Jack's sole concession to court fashion was to replace his customary singlet with a clean T-shirt, albeit one with a Rocket Bar logo splashed across its front. His shorts were faded, his cross trainers scuffed and stained. He didn't wear socks. He tried never to wear socks.

Trevor smashed the ball. Jack caught a break. He was leaning to his right and that's where the serve was aimed. He took two steps, planted, and wired back a thundering forehand. The ball was a green flash as it blasted past a startled Maddy, eluded a straining Trevor, and caught the far corner. Service broken. Mission accomplished.

"Nice shot, Jacques," Larouche grinned. "Magnifique."

"You've been speaking French all morning," Jack said.

"Oui," Larouche nodded. "Is there a problem?"

"Of course not," Jack shook his head. "It's just that I thought you were from Belgium."

"I am," said Larouche. "But we speak French in the region where I live. Do you understand the language?"

"Not really," said Jack, bouncing a ball as the Owensbys discussed their defensive strategy.

"But you are from Canada originally, non?" Larouche looked puzzled. "Do you not have a French province? Quebec?"

"I'm from the west coast of Canada," Jack said. "We coasties hate the Quebecois."

"Pourquoi?" Larouche asked. "But why?"

"Because they're a bunch of whingers," Jack said, bouncing the ball harder. "They coerced the federal government into making French a mandatory subject in schools right across the country, then employ a language police to control the use of English in their own province."

"Language police? Merde."

"And then every couple of years, Quebec starts bleating about independence, how it wants to separate from the rest of the country."

"But that would not be good," Larouche said.

Jack took up his serving stance. "Personally," he said, "I'd love to see the lot of them just bugger off. If only to stop all the bitching."

Jack tossed the ball into the air. Crashed his racquet down. Found the sweet spot. Delivered smoke. Trevor never moved. Ace.

"Good on you, Jack," Maddy called over, saluting him with her racquet. "You're getting better every time out. Bon."

Larouche winked at Jack again. "See, even Madame Owensby speaks French, and she's from New Zealand."

Jack smiled grimly. Larouche was only an adequate player at best and Jack needed him to be serious about the game if they were to have any chance of emerging with a win. There would be plenty of time later in which to debate the politics of language. As if reading his thoughts, Larouche momentarily abandoned his side of the court.

"Have you made plans for after the match?" he asked as he approached Jack. On the other side of the net, Maddy and Trevor straightened out of their stances, looked at each other, and shook their heads. Amateurs.

Jack flipped through his mental daytimer. It didn't take long. "Not really," he said. "I've got to pick up my flatmate from work, but that's not until later this afternoon. Why?"

Larouche ran a fingertip over the outline of his goatee. "I would like to invite you to lunch," he said. "I've rented Mark Anderson's house at Black Rock and I'm forever seeking excuses to show it off. Do you know it?"

"I've driven past it a million times," Jack said. "But no one's ever invited me inside."

"Well, now you have been invited. It would be my honor to give you a guided tour."

"My dear boys," Maddy called across the court. "Are you trying to win by boring us to sleep? We're supposed to be playing tennis here."

Larouche displayed a pretentious smile. "Pardonner a moi, madame." He gave a shallow bow. "But I was just inviting Jacques for lunch. Would you and your husband care to join us?"

Maddy looked at Trevor. He gave his head a quick shake. "Sorry," Maddy said. "But we have a prior engagement. Another time, perhaps?"

"But of course."

Jack rolled his eyes. The guy was smooth; he had to give him that much. The great unanswered question was what exactly Larouche hoped to gain from being so obsequious.

"Let's go." Jack nodded at his partner, and Larouche returned to his position at the net.

His second serve wasn't as powerful. Maybe a random gust of wind caught the ball. Maybe Jack's timing was slightly off. Whatever. It was a poor delivery and he knew they would pay for it.

Maddy devoured the service. She pounced on the ball. She cocked her racquet and aimed with a deadly deliberateness. Jack, drifting to his left, tensed. Larouche, seeing Maddy wind up, relaxed. This volley would be all Jack this time.

Maddy fooled them. She calmed, she took the muscle out of the swing. Her trained eye computed how Jack and Larouche were reacting and drew a bead on where the ball would do the most damage.

She turned her wrist. She introduced spin to the ball. She dropped it right in front of a surprised Larouche. The Belgian's eyes popped with surprise. The ball thudded onto the tar seal. It bounced. It shot off wildly to the left. Larouche shifted his thought processes and went to his backhand. Body weight shifted. He swung, missed, stumbled. His right ankle turned. He screamed, then crashed down awkwardly on his side.

Jack cringed as Larouche rolled on the court, hands clutched to his damaged ankle. Maddy gasped loudly and rushed around the net to kneel by his side. Trevor followed closely behind. Jack propped his racquet against the chain-link fence and trotted over.

Larouche sat up. His eyes were slitted by pain, his tanned face now pale from shock. His breath whistled through clenched teeth.

"Oh my, oh my, oh my," Maddy intoned, one hand clamped to her cheek in consternation.

Jack bent down. "Are you alright?" he asked, knowing it was a moronic query even as he spoke.

The look on Larouche's face confirmed his thought. "What do you think?" he hissed.

Trevor Owensby ran a careful hand over Larouche's injured ankle. "I don't think it's broken," he said.

"Thank God," Maddy said. Her hands fluttered aimlessly. She was obviously upset by this sudden turn of events.

"Hopefully there's no ligament damage," Jack said. "Did you hear a pop or a snap?"

This time Larouche managed a weak smile. "Only the sound of my ego being bruised," he said. "I was caught flat-footed. Le fou."

"It's my fault," Maddy said. "I should have gone deep."

"Non, madame," Larouche said. "Do not reproach yourself. It was an accident. Part of the game. No one is to blame."

"Oh you poor, poor dear."

Larouche shifted, winced. "I'm afraid I've taken your invitation to participate in Nearly Dead Friday a little too literally."

Maddy twittered nervously. Trevor caught Jack's eye and jerked his head. *Come here.*

Jack hunkered down beside Trevor. "He's hurt himself pretty good," he whispered, turning away from Larouche and Maddy. "He really should go to the hospital, but he can't drive himself, not with his gas foot buggered. Can you take him? I've given up my licence and I think Maddy's too upset to drive right now."

"No problem."

"What are you two conspiring about?" Larouche asked.

Trevor stood. "I was explaining to Jack how your ankle's starting to swell up. We both agree that it needs to be attended to. Maybe even X-rayed."

Jack pivoted back to Larouche. "I'll give you a lift to the hospital," he said. "Dr. Rangi will take good care of you."

"Non." Larouche waved his hand forcibly. "Just take me to my house, s'il vous plait. Dr. Charbonneau, the ship's physician, is there. He's become rather an expert on these old bones."

"Are you sure?" asked Jack.

"Is that wise?" asked Trevor.

Larouche brought his knee up and tentatively applied weight to the ankle. "Oui, oui. I've done this before, I'm afraid," he said. "The ankle was weak to begin with. It was silly of me not to have taped it before I tried to play."

A groundskeeper hurried over with a bag of ice wrapped in a towel. Jack thanked him, then undid Larouche's shoe and gently removed it. He started to roll down the sock. Larouche lurched forward, hand outstretched. Trevor, thinking he was reacting to the pain, grabbed onto Larouche's shoulders, steadying him.

Jack tugged the sock off and whistled in astonishment at how quickly the ankle area had swollen up and discolored. The whistle died on his lips as he elevated Larouche's foot to place the towel under it.

He stared. He whipped his head up and met Larouche's glare. Dropped his eyes back to what he had seen on the top of Larouche's foot.

A tiny perfect tattoo. A jackal.

TWENTY-FOUR

"Kia orana."

"Uh? Yeah, OK. You speak English, right?"

"Sweet as."

That was a close one. For one terrible second, Shel Freeburg thought he might actually have to deal with a foreign language. He was still fuming at being stuck with researching *Blood and Ruins*; having to also hunt down a translator would have been more than just cause for ringing his union rep.

"OK, good."

Shel could hear the agitation in his own voice and chided himself for it. He was the one who was supposed to be controlling the situation. After all, he was the media, for chrissakes. That alone should command authority. And servility.

"Listen," he continued. "This is Shel Freeburg calling from *Silver Screen Weekly* in New York City. You know where that is, right?"

"Gee, let me think. Didn't you guys get bombed or something a couple years ago?"

"Or something," Shel muttered. "Look, I'm trying to reach a writer named Jack Nolan. Do I have the correct telephone number?"

"Yes."

Shel frowned. "Well, may I speak to him then?"

"No."

"Excuse me?"

"He's not home right now."

Shel slammed his pen down on the desk. "Why didn't you say so in the first place?"

"You didn't ask."

I am Shel Freeburg, he thought, his head starting to pound. *I am the most talented writer at the No. 1 weekly entertainment magazine in the entire world. I AM IMPORTANT!*

Then why am I allowing this person—on some insignificant little speck of an island thousands of miles away—to piss me off?

Shel looked at his watch, then down at the list of people he had yet to interview. So far the process had been a ghastly nightmare of answering machines and pagers. And people like Jack Nolan who, for some ungodly reason, had insisted on abandoning the creature comforts of civilization.

Shel had yet to speak to Paris. The elusive director was currently on a closed set in Prague directing the umpteenth sequel featuring the ubiquitous boy wizard. Its working title was *Harry Potter and the Black Head of Puberty*, or some such nonsense.

Among the minute tidbits of information that Shel had managed to gather was the fact that, as of six months ago, Paris had once again changed his name. This time to a mathematical formula that no one could remember much less pronounce. In typical journalistic shorthand, North American writers simply referred to the director as IWISA, or the Idiot Who Is Still an Asshole.

Shel had actually caught a lucky break when it came to Jack Nolan. One of the writer's nephews had answered the phone at Porter Nolan's house and Shel managed to ferret out the fact that Uncle Jack was currently living in the Cook Islands. But that was the full extent of the information he'd ascertained before Porter picked up the extension, growled a curt "No comment" and severed the connection.

Come to think of it, he'd had better luck with Nolan's six-year-old nephew than he was having now with his call to the Cook Islands.

"Will Jack be home soon?"

"Don't know."

"Are you a friend of his?"

"I'd like to think so. Jack may have a different opinion."

Shel dropped his head into his free hand. The world was filled with morons. That was a granted. But why did he have to meet them all?

It was his experience that people practically begged to be interviewed by someone with his reputation. So what was the problem here?

A light flashed on his telephone set. Someone was holding on the other line. He had to make this quick.

"Do you mind if I ask you a few things about Jack? It won't take long."

"Go for it."

Shel ran his pen down the list of questions he had prepared earlier. He quickly crossed off most of them. He might just have to fill up Jack Nolan's article with pre-digested information that had been printed during the novelist's short tenure on the throne of public opinion. He had a backup plan, though, just in case: the number for Jack's ex was somewhere on his desk. Surely Nile Ramsay wouldn't mind fleshing out the story with a few quotes. From what he understood about her current situation, Shel was reasonably confident Nile would be only too thrilled to see her name in print again.

At least *someone* understood how this game was supposed to be played.

Besides, Nile Ramsay was still living in California. That three-hour time difference meant he could squeeze in several other interviews before he called upon the former Mrs. Jack Nolan.

"Hello? Mr. New York? You still there?"

Shel had no idea what time it was in the Cook Islands. He could care less.

He sighed, flicked on his micro-cassette recorder, and launched into the interview.

"Are you sure about that last part?" he asked several minutes later.

"I've seen it with my own eyes."

"Super." Shel dropped his pen, switched off the recorder, and sat back hard. "You've been a great help."

"No worries."

"Alright," Shel said. "Bye now."

"Aere ra," said Maina.

"Yeah, whatever."

Shel snorted derisively as he punched into Line 2. Ignorant, bloody savages. Never get anywhere in life if they insisted on speaking their own language.

TWENTY-FIVE

The villa was enormous. It was an anaconda. There was no logical reason for it to be that huge, other than it gave Mark Anderson another opportunity to showcase his wealth.

The wanker didn't even live there, Jack fumed, shifting to a lower gear as the Toyota started to labor on the steep climb to the villa. Anderson, whose chief residence was farther along the west coast in Arorangi, leased the property to bloated Yankee gentry and heroin-gaunt Eurotrash. Anyone whose country's exchange rate made a mockery of the New Zealand dollar.

Anderson was a Kiwi who had made his fortune in the Cook Islands, some of it even legally. He'd started with a fleet of commercial fishing boats, put the money up to open the Smiley Mart grocery store, then segued into property development. His specialty was acquiring the leases on land put up as collateral by locals who had defaulted on loans. His specialty did not make him a popular man.

The Black Rock project was his personal masterpiece.

The villa hunched on a craggy outcrop like a Japanese horror-movie monster overlooking the beach. It was the incongruous and grotesque love child of dusty New Mexican adobe and Indonesian rain-forest timber.

Jack drove by the villa several times a week. Originally intrigued by its mad grandeur, he no longer even bothered to glance up when passing through Black Rock. The locals had come to ignore it as well, those who weren't hired as housekeepers or landscapers. It represented a wealth beyond their capacity to imagine. It was more science fiction than architecture, a burnt-umber blight.

The villa emerged from its surrounding greenery as Jack gunned his truck up the tar-sealed driveway. He braked in front of an oversized wooden door armored with wide strips of burnished steel. Started to help Larouche out of the cab, was brushed aside by a hulking brute.

Blond-white hair, complexion like salted leather, nasty lump of scar tissue. Jack flashed back to Captain Tai's Mountain Motor Tours outside the Outrigger Villas. The rather large fellow who appeared to be in charge of the other passengers. He flashed back to Maina's description of the man who sat with Rev. Moses Akimo at the café.

There was only time for a quick introduction—"Jack, this is Tor."—before Larouche was swept up and carried inside. He leaned back over the big man's shoulder and waved Jack to follow.

Stucco. Wood. Twelve-foot ceilings. Block ventilation. Living room: an array of overstuffed furniture, slate floor, a scattering of Persian rugs. Tiffany-style lamps. South Pacific art on the walls. Jack noted an Andrew Tuara piece. Someone had good taste. Not enough to offset the villa's excesses, however.

One view: the lagoon, turquoise and cobalt. Second view: courtyard with pool and fishpond. Third view: the gardens, flowers and fruit. The fragrant scent of pitate and tipani.

Jack's neck swivelled. He gawked. He rolled his eyes. He had been subjected to pretentious magnificence during his time in LA. But that's where it belonged, in Fantasy Land. This villa had nothing to do with the Cook Islands. No connection to cinder block and tin sheets and kikau. No connection to reality.

Tor placed Larouche on a couch and propped a throw pillow under his leg. Jack saw the tattoo again. Frowned. The drive from the Ocean Beach Resort to Black Rock had taken 10 minutes. Neither man had spoken during the trip. Jack watched the road, thought of the jackal tattoo, and recalled the look on Larouche's face. Knew that he'd seen something that was supposed to remain hidden. Knew that he was seeing too many jackal tattoos for it to any longer be a coincidence. What was the connection?

Tor left the room and returned with another man in tow. Older, glasses: Dr. Charbonneau.

Charbonneau clucked over Larouche as he examined the ankle with a light-handed thoroughness. They conversed in a mixture of English and French. Jack grasped enough to understand that Larouche had suffered a sprain. Painful, yes, but not debilitating. Rest and cold treatments were called for. The doctor taped an ice pack over the swelling and was gone.

Tor remained. He filled the room; he was a *presence*. Tor embodied the villa: bulging, ugly, alien. He made Jack nervous.

Larouche rubbed his eyes. He had waved away the doctor's painkillers but it was obvious that he was hurting. He looked across the room to where Jack had lowered himself into a chair. Larouche smiled, his lips thinned by discomfort.

"I apologize for the inconvenience," he said.

Jack's eyebrow jigged. He face-talked: *Don't mention it.*

"Thank you for the lift, Jacques," Larouche said. "Now I really do owe you lunch."

"Maybe we should do it another time," Jack said. "When you're feeling better."

"Non," Larouche said. "Please stay; I insist. We sail for Vanuatu on Monday morning and I'm afraid that I may be too busy after today to be a decent host."

Jack spread his hands in mock surrender. "Alright," he said. "You've talked me into it."

Larouche smiled again. "Perfect. Now can I start you off with a coffee? The kitchen here is equipped with an espresso machine that rivals that of the esteemed Monsieur Muldoon."

"That would be great," Jack said. "Although I'm guessing it would be too much to expect that a place like this would stock Starbucks coffee."

"Regrettably, non."

"Right." Today's lesson: money doesn't buy everything after all. "In that case, I'll have a long black, thanks."

Larouche nodded at Tor and waved two fingers. Tor ducked out the door. There was suddenly more air in the room.

"Your friend should be a professional wrestler," Jack said.

Larouche shifted on the couch and wheezed with the effort. "Tor is rather grande, isn't he?" Larouche said. "He has served me faithfully for many years."

"Is he a member of the yacht's crew?"

"Oui," Larouche said. "He is actually a very good sailor. Formidable. I believe he could handle the *Chacal* all by himself if I allowed it. But I don't want a man of his specialized talents being wasted on menial tasks."

"Why is that?" Jack was being polite. He was killing time. He didn't give a shit about Tor.

"He has other skills besides sailing that I prefer to take advantage of."

"Such as?"

"Such as his powers of persuasion," Larouche chuckled. "Not too many people say non to Tor."

"I bet." Jack settled deeper into the chair's depths. The leather was cool against his skin. The house might be an abomination in a country where the starting wage was $4 an hour, but there was no denying that its creature comforts were seductive.

Jack had forgotten what luxury felt like. That was OK. He liked that he'd forgotten. His life on the island had new definitions for luxury now. Picking fresh pawpaw off a tree in his backyard, for instance, or a fish burger at Sunset Takeaways. The friendly faces he encountered every day.

These wonders represented real life. This villa was a sham, a soulless composite of glass and plastic, of metal and wood. You came to a place like this to escape from something. Jack wondered what might be nipping at Larouche's heels to cause him to hole up here.

A local man entered, bearing their coffees on a silver tray. He flashed Jack a look of surprise. His forehead crinkled. He face-talked: *What are you doing here?*

Jack shrugged, then sipped at his coffee. Fought the urge to spit the bitter black goo back into the cup. *Espresso machine, my arse,* he thought. *This tastes like raw sewage.*

He forced himself to swallow, and grinned appreciatively at Larouche. Made a show of blowing on his coffee—too hot—set the cup down on a small glass-topped table. Abandoned it.

Tor was back. He loomed.

"Lunch in 30 minutes," he said, his voice deep, cold, accented. It sounded like a Scandinavian blizzard.

"Perfect," said Larouche. "That gives us the opportunity to work up an appetite with conversation."

Jack constructed another smile. He resisted the urge to look at his watch. What time did Maina finish her shift? He watched Larouche sip daintily at his coffee. His own long black grew cold beside him. Maybe they could patch the tar seal in the driveway with it later.

"I have a proposition for you, Jacques," Larouche said. "One that may prove to be very lucrative for both of us."

Here it comes, Jack thought, the real reason why I'm here. The real reason why this mere mortal had been allowed entrance to Mark Anderson's palace of sins. "Fire away," he said.

Larouche took another noisy mouthful of coffee, then handed the cup to Tor. Jack watched the big man spring into action. He was fast for his size. That was scary.

"As I told you at the party, I am simply an employee of the corporation that owns the *Chacal*," Larouche said, swiveling on the couch to face Jack directly. "This particular corporation is involved in several business ventures. For instance—and this is the main reason we have come to the Cook

Islands—part of our mission statement mandates that we distribute educational material to various, shall we say, less-fortunate countries. We also conduct instructional seminars on how best to use this material."

Jack flashed back: the seminar that no one else on Raro seemed to know about.

"Who attends these seminars?" he asked.

Larouche shrugged. "I'm not sure exactly," he said. "Teachers, I suppose. Administrators. I'm not directly involved with that end of the operation. Pourquoi?"

"Two days ago the police pulled a body out of a motel pool," Jack said. "My sources tell me the dead man had some connection to those educational seminars you just mentioned."

Larouche nodded solemnly. "Ah, oui," he said. "That terrible incident did involve one of my employees. According to the police, the man made the unfortunate decision to combine excessive amounts of alcohol with your otherwise delightful tropical heat. He must have forgotten that he couldn't swim. Tres tragique."

The man? Jack perked up. "You don't even know his name?"

A crack spidered across Larouche's ice-cool demeanor. For a moment he actually appeared confused. His hands jittered in his lap. He quickly folded them together.

"Forgive me, Jacques," he said. "That was rather callous, wasn't it? I'm afraid that the pain in my ankle has somewhat addled my brain."

He made a show of pulling a light blanket from the back of the couch and draping it over his bare legs.

"The man's name, by the way, was Gert Junger," Jack said. "Ring any bells?"

"But of course, Herr Junger," Larouche said, returning his attention to Jack. "Thank you for that. My problem, you see, is that we have a large number of instructors on board at the moment. In fact, I believe there are at least 10 right now, who are also working as crew. We tend to hire them on short-term contracts, so the personnel is constantly changing. Obviously, I'm not always able to keep track of them all."

Jack had pushed a button. He liked what it did to Larouche. He decided to push it again.

"All those instructors and yet no one I've talked to knows anything about an educational seminar being hosted on the island."

This time Larouche's face remained blank. The crack had sealed. He had regained his composure. *Damn.*

"Am I to assume that you've talked to every single person on the island?" he asked pointedly.

"Only the ones who are paid to know about such things," Jack shot right back.

Larouche waved Tor over and pointed to his ankle. Tor adjusted the ice pack, tightened the bindings, and replaced the blanket.

"All I know, Jacques," Larouche continued, "is that the commitment to improving education on a world-wide basis is something my company takes very seriously."

Larouche was on the defensive. He was ducking away from Jack's line of questioning. Jack let him go. For now.

"But it's not the only project this company of yours is involved in?"

Larouche nodded energetically. He was obviously pleased with this question.

"Exactement," he said. "For example, we are very active in futures trading. Coffee, mainly. We also dabble in offshore investments, real estate, import/export, e-commerce, and the creation and maintenance of Internet sites. All very lucrative, I'm pleased to report, if not always approved of by the various government agencies we've encountered in our journeys."

"Which explains why you conduct most of your business from the sanctuary of international waters."

Larouche's eyes widened. Jack smiled. "I'm not as dumb as I look," he said.

Larouche laughed and made a grand gesture of applauding.

"Bravo, Jacques," he said. "Yes, the ship, she does serve as more than just transportation. It's an unfortunate fact of life that those who are aggressive in their pursuit of success are not always appreciated. Especially by those who stubbornly insist on adhering to antiquated rules and customs."

"Speaking of making money," Jack urged.

"Of course, of course," Larouche said. "Cut to the chase, as it were. Always an admirable quality."

"Just one of many."

Larouche cackled. "I like you, Jacques. I like you so much, in fact, that I want to hire you as a freelance writer."

"You're hoping that I write better than I play tennis?"

"You are being modest, Jacques," Larouche said. "I've read your book. In fact, I'm sure I saw a copy here in the house library."

"Stop it," Jack said, "before I change my mind about what a turd Mark Anderson really is."

"My company also operates an Internet publishing company," Larouche continued. "We hire writers and photographers to provide the material, then charge interested parties an annual subscription fee to access it."

Jack suddenly had an uncomfortable feeling about where this conversation was heading.

"What kind of material are we talking about here?" he asked.

Larouche flashed a coy smile and slid his eyes around the room. Returned to Jack.

"We prefer the term 'adult entertainment,'" he finally said. "Although it's also known as erotica."

Jack groaned. He was disappointed; he was *hurt*. Had the luster of his modest fame faded so quickly? Is this what happens to one-hit wonders?

"Erotica?" Jack said. "By that, I assume you mean Internet porn. Jerkoff journalism."

Larouche waggled his hands in a negative gesture. "I would never presume to argue semantics with a writer of your proven ability, Jacques."

"So what gave you the idea that I would have any interest whatsoever in doing that style of writing?"

"I've read *Resurrection Waters*," Larouche said, the flesh around his eyes puckering in delight at the memory.

"You already mentioned that," Jack said. "And?"

"And I found it fascinating," Larouche said.

"Get your nose out of my arse and get to the point," Jack snapped. He was feeling insulted. He was feeling irritated.

Larouche gasped at the insult. Tor shifted towards Jack, hands flexing: open, closed. The motion disturbed the room's gravity. Jack's flash of anger was replaced by a sudden flare of anxiety. Screw lunch; it was time to leave.

Jack eyed the door. *How quickly can I make it out of this house?* he thought.

Larouche calmed himself and waved Tor off with a flick of his head. Tor uncoiled, but remained close to Jack. Larouche cleared his throat, collected his thoughts. He decided to ignore Jack's rude behavior. The poor man had obviously been on this island far too long. His manners, his civility, had atrophied. The brute in him was showing through the creases.

"The *point*," Larouche said, "is that I found myself intrigued by the fact that your book's heroine was significantly younger than your main character.

What was his name again?"

"Billy Apollo."

"Ah, yes. Lucky, lucky Billy," Larouche said, absently stroking his goatee. "I assumed—"

"That I was some kind of pervert?"

Larouche's eyes widened again, this time in a forced display of shock that Jack didn't buy for an instant. "Oh non, mon ami. Of course not," Larouche sputtered. "I simply assumed that you have an open mind. That is all."

Jack nodded. Yeah, right.

"Sorry to disappoint you, *my friend*," he said, his edginess now replaced by the sharp jab of sarcasm. "But the age difference between the two characters was strictly a plot device. I simply wanted them to be coming to the same place from different backgrounds. So they would see and interpret things in a contrasting manner."

"But of course," Larouche said, steepling his fingers in front of his face. "I understand fully."

Jack saw disappointment cloud the older man's face. What had he expected? Thought wheels turned. Thought sprockets linked. Thought connections sparked.

"Oh shit," Jack blurted. "You thought I was into kiddie porn!"

TWENTY-SIX

Bloody tourists!

Dennis Katu swiveled in the driver's seat and addressed the tightly packed, sweaty throng jammed into his bus.

"Folks, please," he said, his tone friendly yet firm. "We can fit everyone on, but I'm going to need you to move as far towards the back as you possibly can."

His route around the circular Ara Tapu should have taken Dennis just under an hour to complete. But he had been on the road for 55 minutes now and had only just reached Matavera. They were still 10 minutes away from the route's termination point outside Cook's Corner, and that was only if he didn't have to make any more stops.

That likelihood vanished when Dennis recognized the person flagging him down outside the Matavera Beach Store. Maina smiled as she climbed aboard and squeezed her way into the crowd clogging the centre aisle.

"Kia orana," she said. "Sparky's Café, please."

Dennis nodded resignedly and flipped the switch to close the doors. He disengaged the hand brake and eased down on the gas pedal. He was careful not to jerk the vehicle too much as he accelerated, but his passengers were wedged in so tightly that he doubted anyone could tip over no matter how erratic he might drive.

Dennis Katu glanced in his rear-vision mirror. The majority of his passengers this morning were tourists. He could tell by the varying shades of pink on their faces and necks and arms exactly how long each of them had been on the island. It was an ability he had acquired during a 20-year career spent driving around what was essentially one big circle. He had also developed a thick skin and an endless reservoir of patience. He drew heavily on both during his five shifts a week.

He willingly accepted the obligations of his position on the front lines of the tourism trade. He enjoyed meeting and talking to the overseas visitors and he understood the major role that tourism played in his country's economy. How all those greenbacks and pounds sterling and euros helped provide an education for his children, helped pay for the equipment in the hospital, helped tar-seal the very road upon which he made his living.

But those same visitors could also be a nuisance. This morning was a perfect example, when it appeared that every tourist currently on the island was determined to board his bus on this particular run.

He made a quick scan of the vehicle's interior. How many more could he possibly cram in? Not many, but he'd try, if only to appease all those who waited patiently at the side of the road. The scary thing was this was only Friday. Wait until tomorrow morning, when activity at the Punanga Nui outdoor market would attract even more hordes with their endless babble of questions. Dennis shook his head in mock exasperation. He needed a raise. Or a bigger bus.

"Driver!" Someone shouting from the back. *Damn!* The bus had just flashed by the Trade Winds dairy in Upper Tupapa. Lost in thought, Dennis had forgotten about the old mama who'd requested to be let out there.

He applied the brakes as quickly as he could without dumping any of those passengers standing at the front onto the engine cowling or, worse yet, up against the inside of the windscreen. *Now where was the mama sitting?* Near the back, of course. It never failed.

Dennis raised his voice. "Sorry, people, but all those standing in the aisle are going to have to get out so we can let mama off."

Maina led the parade to the shoulder. She glanced at her watch. She was also concerned about how far behind schedule the bus was running. She knew that Muldoon understood the vagaries of island time and wouldn't be growling her, but it was not in her nature to be late for work. She had learned that in Pukapuka. She had learned many things in Pukapuka.

The mama, her arms laden with shopping bags, flashed a toothless grin as she limped down the aisle, then stepped from the bus and bustled off toward the store. The passengers, who had stood aimlessly beside the bus as the aisle emptied, trudged back on. At least one of them now had a seat.

Maina was the last one in again. Dennis lifted his eyebrows. He face-talked: *These people are driving me maki maki.*

Maina nodded twice in quick succession. She face-talked: *I know the feeling.*

"Sorry I'm late!" Maina rushed past Muldoon.

"Your favorite customer is waiting for you," he mumbled around his cigarette as he filled the espresso machine's porta filter with freshly-ground coffee. Maina adjusted her apron as she peered over the bar in the direction Muldoon had indicated. She picked out the back of a bald head. She groaned.

Rev. Moses Akimo.

"He won't let anyone else take his order," Muldoon chuckled as he fitted the porta filter into place. "Looks like someone has a fan club."

Maina rolled her eyes. "Eh?" she said. "I don't think so. The guy is such an egg."

"How so?"

"He thinks he's it."

"Well, *I* think he needs to be served," Muldoon said. "Better hop to it."

Maina hesitated. It was starting to feel as if the reverend never left the place. He always sat in her section. Always ordered the same coffee. Spent his entire time leering at her. She wasn't sure how much longer she could put up with his blatant staring.

Maina shuddered. He creeped her out. He made her skin crawl. His eyes undressed her. At least he was alone today. No sign of his hulking, silent friend.

A tiny smile crept across her lips. If Akimo insisted on perving her, maybe it was time to give him a show. One that he wouldn't soon forget.

"I'll be right back," she said to Muldoon.

Maina ducked into the storeroom. She untied the apron, slipped it over her head, and hung it on a nail. Pulled up the back of her T-shirt, unhooked her bra. One side at a time, she reached up inside the sleeves of her shirt and pulled the bra straps over her hands. Lifted the front of her shirt, pulled the bra out, and stuffed it in a pocket of her cargo shorts.

She hoisted the front of the T-shirt until it sat just below her breasts, then fashioned the material into a knot. She looked down, arched her shoulders, and stuck her chest out. Perfect.

She pulled her braid apart, shook her hair loose. It hung down nearly to her waist.

It was show time.

Muldoon was stretching the milk with the steam wand when Maina walked by on her way to the seating area. He glanced up at her, down to the milk, then snapped his head back up. He stared. His jaw dropped. The cigarette teetered on his lower lip for an instant, tipped off, and plunged into the metal container of foaming milk. Ash, paper, tobacco all rotated in a small, perfect whirlpool.

Conversations ceased as Maina passed tables. Cups, glasses, cutlery freeze-framed. Pastries dropped silent crumbs from stilled hands.

Maina came up behind Akimo. She touched him lightly on the shoulder. As he turned, she leaned in close, pressing the side of her left breast to his ear. She heard his breathing stop. She heard him swallow hard. She loved it.

Maina swung in front of Akimo, put a foot up on an empty chair, and thrust herself into his space. Akimo's eyes bulged. His field of vision filled with the soft brown contours of Maina's bared abdomen, the twin bumps of her nipples plainly visible under the T-shirt.

He swallowed again. The skin on his head grew slick with sweat.

"I heard you were waiting for me," she said. "I was tied up," she purred. "If you know what I mean."

Akimo blinked. Very rapidly. A vein in his forehead pulsed in a blue frenzy. Maina teased him. She played him.

She reached down and put a light hand on the thigh of his navy-blue dress pants. "The usual, reverend? Or do you want to try something a little hotter this time?"

She cupped her hand around his ear, used it as a handle. Pulled his face close, bounced his nose off a nipple.

She tilted his head, looked into his eyes. "You have no idea who I am, do you?" Her voice was an ice pick. It probed.

She felt Akimo shiver. *No, he didn't.*

She moved in even closer, her lips hovered over his ear. "I'll be right back," she whispered. "Don't you go soft on me."

Maina pivoted out and away, winking conspiratorially at the other customers. They laughed. They applauded. They had another story to tell. The coconut wireless would hum tonight.

Akimo was a statue. He was cemented in place. Eyes round and white, unblinking. Hands flat and damp on the table. A fat, oily bead of sweat formed at the very top of his shiny skull. It rolled lazily down the back of his head. It gathered speed, disappeared into the bulging collar of his white shirt.

Akimo moved. He jacked straight up, snatched his coat from a chair, and marched out of Sparky's Café, trailing whispers and giggles in his wake. He didn't look right, he didn't look left. He most certainly did not look back.

A customer nodded in admiration as Maina skipped away.

"You are evil," the man said.

"Oh, you don't know the half of it," Maina laughed.

Exaggerated clapping sounded from a corner table. Maina smiled at the woman who was applauding. She had striking red hair; she wore a nurse's uniform.

"That was quite the show," the nurse said as Maina approached.

"Thank you." Maina curtsied.

"Do you behave like that at home as well?"

Maina looked closer at the woman. "Do I know you?"

"The locals call me Nurse Heather. I'm a good friend of Jack Nolan."

Maina nodded. "Jack says nice things about you."

"I'm surprised he still has the ability to speak with you prancing around the house half-dressed."

Maina blushed. She fumbled. "Oh that," she said. "I was only—"

Heather cut her off. "I know what you were doing, Maina," she snapped. "And I'm guessing you had a very good reason for embarrassing Rev. Akimo in front of all these people."

"He deserved it." Maina grew defensive. "The guy pervs me every day."

Heather looked Maina up and down. "Do you blame him?"

"Not really," Maina said, a catty edge creeping into her voice. "I suppose it comes with the territory when you're young and pretty. But then you wouldn't know anything about that, would you?"

Heather's eyes pinched into slits. Flames shot from between her lids. "That's quite the mouth you have there girl."

"No one's complained yet."

"Too busy getting their penicillin shots, I reckon."

Maina put her hands on the table and inserted herself into Heather's personal space.

"Why are you winding me up like this? Have I pissed you off somehow?"

It was Heather's turn to lean forward; their noses nearly touched. "Keep your distance from Jack," she hissed.

"I'm sorry," Maina smirked, "but I must have missed the sign around his neck that says 'Property of Nurse Heather.' Maybe I need glasses."

"You're going to need medical attention if you get any cheekier." Heather's smile secreted malice. "And guess who's going to be right there when you're admitted, enema bag in hand."

Maina blinked first. The emotional high she'd experienced after belittling Akimo had dissipated.

Heather glared. "I don't trust you, missy," she said. "I know you're up to something; I just haven't figured it out yet."

She grabbed her bag and stood up. "Now, if you'll excuse me, some of us have real jobs."

TWENTY-SEVEN

Jack extricated himself from the leathery depths of his chair. "I gotta go," he said, chagrin obvious in his body language.

Larouche swung his legs off the couch and sat up stiffly. The ice pack shifted, then dropped to the floor. Tor reached for it. Larouche waved him away.

"Don't leave, Jacques," Larouche said, his face strained from the exertion of moving his injured ankle. "I apologize if I have offended you in any way. That was never my intention. It was a misunderstanding, nothing else. Finish your coffee, s'il vous plait, and we will retire to the dining room."

Jack hesitated. His anger felt justified. He didn't appreciate having his integrity questioned. Still, there was no denying that he was intrigued by what was transpiring in this room. If he stormed out now, wounded pride clutched tightly to chest, he would be allowing too many questions to remain unanswered. Starting with the significance of the jackal tattoos.

The room was thick with anticipation. Even the act of breathing, it seemed, had been momentarily suspended. Jack looked at Larouche. Jack glanced at Tor. Both men watched him closely. They were wary. They seemed on edge. *Let's find out why.*

Jack sat back down.

Larouche exhaled. "Merci, Jacques."

"Don't thank me yet, Andre," Jack said. "I'm only staying because you haven't finished pitching your job offer."

"But you said—"

"I expressed disgust at the thought of disseminating kiddie porn," Jack said. "People who do that should be castrated. People who do that on this island *are* castrated. But I said nothing about my feelings for your so-called erotica. I'm not a fan of that form of quasi-literature, but anything that encourages reading can't be all bad, can it? And besides—"

"You could use the money?"

Jack chuckled. "Money is always good," he lied. "Paradise may be beautiful, but it ain't cheap, if you know what I mean."

"I understand completely," Larouche said, hefting his legs back onto the couch, smoothing the blanket over them.

"So?" Jack prompted.

Now it was Larouche's turn to suspend the conversation, to conjure silence while pondering his next move. His brow furrowed, his eyes narrowed. His fingers worried at the edges of the blanket.

He's deciding how far he can trust me, Jack thought. *I was right; there is more here. And it's nasty.*

Larouche looked up, met Jack's determined gaze, and held it.

"You are an interesting fellow, Jacques," he said. "I am sorely tempted to take you into my confidence, if only because I'm convinced that your considerable skills will prove invaluable."

"So what's the problem?"

"The problem," Larouche said, "is that I'm not entirely convinced that you won't take advantage of my hospitality, thank me graciously in that polite way of all Canadians, and then drive straight to the police station."

Jack smiled. "You're just going to have to take that chance now, aren't you?" he said. "Besides, I've haven't heard anything here that the police might find remotely interesting. Not yet, anyway."

Larouche's eyes never left Jack's face. He deliberated; he weighed options. He came to a decision.

"Have you heard of the League of Jackals?" he asked.

Jack's adrenaline gland squeezed off a shot. Pure joy juice. Excitement coursed. Jack fought to keep a straight face. *Here we go.*

"No," Jack said. "But does it have something to do with that tattoo on your foot? With the tattoo I saw on Gert Junger's leg?"

Larouche nodded. "The tattoo, it is a symbol of membership," he said. "Less ostentatious than a ring, and not so prone to being lost or stolen. Or ignored."

"It was hard to ignore Chaka Tane's tattoo."

Larouche's head bowed. "Ah, oui, the esteemed member from Rapa Nui," he said in a resigned tone. "She serves her purpose, but she must learn to be a little more, shall we say, discreet."

Questions bumped up against each other in Jack's brain. *Don't appear too eager,* he cautioned himself. *He wants to talk; let him.*

"The members of this league of yours," he said. "I'm betting that we're not going to see them riding minibikes in a parade any time soon. No silly hats? No donations to hospitals?"

Larouche nodded. "We are not philanthropists, neither are we a service group," he said. "The League of Jackals is instead an elite collection of individuals dedicated to the same basic goal."

"Which would be?"

"To glean as much pleasure out of life as possible," Larouche answered, a carnivorous smile splitting his face. "It's as simple, and as complicated, as that."

"Define pleasure. Money? Power?"

Larouche shook a finger. *No.* "Fortunes come and go, as the stock market proves on a boringly regular basis," he said. "And power is highly overrated. Too many strings attached. Too many favors owed at the end of the day."

"Drugs then?"

Larouche grimaced. "We leave such abhorrent habits to the more uncouth elements of society," he said. "The dregs of humanity, if you will."

"I guess that just leaves sex."

"Exactement!" Larouche grew animated again, his sore ankle seemingly forgotten in his display of excitement. He practically vibrated on the couch. "Carnal pleasure—now that is worth any price, any exertion, any *pain* to achieve."

"Is it also worth dying for?"

"Excuser moi?"

"I'm talking about the late and apparently only slightly lamented Gert Junger," Jack said. "Blame it on the wild imagination of a fiction writer, but I can't help wondering what pleasure he might have been gleaning from the bottom of a swimming pool."

Larouche and Tor exchanged glances. More adrenaline sluiced. Jack buzzed.

"It is a universal truth that no goal is ever attained without discipline," Larouche recited calmly, his eyes never leaving Tor's face. "Guidelines must be installed and then adhered to very strictly, so that order does not descend into chaos."

He pivoted back to Jack. "Those who choose to disregard these rules—who, in doing so, foolishly endanger the safety of others—must be culled for the good of the whole. It's the foundation upon which our entire code of conduct is constructed."

Jack saw Tor smirk. Even his teeth were huge.

"Wait a minute," he said to Larouche. "Are you telling me that you had one of your own employees killed because he somehow stepped out of line?"

Larouche emitted a dry laugh. "You were right about your imagination, Jacques. That's why I'm so eager to hire you."

"You didn't answer my question."

Larouche stopped laughing. His eyes were flints. "Did I order someone killed? Is that what you are asking?"

Jack nodded.

"That is absurd," Larouche sneered. "I would do no such thing. And I certainly did not imply that to you; Tor can vouch for that. The Jackals may be hedonists, but we do not kill people. I simply meant that, as with anything in life worth achieving, the Jackals are prepared to make certain sacrifices in order to attain the maximum degree of gratification. Our members not only understand this logic, they actually thrive on it. Unfortunately, there are times when someone who has failed the group in some manner has their membership revoked. We can't possibly be held responsible for how a person reacts to losing that privilege."

"What did Junger do that was considered too debauched by people who get their jollies by fucking everything that moves?"

Larouche feigned a sudden interest in the fingernails of his right hand. "I'm not at liberty to discuss that," he said.

"What a surprise," Jack said. "The bottom line is that there's more to this visit of yours than just throwing some textbooks on the beach in the name of education."

"There's always more to something than initially meets the eye," Larouche said. "You're the writer, Jacques, you should know that."

"OK," Jack nodded, "so let me get this straight. You're seeking this ultimate pleasure of yours here in the Cook Islands?"

"The Cook Islands, Vanuatu, Samoa, Tahiti, Tonga," Larouche said, arms spread wide to encompass the entire room. "Anywhere in the South Pacific that we can find it, actually. We want to savor the sweet delicacies of each island nation, to write about them, film them, to share our adventures with others, in all their sensual glory."

"But why here?" Jack asked. "Why now?"

"You work for a newspaper, Jacques," Larouche said. "Even that one solitary TV channel you have here shows the international news."

Jack's brows knitted. "You've lost me."

"Think about it," Larouche said. "The League was originally formed in Cambodia, to take advantage of that country's blind-eye attitude towards the tourist sex trade. It was a never-ending orgy for us. Beaucoup decadence. Imagine this: entire villages created for the sole purpose of providing housing to the young girls who sold their bodies to foreigners. It was a smorgasbord of fornication and we Jackals gorged ourselves at every opportunity."

Jack leaned forward. "Cambodia? Please don't tell me you've got Gary Glitter stashed on your boat somewhere."

Larouche made a face. He looked like he'd just stepped in something. "Jacques, please," he said. "We consider ourselves mannered gentlemen."

"Mannered gentlemen who saw the local authorities bow to international pressure and steadily clamp down on their favorite pastime."

Larouche nodded sadly.

"Your playground has grown too hot for you."

Larouche continued to nod. "Sad, but true," he said. "But all good things must end, non?"

"So now you're turning elsewhere to get your rocks off. Some place else to conduct your sex tours."

"Oui," Larouche said. "The League considers the South Pacific a fertile playing field ripe for tilling. The women here are really quite delightful, and we can be very appreciative."

"So there never was an educational seminar. Just your men on a scouting mission."

Larouche shrugged. "The books are genuine," he said.

"I don't know if I like the idea of you using the island as your personal brothel," Jack said. "This isn't Club Bed."

"Remove your head from the sand," Larouche said. "How are we different from any of the other tourists who fly in each day? Do you think they are here for a sunburn and a carved Tangaroa? Hardly. Brown skin is an aphrodisiac for the white man. Think of the Island Night performances: the frenzied dancing, the hypnotic pounding of the drums. Don't tell me that isn't meant as seduction."

Jack was gutted. He felt ill.

The island was his home now. The locals were his friends, they were his neighbors. He liked them. He admired them. He even loved some of them. What Larouche was proposing felt so deliberate, so impersonal. So *mechanical.* A commerce based on the exchange of bodily fluids. No other attraction to the country or its inhabitants other than a receptacle for ejaculate.

In Jack's mind, this league represented salaciousness in its basest, crudest form. Sick, perverted bastards, the lot of them.

Larouche picked up on his discomfort.

"I don't mean to be disrespectful," he said. His words were oily, slick.

"But I am only stating the obvious."

"I don't think I much care for your obvious," Jack said.

Larouche licked his lips. "Tell me this, mon ami, have you ever made love to a brown woman?"

"Of course," Jack said warily. "Several times, actually. What's your point?"

"How was it?"

"The sex?"

"Oui."

"The best I've ever had," Jack said. "But that doesn't mean that every wanker with a jackal tattooed on his arse is automatically guaranteed to get laid in the Cook Islands. Unlike your experiences elsewhere, there are laws here. There are standards and morals. Or were you too busy cruising the colleges to notice all the churches on the island?"

Larouche cackled.

"I'm glad you find all this amusing," Jack said.

Larouche held up a hand and fought to check his laughter. "Pardonner a moi, Jacques," he said. "But your naivete really is priceless."

Jack didn't appreciate being mocked. "What are you talking about?" he snapped.

"My men have frequented the nightclubs on the island," Larouche said. "They have visited your bars in the company of your moralistic islanders. And, according to their reports, they haven't encountered many refusals from those they propositioned. Male *or* female. Face it, Jacques, your adopted home is not exactly swarming with saints."

"Of course not," Jack asserted. "I never said it was. But that doesn't mean we need the likes of you to lead us into any further temptation."

Larouche cocked his head to one side. A thought had struck. "Un moment," he said. "I believe that I see the problem here."

"Do you now?"

"Oui," said Larouche. "You don't like to share."

"What I don't like is foreign shitrats who think they can just sail in here and fuck with an entire country and its population," Jack hissed.

Larouche's face pursed. It hardened. It *compressed*. "Then my advice to you, mon jeune ami," he said, "is that you either learn to like it, or learn to stay out of the way."

Jack's face blistered. His fingers curled instinctively into fists. He usually made a point of avoiding confrontations, but Larouche had put his back up.

"And if I don't?"

A smile slowly rippled across Larouche's countenance. It was the look a vampire's victim sees just before the fangs descend. Jack's orifices tightened an extra notch.

Larouche tilted his head in Tor's direction. "Those who interfere with the League of Jackals inevitably come to regret their impudence. I would hate you to have such regrets, Jacques."

TWENTY-EIGHT

Rev. Moses Akimo hiked the perimeter of the library. He marched, he tramped. He pulled a wadded handkerchief out of a pocket and mopped his face, throat, the back of his neck.

He stopped. He squinted at the books on the shelves. They were mostly mystery novels featuring ingenuous forensic investigators or crafty lawyers. Akimo shook his head in disgust. The devil's work. Into the rubbish bin with the lot of them.

Patience is a virtue. That was Akimo's mantra this particular afternoon. It was a lesson drilled into him by his father, the Rev. Dante Akimo, may he rest in peace. Another invaluable skill—this one also impressed on him during his youthful days at study—was the ability to recognize a potential benefactor. And, having targeted a wallet that was about to be opened, to ensure, by whatever means necessary, that the funds flowed freely and without interruption.

By whatever means necessary. Even if it meant loosing the serpent into his own garden.

It was only the expectation of a sizable contribution that kept him here, in this airless room reeking of wicked, wicked words. He was agitated, he was distraught. He choked back a scream of frustration. The physical exertion of striding from wall to wall seemed to help.

He'd considered himself cunning when this opportunity was first presented. He no longer felt that way. Now he just wanted what was owed to him so he could be left in peace.

The library door opened. Akimo braked. Tor appeared and flicked his head: *He's ready for you.*

Akimo followed Tor to the end of the hallway and down a set of stairs to a dining room on the first floor. Andre Larouche looked up from his meal. He carefully placed his utensils beside his plate and patted the edges of his mouth with a cloth napkin. He waved Akimo closer.

"Sit beside me," Larouche said. "Can I offer you something to eat? The poke is particularly tasty today."

"No thank you," Akimo said. He looked around. "Where's Jack Nolan?"

"Gone," Larouche said, reaching for a glass of wine. "He practically shoveled down his meal then begged off without even sampling the dessert. Frankly," Larouche guzzled wine, "I'm worried about the man's digestive system. It can't be good for you to eat that fast."

"I'm worried as well," Akimo said. He watched as Larouche resumed eating. "Nolan could be a problem."

Larouche patted Akimo's arm. "Forget about him," he said around a gummy mouthful of pawpaw pudding. "He was curious—which is a necessary evil in a writer—but he was so intent on being petulant that I doubt that he had the time or the energy to entertain suspicions as well."

Larouche chewed thoughtfully, swallowed, then continued. "Monsieur Nolan has been on this island for far too long, I'm afraid. Too much sun, too much beer; his brain has atrophied. He might be a nuisance but he will not be trouble. Trust me. I know about such things."

Akimo wasn't convinced. "I wish I could be so sure," he said. "The last thing we need is Nolan running to Lloyd Dempster and Jordan Baxter. Our, uh, business transaction is so close to being completed that if the media got wind—"

"I thought I told you to relax." Larouche clamped a rough hand on the top of Akimo's shoulder. The reverend squirmed. "I promise you that Nolan is the least of our worries."

Larouche's grip relaxed. Akimo shifted away.

"Now let's talk about payment for your new church," Larouche said. "Tor tells me that your contacts have proven very beneficial. Rest assured that your loyalty will be rewarded most handsomely."

Akimo sweated. He was vexed. He was anxious.

Larouche sighed. "You're still thinking about Nolan."

"Yes," Akimo said. "You don't know him like I do. He's made many friends during his time here. Influential people who could scuttle this entire enterprise before it's even properly begun."

Larouche ignored his meal, and stared at Akimo. "Nolan can be controlled," he said slowly, firmly, emphatically. "I know enough to know this."

"But how can you be so sure?"

"It's very easy, mon ami." Larouche's eyes glowed. "If Nolan is so foolish as to cause trouble for us, we simply turn our attention to his young friend. We let him know, in no uncertain terms, that should he do anything impetuous, Maina will be the one who suffers for it. She is his weakness."

Maina. Akimo flashed back: he felt her hand on his skin, her breasts

pressed against his face. He smelled her hair.
He heard the laughter at the café. His face fell.
"She's a wicked, cheeky girl." Akimo grimaced. "I don't like her at all."
"Then you won't mind fucking her," Larouche said, "should Nolan need to be taught a lesson."

TWENTY-NINE

Karl Lamu picked at his teeth. He yawned. He made a grand production out of checking his watch against the clock situated on the wall over Jack's shoulder.

Jack talked in excited tones. He expounded on chaos theories. He predicted hellfire and the end of civilization on the island. Rev. Albert Smail would have been impressed with Jack. Rev. Albert Smail would have taken notes.

At one point, Lamu leaned forward. He shoved his hand down the back of his uniform shorts. He scratched.

Jack finally bolted from his chair and slammed his hand down on the Chief Inspector's desk.

"Have you heard a single word I've said?" Jack snapped. He was exasperated. He was frustrated. He was banging his head against a cinder block wall.

Lamu calmly examined the splintered end of his toothpick, flicked off a chunk of half-chewed something, twisted in his chair, and dropped the toothpick in a rubbish can.

He looked at Jack.

"You're drawing a long bow here, mate," he said.

Jack threw up his hands in surrender. "I don't fucking believe this."

"Eh!" Lamu said. "Do not use that language in my office. I'm a Christian."

Jack retreated. He stepped to the office window and worked at calming himself by observing the street from two storeys up.

He had wolfed down his lunch, his brain working as quickly as his fork. He thanked Andre Larouche for the meal, then fled the villa. He drove to town, to the police station, determined that the Belgian and his League of Jackals had to be prevented from running amok on Raro. Convinced that their warped fantasies must never be unleashed on his adopted country.

Jack brushed past Jimmy Tauranga at the front desk, and climbed the stairs to Lamu's office. He was breathing fire. He was incensed. He would demand that Lamu put a stop to the depravity.

Lamu's indifference was deflating; it extended beyond disappointment.

His zeal dampened, Jack stood by the window musing on his choice of words, on his tone of voice, on his desk-thumping antics.

Maybe he should have been less demanding. Maybe he should have been more diplomatic. Maybe he should have driven the long way to town.

He watched the traffic. He saw a local man on a bike. A dog perched on the gas tank. The wind blew its ears straight back. He saw mommas carrying babies, doing their shopping. He saw young men wearing woollen beanies pulled low on their heads. It was 30 degrees outside. They sweated to look as cool as the American blacks they saw in music videos.

He saw tourists gesticulating, pointing. Confused. *It's not that big of an island, people. No one has ever gotten lost here. Relax You're on holidays. No worries, no hurries.*

Maybe he should listen to his own advice.

His heart rate eased. His breathing slowed. He turned back to Lamu.

"Larouche and his people are criminals."

"So you've said. A number of times, actually. I'm still waiting for proof."

"The educational seminar is a smokescreen—Tommy Niomare can verify that. This organization is only using it to gain our trust while they track their prey," Jack said. "Why can't you see what's right in front of your face?"

"Actually, Jack, my eyes are working just fine," Lamu said. "And what they saw was the box of school books that Larouche brought to Lloyd Dempster's party. The prime minister and the French ambassador, to name just two, were quite impressed. I'm sure they will be very disappointed to now hear that our children will be reading through a smokescreen."

"What about this master plan of theirs?"

"To have sex in the Cook Islands?" Lamu shrugged. "If there was a law against that, this island would be empty. We might even have to deport you, Jack." He winked. "As long as it involves only consenting adults, there's nothing the police can, or should, do about it."

"And if it doesn't?" Jack asked. "If they start to treat us like we're another Cambodia? If they start hanging around the primary schools?"

"Should that come to pass," Lamu said, "my constables will be on them like an island dog on a fish head. I'll even let you take the photos when we make the arrests."

"Alright," Jack nodded. "That's all I'm asking, that you keep an eye on these people. But that still leaves a dead man in the Outrigger pool."

Lamu opened a desk drawer and selected another toothpick. Returned to excavating molars. Spoke around wood. "All you've told me is that his employer isn't exactly gutted. No law against that either, Jack."

"But the bruises," Jack said, running a hand through his hair. "We both saw them. Dr. Rangi saw them. Didn't they make you the least bit suspicious?"

"Dr. Rangi estimated that the bruises were at least a day old," Lamu said. "And I've always been inclined to agree with those who know what they're doing."

"But—"

"He drowned, Jack," Lamu said. "Let it go. Let it all go. The dead man. This league of whatever. Go home. Have a siesta. It's too hot to be getting all worked up over nothing."

"I hope that this 'nothing' doesn't come back to bite you in the arse," Jack said. "Because you weren't in that villa with Larouche. You didn't see the look on his face when he was talking to me. The bastard was practically *gloating* at what he and his mates are planning for Raro."

Lamu twirled the toothpick between his fingers. He sat up, pulled a pen from his shirt pocket, and scribbled on a piece of paper. Sat back.

"There," he said, indicating the paper. "Your concerns are duly noted. Now, unless you have any concrete evidence—the sort that would stand up in a court of law for instance—I think you should stop wasting my valuable time."

"A real policeman would get on the phone to New Zealand and call in a scene-of-crime officer and a forensic team."

"Careful, Jack." There was steel in Lamu's voice now. "You're beginning to try my patience."

"I'd rather you tried a murderer."

"There hasn't been a murder here in eight years," Lamu said. "When, and if, there is another one in the Cook Islands, I assure you that I will be relentless in my investigation." He reached for his phone. "I think we're done here."

"Willie Laofia."

The phone dropped into its cradle.

"What did you say?"

"You heard me."

Lamu leaned back in his chair. He hooked his thumbs in his belt loops. He regarded Jack. He studied him. Jack regarded right back. He refused to blink.

"What's your point?" Lamu asked.

"That was murder," Jack said. "I took the photos for the paper, remember? So I saw the poor bugger lying in that taro patch with his dick shoved down his throat. I don't remember any talk of a relentless investigation at that time."

There was midnight in Lamu's eyes. There was nightfall in his face. "Willie Laofia wasn't murdered," he said slowly. Deliberately.

Jack cocked an eyebrow. He face-talked: *Oh, really?* "Then what would you call it?"

"It's called island justice, Jack," Lamu said. "The day you understand that, is the day you will truly belong in this country."

Jimmy Tauranga worked the stapler. He pounded it. He punched it. He hung posters on the corkboard near the front desk. Wanted posters. Tourists loved them. Tourists had their pictures taken next to them while they waited for their Cook Islands driver's licences to be processed. Tourists will take photos of anything. Tourists were why Pacific Photos stayed open late seven days a week.

"I know that bastard."

Jimmy nearly dropped the stapler. "Sweet Jesus, Jack, you can't be sneaking up on people like that."

Jack was at the bottom of the stairs. He was looking through the doorway into the reception area. He was looking over Jimmy's shoulder. He was looking at the Wanted poster.

He came into the room. He held out his hand. "Let me see that."

Jimmy looked at the sheet of paper he was holding. The photo was of a broad-faced man with light, curly hair and a full beard. Polar eyes. Thin lips. Scar tissue. A bad man.

The photo had been scanned, enlarged, manipulated to fit on a replica of an Old West Wanted Dead or Alive poster, then printed. Clarity had been lost in the process—pixels had blown out—and the image was fuzzy. The scar on the man's cheek was a smudge of ink.

Jack snatched the poster away.

"Eh!" Jimmy yelped. "What's with you?"

Jack examined the poster, turning it so the light from the front window fell on it. "I know this man," he repeated.

Jimmy looked closer. "What, from North America?"

"No." Jack waved the sheet under Jimmy's nose. "From here. From Raro."

Jimmy laughed. "Eh, bro," he said. "You winding me up?"

"I'm serious here, Jimmy," Jack said. "This is Andre Larouche's henchman. His name is Tor."

"Eh?"

"Big guy," Jack said. "You must have seen him around town. Hard to miss, actually."

"I've seen the man you're talking about," Jimmy nodded. "At Sparky's with Moses Akimo. But," he looked again at the poster, "he doesn't look anything like this guy."

"Sure he does," Jack said, stabbing a finger at the paper. "He's shaved, of course, and cut his hair. But it's him, alright."

"I don't know, Jack." Jimmy pushed back his peaked cap and scratched his head.

"Look at that scar," Jack said. "I'd recognize that mark anywhere."

"Lots of people have scars, bro," Jimmy said. "Including your new flatmate."

Jack was agitated. The paper shook in his hand. He was certain that the man in the poster was Tor.

"Where did this come from?" he asked.

"We make them up for the tour—"

Jack cut him off. "I know that," he said. "But where's the original that you worked from? I need to see that."

Jimmy backed away from Jack. His forehead jumped. He face-talked: *You're acting a bit maki maki here, bro.*

Jack raised a hand. It was a gesture of apology. He shucked his chin. He face-talked: *Sorry, mate.*

Jimmy moved behind the counter. He opened a drawer. He pulled out a sheaf of papers, licked a finger, and started to sort through them. Stopped. Pulled one out.

"Here's your man," he said.

Jack reached. Jimmy pulled the paper away. "Not so fast, bro," Jimmy said. "Official police document."

"Fine," Jack said. "But you can tell me what it says, right? Or is that top secret as well?"

Jimmy skimmed down the sheet. His lips moved. His eyebrows wobbled. He face-talked: *This is interesting.*

"What is it?" Jack shuffled his feet, growing impatient. If Tor was a wanted criminal, then Karl Lamu would finally have his reason for getting off his arse and doing something. And, with his goon behind bars, Andre Larouche wouldn't be quite so cocky. He might be persuaded to sail away as quickly as the trade winds could carry him. And take his bloody horny pirates with him.

Jimmy looked up, then waved the paper. "This was issued by Interpol," he said. "The man's name is Gablehaus. Markus Gablehaus. He's from Sweden." Jimmy's face brightened. "Volvo," he said. "Ikea. *ABBA!*"

"I don't care where he's from," Jack spluttered. "Why is Interpol so interested in him?"

Jimmy returned to the paper. "It's something to do with an Operation Ore," he said. "Which, coordinated with the National Crime Squad, appears to be the English wing of an FBI action called Operation Candyman."

"And what's the purpose of this operation?"

Jimmy looked up. "They're hunting down pedophiles," he said. "Internet pedophiles."

Karl Lamu punched numbers on his phone.
"Hello?"
"It's me."
"Chief Inspector. How very nice to hear from you."
"Drop the cute act," Lamu said. "It doesn't work for you."
"Fine. What's up?"
"You're always whinging that I never call you about anything," Lamu said.
"So now you're going to finally tell me something?"
"Jack Nolan was just in my office."
"And?"
"And," Lamu said, "he insists that Rarotonga is about to be invaded by the devil incarnate seeking sexual favors from our women."
"And how is this news?"
"My point exactly," Lamu sighed. "But Jack was very insistent that action needed to be taken before we become the Sodom of the South Pacific."
"Did he happen to mention where these invaders are coming from?"
"Apparently the first wave is aboard that superyacht in Avatiu Harbor."
"The *Jackal?*"
"No, I don't think that's it," Lamu said. "This ship has a foreign name of some kind."
"Sorry, you're right. It's actually the *Chacal*, isn't it? That's French for jackal."
"How very enlightening." Lamu rolled his eyes.
"What do you think of his allegations?"

"Personally, I think he's overreacting to a comment made to him by the yacht's owner," Lamu said. "But he's one of yours, so I thought you might be curious as to what he's up to. I'm just trying to protect all of our arses. If any of what he's saying actually turns out to be true, I want both of us to be forewarned."

"I appreciate that. So where's Jack now?"

"I don't know. He stormed out of my office when I refused to call in the New Zealand navy for a full-scale assault. I suggested he go home and cool down."

"You don't think he'll do anything stupid, do you? Try to take the law into his own hands or something along that line?"

"He was ranting a fair bit, but I think he blew himself out by growling me," Lamu said. "Jack may like to imagine himself as some kind of cowboy, but I don't see him becoming a vigilante. He's a Canadian, for heaven's sake. What do they know about violent behavior?"

"Exactly. But, hey, thanks for the tip about the superyacht. I'll see what I can find out about it."

"This is a one-off, OK?" Lamu said. "So no more complaining to the PM that I'm not doing my job properly. OK?"

"Good as gold," said Jordan Baxter. He hung up his phone. He flopped back in his chair. Put his hands behind his head. Smiled evilly. This was starting to be fun.

SATURDAY

THIRTY

"Pa pa!" Andrew Tuara barked.

The five men sitting ahead of Andrew in the vaka snapped to attention.

"Ki mua!"

Jack, seated fourth, cocked his left arm and raised his paddle until his right knuckle nearly touched his forehead. His teammates did the same.

"'Uti!"

Six wooden paddles knifed into the lagoon's surface, three to the left, an equal number to the right. The outrigger canoe shot away from the beach, its supporting ama cutting a white swath through the liquid turquoise.

Jack dug deep. Exhaled through his mouth as he plunged the paddle, pulled it through the water. Inhaled through his nose as he lifted the paddle, quickly raised it for the next stroke.

Ten strokes. Then: "Ii!" and the six men expertly shifted their paddles to the other side. Jack went right. Ahead of him, Big Suga Makara switched to the left.

Jack could hear Jimmy Tauranga breathing hard behind him in the Number 5 seat. Jimmy leaned forward to speak, his words coming in blurts as he talked through the exertion.

"How are you today, bro?" Jimmy asked.

Jack glanced over his shoulder. He caught a glimpse of Andrew Tuara in the Number 6 seat, the steering position, the command position. He didn't like it when his paddlers talked in the vaka. This was serious work. This was competitive training. Talk could wait until they were back on the beach.

"I've calmed down," Jack said. "If that's what you mean."

"I thought you were going to blow out an artery on me there yesterday," Jimmy laughed.

"'Ii!" Andrew growled from behind them. Paddles changed sides again.

"I was a bit of a wild man, wasn't I?"

"Work hard, you two," Big Suga snapped.

"Are you still on a witch-hunt for pervs?" Jimmy whispered.

Jack's hands were already slippery from sweat and seawater. He tightened his grip on the paddle's shaft. "No," he said. "I'll leave that to you boys."

"Choice."

Andrew dragged his paddle, the vaka turned left. The launching area, where Heather and Maina had helped them carry the craft down the embankment to the beach, fell behind. Now they flashed horizontally across Muri Lagoon, running parallel to the beach on their left and the coral reef to the right.

Tourists relaxing on the deck of the Ocean Beach Resort paused in their sipping of lattes and long blacks to wave encouragement. Windsurfers leaned precariously, their boards barely touching the wave tops as they skipped like stones across the surface of the lagoon. Children laughed and screamed as they played and splashed in the shallows near the shore. Snorkellers, sporting candy-colored rubber fins, duck-walked into deeper water.

The vaka continued to glide north, past the volcanic motu called Taakoka, past the three sand cays: Koromiri, Oneroa and Motutapu. The beach to their left was now filled with guests of the Seven Palms Hotel, relaxing on plastic loungers or large towels spread near the lagoon's edge. The brightness of their swimming togs flared against the white sand.

The sun hurled its heat down on the paddlers. While his five teammates, all locals, were dressed only in shorts, Jack still wore his blue singlet. His arms, legs, the back of his neck, tips of his ears, even his nose were all slathered with sunblock. He wore a Rocket Bar cap pulled tightly down on his head. His skin had gradually browned during his five years in the tropics, but he wasn't taking any chances. Heather had made him look at photos of skin-cancer victims. The photos were in color. He never wanted to see that again.

Andrew dragged once more. The vaka made another wide, swooping turn. The beach was to their right now. Ahead, in the distance, they could see the launching area. A single canoe pushed out from shore. Its occupant wore yellow: Heather.

The men grunted in unison. Tendons strained. Muscles bulged. Tattoos shimmered and rippled. Sweat met sea.

Jack worked his paddle. It was an instrument. It cut into the lagoon. It was a sharp knife. A smooth sweep back—not too far—then out, careful not to spray Jimmy in the seat behind him. Then elbows high again for the next stroke. And again. And again. Now the changeover. Make it clean. One fluid motion. Don't hit Big Suga. Don't miss a beat.

To the visitors sucking back their umbrella drinks on the sand, none of this looked terribly difficult. They were wrong. Competitive paddling took balance, timing, strength, and endurance. It built teamwork. It built muscle. It worked cardio. It burned fat. It had no effect on Big Suga.

It had taken Jack months of practice before Andrew Tuara stopped growling him for mistakes. Even now he refused to equate his skill level with that of his fellow paddlers, but his team had won too many inter-club races for there to be any weak links onboard. Now there was even talk of traveling to Tahiti or Hawaii to compete internationally, if they could raise the money to cover expenses.

Jack's body was a paddling machine. It reacted instinctively to Andrew's commands, to his pace. The mechanics freed Jack's mind. It allowed him to think. Sometimes that was a good thing.

Sometimes it wasn't.

He chewed over yesterday's events as if they were cud. He tasted his leftover emotions; they were still bitter. But Jimmy was right. He had reacted badly. He'd been an arsehole in his meeting with Karl Lamu. After all, Andre Larouche hadn't exactly proposed a scorched-earth policy of rape and pillage. If visitors to Rarotonga found willing sexual partners during their stay, it was nobody's business but their own.

It was Larouche's *attitude*, more than anything, which burned Jack. The man was so overbearing, so swaggering, so *almighty*. Larouche needed a good dose of dengue fever. That would fix him. Or a centipede in his drawers. Jack smiled. That would be even better.

He'd been smart not to return to Lamu's office with the Wanted poster. Instead, he thanked Jimmy for his help and drove home. This time he did take the long way. He pulled the mower out of the shed and attacked the lawns, both front and back. He kept going, right onto the Matavera Beach Store's property, much to Mama Rosie's surprise.

He hated cutting the grass. He hated the lawnmower. It was loud; the exhaust reeked of two-stroke oil. But by channeling his energy into physical labor, by gritting his teeth and putting his head down and just *doing* it, he managed to momentarily forget about Andre Larouche and the League of Jackals. He forgot about Tor, or whatever his real name was.

He had picked up Maina after her shift at the café. He prepared their tea and made a token effort at conversation while they ate. Then, with the hour still early and the evening still bright, he simply went to his room. Shut the door on Maina's mixed expressions of curiosity and concern. Lay down on his bed. Slept. He did not dream. A small mercy but a mercy nonetheless.

He thought about his new book. He'd made a start and that was encouraging. It was set in the Cook Islands, obviously; that was a no-brainer.

For the first time in years, plot ideas and character traits were beginning to swirl in his brain. For the first time in years, he felt excited about facing his computer. Now he just had to finish the book before that feeling disappeared again.

He thought about Maina. She'd mentioned over breakfast that she had the day off from the café. Jack, feeling bad about his behavior the night before, asked if she wanted to go to the beach with him. If she was lucky, she might even have an opportunity to paddle in one of the vakas.

She disappeared into her room. Was back at the table five minutes later wearing board shorts and a bikini top featuring electric-orange seashells on a white background.

When they reached Muri Beach, he expected her to remove the shorts. He was surprised when she paused only to kick off her jandals before charging into the lagoon's warm embrace. When she emerged, drops of water dripping off her face, hair slicked wetly down her back, he asked what had happened to the bottom half of her swimming togs.

She blinked water out of her eyes and looked down at her shorts. "This is it, mate," she said. "Do I look like a freak or something?"

"No," Jack said. "But the top is so nice, I just thought you'd want to wear the bottoms as well."

"Nah, left them at home," she said. "Couldn't be bothered."

"Couldn't be bothered putting them on?"

"Couldn't be bothered shaving."

Maina saw Jack's face redden. It was too good to let go.

"You ever had an ingrown hair, Jack?" she asked. "Let me tell ya, they hurt like a bitch. Especially in an area that's so tender already. So I just save myself the agony and wear the shorts instead. But, if you want, I can show you the rest of the outfit when we get back to the house."

Jack blushed again. Looked away. Was suddenly very interested in a gaggle of tourists that had just emerged, chattering to each other in German, from a tour bus.

Heather approached from the direction of the Ocean Beach Resort. He had spotted her there earlier, standing sentinel on the balcony, surveying the beach.

"Heather," he said. "We were—"

Heather ignored him. She muttered, "Not on my shift." She brushed past Jack and Maina, the tail of her yellow shirt flapping behind her. A caution flag. Jack exchanged a puzzled look with Maina, then ran to catch up.

Heather didn't break pace as Jack drew even. Instead, she zeroed in on a large piece of driftwood strewn on the beach. It rested midway between the water's edge and a small grove of palms. Jack tried to speak; she waved him to silence.

He examined the piece of wood as they drew near. It was huge. It was amazing what the tide could deposit on the beach, despite the protective barrier of the coral reef.

Heather stopped at the log and put her hands on her hips. Jack stopped beside her, at first too bewildered by Heather's actions to take notice of what she was glaring at. He finally followed her gaze. To the driftwood log. To the other side of the log. To where a woman lay on her back, sprawled on a large white towel.

A paperback novel sat to one side, a small shell marking a page. An empty glass bearing the Ocean Beach Resort logo was jammed into the sand. A tube of sunscreen lay on its side beside the towel. A large straw hat obscured the woman's face. A billow of raven hair spread out from under the hat like an oil spill. Her skin was brown and taut. It glowed under a thin gloss of sweat. It quivered under the caress of the soft breeze murmuring off the lagoon.

She was topless.

Jack was riveted. Heather caught him. She punched him hard. He winced. He face-talked: *Ow! What was that for?*

"Excuse me young lady," Heather snarled.

The woman lifted an edge of her hat and squinted. "No more drinks," she said. Dropped the edge of her hat.

Heather looked at Jack. She face-talked: *Do you believe this bitch?*

Jack flicked an eyebrow. He face-talked: *Cheeky, eh?*

Heather nudged the woman's hip with a sharp toe. "*I said excuse me*," she growled.

The woman sat up. Jack stumbled back. The woman swiped the hat off her face. "I said I'm fin—Oh, hello, Jack."

Heather spun on him. Lightning launched from her eyes. She face-talked: *Hello, Jack? You know her?*

Jack lifted his eyes to the woman's face. "Chaka! How are you?"

His voice was too shrill. Beads of sweat popped on his forehead. He should have recognized Chaka Tane's body. Maybe it somehow looked different in the white light of morning. He might have to do a bit more research.

A sharp elbow to his ribs. It said: *Introduce me to your friend.*

Jack took a deep breath. "Heather Flynn, Chaka Tane," he said. "Chaka's from Rapa Nui. She's here filming a documentary about surfing in the South Pacific."

Chaka smiled up at Heather. "Nice to meet you," she said. "How are you?"

Heather did not smile down at Chaka. "I'd be a lot better," she said through clenched teeth, "if you'd put your top back on. It's considered an insult to the locals to let your titties flap in the breeze like that."

Chaka's smile vanished. Jack groaned, looking away. "I assure you, Heather," Chaka said, "that my *breasts* have never flapped. That may be because some of us are still young and firm."

Jack took another step back. *Here we go,* he thought: *cat fight.*

Heather didn't reply, but Chaka caught the tropical storm that flashed across her face. She wisely decided to disengage. "I'm sorry if I've offended anyone," she said. "I guess I've spent too much time in Tahiti, where even the school girls go topless at the beach."

She rolled over and showed her bare back to Jack and Heather. "Is this better?"

"Thank you," Heather said. "Just be careful of the sand fleas. They're particular to silicone."

Chaka squealed. Jack grabbed Heather by the arm, pulling her away.

"There aren't any sand fleas on Muri Beach," he whispered.

Heather glanced back over her shoulder. Chaka had wrapped the towel tightly around her torso. She was swiveling in a series of jerky motions, scrutinizing the sand around the log with a panicked expression. "Your girlfriend doesn't know that."

"She's not my girlfriend," Jack said. "Jordan Baxter has already staked his claim."

"How are your eyes?"

Jack blinked rapidly. "Fine," he said. "Why?"

"Not that I care," Heather pulled away, "but I didn't see you blink once while you were examining every minute detail of that woman's body. I thought maybe you might have sunburned your retinas."

Jack shook his head in denial. "I was as shocked as you," he insisted. "And just for the record—and not that it's any of your business—but I've already seen Chaka naked."

"Some guys have all the luck," Heather said, marching purposefully back across the beach.

Maina met them. "What was that about?" she asked.

"You might want to ask your flatmate," Heather said without breaking stride. "King Perv."

Maina scowled at Jack. She face-talked: *What have you done now, you stupid bloody man?*

The vaka caught up to Heather, slid past her. Jack took a quick look at her. Hoped to catch her eye. She stared straight ahead, chin resolute, paddling strongly. She was still pissed. This was going to cost him. Big time. Again.

"Whoa," said Andrew, and the six men stopped paddling. The vaka glided silently under the momentum of their final thrust. The crewmembers took advantage of the break to sip at water containers. They hunched forward, and sucked hard to catch their breath.

Jack looked left. Heather had maneuvered the single vaka nearly to the reef line. Jack looked right. Suddenly straightened up.

Maina sat at the water's edge; waves gently washed her bare feet. The morning sun was good on her face. She glowed. She looked content. She looked untouched by nightmares.

She wasn't alone.

A man approached and squatted beside her. Young, from what Jack could make of him. Facial hair. Buzz cut. He was talking intently, gesturing with his hands. Maina didn't look at him, stared instead at the lagoon. But she nodded at what he was saying.

Jack felt a stab of distress. He wasn't sure why. Maybe he didn't trust strangers after his talk with Larouche. Maybe the young man's body language was too intense. Maybe it was the way Maina's expression changed as the man bent to her ear. She appeared to face-talk: *I don't like this.*

Was it directed at Jack? Was it a silent plea for help? He couldn't be sure.

The vaka glided past the launch area. Jack twisted to keep Maina and the young man in sight. Jimmy Tauranga looked up. "You alright, bro?"

Jack strained to look past Jimmy, but Andrew Tuara was already steering the craft away from the beach. Maybe he should hop out and check on Maina. She definitely did not look comfortable. She might be—

"Help!"

Jack spun around in his seat. His teammates did the same, searching for the source of the distress call.

"Over there!" Big Suga shouted, pointing a beefy finger at the distant coral reef.

Jack squinted. The sun glancing off the dancing waters interfered with his vision. But he spotted it as well. A waving arm. A flash of yellow. *Heather!*

"Ki mua!" Andrew barked. The command to ready your paddle for the first stroke. Then "'Uti," and the vaka leaped ahead. Maina was momentarily forgotten as Jack joined the others in propelling the canoe up to full speed as quickly as they could.

They were at Heather's side within minutes, each man anxiously looking overboard for the source of her problem. Heather was standing, the water nearly to her neck, holding onto her canoe with one hand.

"What is it?" asked Andrew. "Has a shark gotten into the lagoon? Is it a jellyfish?"

"No." Heather shook her head.

"Have you stepped on a stonefish?" asked Jimmy. "Or touched stinging coral?"

"No," Heather said.

"Have you cramped up?"

"No."

The six men looked at each other. Jimmy lowered his head, nodded up at Jack. He face-talked: *She's your friend, bro. You deal with it.*

Jack trailed a hand in the lagoon. It was warm. It was bath water. "Then what's the problem?" he asked.

Heather bobbed on the tide. She looked embarrassed. She looked sheepish. "I dropped my car keys," she said.

The men in the vaka groaned. *This* was the emergency?

"Your car keys? That's it? That's why you're screaming for help?"

Heather's look shot arrows at Jack. "I wasn't screaming," she said, her voice thick with bubbling anger. "And unless one of you gentlemen plans on driving me around the island for the rest of my life then, yes, this is rather an emergency."

Jack sighed. "What do you want us to do?"

"I hopped out as soon as I felt the keys slip out of my pocket," Heather said. "So they can't be far away. But I can't dive down to look for them and keep the vaka from drifting away at the same time. So you can either hang onto the canoe or show me what great swimmers you are."

Big Suga laughed. "If I get out now, I'll never get back in. You'll have to tow me to shore."

Jimmy put his paddle down. "I could—"

Jack was over the side in one fluid motion. He used his arms to propel himself to the bottom, then did a slow circle of Heather's legs. As he pulled away, he gave her a quick pinch for good measure. She lashed out with a foot. Jack smiled. It was worth wasting precious oxygen.

He used rocks and outcrops of coral to pull himself along, careful not to disturb a stonefish. Nothing. Lungs bursting, he surfaced, shook his head at Heather, sucked in another deep breath, and submerged again.

This could be a needle in a wet haystack. Surely Heather could have another key made. Even if she didn't have a spare at home, it was not uncommon for someone else's key to open several vehicles, and not necessarily of the same make. An outsider might consider this a lack of security. A local would ask why anyone would bother stealing a vehicle when there was nowhere to go but around and around and—

There! A glint of sunlight on metal. Jack had almost missed it. Was turning away and about to give up when his eyes were attracted to the brief flash. He used his last reservoir of air to reach down, fingers scrabbling in the loose sand. The car key was attached, along with several others, to a tiny surfboard. It was unmistakable. It was Heather's.

Holding the keys aloft, Jack breached in a dramatic spray of water. Jimmy and the others clapped: his discovery meant that they could now continue with their training. Heather was sitting in her vaka. She took the keys from Jack, consigned them to the safety of a zippered pocket of her shorts, and closed the zipper with a flourish.

"Am I forgiven?" Jack asked.

Heather splashed him as she paddled away. "Let's just say your probation period just got a little shorter," she called back.

Jack's teammates laughed. He scowled at them. He swam to the vaka, put his hands on the edge, and lifted himself. Big Suga grabbed the back of his shorts and heaved him aboard while Jimmy, Andrew and the others leaned in the opposite direction to maintain balance.

They churned back and forth across the lagoon for another hour before Andrew steered them back to the beach. They'd stayed in the deeper water near the reef. Jack tried to look again for Maina, but they were too far away, moving too fast, for him to make out any details.

Muscles aching, suffering from the early symptoms of dehydration, the crew stepped wobbly-legged out of the vaka, handed it over to the next team waiting to train. Sharing was common practice for the various paddling teams; there were never enough vakas on the island.

While the rest of his teammates slumped to the sand or stretched to loosen leg cramps, Jack scanned the launch area. Several children squealed with delight as they skipped through the waves. He asked one of them about Maina, and was directed to the driftwood log where he and Heather had encountered Chaka.

Jack stepped around the log. Maina sat cross-legged on the sand, idly braiding her hair. She looked up when Jack's shadow fell across her. "Hey," she said. "Good paddle?"

Jack sat on the log. "Andrew worked us hard."

"Heather said to tell you that she's at the OB." Maina nodded at the Ocean Beach Resort. "Said something about keys and shouting you lunch."

"What are you doing over here? I was worried when we came in and I couldn't find you."

"At first I came to see what Heather was so upset about," Maina said. "And later I just wanted to get away from those noisy kids."

"Did you see the woman who was here?"

"Yeah," Maina said. "For about two seconds. She seemed quite upset about something. Just packed up her things and ran off."

"Did she put her top on?"

"Is that what Heather was so upset about?" Maina shook her head. "I can't believe you people and your uptight attitudes. On some of the Outer Islands, the children run around naked all the time. They only put clothes on when the boys get hair and the girls grow titties."

"Heather doesn't want the locals to be upset," Jack said.

"They wouldn't be upset if the missionaries hadn't told them to react that way." Maina kicked at the sand with angry toes.

"I saw you on the beach," Jack said.

"You're supposed to be concentrating on your paddling, not watching me," Maina said. She finished with her hair, stood up, brushed sand off her shorts, and sat on the log beside Jack. Leaned against his arm.

"Who was that man talking to you?"

Maina pulled away slightly. Her eyebrows knitted. She face-talked: *What man?*

"Young guy. Short hair. Seemed to have something important to say."

Maina's eyebrows relaxed. "Oh, him," she said. "Just some tourist asking questions. Terry, Barry, Jerry. Something like that. Sounded like a Yank."

"Did he say anything about being a crewmember of that superyacht in Avatiu Harbor?"

"No."

Jack swallowed. "Did he have any tattoos?"

"Tattoos?" Maina wrinkled her nose. "What kind of tattoos?"

"Like an animal of some kind." Jack said. "Something small, done in red and black ink."

"Not that I saw," Maina said. "He just wanted to know if he could get pizza somewhere in town."

"That's it?" Jack pressed. "You're sure?"

"You're starting to weird me out here, Jack," Maina said. "Is there a point to this interrogation?"

Jack put on his serious face. "Just bear with me," he said. "Please. Now did this American fellow say anything else, anything that might have made you feel uncomfortable?"

"No." Maina looked down. "But he did tell me I was pretty," she said, stroking a braid. "He said he liked my hair."

"So he was hitting on you?"

"Get real," she said. "He was just being nice. Unlike certain pervs I know."

Jack nodded. He conceded the point. "Fine," he said. "Anything else?"

Maina cocked her head to one side and pursed her lips. "He asked if I was a dancer, because all the dancers he's seen at Island Nights have long hair like mine. I told him if he wanted to see real dancers, he should stop in at the auditorium and watch Maeva and Teina."

Jack said nothing, but Maina felt him tense up under her touch. His gaze shifted from her face as he looked back down the beach to where Heather, Big Suga and several other paddlers had commandeered a table on the Ocean Beach Resort balcony.

"Are you jealous?"

"What?" Her question ambushed him. "No," he said, "that's not it. *No.*"

"But something's bothering you or we'd be eating kai by now."

Jack rubbed the back of his neck. It felt gritty and hot under his fingers. He'd burned after all. "I'm just concerned," he said. "There are some nasty people on the island right now and I want you to be careful until they leave."

Maina gave Jack's arm an impish squeeze. "Don't worry about me, mate," she said. "I know all about handling bad men."

I know you do, Jack thought. *And that's the sad part.*

THIRTY-ONE

"Why does God give money to stupid people?"

Roger Henderson slid bottles of Lion Red across the bar to Jack and Captain Tai. Beads of water glistened invitingly on the bottles' chilled glass surface. "Present company excluded, of course," Roger added, winking at Jack.

"I hope so," said Jack, raising his bottle to Heather. She returned the salute. "According to a story published years ago in the esteemed *Silver Screen Weekly*, and quoting the usual unnamed sources, I was once in the possession of a shitload of greenbacks."

"'Once' being the operative word," said Heather.

Jack swallowed thirstily and smacked his lips. "Sadly, you are correct."

"Did I hear someone take my employer's name in vain?" Rev. Albert Smail dropped onto a barstool beside Heather. He pointed at her beer and nodded to Roger.

"Sorry about that, padre," Roger flashed his best teen idol smile. Best not to piss off the Lord or any of his earth-bound representatives. "But I wasn't expecting to see you on a weekend. What did you do, run away from home?"

"I told Apii that I needed to visit some of my parishioners," Albert said. "Now what were my most dedicated parishioners just talking about?"

"Jack was telling us about his meeting with that Larouche idiot stick."

Albert nodded. "Ah yes, the fortunate son with the massive boat. Pray tell, Jack, what mischief is our esteemed foreign visitor up to these days?"

Jack gave the down-and-dirty version of his previous day's conversation at Larouche's Black Rock villa.

"That is rather nasty, isn't it?" Albert said when Jack was finished. "It's as if God gathered up a collection of evil people, put them in a paper bag, gave it a good shake to piss them off, and then dumped the lot of them on our island."

Heather clapped. "That was very good."

Albert looked up from his beer in surprise. "It was, wasn't it? Where's my pen?" He patted at his jacket pockets. "I must write that down for tomorrow's sermon." He pointed deliberately at Jack. "And don't even think of stealing it. I know all about you plagiarizing writers."

Jack expressed feigned outrage as Roger produced a pen. Albert grabbed a cardboard coaster and began scribbling.

It was miserably hot outside. It was fry-the-bottom-of-your-feet hot outside. The air-con in the Rocket Bar clattered in a furious attempt to pump out cold air. The shades were drawn against the sun's glare. Most of the lights had been turned off. Anything to help cool the bar.

Jack swivelled on his stool, surveying the room. A quartet of tourists wandered onto the outdoor deck to nurse their drinks over the water. Two tables away, a middle-aged man sat by himself, reading. He held his book close, squinting at the pages in the low light. Two local women servers stood in a corner, heads bowed together, gossiping. Conserving energy for the evening's rush.

Jack turned back. He hadn't planned on spending the rest of the afternoon in the Rocket Bar. But after dropping Maina off at the auditorium to watch another rehearsal, he'd spotted Captain Tai in the bar's parking lot. The tour operator waved Jack over. Heather, who had followed him from the Ocean Beach Resort, joined them.

"So what were you saying about cash and a lack of brains?" Albert slid his empty bottle towards Roger and signaled for another.

Roger Henderson shrugged. "I realize I'm probably not the one who should be talking, considering how many mortgage payments I made for my drug dealers, but it just makes me sick when I see all these pseudo-celebrities—with their inflated egos and entourages of professional goons—acting like they're fucked in the head. Pardon my French, padre."

"I'm not following you," said Captain Tai, picking a speck of pawpaw out of his beard.

"My point is this," Roger said, "a lot of these people are goofs. Not a clue, not a brain. Completely devoid of humanity or even manners, most of them. If they didn't have money—if the media didn't encourage us to worship them for that very reason—you wouldn't look twice at them. And you certainly wouldn't want them as a mate."

"Money has never impressed me," said Heather. "Unless, of course, it's mine."

"I agree," said Jack. "But Roger has a valid point, as much as it pains me to admit it. Because these people can sing or run with a ball or spout lines on cue, the press tends to fawn all over them. And the more attention they attract, the longer the line grows of people who insist on throwing cash at them."

"And then what do they do?" Roger jumped back in. "Engage in drunken brawls in public. OD on drugs. Blow their brains out. What a waste."

"Of money?" asked Albert. "Or life?"

"Both," Jack said.

"Don't get us wrong," Roger said. "Me and Jack, we're not pointing fingers without looking in the mirror first, but when I hear of this… this…"

"League of Jackals," Jack filled in the blank.

"League of Arseholes is more like it. But when I see that ocean liner they're sailing around in and then hear about their twisted perversions, it makes me question the logic behind the distribution of wealth."

"This reminds me of another papa'a," said Captain Tai. The others turned to him.

Captain Tai took a long swallow. "This was before your time, Jack, and maybe even yours too, Heather," he said. "But the reverend and Roger will remember Lonnie Maxwell."

Albert Smail rolled his eyes. He face-talked: *I remember, and it's not a good memory.*

"Oh, that prick," Roger mumbled.

"Lonnie Maxwell?" Jack said. "Who was he?"

"In a word: pig," said Roger, "but I'll let the captain tell you the story."

"Thank you," Captain Tai said. "Lonnie Maxwell was a Kiwi property developer, or some such nonsense."

"Something like Mark Anderson."

"Exactly. Those two buggers even made some noise together about reviving the Endeavor. The point is, Maxwell was loaded. Millions, apparently. So much money, in fact, that he was able to basically buy himself entry into the country despite being on bail at home on some sort of drug charge."

"Is that legal?" Jack asked.

"Money talks, Jack," Roger said. "And in Maxwell's case, it was said 'free ticket.'"

"How long was he on the island?" Heather asked.

Captain Tai shook his head in disgust. "Long enough to mangle a rental car or two," he said. "Long enough to trash several hotel rooms. Long enough to make those whose pockets he'd lined regret the day they let the bastard out of the airport in the first place."

"So what happened to him?"

"He finally had no choice but to go back to New Zealand," said Albert. Seeing Jack's raised eyebrows, he continued. "Accommodation operators eventually refused to provide him with a room or a house, fearing that he would destroy it. He couldn't even rent a car to sleep in. So, with no place to stay, and it being very obvious that he was not welcome in what is universally considered the friendliest country in the world, the good Mr. Maxwell had no choice but to depart."

"I think they held a parade when his flight took off," said Roger. "Or, if they didn't, they bloody well should have."

"So where he is now?" Jack asked.

"If there is a God—and you already know my feelings on that one, Albert," said Roger, "then Maxwell lost all his money, his wife *and* his mistress left him, and his dick fell off. In no particular order."

"I'll drink to that," said Captain Tai. They all did.

"So your point about money and stupid people?" Jack winked.

Roger spread his arms wide. "I rest my case."

Jack laughed and went back to finishing his beer. He caught movement out of the corner of his eye. One of the servers had done the jandal shuffle out of the shadows. She now stood beside the reading man, taking his order.

"A Beach Burger," the man said. "But please hold the beetroot. And lots of ketchup, um, tomato sauce. And I'll have a large Coke, please."

The man had a North American accent. Nothing unusual about that. But something tugged at Jack. A memory synapse sparked, attempted to make a connection.

Jack took another look at the man. He'd gone back to his reading. Fortysomething, receding hairline, soft sliding to fat. The Beach Burgers were taking their toll. Glasses, which kept sliding down the bridge of his nose as he bent over his book. Pareu shirt, black shorts, sandals. A rather ordinary fellow. Thousands just like him arrived on the island every year. But judging by the color of his arms and legs, and particularly the domed extent of his forehead, the man had obviously been subjected to the tropic sun for some time.

Rubber slapped against bare heels as the server drifted over with the man's drink.

"Thanks," he said, and that one word finally pulled the memory trigger. *Gotcha!*

With his friends engaged in idle conversation, Jack slid off his stool and approached the man's table.

He stood behind him. The man sensed his presence and turned slightly.

"May I help you?" he asked, no sense of alarm in his voice. He had noticed

Jack at the bar and had already gauged that he wasn't the sort to bash strangers.

"I know you," Jack said, without moving.

"How so?"

"I'm not sure," Jack said. "But there's something about you I can't quite put my finger on."

"Have we met before?"

"No, I don't think so," Jack said. "But maybe if you did something for me, it might help jog my memory."

"Shoot," the man said.

Jack chuckled. "I'd like you to say, 'This is the Great and Wonderful Johno, and you're listening to Teen Scene, the island's favorite radio request show'."

The man put his book down and laughed heartily. Heather turned from the bar and crinkled her forehead. She face-talked: *You OK over there?*

Jack waved to her, walked around the table, stuck out his hand, and introduced himself. The man took Jack's hand and gave it a firm, friendly squeeze.

"Busted," he said. "And, just for the record, my real name is John Redden. I'm Canadian, in case you were wondering about the accent."

"I'm from British Columbia myself," Jack said. "So I'd already figured that part out. But if I hear you say 'aboot' instead of 'about,' I'm going to kick your arse all the way back to the Great White North."

"So you get that crap as well?"

"All the frigging time. A handful of bloody Newfie fishermen in some remote village in the armpit of the country say 'aboot' and we all get stereotyped." Jack pulled out a chair. "May I?"

"Please do." John smiled.

Jack cocked his head and studied the man across from him. "What?" asked John, grinning crookedly. "You're starting to make feel very self-conscious."

Jack gave his head a quick shake. "Sorry, mate," he said. "I was just thinking how I should have my hearing checked one of these days."

"Come again?"

"I must be growing a bit deaf in my old age," Jack said, "because I'm sure I heard the Great and Wonderful Johno tell the entire country that he's 19 years old and single. And yet I'm looking at a wedding ring and what surely must be the oldest teenager this side of Dick Clark."

John nodded. "See this?" he said, touching his chin. "It's a face made for radio. And it's why I'm a radio jock, because the job comes with a built-in anonymity factor. When I'm wearing the headphones and working the mike, I can be anybody, and any age, I want."

"Because no one can see you."

"Exactly."

The waitress slid a burger platter onto the table. John moved his book to an empty chair to make room. The woman hurried away as he began to peel back the burger's various layers.

"I knew it," he muttered, extracting a thick slice of beetroot. He plopped the juicy purple invader on the side of the plate. "It never fails."

"Comes with the territory," Jack laughed. John shrugged and took a bite. "Next time," Jack said, "ask for extra beetroot and you won't get any at all."

John smiled around a greasy mouthful.

"You're very popular with the teens on the island, no matter how old you really are."

John wiped sauce off his mouth. "At the risk of sounding immodest, I believe Teen Scene is the highest rated show on Radio Raro."

"And why is that, I wonder."

John gazed over Jack's shoulder for a long second. Laughter drifted through the room from the outdoor deck.

"Couple reasons, I suppose," he said. "Most of it is the music we play. It's all by request, so it's exactly what the kids—and a goodly amount of adults—want to hear. We're always sending out greetings and personal messages, so that tends to attract an audience as well. And my personal secret is to not talk for very long between songs. Say something funny or profound, or even outrageous, then get the music back on. No one wants to hear me prattle on like those wankers in North America or New Zealand."

"What about the co-hosts?"

"They're great," John said, lowering a fry into a small bowl of tomato sauce. "They certainly add an element of enthusiasm, although they can be a bit shy at times. Plus most of them can speak Cook Islands Maori, which comes in real handy when listeners ring from the Outer Islands."

Jack crossed his arms on the table and leaned on them. "But surely your co-hosts know the truth about you."

John shrugged. "Sure they do," he said. "But they play along with me because it's fun. It's like our little secret. That sort of thing."

Jack nodded. "So these co-hosts," he said, "where do they come from?"

John took another large bite of his burger, chewed enthusiastically for a minute, and swallowed.

"Lots of places," he said. "We have a roster and a waiting list because some of the kids literally wander in off the street asking to go on the radio with me. Others are friends of the current co-hosts. Some are sent to us from the colleges because they've shown an interest in a broadcasting career. Others belong to various social groups on the island."

"Really? Which ones?"

"Several of the more confident girls actually come from Rev. Moses Akimo's church group, Virgin Brides Saving Themselves for Christ." John took another bite. A slice of tomato, chewed in half, dropped to his plate.

"That's quite the mouthful."

John stopped in mid-chew. He looked distressed as he contemplated his half-eaten burger.

Jack held up his hands. "Sorry, mate," he said. "I was talking about Akimo's youth group."

John nodded, reached for the Coke.

"Look, I didn't mean to interrupt your meal," Jack said. "But I've just heard so much about this Great and Wonderful Johno bloke that this is almost like meeting an island celebrity."

John blushed. "Please," he said, "you're embarrassing me."

"So what are your plans for the future?" Jack asked. "Are you still going to be passing yourself off as a teen when you're 60?"

John spluttered into his glass. "Oh God, I hope not," he said, wiping Coke off the end of his nose. "Another year, maybe two, and then I'll probably go back to Canada. See if I can't use this broadcasting experience to find a job there."

"So this is a new thing for you, this radio host gig?"

"I've been very lucky," John said. "The station's owners were kind enough to teach me how to operate their equipment. It's been an invaluable learning experience and I'm eternally grateful."

"So do you have any candidates to take over Teen Scene for you?"

"A couple of local girls are really quite keen," John said. "They barely let me talk sometimes and it's my show. If I wasn't operating the control panel, they would probably kick me right out of the booth."

"I'm relieved to hear that the show will be left in capable hands."

"No worries about that," John said. "In fact, management has asked me to start grooming one of those girls as my replacement. Her name's Teina McCrystal; you might have heard her on the show with me. As a matter of fact, she's one of Rev. Akimo's Virgin Brides."

Teina. Another memory twitch. "Is she a dancer as well?"

"Yes." John nodded. "And quite a good one, from what I hear. She's been very busy lately practicing for the Constitution Celebration."

Jack flashed back: *Her name is Teina. She dances with Maeva. She's met someone and she thinks it might get serious. She hopes it gets serious.*

"So now you know all about me," John said, wadding his soiled napkin. "But other than your name, which I know I've heard somewhere before, I don't—"

Heather tugged on Jack's sleeve. "We're leaving," she said. "Sorry to interrupt, but Roger wants us to settle the bill. Something about not trusting foreigners."

Jack pushed his chair back and stood up. The men shook hands again. "Gotta go," Jack said.

"Take care. It was nice to meet you."

"Hey," Jack said, "you ever play anything from the last century?"

"Are you making a request?"

Jack laughed. "Yeah," he said, "I guess I am."

"What would you like to hear?"

"BTO," Jack said. "Or the Guess Who. Something Canadian. Something to remind me of my childhood."

"Celine Dion?"

Jack's eyes widened in horror. "We've known each other for—what? Five minutes?—and already you're insulting my intelligence?"

"Sorry, dude." Both men laughed.

"Jack!" Heather called from the bar. Jack dug out his wallet as he joined her. He pulled out several bills and placed his wallet on the bar while he sorted through the money. He hoped he had enough. "How much you ripping us off for today, Roger?"

"Don't star—"

The door to the bar crashed open. Jordan Baxter was little more than a black silhouette framed against the glare of the afternoon sun.

"Jack!" he bellowed into the room. "I can't see you in here, but I know that's your truck in the parking lot."

"Over here, Jordan," Jack said, quickly zipping his money into a pocket as he moved towards the door. There was a sense of urgency in Baxter's voice that was alarming. "What's wrong? What's happened?"

Baxter's head bobbed as his eyes struggled to adjust to the semi-darkness.

"Please tell me you have your camera with you."

"It's in the truck," Jack said. "I take it everywhere I go. What's the buzz?"

"The paper just got a call from the police," Baxter said breathlessly. "Karl Lamu has called a press conference at the National Auditorium."

"A press conference?" Heather joined the two men near the door. "Lamu never does things like that. Did he say what it was about?"

"I don't have time to explain," Baxter said. "But it's something about a young girl who's gone missing. Let's go!"

Jack sprinted out of the cool, dark interior of the Rocket Bar into the blast furnace of the parking lot, legs pumping, mind whirring. Already thinking about shutter speeds and fill flashes and camera angles. What he wasn't thinking about was his wallet, left sitting on the bar behind him.

THIRTY-TWO

Poto Rao yawned. He struggled to keep his eyes open. It had been a long busy night and he was exhausted.

Poto thought about the Russian doctor who was the cause of his fatigue. Natasha had an unexceptional face, but there was nothing ordinary about her lovemaking skills. Poto hadn't realized how stimulating a prostate exam could be.

He smiled at the passengers filing out of the Arrivals area of the Rarotonga Airport. In his mind he once again heard the snap of the rubber glove against Natasha's fist. His smile broadened.

Poto waved a handful of flyers. They were photocopied ads for his act.

"Come watch the legendary God of the Sea capture live fish with his bare hands," he recited in a bored monotone. "You won't believe your eyes. Rated the best show on the island. Includes a barbecue lunch. If you do only one thing on Rarotonga, you must see the world-famous Poto Rao in action."

He scanned the exit doors with bloodshot eyes. "God of the Sea," he mumbled. "Best show on the island. World-famous."

Because of the terminal's design, Poto Rao and his fellow small business operators, hawking everything from car rentals to backpacker lodgings to fishing expeditions, had a captive audience.

Every person who disembarked on Rarotonga had to use the same exit after passing through Customs. Returning locals and permanent residents would step through those doors to be greeted by family and friends, or to disappear into the car park. Poto and the others ignored these travelers; there was no money to be made from anyone who actually lived on the island.

It was the tourists they sought. And they were easy to distinguish. The stunned looks was always a dead giveaway, as was the herd mentality as they bumped around the reception area, blinded by the intensity of the tropical sun, brains thick from too many hours spent wedged into a narrow seat.

The heat dropped on them like a heavy, wet towel. They suddenly were wearing too many clothes. There were unfamiliar smells: the perfume of tropical flowers, the sweet stench of rotting vegetation. Sweaty bodies; vehicle exhaust. A foreign language or, at best, heavily-accented English.

Confusion was rife: *Where do we go? Are you sure the package deal included transfers? Yes, dear, our travel agent specifically assured us that they no longer eat people here. Do they eat dogs? Now that I'm not so sure about.*

This was the quarry that Poto Rao tracked with the finely honed skills of the natural promoter. He was in their faces before they could properly adjust to their new surroundings, shoving his colored sheets of paper into hands or pockets or purses or hand luggage. Talking, always talking. Doing the spiel. Doing the huckster thang. Smiling, always smiling.

Welcome to the Cook Islands, he would say. *Paradise on earth. The shuttle for the Ocean Beach Resort? Just follow this lovely lady in the orange pareu. And don't forget the God of the Sea show. Legendary. World-famous. Not to be missed.*

Poto kept one eye on potential customers, the other eye on his competition. He watched as they trolled. He measured their success rate: how many discarded brochures fluttered, unread, to the dirty lino floor, or were shoved into the nearest overflowing rubbish bin.

He also noted the young men who lounged nonchalantly along the walls, eyes hooded, casually feral. Waiting for aunty, maybe, or cousin. Returning from North America, perhaps, or Europe, bearing outrageous tales of civilization.

Poto knew these boys. Knew how appearances can deceive. Knew how quickly they could transform from slack-boned indifference into shiny-eyed barracudas with the razor teeth and single-mindedness of purpose to match. All it would take was the sight of a woman, preferably on her own, who seemed even slightly bewildered. Just a hint of hesitancy on a smooth, round, *white* face was chum to the predators who staked out the airport whenever an international flight arrived.

Forgive my boldness, dear lady, but I just wanted to tell you how manea, how beautiful, you are. Your boyfriend is a lucky man. Eh? No boyfriend? How can this be? It is a mortal sin that a goddess like you should be alone in paradise. Allow me to be your guide. Let me find you a place to stay. Show you the wonders of my country. Take you down to the starlit beach and give you some brown sugar.

When your return flight drags you home, I will summon genuine tears at the airport as you are torn from my arms. I will swear on my mother's grave never to forget you.

And then I will lean here against the airport wall until your replacement arrives on the next flight.

Poto hated the barracudas. Not because they took such obvious advantage of the naïve and the stupid. No, he hated them because, as he had grown older, Poto had been forced to work harder for his share of the naïve and the stupid. For his share of the fresh meat.

He caught a ripple. It started near the cafeteria entrance, worked its way around the open-air reception area. The barracudas shifted. They straightened. They became alert.

Incoming.

Poto scanned the crowd, frantically sidestepping an older couple who had stopped to ask for one of his handbills. He glanced again at the barracudas, and tried to determine the direction of their focus. He craned his neck; he went up on tiptoe. He forgot how tired he was. There was prey to be had. The game was on.

He saw her.

The herd of tourists miraculously parted. They shifted aside and, in the process, effectively obstructed the progress of the barracudas who had converged from their reconnaissance positions. The result: for one long, exquisite second, it was just Poto Rao and the woman. Face-to-face. The hunter and the victim.

She was older than the vaines who normally caused the barracudas to become this agitated. But there was no mistaking the attraction: blonde, willowy, stacked. She would look good in a coconut bra. She would look better out of a coconut bra.

There was an air of refinement about her, the unmistakable attitude of someone accustomed to life's finer things. It was there in her expensive clothes, in her expensive sunglasses, her expensive luggage.

Dr. Natasha was forgotten. His bruised prostate was forgotten. Last night was flushed from his mind in its entirety. Poto Rao was in love. For only the first time that day.

He could hear the commotion as the barracudas forced their way through the crowded terminal. They were closing in. Drawing a bead. He had to be quick.

He approached her. Mouth curving. Teeth baring. Charm exuding. Body language: open, friendly; no threats here. The faded tattoos on his arms mere objects of curiosity. Nothing to be alarmed about. He was the very picture of island hospitality.

He batted his eyes at her. He nodded his head at her. He felt himself getting hard. He opened his mouth to speak to the stunning creature.

"Don't even think about it, Coconut Face," the stunning creature snarled. She brushed past him with such hasty determination that Poto actually had to leap out of the way or risk his toes being crushed by the woman's luggage trolley.

His mouth hung open. His dick hung limp. What the hell had just happened?

The woman could see daylight ahead. She could see cars and minivans and small buses. She could see the end of a long trip.

Then she saw them. Picked up the approach of the barracudas on her feminine radar. Spotted their too-eager faces cutting through the eddy of the departing passengers. Saw wet tongues lick pink lips in quivering anticipation of the feast. Saw hungry saliva shimmering on ivory fangs.

She slowed. She hesitated. She did not—repeat: *did not*—need this shit. Not now. Not when she was on a mission. Not when it was so fucking hot.

She made a quick inventory of her options. The barracudas were closing in from nearly every direction. The only clear avenue of escape was behind her. She reversed. Barged into Poto and nearly knocked him to the floor.

Poto staggered. The woman staggered. They looked at each other. She: panicked, desperate. He: crushed, wounded.

She looked over her shoulder. The pack moved towards her, relentless. She rolled her eyes, took a deep breath, and made a decision.

She hooked her fingers in the chest hair sprouting from the top of Poto's singlet and put her nose right to his.

"Let's start with the easy stuff," she said. "You understand English?"
Poto nodded.
"Good boy," she said. "Next question: you got a vehicle?"
Poto nodded.
"You know where the Kia Orana Lodges are?"
Poto nodded.
"You know where a lady can get a cold drink?"
Poto nodded.
"Then get me the hell out of here."
Poto nodded. He was getting hard again. His prostate throbbed.

THIRTY-THREE

Jack stared at his laptop screen, chin cradled in his hands, elbows on the kitchen table. The cursor flashed forlornly in an empty grey expanse. Jack had been in this position for the better part of an hour. He had yet to produce a single word. Instead, he flashed back to Karl Lamu's press conference, replaying the event in his mind. Replaying the name of the missing girl: Teina McCrystal.

Jack had been talking about Teina with the Great and Wonderful Johno just before Jordan Baxter dragged him out of the Rocket Bar. How freaky was that?

A section of his brain registered that the TV had been turned off in the lounge.

A barefoot Maina padded into the kitchen. She gave his cheek a quick peck. Looked over his shoulder at the computer, pulled up a chair beside him.

"Stuck?"

Jack didn't answer. Maina touched his arm and gave it a gentle shake. Jack snapped back to the present.

"I'm sorry," he said. "Did you say something?"

"Where were you just then?"

Jack shook his head and rubbed a hand over his face. Maina ran a finger through the hair on his arm and traced a line between freckles. "You're still thinking about Teina, aren't you?"

Jack nodded. "I don't like it when bad things happen on the island," he said. "The population is so small that it tends to have a negative effect on everyone. I had to take photos of her parents sobbing today and I'm having a hard time shaking that image. Imagine the reaction when the paper runs that shot."

"They were pretty upset, weren't they?"

"Wouldn't you be if your daughter had just vanished into thin air?" Jack said. "I'm surprised that you're taking this all so calmly. Wasn't she one of your mates?"

"Not really," Maina said. "I just met her the other day when Maeva introduced us. It's Maeva you should be worried about. She's absolutely gutted about this."

"I know," Jack said.

Jack was on Jordan Baxter's bumper during the entire drive from the Rocket Bar to the National Auditorium. His guts sputtered as he tried to imagine why Karl Lamu had summoned the press. Heather was right: Lamu never did things like this. The Chief Inspector of Police had little use for the media. After yesterday's blowup in his office, he would have even less use for Jack Nolan.

Jack pulled into the auditorium's parking lot and braked beside Baxter. Several of the dancers, including Maeva, stood nearby in a tight, quaking mass, clutching onto to each other. Their faces were wet and swollen. They looked dazed, scared, incapable of comprehending the events unfolding around them.

Karl Lamu was positioned near the main doors. Around him swirled a vortex of people: several policemen and locals all insisting on speaking to him at the same time. Jack grabbed his camera bag and sprinted from his truck. He was changing lenses on the run when Maina materialized at his side. Her eyes were dry, but her features were pinched and pale. She looked anxious.

"Jesus," Jack puffed. "What's going on?"

"I'm not sure," Maina said, hurrying to keep up. "The rehearsal was nearly over when I saw this man and woman walk in. I didn't pay much attention to them because lots of people were arriving at that time. They sat down with the other parents to watch the dancers for a few minutes and then the next thing I knew, they were running through the stands and shouting out for Teina. They started asking if anyone had seen her. And then there was all this yelling and crying and I thought Maeva was going to faint."

Jack nodded as Jimmy Tauranga trotted past and disappeared into the building.

"Is this the same Teina who asked you to score condoms for her and her older boyfriend?"

"Yes."

"And this boyfriend, you said he was some kind of sailor, right?"

"I... I think so."

"Not good," Jack muttered as he activated his camera's flash. "Not good at all."

Jack and Maeva stopped in front of Karl Lamu. Jordan Baxter arrived seconds later, frantically popping a fresh tape into his recorder. Simon

Winthrope, a freelance travel writer who worked as a stringer for the *New Zealand Herald*, was already taking photos of a beleaguered Lamu. Jack decided to wait until Winthrope was out of film before stepping in. Judging by the frantic whirring of the Kiwi's motor drive, it wouldn't be long now.

Lamu chucked his chin at the three men and waved his arms to disperse the crowd. He removed his peaked cap and ran thick fingers through his hair. Winthrope machine-gunned the shutter release button again. Jack shook his head. Amateur.

He stepped past Winthrope, raised his camera, framed Lamu, and fired off a single shot. Checked it quickly on the LCD display screen. Good start, but nothing worth printing.

"What's happening here?" Baxter asked, shoving his recorder under the Chief Inspector's nose. Lamu cleared his throat and adjusted his hair again. Winthrope cursed. Out of film. Jack smiled and moved in closer. Maina stayed right with him. He could feel the pressure of her body. As Lamu talked, and Jack's blood chilled with each word, it felt good to have Maina that close. It was a comfort.

Teina McCrystal, Lamu told them, received permission to stay the night at the home of her friend and fellow dancer, Jewel Tangata. The two of them would spend the next morning helping each other with homework, then attend the Constitution Celebration practice at the National Auditorium. Teina's parents were to pick her up there, after the rehearsal.

That was how it was supposed to play out. What actually happened, according to Lamu, was that Teina never arrived at the Tangata house. Thinking that Teina had changed her mind about sleeping over, Jewel's first instinct had been to ring and give her a growling. But her brother was on the Internet and tying up the phone line, so she decided to wait until the next day's practice before confronting Teina.

When Teina didn't show up at the auditorium, Jewel assumed she was crook. It wasn't until the practice session was nearly finished, and Teina's parents showed up to give their daughter a ride home, that Jewel realized that something was wrong. After a hasty, tearful conversation between the parents and the best friend, the police were alerted.

"Are there any clues as to the young lady's disappearance?" Simon Winthrope asked Lamu. The freelancer had replaced his camera with a notepad.

Lamu cleared his throat again. "The investigation is still in its early stages," he said in his most authoritative tone. "What we do know is that Teina McCrystal was last seen Friday evening at approximately 19:10 hours. She left her family home wearing a light-blue hoodie, black board shorts and yellow jandals. She was carrying a small black sports bag that, supposedly, contained a change of clothes and the toiletries she'd need to spend the night at her friend's house."

"Are you suspecting foul play?" Winthrope asked. Both Jack and Baxter rolled their eyes at the man's tabloid sensibilities.

Lamu shook his head emphatically. "Absolutely not," he said. "We're treating this as a probable runaway. We do know that Teina had several recent arguments with her parents about being allowed to go on dates. We assume that she is hiding somewhere with a boy, probably a local. I'm asking the media to alert everyone on the island to immediately report any sightings of these two young people."

Winthrope's pen halted. He looked up, puzzled. "But if you think that this is two kids sneaking away for a shag, why do you want me to send the story to *The Herald*?"

"Because he's thinks they may be leaving the island," Jack piped up.

Lamu glared at him. Baxter turned in surprise. "What do you mean?"

"Hey, who's in charge of this police investigation?" Lamu snarled. "Jack Nolan or me?"

"Ask him if he's searched Andre Larouche's superyacht yet," Jack said, his eyes welded to Lamu's face.

Lamu didn't back down. "Ask *him* who the reporter is," Lamu said, "and who's here just to take the pictures. And while you're at it, ask him how much he's had to drink this fine afternoon."

"Who's Andre Larouche?" asked Winthrope, suddenly feeling ignored.

Jack felt Maina cringing against him. The confrontation was getting ugly and she didn't like it.

Lamu concentrated on Baxter and Winthrope. "Please include the police station's 24-hour contact number in your story. I've already had my office e-mail a photo of Teina to both of you. That's all for now."

Lamu spun on his heel and stomped away.

"But—" Winthrope waved his pen. No use. Lamu was gone.

Jordan Baxter scowled at Jack. "Mind telling me what that little show was all about."

"Lamu's not telling you the entire story," Jack said.

"Oh, really." Baxter was skeptical. "And what makes you think that?"

Jack glanced at Maina. "I have my sources," he said.

Baxter looked at Maina. She casually shifted to the other side of Jack, away from the reporter's prying eyes.

"And what does the coconut wireless have to say about all this?" Baxter asked, pulling Jack out of Winthrope's hearing range.

"Let's just say that this all fits in with rumors I've heard about Larouche and the real reason why he's here on the island."

"He's kidnaped Teina McCrystal to help him distribute textbooks to Vanuatu?"

"I'm serious here," Jack glared. "The only education Larouche and his crew have on their agenda is to teach us a lesson in degradation."

Baxter shook his head. "So far, mate, you're not making a whole lot of sense," he said. He turned his wrist and flashed his watch. "Dempster wants the guts of this story today, so I don't have a whole lot of time to be standing here listening to you talk like you're maki maki."

Jack waved his camera in an agitated gesture. "I'm just doing the maths here," he said. "I've talked to Larouche. First of all, he offered me a job writing porn, and then got into the juicy stuff."

"Such as?"

"He's part of an organization, a *league*," Jack said, "which is determined to convert Rarotonga into the new Cambodia, a sex destination for degenerates."

"I'm not sure what all this has to do with the missing girl," Baxter said, "but I'm still listening."

"Just bear with me for a minute," Jack said, closing his eyes. Concentrating. Trying to gather together all the wild ideas and theories and facts that were whirligiging around in his brain. *Make them line up. Make them make sense.*

"Larouche's yacht has a crew," he said, eyes still closed. "They're here for no other reason than to get laid. The books are nothing more than a ploy, a trick they use to gain entry to a country. Teina tells her mates that her new boyfriend is a sailor. That he's significantly older. She asks her friends to supply her with condoms. There's how the sex piece fits into the puzzle."

"You're pushing on that one," Baxter said. "Because people have been known to have sex without kidnaping their partners. But if this boyfriend is from the yacht, how does he hook up with Teina? Because I'm assuming that her parents would *not* be allowing their daughter to hang around the harbor propositioning sailors, nor would she be allowed into bars and nightclubs. A good girl like her goes to school and goes home. Anyplace else, she's under constant family scrutiny. Church, the market, the dairy down the road. Where do they meet?"

Jack flashed back once: The Great and Wonderful Johno: *Her name's Teina McCrystal; you might have heard her on the show with me. She's one of Rev. Akimo's Virgin Brides.*

Jack flashed back twice: Maina: *Akimo meets another man at the cafe and the two of them huddle together and make notes of some kind.*

Jack nodded to himself. "Teen Scene," he said, opening his eyes.

"What?"

Jack felt Maina pull away from him. He looked at her and saw something flash across her face, as quick and surprising as sheet lightning. It was a look that suggested that she too had thoughts that wouldn't lie still, that flapped and tangled like drying laundry in the wind.

"Teen Scene," Jack repeated. "Teina is on the radio; Johno says she's one of his best co-hosts. But how does she get on the radio? Because she belongs to Moses Akimo's youth group." The words were tumbling out of his mouth now. "And who has Akimo been chumming around with lately? Having coffee meetings with every day?"

"I'm waiting."

"Tor."

"And Tor is who?"

"Tor is one of Larouche's henchmen." Jack grinned. It all seemed so clear now. "One of his *sailors*. Just like Teina's boyfriend. Don't you see? Akimo and Tor must have worked together to arrange for the reverend's youth group to meet the crew from the yacht. That's how Teina and this fellow could get together without setting off any alarm bells with her parents."

Baxter didn't look convinced. "I don't know, Jack," he said, stuffing the tape recorder in a pocket and fishing out his car keys. "This theory of yours seems a bit farfetched, if you ask me. That's a *whole* lot of degrees of separation."

"You're saying that I'm full of shit?"

Baxter shook his head. "I'm saying wait a day or so, and then we'll see two hungry, dirty kids wander out of the jungle with big, stupid grins on their faces. And we'll all shake our heads at how this new generation is going straight to hell, and marvel at all the effort they went to just to lose their virginity. They'll both get a good bashing and, a week later, it will all be forgotten."

"You're making the same mistake Lamu did," Jack said.

Baxter clapped Jack on the shoulder. "Tell you what, mate," Baxter laughed. "You go home and use that wild imagination of yours to write another bestseller. As for me," he stepped away, "I'm going back to the office to listen to this tape, and write no more than three paragraphs about this false alarm. And then I'll wait for Lamu to ring saying that Teina McCrystal has just been located in someone's shed with her knickers around her ankles and wondering why everyone makes such a great fuss about sex when it's over so quickly."

THIRTY-FOUR

Jack clicked the mouse. Hit Start. Hit Shut Down. Hit OK. Closed the laptop cover and pushed the machine aside.

He turned from Maina, gazed out the window beside the table. Saw that the streetlight outside the dairy was glowing into life. Twilight blinked—a tenuous, aubergine wedge between the spheres of day and night—and was gone. Darkness dropped.

Jack had followed Jordan Baxter back to *The Tribune* office, wordlessly handed his camera to Mona Vaevae to download, then waited in his truck with Maina. They sat in silent contemplation, staring straight ahead through the windscreen.

Mona brought the camera out and handed it through the driver's-side window.

She looked at Jack. She leaned past, looked at Maina. "You OK, mate?" she asked.

"Never better," Jack said.

Mona shuffled her feet beside the truck and glanced at Jack again.

"Listen, bro," she said. "Sorry to keep bringing this up, but you really do need to do something about that skylight filter. I'm spending way too much time PhotoShopping that scratch out of all of your pictures."

"Sorry," Jack said, turning the ignition key. "I'll stop in at Pacific Photos first chance I get."

He put the Toyota into gear, but kept the clutch engaged as he watched Mona return to the production office. The engine idled while Jack deliberated. Maina turned to him, confused by his hesitation.

"Jack?"

He turned the truck off and hopped out. "I'll be right back," he said.

Jordan Baxter had his earphones in. He was nodding in rhythm with his typing as he transcribed his interview with Karl Lamu. He saw Jack approaching, pressed Pause, and removed the earphones.

"Hey, Jack," he said. "Loved your shots of Lamu. Especially the one where his mouth's open and his eyes are closed. Makes him look exactly like the moron that he is."

Jack grabbed a chair and pulled it up tight to Baxter's desk. "Are you still seeing Chaka Tane?"

Baxter frowned at Jack's bluntness. "If you're asking if we're still dating, then the answer is yes," he said. "If you're asking if we're sleep—"

"How well do you know her?"

"What's with the questions, Jack?"

"How well do you know her?"

"Jesus already." Baxter hitched his chair back in reaction to Jack's intensity. "We haven't exactly gotten around to comparing favorite footy players yet, but other—"

"I'm almost certain that she has a connection to Andre Larouche, the yachtie I was telling you about at the auditorium."

"I know."

"You know?"

"Easy, mate." Baxter tried to soften Jack's blowtorch glare with a smile. It didn't work. "Chaka told me that Larouche's organization finances a lot of the filming that she does. They're partners in a company that's won a number of awards for short subjects. That's one of the reasons why she's here now, to pitch her next project to him."

"So they're just business associates? That's it?"

"Yeah," Baxter said, his tone suddenly frosty. "Why? What else would they be?"

"Have you seen her tattoo?"

Baxter laughed. "I've had sex with the woman, for Christ's sake," he said. "I've seen everything."

"Did you know that Larouche has a matching tattoo?"

"This conversation is going somewhere, right?" Baxter said. He pointed to the tape recorder. "Because I do have work to do."

Jack pressed on. "Aren't you the least bit curious as to why your girlfriend and the man who is determined to wreak havoc on this island just happen to have the same tattoo?"

Baxter picked up the earphones and pushed in the left one. "Chaka says the jackal image is the logo of the film company they've formed together. All the members of her film crew have them. It's supposed to be symbolic of how dedicated they are to producing quality product."

"And you believe her?"

Baxter stopped fiddling with the earphones. He stared at Jack. Saw the white circles around his eyes, the disheveled hair, the beads of sweat on his upper lip. "You keep this up, Jack," he said, "and I might start believing that Lamu was right about your drinking problem."

"You need to ask her again about the tattoo."

Baxter stared at the ceiling. Counted to three. Counted to five. "Why?" he finally said.

"Because that's the second explanation I've heard for someone having one," Jack said. "Every person I talk to has a different story about their significance."

"Tell you what, mate," Baxter said. "The next time you see Chaka— preferably with her clothes on—*you* ask about it. Then maybe you can stop with the fairytales about the Big Bad Jackal and return to the real world where the rest of us live."

Jack swiveled away from the kitchen window, then back to Maina. "Whose turn is it to make tea?"

Maina shrugged. "I'm still crook, so I'm not that hungry," she said. "But good luck finding something to eat in this place."

"Time to do the shopping?"

"I reckon."

Jack stood up. "In that case, what say I shout us takeaways from the Sunset? Unless, of course, you're too crook for some of Moe's fried wonders."

Maina nodded enthusiastically. "Maybe I could squeeze down a bite or two," she said. "You drive into town, I'll set the table and make us something to drink. I'm sure we have at least one or two lemons around here somewhere."

"Choice." Jack patted his pockets and frowned. He disappeared into his bedroom for a moment. When he emerged, the frown had deepened.

"You haven't seen my wallet anywhere, have you?" he asked, taking a quick visual sweep of the lounge as he passed through it.

Maina, reaching for plates in the cupboard, looked over her shoulder at the telephone stand. "Don't see it in here," she said. "Did you leave it in the truck?"

"I'll check."

Maina heard doors open and shut. Jack was back in the house. "Shit," was all he said.

"That's weird." Maina squatted to peer under the kitchen table. "I hope you didn't have much money in it."

"Money, bank card, credit cards, driver's licence," Jack muttered. "Pretty well the entire lot. I'm such an idiot."

Maina stood in the centre of the kitchen, hands on hips, head slowly turning, scanning. "No one could have stolen it, because I know you always keep your pockets zipped," she said. "And that means that it didn't just fall out either. You must have left it at the last place you used it."

Jack backtracked. Where had he been today? He flashed back: Jordan Baxter's excited entrance. The Rocket Bar. Settling his bar tab.

"Maina," he said, grabbing her shoulders and planting a kiss in middle of her forehead, "have I told you what a genius you are?"

"Not nearly enough," she said.

Jack bounded up the stairs to the front entrance of the Rocket Bar. Traffic had been scarce and so he'd made good time into town. Those people he had seen on the road seemed in a hurry to reach their destination. They wore looks of apprehension, of fright even. Obviously word of Teina's disappearance was spreading quickly.

The bar's parking lot was nearly deserted. Not completely unusual for this early in the evening, but Jack wondered how much business Roger would actually do before he had to close at midnight out of respect for the Sabbath.

Jack recognized Poto Rao's Jeep parked next to the building. There was no mistaking it, not with 'God of the Sea' painted in large fluorescent letters on both panels.

Roger, seeing Jack enter, fished under the counter and slapped down something brown and ragged. Jack smiled broadly and scooped up his wallet.

"Thank Christ," he said in obvious relief.

"That thing go through Operation Desert Storm?" Roger asked.

"It is pretty beat up, isn't it?" Jack laughed, examining his wallet's mangled exterior.

"Might be time to break down and buy a new one, mate."

"Nah," Jack said. "This old bugger's a keepsake. My agent gave it to me. Said it was a gift, then told me to look inside."

"What'd you find?"

"My first royalty payment for the book," Jack said. "Now every time I open my wallet, I remember how thrilled I was that day. It must be how a father feels when his child is born."

"Only you can throw your wallet away when you don't want it anymore," Roger said. "Kids are a bit harder to get rid of."

"So I'm told," Jack said. He dropped the wallet into a pocket of his board shorts and zipped the pocket closed.

"Aren't you going to check that everything's still there?" Roger asked him.

"No worries, bro," Jack said, sliding onto a stool. "I trust you. Besides, I already know that you've taken out what I owe you. I just hope you left me enough to buy tea."

"Unless you're shouting for the entire Wednesday night gang, I'm guessing I left you enough for kai *and* a beer."

"That sounds awful tempting, but I've got to get home." Jack patted at the wallet in his pocket. "Thanks again for tucking this beast away for me. I almost had a panic attack when I couldn't find it."

"Lucky for you that it was me who found it," Roger said. "Sometimes I think that the number of people you can trust grows smaller with each passing day."

"I hope you're wrong," Jack said. "That would completely destroy whatever faith I still have in humanity."

Roger nodded at the tables behind Jack. "Well, you're not going to find much in the way of humanity in here tonight, I'm afraid. This missing girl thing has certainly sent a ripple through the island. It's spooked all my customers into staying home and locking their doors for the first time in their lives."

"I feel sorry for Teina's parents," Jack said. "They were bordering on hysterical when I saw them at the National Auditorium."

"I can only imagine what they're going through right now." Roger shook his head sadly. "I know I'd be climbing the walls if this happened to my Lindsay. Not knowing where your daughter is, whether she's still alive or not. What kind of freak torments innocent people like that?"

Jack swivelled on his stool. "Speaking of freaks, Poto Rao's truck is parked outside, but I'm not seeing the legend in here anywhere."

Roger leaned out from the bar and peered around at the few tables that were occupied. "That's strange," he said, frowning. "He was just here. And he had a sweet-looking blonde with him who seemed quite happy to throw back all the shooters he was willing to shout."

"I can't believe that Poto's still pulling that shit," Jack said. "He's one day older than God, for chrissakes, and the bastard's still scoring."

"Apparently he looks better the more you drink," Roger laughed.

Jack hopped off the stool. "What I don't understand is why his wrinkled old dick hasn't fallen off."

Roger shrugged. "Some guys have all the luck," he said. "I just hope I'm walking when I'm his age, never mind getting wood."

Jack tapped the bar with his knuckles. "Gotta go," he said. "Promised Maina I'd bring her home a Sunset Special."

Roger winked. "Sounds good to me. Later, dude."

Jack stood at the top of the staircase for a minute, facing the sea. The water was ink, but he could make out whitecaps as the waves raced towards shore. The tide was out and Jack could smell the salty tang of seaweed starting to dry among the rocks. A lighted buoy bobbed just offshore, marking a boundary of the narrow shipping channel that cut through the coral reef.

He stopped when he reached the parking lot and dug out his keys. A bus drove past. Its interior lights were on and Jack saw that it was nearly empty. He glanced again at the garish paint job adorning Poto's Jeep, then stepped past it towards his own truck.

Stopped. *What was that?*

Jack cocked his head. Looked around. He'd heard something. A muffled scream? A cry for help? Was it Teina McCrystal? Was she in trouble?

He turned back to the Rocket Bar. Glanced up at the first floor. There were lights on in the Hendersons' living quarters and Jack could detect movement behind the closed curtains. Gracie and Lindsay. One floor above them, someone had dropped a coin into the bar's jukebox. Bruce Springsteen wailed about the road to the Promised Land.

Was it the music that had caught his ear? No. He was sure that it was a female's voice that he'd heard.

Again! Louder this time. More of a high-pitched moan. Accompanied by something else. Another sound. Lower in octave. Almost bestial.

Jack walked around to the side of the building. The exterior wall was clad in treated plywood sheets stretching down the beach to a piling that supported one end of the bar's outdoor deck. The seaward side had been left open, to allow the tide to reach its high-water mark unimpeded. But the resulting gap gave access to mischief-makers as well.

The noises were louder now, more distinct. The female moaning and yipping. The male making guttural sounds, muffled and indistinct. A wave of prickly heat flushed through Jack's body. He recognized the sound. Realized that what he was hearing was not an attack in progress, not a victim begging for rescue.

It was sex.

Jack looked over his shoulder. Several tourists had just arrived and were making their way towards the bar's stairs. They were speculating about the menu's catch of the day. One of the men grumbled about not being able to order his favorite beer in this uncivilized backwater. In a minute, they'd be demanding all of Roger's attention. Jack looked up at the lights of the apartment and recalled Roger complaining about how copulating couples under his building disturbed his family with their noisy antics.

He remembered the immense relief he'd felt at being handed his missing wallet. Here was the perfect opportunity to return the favor.

Jack would flush out the lovers himself.

The sand was still wet from the tide and Jack found the going slow as he made his way towards the ocean end of the building. He sank several centimetres with each step, and was forced to lift his feet high in an exaggerated stride.

The noise from the lovemaking faded as Jack moved down the beach toward the water, the moans and grunts muffled by the splash of breaking waves, the soft metallic clanging of the buoy as it rose and dipped at its mooring.

Jack reached the end of the wall and put his back against the piling. Took a deep breath, leaned around the piling and squinted into the space under the building. His eyes adjusted, pupils flaring to maximum aperture. He blinked, adjusted aperture.

Cracks in the ceiling allowed thin beams of light to leak down from the rooms above. The buoy's flashing beacon also provided a degree of illumination. As a result, Jack wasn't facing the total darkness he had expected.

Guided by the moaning and grunting, now building in volume and frequency into a demented tempo, he crept ahead, moving sideways: a human crab. Concrete pillars, used to support the structure above him, served as both guides and concealment.

Movement near the back of the enclosure. Jack stopped behind the final support. Craned his neck around the column's rough surface, and poked his head out only far enough to focus on the action.

The man was facing away from Jack, but there was no mistaking his identity; the electric yellow lettering on the man's dark singlet was a dead giveaway. The God of the Sea's shorts were lowered to his knees and his bare, brown arse dimpled with every thrust he made into his partner.

A narrow shaft of light fell across the woman's head as it lay tucked into Poto Rao's shoulder. Her hair was blonde. Obviously the woman from the Rocket Bar. Settling the bill for the shooters she'd consumed.

Poto had her pinned against the wall, but there was a blanket between her back and the rough surface. That way she'd still have some skin remaining when they were finished. *How very thoughtful,* Jack smirked. The woman's legs were locked around Poto's hips. Her knickers dangled from one ankle, trembling like a wispy pennant.

Poto oinked with every lunging motion. His partner squealed a corresponding refrain. Jack's face grew hot. He didn't want to watch, and derived no thrill by playing the voyeur. It was embarrassment that had him as paralyzed as if the soles of his sandals had been welded to the sand.

An irritated pounding came from above; Gracie had obviously had enough of the amorous clamor beneath her feet. The noise didn't faze Poto or the woman—their lovemaking continued unabated—but it served to startle Jack out of his state of immobility. He drew a deep breath of determination and stepped out from behind the pillar. Advanced with a resolute stride that belied the nervous chattering of his teeth.

What exactly was he going to say? *Excuse me, but you know this, uh, activity that you're engaged in? Well, could I ask you to take it someplace else?* Oh, yeah, that would really grab their attention.

Poto gasped for air as the woman's fingers raked his back, urging him on. His thrusting became harder, faster, more intense. The short strokes. The angry strokes. The power strokes. Jack had to hurry.

The woman cried out again and threw her head back. Upper teeth bit into lower lip as the intensity of her pleasure magnified. Arms clutched Poto's shoulders, hips arched to take him deeper. Eyes squeezed shut. Her knickers, knocked loose in the fury, fluttered to the sand, an insignificant mound of black lace and elastic and silk.

The narrow beam of light from above fell across the woman's face. Jack froze again.

She opened her eyes. They glowed with the high-octane intensity of her impending orgasm. She saw him standing in front of her. Smiled. White incisors in the purple murk.

"Hello, Jack," she gasped.

"Hello, Nile," he said.

THIRTY-FIVE

Maina poured herself a glass of fresh lemonade and carried it into the lounge. She dug the remote control out from under the chair cushions and turned on the TV.

The local news was just starting. Teina McCrystal's disappearance was the lead story. Maina sipped at her drink as she watched. Her stomach growled. *Easy, girl,* she thought, glancing at the digital clock on the video deck, *Jack will be home soon.* She could almost taste the Sunset Special.

Jack stood silently as he watched Nile having sex with Poto Rao. Shocked by this unexpected encounter with his ex, Jack felt curiously detached, as if he was merely a neutral, clinical observer to the mating habits of humans. There was nothing erotic about the performance he was witnessing. He experienced neither stimulation nor arousal. It was all physics, really: heat and friction. A fusion of hormones and opportunity and hydraulics: raw, ignoble, noisy, and ultimately quite messy.

It was muggy in the close quarters under the bar and, in the faint light, Jack could pick out tiny streaks of perspiration working their way across the planes and contours of Nile's face.

He noted how her eyes, once fixed on him, now rolled back in their sockets. He watched Poto flex his knees, then curl his toes to gain better purchase in the sand. So he could grind harder. Grind *deeper.*

The fog in Jack's head began to lift, and was replaced by a stomach-churning disgust. His knees no longer felt as if they were constructed of cartilage and ligament and bone and skin. Instead, they were made of air. He staggered, and was sure that his legs would give out completely and drop him to the sand.

He'd been aware, before venturing under the deck, that he stood a good chance of happening upon someone he knew from the island. But he was gutted to stumble across Nile Ramsay. He had long since resigned himself to never seeing her again. Not in California. Surely never in the Cook Islands. And definitely not being impaled by the wrinkled idiot stick of Poto Rao.

Jack felt sick to his heart. Something burned in his chest just at the sight of Nile. That he had found her in such a crudely compromising position only heightened the anguish. She'd spent his money at a reckless pace, then abandoned him at the first sign of trouble. Had only been willing to stand by her man just as long as she was standing on his wallet. When he truly needed her support, when he was at his most vulnerable, she had simply abandoned him.

But right now, at this instant, in the sticky-hot confines under the Rocket Bar, none of that sordid history seemed to matter. The fact remained that she'd been his first love and first loves leave indelible traces. Beneath your fingernails. On your skin. In your head. *In your heart.*

It wasn't fair. She didn't deserve to be disturbing his thoughts. Not after five years. She didn't deserve his sympathy. Not after the way she'd deserted him.

But neither did she deserve to be shagged by the likes of Poto Rao.

Jack grabbed at Poto's arm. The God of the Sea grunted, annoyed, and tried to shrug Jack off. Jack's fingers tightened.

"Wait your turn, eh," Poto panted. "I'm nearly finished with the bitch. Then you can have her."

Jack ground his teeth and lowered his head. A scarlet haze obscured his vision. His limbs vibrated with anger.

He reacted.

Took hold of Nile's ankles, unlocked them with a single twist. Grabbed Poto by the shoulders. Tugged him backwards with such force that Poto was spun completely around. Off-balance, the God of the Sea sprawled facedown, his erection gouging a narrow furrow in the sand. He wasn't wearing protection.

Poto howled in pain. He clutched at his genitals, rocked from side to side.

Jack gasped raggedly, jaws clenched, eyes bulging. Never a violent man by nature, he was now uncharacteristically consumed by the blood rage of the berserker. He kicked Poto hard in the ribs. And again. Poto bucked. He whimpered. He tried to crawl away, shorts still around his knees.

Jack planted his sandal in the man's arse. The force of the impact lifted Poto into the air. He scrambled to his feet. Clutching his shorts, he staggered to the end of the building and skittered out of sight around the corner. Seconds later, Jack heard his truck start. Tire rubber burned for the entire length of the Rocket Bar's parking lot.

Jack turned to Nile. Suddenly freed from the pinning pressure of Poto's body, she had momentarily slumped down against the back wall. Now upright, she shook sand out of her knickers and casually pulled them on.

"You OK?" he asked.

"Oh, I'm just peachy," she said. "That was consensual, by the way." She nodded after Poto. "So you could have saved your white knight routine for a real damsel in distress. I doubt there's enough left of my honor or dignity to be worth rescuing anyway."

Jack put his hands on his hips and waited for his lungs to relax. "You're welcome," he gasped.

Nile gently touched the back of his head with her fingers. "Since when did you turn into a hero?" she asked. "I thought you only wrote about all that noble shit."

"I've been looking for the opportunity to bash that bugger for years now," Jack said. "You just provided the distraction I needed."

Nile snatched her fingers away. "Whatever," she said. "But I gotta admit that I'm impressed with your new, improved balls. Maybe this place has been good for you after all. Now let's get the hell out of here."

Jack followed her. "Where we going?"

"Back up to the bar," she called over her shoulder. "If you're going to ruin a perfectly good orgasm like that, the least you can do is buy a girl a drink."

Maina jerked awake in the chair. She stared bleary-eyed at the TV. *Shortland Street* was on; it was after 8. Jack had been gone for more than an hour. Sunset Takeaways was popular with the locals, but it should never take this long to be served. Had something happened to him? Had Jordan Baxter flagged him down for another assignment? Was he dead in a ditch somewhere?

Maina wandered into the kitchen and turned on a light. The sudden brightness startled a moko above the sink. It scuttled under the wall clock.

Jack often joked about how he'd have to leave the clock behind if he ever moved out, because he wouldn't have the heart to take the lizard's home. That was Jack for you: he could be a misery and a grouch at times, but under all that growling there was a soft, caring side. This was the Jack that Maina felt drawn to by a powerful force she could never express verbally. Call it instinct or intuition, but she knew Jack Nolan was a good man, and the presence of good men had been a rare occurrence in Maina's short life.

She had a sudden urge to hug Jack. Right after she strangled him for taking so long to fetch her meal.

Roger Henderson was transporting eight open bottles of Lion Red between his fingers when Jack and Nile walked into the Rocket Bar. Startled by their appearance together, Roger nearly dropped the entire load on the table. Only some frenzied juggling and the eager hands of helpful customers managed to avert a disaster.

Jack glanced over at the sound of clinking glass. Roger's cocked eyebrow nearly reached his hairline. He face-talked: *What the hell?*

Jack cut his eyes. He gave his head a quick shake. He face-talked: *Don't ask.*

Roger collected the money for the beer. He barely looked at the notes and gold coins being pushed into his hand as he tracked Jack and the woman as they claimed a corner table well away from the cluster of tourists and locals near the dance floor.

Roger returned to the bar and shoved the money into the cash register. His eyes remained locked on the far corner.

"Are Saturdays now self-serve?" Captain Tai was perched on a stool to Roger's left.

"Eh?"

"I'm fair parched and you've left me sitting here for a good five minutes when I could be helping you empty the cooler instead."

Roger cracked a beer, set it on a coaster.

Captain Tai took a long, hard pull at the bottle and wiped foam out of his mustache with the back of his hand. "That's better," he announced. "Eh! What's hooked into you tonight, mate?"

"Jack Nolan's at a table over your left shoulder."

"So what?" Captain Tai said, running his fingers through his beard to dislodge assorted food scraps. "Jack practically lives here. We all do, come to think of it."

"But he's got someone with him," said Roger. "A woman."

"Eh?" Captain Tai spun on his stool, peering past the tables in front of him. Found Jack and his companion. Whistled between his teeth.

"You seen her before?" asked Roger.

"Can't say I have," said Captain Tai. "And, believe me, I'd remember."

"She was in here earlier with Poto Rao," said Roger. "She left with the old bastard and the next thing I know, she's waltzing through the door with Jack in tow."

Captain Tai made a face. "I know Jack isn't getting much these days, but Poto's sloppy seconds? That's just plain nasty."

Roger blanched. "Jesus," he muttered. "I think I'm going to spew."

"Suck it back, bro," said Captain Tai. "Here he comes."

Jack saw the eager looks on his friends' faces. He held up his hands, shook his head.

"It's a long story," he said as he sat down beside Captain Tai and asked Roger for two drinks.

"You do realize," Roger said as he mixed, "that your new lady friend was in earlier with the God of the Sea himself, right?"

Jack sighed, dropped his head in his hands. "I know," he said. "I found them. *Together*."

"Yeah?"

"And let's just say that Poto Rao will be waking up tomorrow with an acute case of blue balls."

"Ouch." Roger winked. "Good on ya, mate." He dropped plastic straws and paper umbrellas into the full glasses and placed them on the bar.

Jack nudged Captain Tai in the ribs. "Look, I'll catch up with you two later, OK?"

"That's it?" Roger said. "You're just going to leave us hanging?"

Jack hesitated, then nodded at the faded photo of Roger and the Rockets over the bar. "Ghosts from the past, Roger, ghosts from the past. You should never lose hope because they tend to turn up when you least expect it."

Captain Tai belched. "So you're not going to tell us what's happening."

Jack glanced over his shoulder at Nile. She waved. "*I* don't even know what's happening," he said.

Jack placed the glasses on the table. Nile grabbed for hers and sucked thirstily on the straw.

"Clandestine sex can really dry a person out," Jack said.

Nile ignored him. "This really is a lovely island," she said. "I'm starting to understand why you've hidden yourself away here."

Jack laughed dryly. "Other than the inside of this bar and Poto Rao's dick, how much of Rarotonga have you actually seen since you arrived?"

Nile gave him a quick glare, then bent her head over her drink. Jack watched her attack the colorful liquid. The way her red lips wrapped around the straw's plastic tip. The way her throat worked as she swallowed without pausing to breathe. The way her cheeks tightened for better suction.

Jack's drink sat untouched. Something fluttered in his stomach. Something that didn't need alcohol. Something that didn't need any more juicing.

Nile disengaged. Sat back. Arched her back. Stuck her chest out. Buttons strained. Heads turned.

"My face is up here," she said.

It was an old trick, but he'd fallen for it anyway. It was her *Look at my tits* routine. Nile employed it whenever she needed to create a diversion. Whenever she needed to change the direction of a conversation. Whenever she felt the urge to mess with Jack's head. It still worked.

Except Jack had purposely dropped his gaze. Because every time he looked at her face he remembered how the sweat had trickled across her brow, how her eyes widened, how her mouth pursed.

How Poto Rao was fucking her.

He siphoned off a small burst of anger. It gave him courage. It made him resolute. It broke Nile's spell.

"Let's cut to the chase," he said. "What are you doing here?"

She opened her mouth to speak. He cut her off.

"We both know how you hate to leave Hollywood because you might miss a party," he said. "So it's obvious that something more important than the lagoon cruise or a real tan has brought you here. I just can't for the life of me imagine what that could be."

Nile dug in her purse, pulled out a small slip of paper, and handed it to Jack. He read the name she had written there: Shel Freeburg.

Jack shrugged: "Is this someone I'm supposed to know?" He dropped the paper to the table.

"He's a writer with *Silver Screen Weekly*," Nile said. "He was trying to find you for some assignment he was working on."

"Eh?" Confusion replaced hostility. "Why would that rag want anything to do with me? As far as the movie industry is concerned, it's been an eternity since I was a legitimate player."

"He said something about a retrospective piece," Nile said.

"Ah." Jack smiled. "I get it now. Since I'm not exactly listed in the telephone book, he rings up the ex hoping that she's still in contact."

Nile nodded. "He asked if I had your number in the Cook Islands. I told him it was news to me that you were even in the Cooks. That I hadn't seen you in years. Our conversation ended very quickly after that."

"I bet it did." Jack smiled thinly. "That explains how you knew where to find me. But it doesn't explain why you bothered to find me."

"I thought you might need some inspiration," Nile said, tilting her head coyly, blinking very slowly.

It hit Jack like a coconut between the eyes. Seeing Nile again had ignited old emotions, had stirred up a whirlwind of questions. But now that the impact of her arrival was wearing off, the reason for her intrusion into his life was suddenly very clear. He shook his head in disbelief, sat back, and smiled to himself.

"What's so funny?" she asked, slurping up the last of the ice shavings from the bottom of her glass. "Aren't you glad to see me?"

"You need money," Jack said, and this time it was Nile's turn to be jolted.

"Excuse me?"

"The reason you're here," Jack said. "It's because you're hoping that I've started to write again. That I might have the next bestseller tucked under my hammock just waiting for a publisher to come knocking with a big fat contract."

Nile started to protest. Saw the look on Jack's face. Shut her mouth.

"Guilty," she finally said. She played with her straw. She avoided Jack's eyes.

"You were awarded more than half of my money." Jack looked past Nile, caught Roger's eye behind the bar. Roger hoisted a beer bottle. Jack nodded, held up two fingers. "You had it made."

"That was then, Jack." Nile traced abstract patterns on the table top with a painted fingernail.

"I'm not following you, Nile," Jack said, bobbing his head in a futile effort to meet her eyes. "I gave you everything your lawyer asked for. What happened to it?"

"It's all gone."

"What?"

Roger brought over two bottles of Cook's Lager and placed them on the table. He could feel the tension between Jack and Nile, and decided to bite his tongue. Nile grabbed her beer, took a huge gulp, and drained nearly half the bottle in one go. She still drinks like a man, Jack noted.

Flickers of defiance swirled in her eyes when she finally screwed up the courage to look Jack in the face.

"What do you want me to say?" Her voice was whiny. Jack hated the sound of it.

"You can start by telling me what happened to the money."

"It just went, Jack, OK?" she said. "For starters, do you have any idea how expensive rehab is these days? Those bastards rob you blind. Plus, I had to have my breast implants removed because somebody told me they could give me cancer or something. And then there was the plastic surgery. Just a nip here, a tuck there. Nothing much, really, but it all adds up."

"OK," Jack interjected. "I get the picture. Now what about the house?"

"Gone."

"The car?"

"Long gone," she sighed. "I found out the hard way that when you're desperate for cash, no one offers you market value. I got hosed, plain and simple. Several times, in fact."

"So how did you afford the ticket to get here?"

"Plastic is a girl's best friend." Nile grinned.

"Jesus," Jack muttered. "But what about Ray Chimera? Porter told me that the two of you were engaged at one time. Or couldn't he afford to keep you in the style that you'd grown accustomed to?"

"I guess you don't get much news here on Gilligan's Island." Nile took another drink. "Ray's dead, Jack."

Jack felt a lurch in his chest. He didn't think anything could ever hurt that tough little bastard. He wondered which vice had finally done him in. Booze? Drugs? Jealous husband? Knowing Ray Chimera, it was probably all three. Just the way he would have wanted it.

"Ray's dead?"

"Oh yeah." Nile casually pretended to read the label on the beer bottle. "His last three movies bombed."

"You mean—"

"It's the truth." Nile nodded sagely. "As far as Hollywood is concerned, he's dead meat. I had no choice but to call off the engagement, if only to save my own reputation."

"You're all crazy," Jack said. "Every last one of you."

A server walked by carrying plates of food. Jack sniffed hungrily at the smell of pan-seared fish. In all the excitement with Nile, he'd forgotten that he hadn't eaten his evening meal yet. He'd have to—

"Shit!" Jack exclaimed, looking at his watch.

"What is it?" asked a startled Nile.

"I'm supposed to be fetching tea," he said, bolting to his feet. "Shit, shit, shit."

"You're leaving?" Nile said, sliding her chair back. "But you've hardly touched your drinks."

"Sorry, Nile, next time," Jack said. "Listen, where are you staying? I'll drop you off on my way home."

Nile flashed a lame smile. "Actually," she said, "I haven't quite gotten around to checking in anywhere yet."

"You're kidding."

"Nope."

Jack looked up at the ceiling. This was getting better and better. "What about when you arrived? Didn't you have to fill out the form asking where you have a reservation?"

Nile grimaced. "I just copied off the fellow sitting next to me on the plane," she said.

"Great." Jack ran his hands through his hair. He couldn't just leave her here; she'd be surrounded by drunks before he was out the door. He made a decision.

"Grab your purse," he said. "You can stay at my place."

Nile stood up. "You sure about this?"

"Yeah," Jack lied. "You can have my bed and I can sleep in the lounge." He held up a hand. "But just for one night," he said. "Tomorrow we find you a proper room."

"That'd be great."

"One more thing," Jack said, keeping his raised hand in place. "This doesn't mean that I'm going to be taking over where Poto left off. I'm still pissed at you."

Nile placed her hand over her left breast. "I promise to behave myself," she said.

Jack led the way to the door. "I just have to make one stop first," he said. "It shouldn't take long. I'll even shout you a burger platter."

"Sounds good," Nile said. "Just as long as you've got something at home to wash it down with."

"I think I've got a can of paint thinner around somewhere," Jack laughed, digging out his keys.

Nile laughed as well. "You're still a dick cheese," she said.

"And you're still a cow."

THIRTY-SIX

He's sitting on the end of her bed again. She's aware that she's dreaming. That she grew weary waiting for Jack to return with the food and crawled into bed for a short nap. She knows that her eyes are closed in sleep. And yet she still sees him, feels the chill of him permeate her bedroom. Smells the ocean in him.

She tugs at the bedclothes in an attempt to warm herself. The dead weight of his rotting carcass traps the sheets in place.

Go away. You don't scare me anymore.

He laughs. It's a damp sound. Water gargles somewhere in his chest cavity.

"There was a time when you cringed at the mere sound of my footsteps," he says.

That's why you deserved what I did to you. I'm only sorry that you didn't suffer more.

"I suffer now," he sighs. "The Old Ones won't let me rest."

Old Ones? I don't believe in that shit.

"Silly girl," he says. "You can no more choose not to believe than you can choose not to breathe."

A thick, noxious vapor envelops him like a cerecloth. The toxic smell of decay makes her gag.

Eh?

"You're a Cook Islander," he says. "The ancient legends are in our blood. Avaiki and Tangaroa and Maui. Ina and the shark. The 12 heavens."

Those are the stories of dead men.

"But," he says, shaking his head sadly, wetly, "I am a dead man."

Then go to hell where you belong and leave me alone.

"Why did you kill me?"

Her breath catches at the bluntness of his question. She starts to cry, brushes the tears away with an angry gesture. She mustn't show him any weakness.

Because you hurt me. Because you raped me.

"I'm a man; I had urges," he says. "I thought your mother explained that to you."

The only thing she told me was to lock my door at night. It didn't help.

"But you never tried to stop me."

What was I supposed to do? She sobs. *You're stronger than I am. I was afraid to resist.*

He shifts closer. He seeks to comfort her. She pulls away.

She sniffs back the tears. *Go away.*

"OK," he says. "I'll leave. But there's something I need to tell you first." *Make it quick.*

"I don't approve of your older friend," he says. "I've never trusted him." *Get real. You don't know anything about him.*

"I know that I don't like him."

You never liked anyone, you miserable prick.

"I don't like the way he looks at you."

Are you jealous?

"I don't like the way he calls you mon chere."

He calls everyone that. Jesus, you're an idiot. Now bugger off.

"I love you," he says softly as the dark outline of his body begins to fade. "I'll always love, my sweet young baby girl."

Shut up, you monster. I was never your *baby girl. You might have figured that one out if you'd stopped drinking for one minute.*

There is silence for a beat. Then noise.

I told you to shut up!

"I didn't say anything."

I heard you laugh.

"That wasn't me," he says. He rises in one fluid motion. She feels his weight lift. Off her bed. Off her heart. *Off her soul.* She dares to breathe again.

"I didn't make a sound," he says. His decaying body shimmers, dissolves, is gone.

"Then who was it?" she demands of the darkness, her eyelids fluttering as she emerges from sleep. "Who is laughing?"

"Wake up," his voice whispers in the hot air, "and find out."

THIRTY-SEVEN

Nile flopped onto Jack's bed. The springs squeaked. Nile squealed.

"Not much privacy in here," she said, bum-dancing on the protesting mattress. "They must hear you getting your rocks off all the way into town."

Jack grabbed for Nile. She pulled away, giggling, nearly spilling the open bottle of white wine she was working on.

"The neighbors are sleeping soundly these nights, I'm afraid," he said.

"Poor little Jackie," Nile pouted. "With no one but Rosie Palmer and her five daughters to keep him company."

"You were always such a class act," Jack said.

"What about your flatmate? No nookie happening there?"

Jack reached again. Latched onto Nile's arm, pulled her from the bed. "I told you," he said. "Maina and I are just friends. Besides, she's only a kid."

Nile waved a reprimanding finger at him. "From what I've heard of these tropical islands, there are no rules of engagement. It's just one big hump fest. It doesn't matter how old you are or even if you're related."

Jack wrestled the bottle out of Nile's hand. Wine splashed. Jack set the bottle aside, pulled off his T-shirt, dropped it to the floor, and used his foot to sop up the mess.

"Well, you heard wrong," Jack said. "The locals are good Christian people who tend to leave the sinning to the tourists."

"I don't know about that." Nile swayed, then plopped down on the bed again. "That Poto fellow was good, but I don't think it had anything to do with being a Christian. From what I can remember, it was me doing most of the talking to God."

"You're drunk," Jack said, tossing the sodden T-shirt into the clothes hamper.

Nile howled. "No shit," she said. "That's what usually happens when men—including, I may add, my former husband—insist on plying me with alcohol. You trying to get back into my panties, Jack? You miss exploring the Nile delta?"

"Like I'd miss having Ebola," Jack said in a fierce whisper. "Now, if you're finished with this whole sloppy seduction act, can you please keep your voice down. I don't want to disturb Maina."

"Sorry, sorry." Nile put a finger to her lips. "I don't blame you," she said. "She'll be pissed that you didn't wake her up to eat with us."

Jack sat beside Nile on the bed. "No use waking her just for a burger. She can have it for breakfast." He stared at the wall separating the bedrooms. "Poor thing. She hasn't been feeling that well since she moved in. The sleep will do her good."

"You were always the gentleman," Nile said, trailing her fingers across his chest. She leaned over him; he could smell the cigarette smoke from the bar in her hair.

"That's quite the tattoo," she said, running the tip of her tongue over the moko design.

He grimaced, pushed her head away, and wiped his arm with the sheet.

Nile's eyes were eager. "You've changed," she said. "I like that you're no longer the scared little rabbit that I married. But," she pulled away, the rescued wine bottle held high, "I like this even better."

"Give me that," he said, stretching out both arms.

Nile planted a hand in Jack's face and brought a leg up to fend him off. Jack found himself staring up her dress, at the black thong he'd already seen once that night. He cursed and struggled to break free. Nile took a quick, dribbling slurp of the wine, then threw her head back. She laughed.

Maina stood outside Jack's room. Through the closed door, she heard the bed springs protest. She heard voices. Urgent voices. Slurred voices. A man. And a woman. She heard the woman laugh: loud, drunk. Maina smelled wine.

She leaned her forehead against the door. What was Jack doing? And with whom was he doing it? Nurse Heather? No. Maina knew there were strong feelings between the two of them, but there had been no indication that they were in any kind of relationship. That they were anything other than good mates. Even the confrontation she'd had with the nurse at the café seemed based more on genuine concern for Jack's well-being than jealousy on Heather's behalf.

Jack hadn't mentioned a girlfriend or even any potential candidates. So was this a one-night stand? Was that where Jack had been all this time, picking up some slut in a bar? But surely Mama Rosie would have warned her if Jack was in the habit of bringing home strays. Would have warned her that Jack Nolan was a Grade A-1 bastard.

Maina's eyes tingled. She'd awakened to a damp pillow, and now her tear ducts, already primed, began to leak again. She turned in the hallway and slumped against the wall. The woman's laughter sounded again at her back.

Maina slid down the wall until she was sitting on the floor. She wrapped her arms around her bent knees, dropped her head on her chest, and unleashed the tears. They were heat on her cheeks. They were salt in her mouth.

THIRTY-EIGHT

Maina heard a vehicle approaching from behind. She snatched a quick look across the lane to her left. The car was small, dark. It glided beside her, matching her pace. She fought the urge to walk faster. Probably just some local boys having fun. Trying to spook her. She wouldn't play their game.

"Hello, Maina."

She stopped and set her duffle bag down. Gravel popcorned as the car pulled onto the narrow shoulder. A man leaned out the driver's window and waved to her. Rap music thumped from the car's sound system. Maina stepped to the centre line and squinted. The driver's face was a pale blur. She drew a blank.

He noted her hesitation. "It's Jerry," he said.

Maina moved closer. Now she could see the goatee, the red hair buzzed to the bone. She flashed back: Muri Beach. Paddling practice.

She nodded.

"Where you headed this time of night?" Jerry asked.

Maina tilted her head towards town. She face-talked: *Away*.

"You sure you want to be doing that?"

Maina looked over her shoulder, back toward Matavera. The woman's laughter echoed in her head. She couldn't go back to the house. Not while she was there. Not while she was there with Jack.

"It's over," she said. "I quit."

"We were afraid something like this might happen," Jerry said.

We? Maina crouched and saw the man in the passenger seat: older, glasses. He looked tired, disgruntled. Maina knew the feeling.

"Get in," Jerry said. "We'll give you a ride."

"You don't know where I'm going."

"I know that you're going with us," Jerry said. "Orders from the big kahuna himself. Now get in."

Maina retrieved her duffle bag and reached for the back door.

"No, take shotgun," Jerry said. "Doc doesn't mind."

The older man hoisted himself out of the passenger seat and held the door open for her.

"Feeling better?" Doc asked.

"I was fine until tonight." She climbed in, tucked her bag under her legs. Jerry turned down the volume on the CD deck. He shifted into first, shoulder-checked, and pulled back onto the road.

Maina sat very still. She watched as the car's headlights picked out peripheral objects: rubbish barrels, palm trees, ragged hedges, fallen coconuts. A stray dog padded into the undergrowth, head lowered, its eyes brilliant yellow marbles. Her guts churned. She concentrated on relaxing. *Don't let them smell your fear.*

"You know you're in shit for doing a runner," Jerry said.

"It wouldn't be the first time," she said. "You call this in on your mobile phone?"

Jerry smirked. "Oh yeah. And we had a very interesting conversation, didn't we, Doc?" He winked at the other man in the rear-vision mirror.

"And?"

"And we've been instructed to teach you a lesson," he said, reaching over to drop a hand on her bare leg. His palm was clammy. *He was sweating on her.* "So you'll never pull a stunt like this again."

"What are you going to do?" She struggled to keep her voice calm, unaffected. "Give me a hiding?"

Jerry smiled. The glow from the dashboard reflected the cruel excitement in his eyes. His fingers nibbled at her thigh.

"Worse than that, I'm afraid." Doc spoke for the first time. European accent. Nasty breath.

"You're going to *rape* me?"

Her heart drummed against her ribs. She couldn't feel her legs. *Be brave.*

"You eggs don't much look like gangbangers to me."

Jerry barked out a laugh. Doc chortled in her ear.

"Then what?" she asked.

Jerry's fingers brushed lower, deeper. Her stomach heaved again. She was going to spew. *Aim for his lap.*

"Young lady," Jerry purred. "We're going to make you a star."

His head flicked. It was the tiniest of motions, but Maina caught it. Knew it was a signal. She reacted. She lurched left. She fumbled for the door handle. Jerry's grip tightened on her leg. His nails furrowed into her flesh. They raked blood.

Doc sprang forward. He reached around and yanked her away from the door. His breath was hot on her cheek as his left arm clamped across her chest. He brandished a cloth. It reeked: something medicinal.

Maina bucked in her seat and slashed her head from side to side. She heaved against Doc's arm. The car swerved as Jerry reached over to help subdue her. She brought her leg up to kick him. Hit the CD deck instead. Ejected the CD. Kicked again; snapped the CD in half. Jerry swore, straightened the car, made a fist, and drove it into her kidney.

The air whoofed out of her. She doubled over in agony. Doc grabbed a fistful of hair, wrapped his fingers tight, snapped her head back, and jammed the cloth over her face.

She held her breath. She had learned to swim before she could walk. *She could hold her breath forever.*

The pressure on the cloth increased.

She could hold her breath for minutes.

Doc pulled her hair again and wrenched her head from side to side, trying to force her to inhale.

She could hold her breath for one more second.

She coughed, she gagged. She drew a deep breath. *Through the cloth.* Her struggles grew progressively weaker as the powerful anesthesia took effect. She convulsed, she twitched. Then her body relaxed. She went limp.

Doc snatched the cloth from Maina's face, gave her head a backhanded clip, and sat back. "Crazy bitch," he muttered.

Jerry tugged the broken CD from the deck and pitched it out the window. "What the hell was that?" he snarled over his shoulder. "I thought you were a doctor."

"What's that supposed to mean?" Doc wheezed, winded by the fury of Maina's resistance.

Jerry swiped a shaky hand across his forehead. "How come that shit took so long to knock her out?"

Doc massaged his left shoulder where Maina's thrashings had cranked it against the doorpost.

"It would have been easier to mix a lethal dose," he said. "It's actually harder to dilute the formula so it will only induce a blackout. Maybe I should have practiced on you first."

"Screw you."

Doc folded his arms across his chest, worked on catching his breath. "How so very mature of you," he said. "Why don't you just concentrate on your driving so we can deliver the star attraction in one piece. Jesus. First Gert and now the girl. It's time to finish this assignment and get the hell off this crazy island."

Jerry glared at Doc in the mirror and gave Maina a nudge with his elbow. Her head lolled, her arms flopped. Her eyes were nothing but white.

"Soon, my little brown pretty," Jerry wagged his tongue at her. "Real soon. Then we gonna have us some F-U-N."

SUNDAY

THIRTY-NINE

"Who does a girl have to blow to get some breakfast around here?"

Jack raised his head off the couch. One eyelid fluttered to half-mast. Nile stood in the hallway between the bedrooms, hands on her hips. She was naked.

"Jesus, Nile," Jack said, his voice cracking from lack of sleep. "You'll scare the chickens."

"You're a real prince, Jack, you know that?" she said. "P-R-I-C-K, prince. I can remember a time when you would have begged for some of this."

Jack winced as a crick in his neck reminded him how poorly the couch substituted for a real bed. He forced both eyes open and struggled to focus them on Nile. Her breasts, the perkiest that Jack's money could buy, defied the laws of gravity, nipples positioned strategically high for maximum advantage. Her pubic hair, what little there was of it, had been appropriately sculpted into the shape of a dollar sign.

Jack's head flopped back. He uttered a frustrated groan. He was tempted; there was little doubt of that. He could already feel his body betraying him. But painful experience had taught him that Nile was a taker. She'd bled him dry once; he'd be a fool to surrender to her fleshy wiles again.

"The only begging I'm doing this time is for you to put some clothes on," he said, swinging his legs off the couch and sitting up. "Before Maina sees you."

Nile glanced to her right. "I don't think we have to worry about that."

Jack's head snapped up. A white flare of pain exploded behind his eyes. "What?"

Nile nodded in the direction of Maina's bedroom. "The door's open," she said. "There's no one home."

Jack was off the couch and crossing the lounge when Nile's gasp stopped him.

"Oh, my," she said, nodding at his boxers. "It looks like someone wants to come out and play with mama after all."

Jack looked down and blushed a deep red. He turned away from Nile and brushed past her to stand in the doorway to Maina's room. The bed was empty, the sheet pulled back, pillows scattered. One of the dresser drawers hung open; Jack could see that its contents had been removed.

An icy panic gripped his throat as he opened the wardrobe. There was nothing in it save for a twist of metal hangers.

"Shit!" Jack charged back to his room and grabbed a pair of shorts. Hopped frantically from foot to foot as he struggled to pull them on. "Double shit!"

Nile stuck her head in. "What's wrong with you?" she asked, her beguiling tone replaced by a mocking concern. "Your girlfriend run off?"

Jack stopped in front of Nile and shoved his face close to hers. At the last second, he crimped his angry rebuke. Shook his head in disgust, charged through the lounge, leaving Nile to slink back into the bedroom. The look in Jack's eyes had frightened her—he was blaming *her* for his flatmate's departure—and her hands shook so badly as she reached for her scattered clothing that she had to sit on the bed for a minute until the trembling stopped.

Jack sprinted through the hedge to the dairy, ignoring the noisy protests of his chooks as they scattered out of his way.

Mama Rosie was serving an old papa when Jack bounded into the shop. He inserted himself between the two, then spoke rapidly, breathlessly.

"Have you seen Maina?" he shouted. "All of her things are gone."

Mama Rosie's fingers froze over the cash register keys. She brought her head up slowly, deliberately, to stare at Jack. She face-talked: *Can't you see that I'm busy?*

Jack caught the message and backed away. Touched the old man on the sleeve. "Sorry, papa," he said.

His heart tapdanced as he waited patiently while Mama Rosie counted her customer's change into his wrinkled palm. The local was shuffling out the door before Mama Rosie finally turned to Jack.

"Jacko!" she said. "That was—"

"Very rude, I know," Jack said. "And I apologize for barging in like that. But I think Maina's done a runner and I need to find her."

Mama Rosie's eyebrow crawled. "Gone, is she? What did you do?"

"Do?" Jack was stunned. "I didn't do anything."

"The girl liked you, Jacko," Mama Rosie said. "Told me so herself. So if she did run off, she must have had a good reason. What were you up to last night?"

Jack felt himself turn crimson for the second time that morning. It was the stupid look. The *man* look.

"I—"

"Yes." Mama Rosie looked down her nose at him.

Jack shifted uneasily. "My ex-wife stayed the night," he said sheepishly, then quickly blurted out an explanation. "Before you start in with the growling," he said, "I assure you that it was all perfectly innocent. Nile needed a place to stay, so I gave her my bed and I slept on the couch."

"If it was all so innocent, why would Maina pack up and leave?"

Jack shook his head. "I don't know," he said. "Nile had been drinking and she was a bit loud at times, but I don't think Maina woke up. But even if she did, there was nothing going on that should have pissed her off."

Mama Rosie leaned across the counter between them. "A loud, drunk woman in your bedroom. That might look bad on you."

"But Nile and I are divorced," Jack protested. "We haven't seen each other for years."

"Did Maina know this?" Mama Rosie asked. "Did she understand that you were just doing a favor for your former partner?"

"I didn't even see Maina," Jack admitted. "Her curtain was closed when we got home and I assumed she had fallen asleep. I decided not to bother her."

This time it was Mama Rosie's turn to shake her head.

"What?"

"You want to know what I think?"

"I didn't come over here half-dressed just to buy chicken bread."

Mama Rosie sat back on her stool. "I think Maina saw, or at least heard, something that she didn't like, and it upset her. A jealous woman is an unpredictable creature."

"I reckon," he said. "But standing here trying to decipher the mysteries of estrogen isn't helping me find her."

"Sorry I can't help you, Jacko," Mama Rosie said. "I've been here since 7 and she hasn't come in."

Jack rubbed his eyes. He could feel a headache stirring.

Why was he so worked up? This wasn't a life and death situation, for chrissakes. Maina hadn't disappeared into thin air like that poor McCrystal girl. She had purposely packed her gear and gone for a walk. No big deal, eh? She'd be back when she calmed down. She'd be back as soon as she was hungry.

Jack took several deep breaths; the headache backed off. He tried on a smile for Mama Rosie. It actually lingered for a few seconds.

"This isn't the way I normally like to start a day," he said. "Not without at least one pot of coffee in my belly, anyway."

Mama Rosie returned his smile and patted his hand in a sympathetic gesture.

"You've talked to her," Jack said, still fishing for clues. "Did she ever mention anything about going someplace else on the island?"

"No," Mama Rosie said. "That's her family house. It's where she belongs. If it was me, I'd go visit a friend, have a cuppa tea and a lie-down, and then come home and kick your papa'a to'e."

Jack laughed for the first time since waking up. "I'd gladly take a boot up the bum if it meant Maina was safe."

He leaned across the counter and kissed the shopkeeper on the cheek. "Thanks, Mama," he said. "I'm going to ring up a few of her mates and ask if they've heard from her."

He was nearly at the doorway. "Jack?"

He stopped, looked back, and raised an eyebrow.

"You really do care about her, don't you?"

Jack looked at the old woman for a long moment.

"Yeah," he said quietly. He meant it.

Nile had a beach towel tied around her when Jack returned to the house. She stood up from the kitchen table, followed him into his bedroom, watched him pull on a singlet, and tuck his wallet into a zippered pocket.

"Going somewhere?" she asked, keeping her tone light. She didn't want to set Jack off again.

"I have to find Maina," Jack said. "There are some very sick bastards on the island right now and I don't like the idea of her wandering around by herself."

"Do you know where she is?" Nile asked. "Where she might have gone?"

"No," Jack said. "But she can't be too far away."

"Why not just ring the police? Let them worry about her."

Jack shook his head. "They've got better things to do right now than be looking for an angry teenager," he said. "Or didn't Poto have time to tell you that a local girl has gone missing?"

Nile let the shot go. She knew Jack was upset, that he wasn't thinking straight. He needed her support now. He needed to know that she wasn't a complete bitch.

"Maybe someone in the neighborhood has seen her," she offered. "We could knock on a few doors, ask some questions."

Jack scowled at her suggestion. "Everyone's nervous enough as it is," he said. "If word gets out that a second girl is missing, it could get real ugly."

"But this has nothing to do with that other girl," Nile said. "This is just some kid with a pout on."

"*We* know that," Jack said. "But you don't know how goss works on this island. Once a story starts to spread, it's not long before fact becomes fiction. No, we need to keep this as quiet as possible. The best thing for me to do is just take the truck and go for a drive. That way, if Maina's decided to go tramping until she cools down, I can bring her back and no harm's done."

"OK," Nile said. "But I'm going with you."

"I need you here in case Maina calls."

"Hello? That's why God invented cell phones."

"Actually, we call them mobile phones here," Jack said. "And I don't own one."

Nile waved a finger at him. "That's exactly why you need me in your life again," she said. "To make sure that you have the essentials."

"The last time you were in my life," Jack said, "you took all the essentials with you."

Nile tilted her head. "And just how is standing here insulting me supposed to help you find your little friend?"

Jack threw up his hands. Surrendered to Nile's damnable logic. "You win," he said. "But I'm not taking you anywhere dressed like that."

Nile hesitated. "We might have a slight problem there."

"Problem?"

"Any chance I can borrow something to wear?" she said. "My dress is pretty much destroyed and the rest of my clothes are in a suitcase in the back of Poto's truck."

"I'll lend you something," he said, "providing you promise not to whine about it not coming from Rodeo Drive."

Nile crossed her heart. "Not a single whine," she said.

Jack rummaged through the shelves in his closet and tossed her a yellow T-shirt and a pair of green shorts.

Nile dropped the towel. Looked down at herself. Looked up at Jack.

He read the message in her eyes. Understood that the two of them still had a connection that time had not been able to completely sever. He measured the distance between them. Between them and the bed. She touched his chest with a tentative hand. His eyes surveyed her body again. It was firm and taut and eager. It was also white and pale. It wasn't the tawny hue of the island women that Jack loved. Nile was not a brown girl.

He walked away.

Nile pulled on Jack's clothes and joined him in the kitchen. She indicated the logo on the front of the T-shirt. "*Survivor: Africa?*" she said. "C'mon. You really expect me to go out like this?"

"What happened to your promise?"

"What happened to good taste?"

"Stay home then," Jack said gruffly, scooping up his keys. "I really don't care."

Nile was on his heels as he crossed the lawn to his truck. "But I look like an idiot," she said.

"Then my advice is to keep your mouth shut," Jack said. "That way, people won't know that it's true."

Maeva Benning was a barefoot angel. Her dress was a radiant shade of white. Matching ribbons seemed to float in her hair. She beamed when she answered Jack's knock, but the edges fell off her smile when she saw his look of concern.

"Wassup, Jack?" she asked carefully. "You going to church with us?"

"Not today, Maeva," Jack said. "Maybe some other time."

"Choice," Maeva said. She stepped aside. "You coming in?"

"Actually, Maeva, I'm not staying," Jack said. "I just stopped by to ask if you've seen Maina this morning."

Maeva shook her head. The ribbons cavorted in the ebony waterfall of her hair.

"Haven't seen her since yesterday," she said. "At the auditorium." Her eyes darkened. "Is everything alright?"

Jack reached out, gently touched the girl's face with his fingers. Mustn't alarm her.

"Everything's sweet as," he said, forcing a smile. "Just like you."

Maeva grinned and dropped her eyes. She was charmed by the attention.

"If you do happen to see Maina today, could you tell her that I have a message for her?"

"Sure, Jack," Maeva said, giving him a quick peck on the cheek. "No problem."

Nile swivelled in her seat as they passed the Endeavor site.

"What bomb hit that place?" she asked, craning her neck for a better view. "Looks like flushed money to me."

"You got that right," Jack said. "And it took a lot of dreams and futures and lives with it."

Nile sat back. "Is that what happens when we shove our wonderful version of civilization down other people's throats?"

"That's what happens when you put your faith in thieves and con men," Jack said. "It's a sad story; too bad you won't be here long enough to hear it."

She pivoted to face him. "What's that supposed to mean?"

Jack glanced to his left, smirking at the arched eyebrows. Nile was an amateur when it came to face-talking.

"It means," he said, "that right after I ask a friend of mine at the hospital to keep an eye out for Maina, I'm going to drop you off at Poto Rao's house. He picked you up from the airport; the least he can do after last night's little escapade is give you a ride back."

"You're telling me to go home?" Nile's voice grew shrill. "But I just got here. We've still got lots to talk about."

"No," Jack said, "we don't."

Jack flashed his headlamps to flag down the Mountain Motor Tours 4WD.

"Hey, Jack," Captain Tai called across the road between the vehicles.

Jack stuck his head out his window. "You haven't seen Maina anywhere in your travels, have you?"

Captain Tai shook his head. His beard swayed.

"Can't help you, mate," he said. "What's she doing out of the house so early? The café doesn't open until after the church services end."

"I'm not sure what she's up to," Jack said, realizing that he was inadvertently telling the truth. "I think she went for a walk, but she must be moving fast because I haven't caught up to her yet."

"Have you checked the hospital?"

"I'm on my way there now," Jack said. "Why?"

Captain's Tai trademark grin was nowhere to be seen. "I heard some goss in town," he said.

Jack's stomach plummeted. "Eh?"

Captain Tai broke eye contact and studied his thumbnail as it worked at the rubber stripping along the top of the doorframe.

"I heard there's a young girl in the hospital," he said. "And she's not doing so well."

Jack struggled to remain calm. "Did you hear a name?"

Captain Tai looked up again. "Sorry, mate," he said. "I didn't."

Nurse Heather's face was grim when she strode into the hospital's waiting room. She saw Jack and smiled thinly. She saw Nile sitting beside Jack. Saw that Nile was wearing Jack's T-shirt. Saw that she wasn't wearing anything under the T-shirt. Heather's face went ashen.

Jack leapt to his feet. One look at Heather—the hollow expression, the bruised pouches under her eyes—and he knew something terrible had happened. But what? And to whom? He'd never forgive himself if it was Maina.

"Jesus," he said, all his questions dying on his lips. He was suddenly very frightened of answers. "What—"

"We had a young girl die on us this morning," Heather said softly, her voice strained by grief.

Jack stopped breathing.

"They flew her in from Aitutaki, but it was too late," she said. "We couldn't save her."

Aitutaki? Then it wasn't Maina. Then it wasn't Teina McCrystal.

Jack exhaled. He reached for Heather; they both sought comfort in the contact. Jack felt an immense feeling of relief course through his body. He still didn't know what had happened to Maina, but at least she wasn't here. At least she wasn't lying in a cold room with a white sheet over her face.

Heather trembled in his arms. He guided her to a seat far away from Nile.

"I'm so sorry," he said. "Do you want to talk about it?"

Heather's head drooped. She was clearly exhausted.

"It's such a bloody awful shame," she said, her tone hushed but emphatic. "Some people should never be allowed to have children."

Jack moved in closer, hugged her tighter. Heather collapsed into him. Used his strength to ward off emotions that threatened to spill out into this over-lit room filled with averted faces and cheap plastic chairs.

She talked into Jack's chest. Told him about the six-year-old Aitutaki girl who had complained of abdominal distress. Told him of parents who trusted in Maori medicine. Who gave their daughter a narcotic concocted from natural ingredients to ease her discomfort. Who massaged the girl with herbal oils because, they believed, this would banish the pain. Who, when the girl fell unconscious, took her limp body to the lone doctor on the island and gave him simple instructions: fix her. Make her better.

An Air Raro turbo prop was just leaving for the main island. The girl was bundled aboard, accompanied by her parents and a nurse. She was still alive when the flight touched down in Rarotonga 50 minutes later. She was still alive when she was hurriedly placed in the back of an ambulance for the screaming ride up the hill to the hospital.

But she was dead when the ambulance arrived.

She'd died from septicemia, Heather said, caused by an appendix that had burst several days earlier. The poison had spread throughout her body even as her parents put their faith in the old ways.

"She didn't have a chance," Heather whispered, looking up at Jack. "I wanted to smack the girl's parents for being so stupid, for believing that the Maori medicine could heal a six-year-old with appendicitis. But I also wanted to put my arms around them and console them because they had lost their child."

Jack's throat tightened. He understood how deeply Heather had been distressed by the girl's death. He knew that, even though health professionals were expected to put aside their true feelings in the execution of their duties, it was never that black and white. Tragedy cuts to the soul. Every soul.

Jack looked over at Nile. She was slumped in a chair, legs crossed, flipping through an old magazine. She looked bored and miserable. She looked *used*. She kept a wary eye on the locals who sat next to her in the waiting room, as if she didn't quite know what to make of them. He watched her pointedly ignoring the laughing children who played around her feet. Realized how much he enjoyed his life now that it no longer included Nile Ramsay or any of the emotional baggage that came with her. It really was time for her to leave.

Heather read his mind. "Who's your friend?"

Jack laughed dryly. "I'm not even sure you could call her that anymore," he said.

"She's wearing your clothes," Heather said. "And not much else, from what I can see from here."

"That's Nile," Jack said.

Heather pulled away from him. "Your ex?"

"Yup. Nice piece of work, eh?"

"She's pretty enough, if you're into plastic," Heather said, not bothering to hide her claws. "But I don't think she's enjoying herself here."

"That makes two of us."

Heather turned back to Jack. "What are you doing here, by the way?"

"Maina ran away during the night, and—"

"And you thought she might be here?"

"I'm driving around the island hoping to find her," he said. "She knows that you and I are mates. I thought she might have come up here to bitch about me."

"About you bringing former wives home to stay the night, you mean?"

"Nothing happened." Jack's voice was firm. "And nothing ever will again. Nile knows I want her on the next available flight off the island."

Heather took a tissue from her uniform pocket and daubed at her eyes. "If I do happen to see Maina, what do you want me to tell her?"

"Tell her that I want her to go home," Jack said. "Tell her I said everything is OK now."

Heather stopped wiping her face and stared hard at Jack. "I'm not sure I like the way you said that," she said. "If I didn't have to go back to work right now, I'd make you sit there and explain exactly what you mean."

Jack shot her a puzzled look. He face-talked: *What?*

Heather stood up. "Just be careful, Jack," she said. "Before someone gets hurt."

FORTY

Jack's elbows were propped on a wooden table behind Sunset Takeaways. He was methodically wolfing down a fish burger without actually tasting it. His mind had been too preoccupied with the day's events to register such trivial details as the passage of time or the needs of his body. It was only when his stomach cramped with hunger that he realized it was now late afternoon and he hadn't eaten since the night before.

It had been a sullen Nile whom he'd dropped off at Poto Rao's house. She slung herself out of the truck, then leaned back in, her face a pinched mask of dismay.

"So this is it, then?" she said.

"'Fraid so," Jack said. "Poto can ring Air New Zealand for the next flight out. You should have no problems changing your ticket."

Nile tugged at the neckline of her T-shirt. "I'll get these clothes back to you."

Jack waved a hand. "Keep 'em," he said.

"More like burn them," Nile answered, but there was no trace of humor in either her voice or her expression.

"I'm going to miss you, Jack," she said.

"No you're not," Jack said, shifting into gear. "Goodbye, Nile."

She stepped back from the truck. "See ya."

Jack glanced at the house as he reversed down the driveway. Caught a glimpse of Poto peeking out from behind a curtain. He had obviously recognized Jack and was in no hurry for a replay of their last encounter. Jack chuckled. Poto and Nile deserved each other. If he could do it over again, he would have left the two of them to go at it under the Rocket Bar. The sick feeling of distress he had experienced since discovering Maina's absence was a nasty price to pay for seeing Nile again.

He lost count of the number of times he'd driven completely around the island. It took just under an hour to do a complete circuit, providing you stayed to the speed limit of 40km/h. Jack had barely approached that pace; the slower he went, the more time he had to scan both sides of the road. To look down beaches and into yards.

He stopped outside several churches and watched as exiting parishioners crossed to the church hall for the customary post-service kai.

He drove up to Wigmore's Waterfall, where he knew the local teens liked to congregate. He saw a group of boys jumping off the rocks into the frigid pool below the falls. He endured the attention of a swarm of voracious mosquitoes, but saw no sign of Maina.

He eyed the cleared walkway of the Cross Island Trek, but doubted she would bother taking to the jungle when there were plenty of other places nearer the coast where she could sit and fume about Jack's antics.

No luck either at Sparky's Café, where Muldoon looked up from whatever designer coffee he was concocting and shook his head at Jack's inquiry. Jack saw ashes fly off the end of Muldoon's cigarette. He didn't want to know where they landed.

Everywhere he went today, he saw policemen. In their cars, on foot. Knocking on doors, tramping through overgrown fields, trudging through the broken rooms of abandoned houses. They were searching for Teina McCrystal and, judging by the sullen looks on their faces and their drooping body language, their quest was no more successful than Jack's was.

And now he was here, at Sunset Takeaways, stuffing his face and not giving a toss what he was consuming. It was ironic that he should end up here—this had been his destination last night before it all went pear-shaped. Maina's meal still waited for her in the fridge at home.

Jack shifted his gaze from the horizon and focused instead on the *Chacal*. There was surprisingly little activity aboard the superyacht considering Larouche had told him that he and his crew were leaving Rarotonga in the morning. Jack picked out only a trio of men engaged in various activities on the decks, but their movements lacked urgency.

Jack stopped chewing. He stared at the vessel. He still considered it plausible that Teina McCrystal had followed her sailor boyfriend aboard the superyacht. Was even now tucked away in his cabin awaiting tomorrow's sailing. Karl Lamu was a fool not to search the ship.

But if Teina was indeed aboard, how farfetched was it to think that Maina might be as well?

The two girls weren't exactly best mates, but they did know each other through their mutual connection with Maeva Benning. If Maina needed to disappear for awhile, if she needed to go somewhere away from the house to sit and think—*if she needed to punish Jack for his indiscretion*—was there not some logic in the notion that she might seek out Teina and her mystery boyfriend and employ their assistance in providing just such a temporary sanctuary?

Jack put his sandwich down. But if Maina and Teina were on the ship, what could *he* do about it? He doubted that he would be able to just casually stroll up the gangplank and request a tour. And if he did somehow manage to sneak aboard, how long would it take him to search the vessel's cavernous depths?

The superyacht could very well be halfway to Vanuatu before Jack had completed his hunt for Maina, and he knew Larouche would be in no mood to return to Rarotonga. No, it would be a long swim home for Jack Nolan.

But something still tugged at his brain. Something about the water. It was why he hadn't bothered with the Cross Island Trek. He just had this gut feeling that Maina would stick close to the sea. She was a beach girl, a lagoon girl. She belonged to the ocean.

Jack's eyes drifted away from the *Chacal* and followed the edge of the harbor to its northern side. Saw the two-storey building standing close to the seawall.

He sat up straighter. Shielded his eyes from the fading glare of the descending sun for a better look. Bolted off the bench seat, abandoning the remains of his meal to the circling mynahs.

Erik Morrison leaned over his desk, brandishing a large magnifying glass. He peered intently at a nautical chart spread out in front of him. Mounds of clutter under the chart gave it an undulating appearance, as if it were draped over frozen waves. Erik marked something with a pencil.

The desk itself was huge and stained and appeared to list slightly to one side. Beside it, an antique ship's compass gathered dust on a carved wooden pedestal. Beyond the desk, the far wall was fashioned almost entirely out of glass, providing a panoramic view of the harbor and its mooring slips.

Several maps and charts, several of them tattered and faded, had been taped or tacked to the other three walls in the harbormaster's office. There were a number of calendars as well, some stretching back more than a decade. They featured scenes of ships and lighthouses and pretty young things in varying states of undress sprawled on idyllic beaches.

Jack took all this in as he stood in the doorway at the top of the stairs. Sensing his presence, Erik's head lifted from his work.

"Ah, Mr. Nolan," the harbormaster said, tucking the pencil behind one ear and waving Jack inside.

"Kia orana," Jack said, shaking Erik's hand.

"Have you come on official newspaper business, or are you just incredibly bored?" Erik asked, reaching to plug in a jug that fought for space on a small counter amidst an assortment of teabags and pink satchels of sugar.

"Neither, actually," Jack said, choosing his words carefully in an effort to appear calmer than he felt. "A friend of mine at the, uh, paper is interested in sailing to Pukapuka, and I said I'd check with you to find out when the next boat is leaving."

Erik was puzzled. "You could have rung," he said. "Or is Lloyd Dempster too cheap to let his staff have phones?"

Jack laughed politely. "I was in the area anyway, so it was just as easy to stop in. Unless I'm interrupting something."

"No, no," Erik said, pushing the chart aside. "Actually it's a treat to have a civilian in this office for a change. I'm more accustomed to being growled by ship captains or Customs agents or fishermen about something that almost always has nothing to do with my official duties."

"I'm not here to complain about anything," Jack said. "I can assure you of that."

"That's good to hear," said Erik. "Now—sorry—what was it again that you wanted to know?"

"The boat to Pukapuka," Jack said. "When does it leave Rarotonga?"

Erik pulled the pencil from behind his ear and used it to scratch thoughtfully at his head for a moment while he surveyed the piles of manuals and notebooks and papers on his desk.

"I know the schedule is here somewhere," he muttered.

Jack frowned at the chaos. He hated mess.

Erik snatched up a sheet of paper and ran a finger down it.

"Just as I thought," he said, then looked up at Jack. "You're a little early, Mr. Nolan."

"Excuse me?"

Erik consulted the paper again. "There are only four sailings a year between Rarotonga and Pukapuka. The next one doesn't leave here for another two weeks."

Jack's mind jittered. *What?* That wasn't possible. Maina—

"That can't be right," he protested. "I met someone this week who told me they'd just arrived on the boat from Pukapuka."

Erik turned to a clipboard on the wall beside his desk. "According to my records, only one ship currently in the harbor has made a recent stop in Pukapuka," he said. "And it's been moored here for more than a week now."

Jack moved closer to the window wall. "Which one is it?"
Erik Morrison pointed. "Right there."
Jack followed the harbormaster's finger. It was aimed at the *Chacal*.

FORTY-ONE

Maina opened her eyes. Blinked. Open. Close. Nothing. The blackness was impenetrable.

It stank. Urine and pungent body odor. And something else. Something she didn't want to think about. Maina covered her face with her hands and forced herself to breathe through her mouth. It didn't help, the ghastly stench was too overpowering to block out completely.

It was damp. Maina was lying naked on a smooth, hard surface. She ran a hand over her body, gently fingered the welts along her arms and legs. Souvenirs of her struggle with Jerry and Doc. She smiled at the memory of the fierce struggle. Her assailants would be hurting as well.

She touched herself. No bruising, no lacerations, no fluids. They hadn't raped her after all. But that only meant that the ugliness was still to come.

Maina sat up and quickly realized the folly in moving so soon after regaining consciousness. Her body, still reeling from the effects of the drug Doc had used to knock her out, reacted violently. Her head felt like it was splintering; her vision filled with a dazzling display of orange sparklers. Her stomach contorted, heaved, then emptied. She barely had time to lower her head and open her mouth before the vomit surged. It hit the floor in chunky splashes.

The retching continued unabated for several agonizing minutes. Maina held her hair out of the way and struggled to her knees so she wouldn't be sitting in her own mess. She marveled painfully at the amount of fluid in her digestive system considering she hadn't eaten dinner.

The spasms in her guts finally subsided. Her throat was raw from the flow of digestive juices. She wiped her mouth with the back of her hand and spit several times in a vain attempt at rinsing out the dreadful taste.

She pushed herself away from the stinking splatter. Moving slowly, careful not to induce another attack.

Maina turned her head from side to side, attempting to see something—anything—in the inky darkness. She stretched out her arms to gauge distance to a wall or another object. Her searching hands encountered only empty space.

Her brain struggled to recall anything between the time Doc clamped the cloth over her face and waking up in this bare expanse of a room. Her memory was an empty receptacle.

How long had she been lying there? Hours? *Days?* She had no way of knowing.

Her head was clotted; her thoughts were ragged, tattered. Where was she? What was this place with only a cold, hard floor? She had to still be on the island. You can't just bundle an unconscious teenage girl onto a commercial aircraft.

Maybe she was on a boat. But there was no motion. Everything felt very still.

Maina drew her knees up and wrapped her arms around her legs. It was her defensive position. It was second nature to her now.

Jerry told her she was being disciplined for neglecting her duties. She understood punishment; it had become ingrained in her bones. The evidence was there in her face, in the scar that bore a mute and jagged witness to the brutal realities of her short life.

She tried not to think about what was about to happen. Her muddled brain coagulated for a moment, seized onto a thought pattern: *they would not break her.*

They would never break her.

And then she cried. It was spontaneous release and she cursed herself for being a weak girl. *Be brave*, she told herself, not for the first time. *Think happy thoughts.*

Think about Jack.

Thinking this: he's awake now. He knows I'm gone. He must know that I'm in trouble. He's looking for me right now. I know it. I *feel* it. I only have to wait here for a little while longer, just until Jack finds me. Then the door to this room will open and he will be standing there. He'll rescue me from this place. He'll rescue me from these demons.

Promise me one thing, Jack Nolan.
Anything, Maina Rima.
Promise that you'll always protect me from the bad men.
I promise.

A noise. To her right.

Maina brought her head up, turned towards the sound. Were her senses playing tricks on her? A rainbow of dust motes danced in her vision. Were her ears just as confused by the utter deprivation of her surroundings?

Maina strained to hear.

"Hello," she called out, her voice cracked, hoarse. The single word sounded inadequate, impotent. It was quickly absorbed by the void.

She tried again: "Is anyone there?"

A pained whimper. This time there was no doubt: she wasn't alone. Someone else was in the room with her. Someone just as frightened and hurt as she was.

Maina gathered her legs under her and began to move towards the sound. She hitched forward on her haunches, one hand on the floor for balance, the other reaching ahead, seeking contact.

"Where are you?"

A rasping whisper: "Over here."

Maina veered slightly, followed the voice. "I'm Maina Rima," she said. "Who are you?"

"It's me," came the reply, sodden with tears. "Teina."

FORTY-TWO

Jack drove by remote control, reflexes on autopilot.

He felt stunned, jumbled, his brain barraged by questions with no perceivable answers. He flashed back to the harbormaster's office, saw himself staring out the window at the *Chacal* while desperately trying to make sense of Erik Morrison's words.

Jack gave his head a shake in a physical effort to realign his thoughts. No matter how many theories he circled, he always arrived back at the same conclusion: Maina had lied to him.

He already knew that there had been misery in her life; that much was evident by her nightmares. But it had never occurred to him that she might be concealing the truth about her reasons for being on the island.

It was now obvious that she could not have been a recent passenger on the inter-island ship. So how had she traveled from Pukapuka?

He kept coming back to the *Chacal*. If Maina had indeed been sailing on the superyacht, the question begged: *why?* What could she possibly have in common with Andre Larouche or any of those other Jackal thugs?

And how long had she been on the island before she showed up on Jack's doorstep? Jack recalled Maeva Benning's reaction on Thursday when he had given Maina a ride to the auditorium. The enthusiasm of that greeting seemed to indicate that it had been quite some time since Maeva had last seen Maina. If Maina had been on the island before she turned up at her uncle's house, how had she managed to avoid making contact with her old friends?

Jack prodded at all the possibilities, examined them from every angle in the hope that a logical explanation would magically appear. Looked for something solid he could grab onto before his world spun completely out of control.

What he tried not to think about—what he *refused* to think about—was this: if Maina had lied about how she had made her way to Rarotonga, what else had she lied about?

I feel safe here, she had said. *I feel like I belong here.*
I love you.

Jack slammed his hand down on the steering wheel. The pain worked to jolt him out of his trance. He blinked the haze from his vision and saw that he was passing through the centre of Avarua. Remembered nothing of his drive up to that point.

A sign caught his eye. Pacific Photos. *Shit!* He really did need to buy a new filter before Mona Vaevae growled him again. But he was too busy to stop now. He had too many other things—important things—on his mind.

He had—

Ah, fuck it. His brain was full; it needed a break.

Jack cranked the truck left and skidded into a vacant parking spot. A short, angry horn blast was a reminder that he hadn't bothered signaling his intent.

Jack looked both ways, then trotted across the road. It suddenly felt very good to have something concrete to accomplish.

Maina struggled to think. Teina? This didn't make any sense. What was she doing here? What did she have to do with any of this?

"I can't see you," Maina called out. "Where are you?"

"Here."

Maina continued to scuttle forward, hand outstretched. She bumped into something soft and naked and trembling.

And then the two girls were hugging each other while molten tears of relief and fear and confusion churned down their faces.

They didn't think they'd ever let go.

Zara and Ebony were behind the counter of Pacific Photos when Jack entered the shop. There were no other customers and the two clerks were taking advantage of the break to restock the film dispensers.

"Kia orana, Jack," they chorused, abandoning their chores to stand side-by-side behind the counter.

"Hello, ladies." Jack smiled back. He hunkered down to look into the glass display case built into the counter. Zara came around to kneel beside him.

"Can I help you find something?"

Jack was a frequent customer and often stopped in just to talk photography with the girls. They were both keen students of the art, eager to learn. Jack was impressed by their enthusiasm.

He had first met them at their college when he'd been asked to speak at a career day. While most of the students had wandered off glassy-eyed after his talk, Zara and Ebony had lingered behind. They elbowed each other playfully, giggling with embarrassment, until Zara finally summoned the courage to step closer and ask questions.

He had passed along tips on which affordable cameras would best suit their specific needs. He explained about film speed and light meters and filters and lenses. If Jack had been instrumental in helping them secure part-time employment at Pacific Photos, he was astute enough to keep that fact to himself. It was the perfect place for photography devotees to work, even if, as the only such business to open on Sundays, the pace was often hectic.

Zara was the taller and more garrulous of the two. She would often playfully growl Jack about the quality of his work in the paper, and never missed an opportunity to touch his arm, or brush her fingers across his hand. All while maintaining an expression of wide-eyed innocence.

Ebony was quieter, almost painfully shy at times. She seemed content to let her best friend do all the talking, but Jack made an effort to include her in the conversation because she possessed a wicked sense of humor that packed a nasty sting.

Zara and Ebony were inseparable, frequently modeling for each other as they quickly built up a sizable portfolio. Jack readily praised their efforts, sincerely impressed with the maturity of their work.

Zara casually leaned her shoulder into Jack. Caught off-balance, he grabbed the edge of the counter to avoid sprawling on the floor. Zara laughed at her own antics.

"What's gotten into you?" Jack grinned back.

"It's almost closing time," Zara said. "That always makes me happy."

Jack scanned the contents of the display case. "I'm looking for a new skylight filter," he said. "There's a nasty scratch on my old one."

Zara put her nose against the glass. It left a greasy imprint. "I'm not seeing one here," she said.

"Me neither." Jack straightened. Zara stood with him.

"We could order you one," she said. "Be here by mid-week."

Jack nodded. "That would be great," he said.

Zara turned to Ebony. "We'll need the order book."

Ebony didn't move. She stared at Jack. Her eyes burned into his.

"Hello?"

Ebony turned to Zara, blinked rapidly, then produced a lined book. She poised a pen over one of the pages but seemed incapable of writing.

Zara came around the counter, snatched the pen away, and used her hip to bump Ebony aside. "Skylight filter," she repeated as she wrote. "Anything else, Jack?"

She looked up, saw that Ebony and Jack had once again locked eyes.

"Jack?"

"What's wrong, Zara?"

"Eh?"

Jack turned to Zara but nodded at Ebony. "Something's up with you two. I can tell by the look on Ebony's face."

Zara scowled at her mate, gave her another nudge. "We're cool as, Jack," she said. "No worries."

"Show him." Ebony spoke for the first time.

Zara dropped her head. "No," she said.

"Show me what?" Jack asked.

"Show him," Ebony said again. Firmer this time.

"We'll get in trouble,"

Ebony's tone acquired authority. "There's already trouble," she said. "Now show him."

"Jesus," Jack said. "You two are starting to spook me. What's going on?"

Zara didn't speak. She knelt behind the counter and pulled open a large drawer filled with bright yellow envelopes.

She flipped through the envelopes, pulled one out. Placed it on the counter's glass top.

"We are going to be in so much trouble if anyone finds out we did this," she said.

She slid the envelope closer to Jack. Kept her hands on it for a beat, then pulled them away. "You might want to take a look at these," she said, then stepped back to stand beside Ebony.

"Where are we?" Maina asked, sniffling through a nose plugged with crying snot.

"I don't know," Teina said. "The last thing I remember was meeting Jerry and—"

"Jerry?"

"My new boyfriend," Teina said. "The one I told you about. Do you know him?"

"Not as well as I thought," Maina muttered.

"What?" Teina reached out in the dark, put her fingers on Maina's face. "You sound angry. Please don't be angry."

Maina stroked the fingers on her cheek. "It's going to be OK," she said. "*We're* going to be OK."

"I don't understand what's going on," Teina said, and Maina could hear the tears returning. "They took my clothes and put me in this... this place. I couldn't find a toilet and so I've—"

"Shhh," Maina whispered, pulling Teina's face into her neck to stifle the sobs. "I'm here now," she said. "No one's going to hurt you. I promise."

"What's going to happen to us?"

Maina rocked her, massaged her back. "Try not to think about it," she said.

"I'm so scared," Teina cried. "I don't want to die."

"Neither do I," Maina said. "Neither do I."

Somewhere a lock shot back. The girls stiffened.

Here they come, Maina thought. *The monsters.*

Jack tapped the yellow envelope. "What's this?" he asked, looking from Zara to Ebony.

"It's a roll of developed film," Zara said.

Jack shot her a look of impatience. He face-talked: *I'd already figured that one out for myself.*

Ebony stepped forward. Her words came quickly, as if she needed to get them out of her mouth before they became sticky and useless.

"We have to look at every photo that comes out of the developer," she said. "Just to make sure the machine is working OK and the chemicals don't need replacing. Most of the time we just sort of glance at the pictures without really seeing them, because we go through so many rolls a day, especially when there are lots of tourists on the island."

"And?"

"And normally we would have done the same with this roll except we knew some of the girls in the pictures," Ebony said. "And then..."

"Yes?"

Ebony looked at Zara; she nodded her encouragement. Ebony took a deep breath. "And then we heard that the man who dropped this film off was dead."

"What?" Jack turned the envelope over, read the name written in pen on the top flap: Gert Junger. The man in the pool. The man with the tattoo. One of Andre Larouche's 'educators.'

"There's more," Zara interjected.

"More?" Jack felt his gut tighten.

"After we heard that Mr. Junger was dead, Ebony and I opened the envelope to take a closer look at the photos," Zara said. "To see if there was anyone else we recognized. Someone we could give the photos to. That's when we started to worry."

"About what?"

Zara picked up the envelope and handed it to him. Jack hesitated. He knew these girls. Knew they were levelheaded. Knew they wouldn't be winding him up.

He opened the envelope, pulled out the photos, set them in a neat pile on the counter top, and started going through them.

The first six or seven were typical tourist shots: the market, the rugged interior peaks, an overexposed sunset. Nothing out of the ordinary. Nothing sinister.

But then the subject matter changed. The shots became grittier, as if taken from a distance using a poor-quality telephoto lens. The hair on the back of Jack's neck rose. A chill shuddered down his extremities.

The next group of photos was all of teenage girls. At bus stops, waiting for their ride to school. At dairies, their young faces captured by the camera in expressions of angelic simplicity. On the beach where wet clothes clung tightly to lithe bodies and wild hair dripped with seawater.

There was one shot of girls standing outside the National Auditorium, laughing and whispering and vibrantly alive. Jack turned the photo to better catch the light. He thought he could see Maeva Benning in the background, but the face was too blurred for him to be sure.

Three photos were left in the pile. The top one had been taken outside a café. In it, a couple reclined in wicker chairs, posing for the camera, their faces partially obscured by a shadow cast by a beach umbrella. Tall glasses of juice sat on a small table between them. The teenage girl was a local Jack didn't recognize. The man, who looked to be in his mid-20s, had red hair cut quite short, and a sparse goatee. His shaded face looked vaguely familiar.

The next photo featured an Island Night revue at one of the resorts. Several girls stretched across the front of a stage, performing a traditional dance in coconut-shell bras and grass skirts. Their hair glistened under the overhead lights; their smiles were radiant.

Two girls dominated the centre of the action. One of them was Maeva Benning. Dancing beside her was the girl from the café photo.

Jack looked at the final shot. His breath caught in his throat. There was a roaring in his ears that had nothing to do with the sound of traffic on the street behind him, or the air-con unit that cooled the interior of Pacific Photos.

In the picture, two local girls posed with their arms around each other. They were mugging for the camera, which had captured them in mid-giggle. The photo had been taken indoors with a flash; the girls' combined shadow was a warped blob on the wall behind them.

Jack looked up at Zara and Ebony. They stood in silence, anxious eyes tight on Jack, knowing what was coming and fearing it no less for that knowledge.

Jack turned back to the photo. The girl on the left was the same one from the previous two shots. The other girl was Maina.

A rectangle of blazing light appeared. Maina and Teina ducked their heads away from the painful brightness. They clutched each other tighter.

"Let's go, you two," a man said from the doorway. "Time for your closeup."

Jack fanned the last three photos out on the counter top. Stabbed down an index finger. "Do you know who this is?"

Zara nodded. "Teina McCrystal," she said.

Jack made a strange noise in his throat. Zara and Ebony looked at each other. They face-talked: *This is serious.*

"That's why we wanted you to see these," Ebony said. "We thought there might be some kind of clue here."

Jack ran a hand through his hair. "But why me? Why not the police?"

"It's been nearly a week since Mr. Junger died," Zara said. "We thought the police might growl us for not calling them earlier."

Ebony broke in, "We kept thinking that a friend or a workmate would come by any day to collect the pictures. And then Teina disappeared and we got scared."

"We were going to take them to the police today, right after the store closed," Zara said. "Honest."

Jack waved them silent. Something was wrong. Something scratched at his fevered brain.

He grabbed up the envelope and turned it over.

"When was this film dropped off?"

"A week ago today," Zara said. "Sunday, first thing. He said there was no hurry, so we didn't even bother processing the film until late Wednesday. The next morning was the first we heard that he'd drowned."

Sunday. First thing. Jack's brain was buzzing again. Sunday. That meant Junger had to have taken the last shot no later than that morning. *Sunday.* Three days before Jack came home to find Maina at his house.

Look, Mr. Nolan. I've just spent two days on the boat traveling from

Pukapuka and I really do need a place to stay.
Two days.
Maina had lied to him from the very beginning.
He picked up the last photo again. Ran a finger over Maina's face. Had there been a kernel of truth in anything she had told him? Had she even made up the nightmares, just to gain his sympathy, his trust?
His finger stopped. He brought the photo closer to his face. *What the hell?*
"You see something, Jack?" Zara asked.
He put the photo down. Tilted his head for a different angle. Picked up the yellow envelope. "Are the negs in here?"
"Yes."
Jack pulled out the sleeve of negatives, held it up to the window. "Please turn on the light table, Zara," he said. "And pass me the loupe."
The light table was built into a section of the counter. Zara flipped a switch and a dulled tube flickered to life. Jack smoothed the plastic sleeve over the light, placed the loupe on the final negative, and leaned in until his eye was clamped tight to the tiny magnifier.
After a moment, he straightened, pointed to the loupe. "Remember what I told you about a negative containing more information along its edges than what is actually printed in a standard photo?"
The girls nodded.
Jack indicated the light table. "Take a look at that."
Zara and Ebony each took a turn squinting through the loupe.
"What are we looking for?" asked Zara.
Jack held up the photo. "See this object behind the girls? How it bleeds off the edge of the photo? At first I thought it was just part of the shadow from the flash. But when I looked a little closer, I realized that it was something else. There's not much of it here, but you can see more of it on the negative."
Zara lowered her head to the loupe again. "You're right," she said. "It looks like some kind of carving. A paddle maybe?"
Jack's heart raced. Zara had confirmed his own observation. It was a carving. An Andrew Tuara carving, actually. And Jack knew exactly where it was hanging. Knew where this photo of Maina and Teina had been taken.
In the rotting lobby of the Endeavor Hotel's convention hall.

FORTY-THREE

Rough hands pawed at her breasts as Maina was hauled to her feet. Beside her, she heard Teina moan as she too was manhandled.

"I'm going to be sick," Teina cried out.

"You barf on me, you little bitch, and you'll be wearing my boot up your ass."

American accent. American slang. Maina recognized it. So did Teina.

"Jerry?" Teina whimpered. "Why are you doing this to me?"

"Just following orders, babe," Jerry said. "Just doing what they pay me to do. Now let's go."

The girls were hauled from the room, down a hallway. They moved toward the light. Maina lowered her eyes to protect them from the glare.

Somewhere ahead of her, there was a murmur of voices. Excited voices. She heard metal scrapping on concrete. She sensed nervous tension. She smelled hot lights.

She realized that whatever had been planned for them, whatever was going to be done to them, it was going to be a public spectacle. She knew the watchers were eager, they were hungry. They would eat her and Teina with their eyes.

Jack slammed through Karl Lamu's door, Jimmy Tauranga hot on his heels.

Lamu looked up from the report he was reading. "Jack," he said, "you really must learn how to knock."

"I'm sorry, Chief Inspector," Jimmy panted. "I tried to stop him."

"I'm sorry too, Chief Inspector," said Jack, smacking a photo down on Lamu's desk. "But you might want to look at this."

Lamu ignored the photo. Looked straight at Jack. "You would try the patience of a saint," he said. "And the Good Lord knows that I have too much time already booked in Purgatory to be considered a saint."

Jack was breathing as hard as Jimmy. There had been quite the little wrestling match at the bottom of the stairs before Jack had broken free and raced away.

"Normally I would take great pleasure in ordering my constable to escort you to the street, preferably in handcuffs." Lamu leaned back, patting his extensive girth. "But I had an excellent lunch that I seem to be still in the process of digesting. And I fear too much excitement at this time would only serve to give me a most unpleasant attack of the cramps."

Jack's eyes widened. What the—

Lamu leaned forward finally, picked up the photo. He sucked at his teeth with his tongue while he examined the faces of the two girls.

"Your girlfriend is very photogenic," he said. "Even with that scar."

Jack closed his eyes. He had one chance here. Get angry, blow it, and he might never see Maina again.

He opened his eyes. Smiled. Pointed at the photo.

"Do you recognize the other person in the picture?"

Lamu nodded. "Of course," he said. "It's Teina McCrystal. The missing girl."

"Actually, both of those girls are now missing," Jack said.

"What?" Jimmy Tauranga stepped into the conversation. "What happened?"

"I'm not really sure," Jack said. "Maina just took off in the middle of the night. I've been driving around the island all day looking for her."

"Why didn't you call us?" Jimmy asked.

"I knew you were busy looking for Teina," Jack said. "And I thought Maina was just angry with me and hiding somewhere to pay me back."

"May I interrupt this little conference?" Lamu said.

The two men turned to the Chief Inspector.

"You've confused me, Jack," Lamu said. "And when I'm confused, I also tend to cramp up. And you do not want to be in this room when that happens. Are you getting the message?"

"Yes, sir."

"So please explain to me why I have once again been blessed with your rudeness."

Jack pointed out the edge of the carving in the photo. "I know where this was taken."

"Eh?"

"It's in the Endeavor."

Lamu snatched up the photo again. "Then these two were trespassing."

"They're still trespassing."

"What?"

Jack drew a deep breath and looked from Lamu to Jimmy. "They've been taken back to the Endeavor," he said.

Lamu lowered the photo, cocked his head at Jack. "Two days ago you demanded that my men tear apart Andre Larouche's boat," he said. "Now you've changed your mind?"

"Two days ago I hadn't seen this photo." Jack could hear the desperation in his voice; he struggled to remain calm. He ignored Lamu's arching eyebrows. "Two days ago I didn't know that Maina and Teina had been in the hotel with someone who was connected to Larouche. But I did know that there was equipment sitting in its convention hall that appeared to have been placed there quite recently. At the time, I couldn't think of any explanation for it, and then things started to get crazy in my life and I just forgot all about it. But now I'm starting to understand that it must have something to do with the girls."

Lamu's eyebrows moved higher. Jack was scrambling; he knew it. He also knew that he had to keep going, he had to say this all now before Lamu blinked. If Lamu had the opportunity to interrupt, to ask questions, to cast doubts, to dismiss him again, then Jack was finished. And Maina and Teina would be doomed.

Maina stumbled. She was pulled upright. They moved farther down the hallway; a larger room loomed ahead. She could hear Teina sobbing behind her.

Maina's eyes were wide open now. She glanced at the men who led her by the arms. She recognized Doc; she knew the other man's face but not his name.

Into the larger room now, lit by the beams of high-intensity bulbs attached to tripods. Vague shapes moved in the semi-darkness beyond the periphery of the lit area. The air smelled of electricity and leaky pores and diesel; a generator grumbled in a far corner.

The strength returned to Maina's legs. She shrugged off the hands. Lifted her chin. She wouldn't show fear. Not to these people. Especially not to these people.

Several of the lights were stationed around a pair of cots that had been set up as makeshift beds. A man holding a video camera knelt by the cots; a red light blinked as he filmed. A second cameraman loitered nearby.

They were going to film her punishment? Why?

The first cameraman stepped away as Maina and Teina were forced to sit on the beds. Teina kept her head down, hid her face behind a tangle of loose hair. She crossed her legs, hugged herself protectively.

Maina smirked, leaned back on her hands, and shook her hair out so that it glowed like raven fire in the harsh glare of the spotlights. *Look at me*, she was saying. *Go ahead. I don't care.*

She tried to catch the eye of Doc and Jerry and the others, to challenge them with the naked ferocity of her spirit. But they refused to meet her stare. They turned away to melt into the nothingness beyond the circle of superheated whiteness.

A large man approached Teina. Maina recognized him: Tor, the silent behemoth, the constant companion to Rev. Moses Akimo at Sparky's Café. Maina glared into the shadows where she knew the spectators were gathered. Was Akimo here as well? Was the holy man party to this trespass?

Tor put his hand on Teina's shoulder, pushed her onto her back. He pulled ropes from a pocket. Tied Teina's hands over her head. Put a noose around each ankle, pulled her legs apart, and secured the ropes to the bed frame. Teina's eyes grew large with fear. Her sobs had mutated into a panicked mewling.

Maina wondered again what Teina had to do with any of this. Was she also being disciplined for disobeying orders?

Tor turned to Maina. She pushed his hand away, leaned back, put her arms up, and opened her legs.

The girls lay on the beds, trussed, spread-eagled, exposed, vulnerable. Their breathing was shallow, harsh. The movement in the shadows around them grew more agitated. Feet shuffled, throats were cleared. Clothes rustled. Chairs scraped. The room grew noticeably hotter.

Teina bit her lip. Blood oozed thickly between her teeth.

Maina stared straight up. She smiled. There was a black vacuum above her. In a moment—when the bad things started—she would dispatch herself into that place. She would hide there, untouched by whatever grotesque cruelties were being visited upon her body below. And while she was in that safe place—that haven—she would envision only pleasant things.

She would remember this: the feeling of sand between her toes as she walked Muri Beach. The first juicy bite into the sweet flesh of a ripe mango. The way the thunder of a pate never failed to agitate her blood.

The way Jack smiled at her.

Footsteps approached. They were uneven, limping. The mutterings ceased.

"What are you people waiting for?" said Andre Larouche. "Let's finish this and return to the ship. We sail in the morning."

Jack took a deep breath. "It all makes sense, when you think about it," he said to Karl Lamu. "It explains why your men haven't found Teina. Or why I couldn't find Maina. None of us thought to look there because the place is a disaster. Because no one goes there. No one is *supposed* to go there. Which makes it perfect."

"Perfect for what?"

Jack waved his hands in frustration. "I don't know," he said. "For whatever sick and degenerate and terrible things the League of Jackals does to young girls. What they used to do in Cambodia before they were finally driven out. What they are going to do all over the South Pacific if we don't stop them here."

Lamu rocked back in his chair. "The Endeavor?"

"Yes."

"Not on the ship?"

"No."

"Jack," Lamu said, "I should lock you up for being maki maki."

"You're right," Jack said. "I'd have to be crazy to think that you'd believe any of this. What could possibly have possessed me to think that today would be different from any other day?"

"Jack?" There was concern in Jimmy's voice. He put a warning hand on Jack's shoulder. Jack brushed it off.

"Tell you what, Karl," Jack said, leaning over Lamu's desk. "I'm going to collect Jordan Baxter and the two of us will solve this mystery at the same time we're reporting on it. I'm sure the prime minister will be very curious as to why his Chief Inspector of Police isn't in any of the photos."

Lamu pointed at his phone. "Good luck getting hold of Baxter," he said. "I've been trying all day."

Jack wasn't backing down. "Then I'll go alone," he announced. "I can write the story myself."

Lamu sat silently, rubbing his gut as he carefully weighed the credibility of Jack's wild theories. He shifted uncomfortably as bowel tissue twitched.

"Take Jimmy," he said.

Jack turned to the constable, then back to Lamu. "What?"

"You've worn me down, Jack," Lamu sighed. "I'm too old and too fat to fight you on this anymore."

"You're serious?"

"Jimmy has his radio," Lamu said. "He can call in if you find anything—not that I think you will. But if this blows up in *my* face, Jack Nolan, I will have your balls as earrings."

Jack shook Jimmy's hand. The two men grinned at each other.

"Jack."

"Yes?"

"Jimmy's in charge out there," said Lamu.

"Fine by me," said Jack.

"I mean it," Lamu said. "No heroics. I don't want any of my men getting hurt just because you're acting like an arsehole."

"Fine," Jack said. "No heroics."

FORTY-FOUR

"Can't you drive any faster?"

Jimmy Tauranga laughed. "Patience, Jack, patience," he said. "How would it look if a police vehicle was flagrantly breaking the speed limit?"

"It would look just fine if the lights and siren were on," Jack grumbled.

"Sit back and relax, mate," Jimmy said. "We'll be there in 10 minutes. Nothing's going to happen in that time."

Jack shut up. This was out of his control now. He had to follow police procedure. But Jimmy was wrong about the time. The Jackals sailed at dawn. Whatever nastiness they had planned for the Cook Islands—either on their superyacht or in the abandoned hotel—it had to be accomplished tonight.

Jack's guts clenched. Chief Inspector Lamu's cramps were contagious.

Larouche continued to bark orders. Maina lifted her head and saw dim outlines as several people scuttled in the gloom beyond the lights.

"Chaka!" Larouche called out. "Is your crew ready?"

A Polynesian woman stepped into Maina's view. The woman from the beach. The woman Heather had growled for going topless.

Chaka Tane was clad in khaki, her hair pulled back into a severe bun. She looked all business as she signaled for the camera operators to join her.

"Which one first?" she asked Larouche.

The Belgian contemplated the girls. He caught Maina's eye, they exchanged looks. Hers: rebellion. His: carnality.

"Start with this one," he indicated Teina. "Draw out the suspense."

Maina strained her neck to look at the other bed. Teina writhed, tugging wildly on the ropes that bound her. Her head thrashed, transforming her hair into a rippled ebony curtain. Sweat jetted. Tears spiraled.

Chaka checked with her crew, then called over her shoulder. "We're ready for you, Jerry."

The young American joined Chaka. He fidgeted nervously with the drawstring of his shorts as she spoke to him.

"This isn't supposed to be a marathon," she explained. "We're just giving our audience a sneak preview. But," she reached out to poke at Jerry's arm, "try to last as long as you can."

"Do I wear a condom?" Jerry asked.

Chaka raised her eyebrow at Larouche. The Belgian shook his head. "No," he said. "We need the money shot."

"Shit," Jerry muttered, staring at Teina's frenzied antics. "She's going to be sandpaper."

Chaka gave him a push forward. "Drop the knickers, eh, and let's get started."

Jerry stripped slowly, his confidence shriveling with every discarded article of clothing. Finally naked, he approached Teina's bed with his hands held bashfully over his crotch. Chaka's crew looked at each other, rolling their eyes in amusement.

One camera operator moved into position at the foot of the bed. The other stood at its head. They were facing, but there was no concern that they might end up filming each other. Their focus would be too tight and specific for that to happen.

Jerry knelt between Teina's legs, then stopped. Maina saw a look of terror dart across his features as he looked down at himself.

"What are you waiting for?" Larouche bellowed. "Get on with it, man!"

Jerry dry-swallowed, then backed off the bed, nearly shoving his behind into the camera lens. He stood nervously; a lost, little boy. He was limp.

"I can't do it," he said.

Chaka was at him in an instant. "What do you mean you can't do it? This is what we're paying you for."

Jerry's face scrunched. Maina thought he might burst into tears. Was this the same hero who had beat on her in the car? Where was that big macho man now?

"I can't have sex with her," Jerry moaned. "She's just a baby."

"You mean you can't get it up," Chaka spat in his face. "What happened to all that big talk you've been spouting for two weeks? What happened to the stallion? I guess that was all bullshit, eh?"

"I'm sorry."

Chaka slapped Jerry. Maina winced at the fury of the blow.

"Get out of my face, you pathetic piece of shit," she spat. Red-faced, Jerry grabbed up his clothes and scampered away.

"What do we do now?" asked one of the camera operators.

Chaka chewed on her lip while she surveyed Teina. Then she crooked her finger at someone standing just out of light range. "I'm going to need you, sweetie," she said.

"Me?" a male voice asked.

"Come on, stud, help me out on this one."

"But I'm only here to watch," the man said. "I don't have any acting experience."

"You don't need experience," said Chaka. "You just need to get it up. Can you do that for mama?"

"You can't show my face. I can't take any chances that someone might recognize me."

"Believe me, honey," Chaka said, "no one's going to be looking at your face. Now, are you going to help me here or what?"

"Anything for the love of my life," said Jordan Baxter, sliding up to kiss Chaka's forehead.

"You never did tell me how you know that carving is here," Jimmy said, straining forward against his seatbelt to look through the windscreen as the police Jeep bounced over the rutted entrance to the Endeavor Hotel.

"Alex Benning gave me an unofficial guided tour," Jack said.

"Did you see anything else interesting?"

Jack thought of the centipedes. "You might say that," he said.

Jimmy sat back. "I'm not seeing anything, bro."

"Keep going," Jack urged. "Before we lose the light."

"We're both going to look awfully silly if you're wrong," Jimmy said.

"Trust me on this one," Jack said. "This is a bad place."

"You must have been talking to some of the former investors."

Jack swivelled his head, willing his eyes to penetrate the lengthening shadows cast by the crumbling buildings. He could sense the adrenaline churning; it felt like he had swallowed battery acid. He only hoped it didn't burn a hole in his conviction that—

"There!" Jack pointed.

Jimmy braked and flipped a switch on the dashboard. The small spotlight positioned on the driver's side of the Jeep's roof flashed to life. Jimmy reached up to turn the spotlight. Shone it into a small grove of rata. Shone it on a collection of vehicles and bikes parked amidst the shrubby trees.

"Oh my," Jimmy whispered. He turned to Jack. "Maybe you were right after all."

Jack was already out of the Jeep. Headed for the reception hall.

"Hold on, Jack," Jimmy called after him. He turned off the Jeep and detached his baton and torch from his police belt. "Remember what the Chief

Inspector said about me being the one in charge."

"You're still the boss," Jack hissed. "I'm just showing you *where* to be the boss."

"You sure you know where you're going?" Jimmy looked around apprehensively at the hotel's wrecked shell.

"Hurry up, Jimmy!" Jack said. "Maina's in trouble. I can feel it."

Jack walked quickly in the failing light. He led Jimmy past the swimming pool, to the main doors of the convention hall. He pulled on one of the handles. The door remained snugly in place. Jack tried the second door. It too refused to budge.

His curse was brief but colorful. "They must have locked it from the inside."

Jimmy tapped the doors with his baton, tested them with a tentative shoulder. Stepped back. "Are there any other entrances?"

"None that I know of," Jack said. "I remember seeing some emergency exits, but those doors only open from the inside."

Jimmy scratched at his head with the torch as he regarded the locked doors.

"Short of chopping down a tree and using it as battering ram, I don't see how we're going to get in."

Jack placed a hand on the doors. How thick were they? Seven centimetres? Five? That's all that stood between him and Maina. Between him and whatever demons Maina was facing.

He formed a fist. He pounded on the doors. Hit the unforgiving surface until he couldn't feel his hands anymore.

"Easy, mate," Jimmy said. "That's not—"

The words died in Jimmy's throat. Both men stood anchored. Saw the wild fear in each other's eyes.

"What the hell was that?" Jack asked.

"Jesus and all His saints," Jimmy whispered. "They're killing people in there."

Teina shrieked when Baxter entered her. She heaved furiously. Screeched again. It was the noise of a damned soul making first contact with the scorching fires of Hell.

Baxter hesitated in mid-stroke, ears ringing. How was he supposed to perform with all this wailing and flopping around going on? Maybe this wasn't such a good idea after all.

"Don't stop," Chaka commanded from somewhere behind him. "We're still shooting."

"Can someone please shut her up?" Baxter implored. "I can't concentrate."

Maina turned away. Closed her eyes. Went to her better place. The place where her nose wrinkled in delight at the fragrance of jasmine. Where her ears filled with the roar of the surf.

That's why she didn't hear Teina's screams. Why she didn't hear the sound of heavy boots approaching Teina's bed. Didn't see Tor grab Teina by the hair. Didn't see him deliver the hammering backhand that broke Teina's nose and loosened teeth.

Didn't see Teina become a flaccid bag of naked flesh under Jordan Baxter, who simply raised himself up on his arms for better leverage and continued with his efforts.

But even in that better place—in that sheltered cocoon of sunshine and coconut palms and shivering rainbow fish you could practically reach out and touch—a vexatious voice still murmured in Maina's brain.

You're next, it said.

"What was that?" Jimmy's eyes threatened to bulge out of his head.

"I don't know," Jack said, stepping away from the door, eyeing it warily as if the very wood still vibrated from the sound.

"Whatever it was," Jimmy said, "I never want to hear it ever again."

Jack stood in front of the locked doors, his hands clenched in impotent fists. That had been the sound of a girl screaming; the bile in his stomach told him so. But which one? It didn't matter. It only meant that all doubt had now been erased from his mind. Maina and Teina were in terrible danger. It was time for action.

He dug the heel of his palm into his forehead. *Think, think!* Had he seen any other entrances during his brief time in the hall? He honestly could not remember. After his encounter with the centipedes, he hadn't exactly been thinking clearly.

The centipedes. Alex Benning. *I may have waited a bit too long to stop.*

Jack spun on Jimmy. "Call for backup."

"Eh?"

"Meet me around the back of this building as soon as you can," Jack said. He sprinted off.

"What are you going to do?" Jimmy shouted after him. "Where are you going?"

"Sorry, Jimmy," Jack called back over his shoulder, "but I've got a train to catch."

FORTY-FIVE

Jordan Baxter pulled out, grunted once, was done. Red lights on two cameras winked out.

"How was that?" Baxter asked, wiping himself with a towel.

Chaka looked at her camera operators. Both men flashed a thumb's-up. Chaka smiled.

"You were great," she said, planting a kiss on Baxter's mouth. "You're wasting your time at that stupid little newspaper."

Baxter grinned, and worked the towel. "Porn star," he said. "I like the sound of that."

"Save your energy," Chaka said. "If this next fool can't get wood, I may need your services again."

Baxter returned the kiss, then padded out of sight.

Chaka shaded her eyes and looked around at the shadowy figures sitting on the metal chairs. "Where is he?"

A man stepped forward, dressed in a spa robe.

"I'm here," said the Rev. Moses Akimo.

Maina floated down. Returned to the container of flesh and blood. She blinked rapidly to recapture her bearings, then turned her head to look at the other bed. Teina appeared boneless. Blood seeped from her nose and mouth. Baxter's pitiful deposit shimmered on her belly as it rose and fell with each shallow breath.

Chaka led her crew to Maina's bed. "Do we need to subdue you as well?" she asked.

Maina smiled. "I'm not even here," she said.

Chaka frowned. "Whatever." She waved her crew into position. "Holy man," she snapped, "let's see that divining rod of yours in action."

"Un moment." It was Larouche. He limped on his bad ankle over to the bed and leaned over Maina. Ran his fingers down the rope around her wrists. Down her arms that were slowly losing all sensation. Across the scar on her chin.

She searched his face for compassion, for pity. Found an impenetrable exterior.

"Why are you doing this?" she said. "Why are you doing this to me?"

"This isn't personal," he said softly. "You are merely an example for the others. I must never be seen to be weak in any way. Order must be maintained or this entire enterprise will implode again. You do understand, oui?"

She dropped her gaze.

"Relax, mon cherie," Larouche said. He eyed the small bulge in Akimo's robe. "All of our obligations will be over very soon."

Larouche stepped back, and flicked his head at Akimo.

The reverend dropped his robe. The bald surface of his head glistened as he advanced on Maina. His tongue flicked nervously across his mustache.

He went to his knees between Maina's legs. Shuffled forward until his face was right over hers.

He leaned in until their lips nearly touched. "You humiliated me in the café," he seethed into her face. "Let this be a lesson in how to treat those who are more powerful and influential than you."

Maina remained silent. Akimo cocked his head. He was confused.

"What happened to that cheeky girl?" Akimo said. "She's not so—"

Maina lunged. Her head shot up. She clamped her teeth on Akimo's mustache. Locked jaws on upper lip.

Akimo howled into her mouth. He tried to pull away; Maina's grip tightened. He shook his head. She hung on.

Akimo brought his hands up, drummed fists on her ribs. Maina refused to let go.

The cot rocked, threatened to tip. Chaka shouted. One of the cameramen backed away too quickly, tripped. His camera clattered to the floor.

Maina tasted blood. It mixed with Akimo's spittle. It sprayed into her mouth, down her throat, and threatened to choke her. She stopped trying to breathe, bit deeper. Clamped tighter.

Akimo cried. Akimo wailed. He roared. He tasted blood as well. His own.

Tor was there. Squeezing his hands between Maina and Akimo, grabbing their throats. He flexed his arms. Pulled them apart with a terrible ripping sound. Chaka gagged and turned away.

Maina's head snapped back. Her mouth was filled with hair. Akimo screamed, reared up, and backed away. He crashed off the bed. A spume of blood arced into the air. The lights caught it, turned it scarlet.

There was a sickening splat as Akimo's sweaty body met the concrete floor. He staggered to his feet and danced in pain. Hands over his face, red leaking through his fingers.

Maina raised her head. Spat hair. Spat flesh. Grinned in triumph. Her teeth were crimson with gore.

"Jesus Christ!" Larouche was beside her again, his face distorted by anger. "You idiots!" he shrieked. "Can't you do anything right? How difficult can it be to have sex with a defenseless girl tied to a bed?"

"If it's so easy, why don't you do it?" Akimo lisped.

Larouche waved his hand and Dr. Charbonneau was beside the reverend, shoving a towel in his face, soaking up the blood, and applying pressure. He attended to Akimo for several minutes, until the wound clotted and he was able to determine that there would be no permanent damage.

"You're going to need stitches," Doc said. "After you're, uh, finished here."

Feeling at his mouth with trembling fingers, Akimo turned on Larouche. "No one said anything about me being attacked."

Larouche shrugged impatiently. "If memory serves, you were the one who insisted on being a participant, mon ami," he said. "I believe you referred to it as payback. But if you are no longer intent on revenge—*if you are too frightened*—then I'm certain that we can find someone here willing to teach this young lady a valuable lesson in good manners."

Akimo continued to dab at his mouth with the towel. "I can finish this," he said.

"Then please do."

Akimo lowered his chin protectively as he made his way to the end of the bed. Maina laughed at him, made exaggerated biting motions. Licked her lips, smearing blood across her chin.

"But I can't do it like this," Akimo announced. "I don't want to be looking at her face."

"Fine," said Larouche wearily. "Then turn her around."

Akimo approached Maina cautiously. She snarled once, then abruptly stopped taunting him. Lay back quietly. Returned to staring at the ceiling, her eyes slightly glazed.

"Behave yourself," Akimo warned, reaching for the rope around her wrists. "Or my friend Tor will make you behave."

Akimo loosened the knots around her ankles, nudged her to turn over. Maina obeyed, rolling on her stomach. After another sharp poke, she rose to her hands and knees.

Akimo left her hands free so she could support herself. Maina's arms tingled and burned as the interrupted blood flow returned to them.

Akimo fussed with the knots around her right ankle.

"Today would be good," Chaka said, her patience rapidly dissipating. Larouche had promised her this job would be a simple exercise in lighting and shooting. It will take no time at all, he'd said. Instead, it had turned into a bloody marathon. Literally.

"All right, all right," Akimo said, his thick fingers fumbling at the rope.

Maina remained still while he worked to secure her ankles. Her head hung low; her hair formed a pile on the cot's thin covering. After her initial aggressive behavior, she now appeared defeated, resigned, ready to be used.

The reality was much different. Staring down the length of her body, Maina regarded Akimo's hurried efforts. She paid rapt attention to every sloppy loop, every careless twist. By the time Akimo finally stepped away, Maina had already formulated how to free herself.

See how the ropes are already sloughing off. You really should have used a better knot. You never were any good with knots.

The ghost had told her that. The ghost was wrong.

Jack's lungs were seared from the fire of his exertion. His legs threatened to buckle. His pace slowed. His mouth gaped opened, sucking desperately for oxygen. Jesus, he was out of shape.

He kept going. Willed his legs to churn. His arms to piston, to claw through the thick night air. He wouldn't stop. He pictured Maina's face. He *couldn't* stop.

He was there. Leaning on the door as he beat with both hands. Then in, and down. Collapsing into arms. Trying to catch his breath. Trying to speak. Trying to play hero.

Jimmy Tauranga keyed the radio mike, called Dispatch, and asked for Lamu.

"I need reinforcements at the Endeavor," Jimmy said, then hurriedly explained about the vehicles and the locked door and the unearthly scream.

"I'm on my way," Lamu said. "Where's Jack?"

"I have no idea," Jimmy said.

"Shit and hellfire!" Lamu roared.

Akimo was on his knees, tucked in tight behind her. His hardness rested on the top of her buttocks, along her tailbone.

"Are you ready, Chaka?"

Chaka looked at her cameramen. They both nodded.

"Go ahead," Chaka said.

"Thank God," Akimo said. "I've got a service at 7 that I have to prepare for."

He leaned back slightly to adjust his aim, and took hold of himself.

Akimo flexed his hips and thru—

"Wait a minute!" It was the camera operator on the left.

Akimo jerked in surprise and rammed himself hard into Maina's inner thigh. He heard her protest at the rough contact. Heard something pop in his groin. Had he snapped something? Something valuable? Was it physically possible to break your penis?

Clawing at his crotch, Akimo scooted away from Maina. He sat back on his heels, then turned to Chaka. "I think I hurt myself," he whined.

"You'll get over it," she said, chucking her chin at the cameraman. "What's the problem, Al?"

Al waggled his camera; there was a rattling sound. "Something came loose when I dropped it," he said.

"Can you fix it?" asked Larouche, looking at his watch. "Because we can always do this with just one camera. It's only for the teaser ads, after all."

Al tipped his camera and gave it a good shake. A small screw dropped onto the floor. He scooped it up, pulled a tool out of a hip pocket, and tightened the errant screw into place.

"Good as gold," he said, bringing the camera up to his eye and moving back into position.

Chaka massaged her temples. Spoke to the other cameraman. "Any problems with your equipment, Gord? Tell me now, before we get started."

The entire camera moved against Gord's face as he shook his head no.

Chaka waved at Akimo. "Our equipment's working, Reverend," she said. "Now let's see if yours can do the same."

Akimo was losing his enthusiasm. His mouth was starting to throb and something was definitely wrong with his member. It appeared to be listing to one side.

He rocked to his knees and sighed deeply. Sex with his wife had never been this painful.

He cradled himself with one hand and hitched forward. This had better be worth it.

Maina watched as Akimo moved closer. *Waited* for him to move closer. He was hot, he was eager. His eyes shone. It would never occur to him to check the bindings on her ankles. It would never occur to him that, while everyone was concentrating on Al and his repair job, Maina had been busy.

No, the Rev. Moses Akimo had only thing on his mind.

Too bad for him.

Now!

Maina shook her right leg free of the rope. Cocked her knee forward. Drove her foot backwards. Rammed her heel into Akimo's scrotum.

For one second, Akimo did nothing but stop and look at her. His expression was an almost comical hybrid: equal parts amazement and shock. As if he couldn't fathom that something else could possibly go wrong. As if he couldn't grasp that his testicles had just been crushed flat.

Then the air gushed out of him as if propelled by a bellows. His eyes distended. He collapsed double. He vomited.

Maina looked back over her shoulder at Akimo. Her hair was plastered to her forehead and cheeks. Her mouth was red. Her eyes flashed savagely. She was the feral child. The wild thing.

She looked into Akimo's face. Saw the gaping, bloody mouth dripping stomach contents. Saw the disbelief writ large in his eyes. The way his skin was more grey now than brown.

He saw her face. It terrified him. He shook his head, he raised a pleading eyebrow. He face-talked: *Please. No.*

Maina's foot caught Akimo flush in the throat. His head snapped back. He tumbled from the cot.

They were shouting outside the ring of light. They were screaming and yelling. Maina pulled her other ankle free. She pounced off the bed and stood facing the shadows. She was naked and bloody and angry and defiant. She howled.

She was the beast. *She was the demon.*

Chaka stepped back. The cameramen dropped their equipment and quickly disappeared into the blackness. Chairs were knocked over. People ran. Larouche cursed in French, cuffed at anyone unfortunate enough to be within range.

There was confusion. It was *her* confusion.

Tor did not run. He stamped towards her. Hands clenching. Biceps flexing. The skin graft on his cheek blazing angrily.

"Look who's out of his cage," Maina snarled. "What a surprise."

"You should have done what you were told," Tor growled.

"The beast actually speaks. Come on then, big man," Maina taunted.

"Let's see how brave you are when the girl isn't tied down."

He reached for her. His hands were the size of roasting pans. Maina twisted. She skittered to one side. She cocked her head and launched a mouthful of spittle into Tor's face.

He staggered. Wiped the back of his hand across his cheek. Trumpeted with rage. Charged in again, fists swinging.

He was fast for his size. But Maina was smaller, quicker. She was slippery. It almost saved her.

She ducked under a roundhouse right. Popped her head back up for a quick look. Saw the cruise missile of a left coming too late to move completely out of its flight path.

Tor's fist clipped her temple. It was a glancing blow; had he connected fully, he would have crushed her skull. He would have killed her where she stood.

The force of his punch spun her. She crashed against the bed. It skidded away. Her momentum dropped her to the floor. One arm landed in an awkward position. Bone does not bend that way. Something snapped.

Her head hit the floor, bounced, and settled. There were no longer any shadows, only continuous, pounding, oscillating light. Her arm was an agony stick. Her brain throbbed. Her vision blurred.

Hold on, Tor, she thought. *I'll be right with you. I just need to lay my cheek down on this nice, cool, concrete floor for a minute and rest.*

She saw his legs. They were hazy, but she recognized the boots. One of the legs disappeared. She knew where it was: poised over her. He was going to stomp her to death where she lay. He was going to kick her until she bled from every orifice. Until she no longer was a cheeky brown girl.

Until she was no longer anything you might recognize at all.

She tried to relax. She tried to leave her tired, broken body. She tried to think of Jack.

The boot began its deadly descent.

And then the back wall exploded.

FORTY-SIX

"My wife's going to kill me," Alex Benning hollered as he continued to goose the throttle on his steam engine.

"Don't worry," Jack shouted back. "This ride will probably kill you."

Jack saw the tracks end. The back wall of the convention hall loomed. Alex was talking to himself. He seemed to be calculating something.

"Hang on," Alex yelled as he applied the brakes.

Jack steadied himself in the small cab as best he could, wrapping his hands tightly around metal railings. He clenched his teeth, and hunched his head as deep as it would go into his shoulders.

At the last second he saw several uniformed figures diving out of the way. One of them was Chief Inspector Karl Lamu. Jack had never seen the man move so quickly. But he didn't have time to savor the image.

Maina didn't know that it was Alex Benning's locomotive crashing through the wall that had saved her life. She knew only noise and motion.

She was lifted into the air as the concrete floor buckled and heaved beneath her. She heard the initial crash of cinder blocks disintegrating and then the deadly whistle as concrete shards and rusted slivers of re-bar arrowed through the air. She heard the dull, sick thuds as these missiles impacted with flesh. She heard the screams of the wounded. The dragon breath of released steam, the frenzied dissonance of running feet and shouting men.

She was bewildered. Reduced to primary thoughts: Tor no longer threatened her. She was surrounded by utter madness. She needed to protect herself. Everything hurt.

Maina located her bed. Crawled under it. Curled into a tight ball. Closed her eyes.

Jack pulled himself upright in the cab. He was battered, he was bruised, but everything seemed to be working. Alex lay beside him. He was bleeding from a gash in his forehead. Jack checked for a pulse. Found one.

From what he could make out, the convention hall was a landscape of destruction. Those lights that still operated barely managed to pierce the murk. Ghostly shapes staggered through dirty clouds of spent steam and concrete dust. Not even the seething engine could drown out the noises in the building. Human noises. Dreadful noises.

Hands reached up to Jack. It was Jimmy Tauranga.

"You are one maki maki fellow," Jimmy grinned. "You could have killed us all."

"I couldn't think of any other way to get into the hall," Jack said, watching as Karl Lamu directed his men through the ragged breach in the outer wall. They stepped carefully over the strewn remains, flicking on their torches as they advanced.

Lamu looked up at the battered cab and shook his head. Disgust? Amazement? Jack couldn't be sure. He did know that he was in line for a particularly enthusiastic growling from the Chief Inspector when this was all over.

He hopped down gingerly and entered the war zone. Maina was in there. He had to find her.

Chaka sat on the floor. Her ears rang. She felt dazed. Her movements were erratic, uncoordinated. She looked around without fully comprehending what she was seeing. At her own left leg, where white bone jutted from ragged skin. Beside her, where Gord lay sprawled on his back, a slender spear of metal protruding from his chest. Someone flopped past her, moaning and dripping darkly.

An object pressed against her hip. Chaka reached back, pulled it loose. It was a head. It was the Rev. Moses Akimo's head. The man's eyes were wide with surprise. His ruined mustache drooped over the smashed hole of his mouth.

Chaka held Akimo's head by one ear, contemplating it. An inner voice—distant, indistinct—told her that she should hurl the disgusting thing into the shadows. Instead, Chaka placed the head beside her on the floor. She was still rubbing her hand over the bald crown when the policemen stumbled upon her.

Andre Larouche leaned against Tor, hopping on his good leg as they made their way slowly, determinedly, toward an exit door. Larouche had twisted his bad ankle again. Maybe even broken the damn thing this time. *Merde!*

"What happened?" Larouche gasped, but Tor only grunted.

"Just get me out of here," Larouche said.

Tor grunted again.

Karl Lamu held Jordan Baxter by the back of his shirt. Gave him a good shake. Baxter yowled.

"Here's a scoop for you." Lamu laughed in Baxter's face. "You're going to prison. For a very long time. And you can quote me on that."

Fingers on her skin. Maina drew her legs up, closer to her chest, and tucked her forehead against her knees.

"It's OK, Maina," a voice said. "You're safe now."

Jack dropped the borrowed torch into a pocket and pushed the cot out of the way. He was dismayed to see that she was naked. What had those monsters done to her?

He bent down. Placed a gentle hand on Maina's shoulder. She shrank from the contact.

"Are you hurt?"

He continued to talk softly, gently pulling the matted hair away from her face, stroking a cheek with the back of his knuckles. Reassuring her.

He felt her relaxing under his touch. She uncoiled. She pulled apart. She turned her face to him. It was swollen and bloody. He took her head and tucked it against his chest. He wanted to squeeze her skin into his, until they were one melded being. Until nothing could ever harm her again.

"It's OK," he repeated. Again and again. "It's OK."

He could feel the tears soaking into his shirt.

He finally pulled away. "Can you move?"

"I think so," Maina said. "My head hurts, and there's something wrong with my arm."

Jack saw the arm. The way it was twisted. He saw the bruises and scrapes and fought the urge to find somebody—anybody—and beat the living shit out of them for what they had done to this girl. To *his* girl.

He gathered Maina up, carried her to the bed, and set her down. She tottered but remained upright. The tumult continued unabated around them, but that involved someone else. Here, in this small area of light, there was just the two of them. They were all that mattered.

Jack knelt in front of her. "Just take it easy," he said. "The ambulance is on its way."

"Jack?"

"Yeah?"

"I'm cold."

Jack stripped off his tear-stained T-shirt and draped it over her shoulders. She hugged it across her chest.

"There you go," he said. "Anything else I can do for you?"

She nodded. "Could you rub my ankles where the ropes were?" she said. "I can't feel my legs."

"Sure." Jack reached for one of her feet. Began to massage it. He tried not to look too closely at the abrasions around her ankles. Tried not to imagine the unspeakable horrors she had faced in this room.

Maina smiled at Jack as his fingers carefully kneaded her damaged skin. She felt safe now, despite the pain in her arm and the wicked headache. Jack was here. Jack had saved her. Just as he'd promised.

She could close her eyes.

Jack watched her. He didn't like the look of the swelling on the side of her head. And whose blood was that on her teeth? He wondered what other injuries she had suffered that maybe weren't as obvious as the broken arm.

He eyes traveled up her bare leg. He pushed aside any feelings of impropriety. Yes, she was naked, but it would save the paramedics valuable assessment time if he could give them at least a preliminary inventory of the damage.

Her knees were raw and scraped, but otherwise appeared OK. He would glance at her pubic area and then be finished, because his shirt hid her upper body.

OK, good. Done. No blood, no—

Maina turned her ankle in his hand. The movement parted her legs slightly, revealing her inner thighs. Revealing what was hidden there.

You ever had an ingrown hair, Jack? Let me tell ya, they hurt like a bitch. So I just save myself the agony and wear the shorts instead.

Now he finally understood the truth. Now he knew what she'd been hiding from him.

Maina felt Jack's hands trembling. She opened her eyes. Saw his face. Saw the emotions that flickered across it.

Shock.

Dismay.

Disgust.

Jack stared.

At the design.

At the betrayal.

At the tattoo.

He pulled his eyes away from the mark of the jackal, then turned them on her face. He expected tears. Saw none. He expected denial. It didn't come.

She reached out for him. He batted her hand away.

Maina held his gaze with a calm resignation. She spoke evenly, quietly, in a tone that contradicted her battered limbs, her bloodstained face.

"I didn't have a choice, Jack," she said. "Andre Larouche is my father."

MONDAY

FORTY-SEVEN

"She's been asking for you," Heather said.

"I don't want to see her," Jack said.

"Then why are you here?"

"I just wanted to make sure that she's going to be OK," he said. "That's all."

"That's all? You almost kill yourself *and* Alex Benning on that stupid train to rescue her, and now you just want to see if she's OK?"

They stood in a hospital corridor. They stood outside a room. *Her* room. Heather in her nursing whites, Jack in a spare police uniform shirt. Someone had handed it to him when he finally left the Endeavor Hotel in the early hours of the morning.

"If you're finished with the lecture, can you please tell me how she is?"

"She's going to be sore for awhile," Heather said. "And she'll have a cast on her arm for probably about six weeks. But she'll heal. I'm actually more worried about the McCrystal girl at this stage."

"That bad?"

Heather nodded. "The dentist is coming in to work on her mouth sometime this morning," she said. "And the doctor suspects she may have sustained a concussion as well as the broken nose and jaw."

"Tor put quite the beating on her."

"It takes a real tough guy to hit a woman." Heather's eyes stormed. "I'd love to get my hands on that rat bastard. I'd teach him a lesson he'd never forget."

"But Teina will recover, right?"

Heather glanced down the hall. The paint on the cinder block walls had faded to a dull white. The lino floor was worn thin by years of busy footsteps.

"It's not her bones I'm worried about, Jack," she said. "It's her *soul*. We know how to fix the body, but how do you repair what's broken *inside*?"

Jack shrugged. "You're asking the wrong person." He looked miserable. He looked shattered.

"The good news," Heather said, "is that she'll live. I can't say the same about some of the others in that building. What the hell were you thinking?"

"I may have been a bit too exuberant with my entrance."

"A bit?" Heather tilted her head. "Jack, five people are dead."

"I didn't mean for that to happen," he said. "I just wanted to get those girls out of that building."

"And now we have bodies stacked like firewood in the morgue," Heather said. "Including the Rev. Moses Akimo. Do me a favor, Jack?" He raised an eyebrow. "The next time you decide to run over people with a train, aim for the skinny ones."

"Is that an example of hospital humor?" Jack said. "Because I'm not laughing."

There was a slight movement in the room across the hall. Someone stood just back from the window, watching. Watching Heather reach out to rub Jack's arm. Recognizing the affection in that small gesture.

"Sorry," Heather said. "It's been a long night. But I get off shift in a few minutes and I promise that I won't be nearly as gruesome after I've had some sleep."

Jack's eyes radiated an anguish that her attempt at levity could not penetrate.

"Look, I know you're gutted that Maina is somehow connected with this whole Jackal thing," Heather said. "And I'm not going to stand here and give you the speech about how I knew she was trouble from the start. But right now she's just a scared little kid who could use a friendly face."

Jack snorted. "Maybe she should ask her father to bring her some flowers and a teddy bear."

"Jack!" Heather scolded.

He leaned his forehead against the room's narrow window. A thin white curtain had been drawn around Maina's bed. He couldn't see her.

"I know," he said. "I'm being an arsehole. But I just feel so... so used."

"Do you know what her role was in all this?"

Jack turned back to Heather. "You'd have to ask her," he said. "All I know is that she's a Jackal, so it can't have been anything good."

"Have you talked to Jimmy again? Have they arrested everyone involved?"

"Everyone except Larouche and his goon Tor," Jack said. "They somehow managed to slip out of the convention hall. But Lamu has vowed that he won't sleep until he has those two shitrats in custody. Their ship has been impounded and is under 24-hour guard, so they'll have to be better swimmers than Gert Junger if they hope to escape."

"So what was the deal with that Junger bloke anyway?"

Jack shrugged. "From what I was able to gather from the police interrogations at the Endeavor, Junger was getting cold feet about the Jackals operating in the Cook Islands. He was making noises about dobbing them in."

"So Larouche had him killed?"

"It's called tying up loose ends," Jack said. "Apparently it's one of Tor's specialties."

Heather shivered. "I'm not sure if I like the fact that those two are still on the loose."

Jack laughed dryly. "You might want to lock your doors tonight."

"That might not be a bad idea," Heather said. "So, has Karl Lamu thanked you yet?"

"Thanked me? For what?"

"For stopping Larouche and his men. For being right about what they were up to."

"Get real," Jack said. "As we speak, Lamu is being interviewed by Lloyd Dempster and I know for a fact that he's taking all the credit for the bust."

"But that's not right."

"I don't really care," he said. "This was never about the glory. Lamu can have the headlines." He looked into Maina's room again.

"So, are you going in?"

"Is she alone?"

"For now," Heather said. "We shuffled patients to give both her and Teina some privacy."

Jack hesitated. "I think I'll go see how Teina's doing first."

He reached for the opposite door. "Is she in here?"

The figure in the room quickly flattened against the wall.

"No." Heather pointed down the hall. "Last room on the left. Her family is with her. Tell them I'll be down in a minute. I'm just going to check Maina's vitals first."

"OK." He moved away. The figure behind the door relaxed.

"Jack?"

He stopped.

"What do I tell Maina?"

Jack ran a hand over his unshaven face and looked down at his police attire. "Tell her I want my T-shirt back."

"It hurts."

"Good."

Maina's eyelids drooped. Heather had just given her another shot of pethidine for the pain. "Please don't be angry with me, Jack," she croaked.

She tried to swallow, couldn't. Reached for a cup of water with a shaky hand. Jack helped, holding the cup while she sipped on the straw.

"Thank you," she said. "I'm so dry." She patted the cast on her left arm. "But I guess that's the least of my worries right now."

Maina looked bad. Her eyes were bloodshot, ringed by a rainbow of bruises. There was a large contusion on one side of her head, just over her ear. Jack knew that, under her borrowed pareu, she sported several other abrasions and welts. He had seen them. He had seen too much.

He wheeled the blood pressure machine off to the side and pulled up a chair. "Tell me everything," he said.

"Now?"

"Right fucking now," Jack snapped. "Or I'm walking out that door and you will never see me again."

Maina flinched at the vehemence in his voice.

"Where do you want me to start?"

"Oh, I don't know," Jack said. "How about with what the hell you were doing at my house in the first place."

Maina nodded. "To begin with," she said, "Nga Rima really is my uncle."

"Yeah?"

"And his brother, Piri, was married to my mother."

"So Piri is your father."

Maina shook her head. "I already told you," she said. "Andre Larouche is my real father. Piri never knew any different. As far as he was concerned, I was his daughter, and that somehow gave him the right to abuse me."

"So how does Larouche figure into this equation?"

"My mother, Repeta, was a very talented dancer, just like Mama Rosie said." Maina leaned into the pillows supporting her back. "She was a member of several dance troupes that promoted the Cook Islands all over the world."

But dancing didn't pay the bills, Maina explained, and Repeta had a lazy drunk of a husband to support back home in Auckland. So when she met this tall, charming stranger one lonely night after a performance in Europe, and he started spending money on her—he started *giving* her money—it was hard to resist his advances.

"They had an affair?"

Maina blushed. "My mother wasn't a bad person," she said.

"Then what was she?"

"A survivor." Maina raised her chin. "Just like me."

"So what happened with Larouche?"

"He stayed close to my mother during that European tour," Maina said. "Never close enough so that the other performers might notice, but he was there. In the background."

"How did it end?"

"The tour finished, and my mother went home to Piri."

"That's it? Larouche just let her walk away?"

"He knew my mother was married," Maina said. "He knew it would be difficult for her to leave her husband. So he let her go. But they managed to keep in touch over the years. That's how he knew she was dying, that I would be left on my own. That's why he came for me."

"So when did you and Larouche finally meet?"

"Only about two weeks ago, when his boat arrived in Pukapuka," Maina said. "He was dropping off textbooks for the schools there. The same books he brought to Rarotonga."

Jack sat back. Combed his hair with his fingers. This wasn't how he'd pictured it playing out. Maina was a Jackal. Maina was one of *them*. She was supposed to be telling him about nasty deeds done in the dead of night. So why was her story instead so warm and fuzzy?

Jack hated. He hated what the Jackals had planned for the Cook Islands. He hated that they had kidnaped Teina and forced her to participate in unspeakable acts. He hated that Alex Benning had nearly ruined his locomotive by ramming into the Endeavor Hotel. He hated that people had died because of that action.

What he really wanted was to hate Maina for being involved in all of this.

But what if she wasn't? The realization staggered him. What if she was simply another pawn in Andre Larouche's master plan?

He had to keep digging. He had to keep asking questions. He had to feed his hate.

"What about your tattoo?"

Maina rubbed at the top of her leg. "That was my father's idea. He said all the crew had one, including him. It's supposed to represent a commitment to teamwork. One of the sailors had a little studio right on the ship. But I don't particularly like the design, so I put it where no one else would see it."

"But the ship was moored in Avatiu Harbor for a good week before you showed up at my place," Jack said. "Where were you all that time?"

"In my cabin," she said. "I was bitten by a dengue mozzie years ago, and every so often, the dengue fever flares up again. I could hardly get out of bed for a week, and I was still feeling crook when I was at your place. You can ask the ship's doctor if you don't believe me."

Jack thought of the five bodies in the morgue. Knew Dr. Charbonneau wouldn't be answering any questions.

"So why bother coming to the house at all?" he said. "Why not just stay on the boat?"

"That was my father's idea," she said. "He sent me ashore to meet up with Maeva and the other girls I knew from dancing. He thought they would trust me more if I was living on the island."

"But these were your friends," Jack said. "Why wouldn't they trust you? Why did they need to trust you?"

"Because my job was to set up dates for my father's employees."

"So you were pimping."

"No," she said sharply. "I was just supposed to ask if any of the girls were interested in spending some time with the crew. Show them around the island. Go out for dinner. That sort of thing."

"Weren't your mates a little young for that?"

"Most of ship's crew are in their early 20s," she said. "Island girls like older guys. Especially if they're papa'a."

"And especially if they have money."

"Look," she said, "it was embarrassing to talk to the girls about it, but my father asked me to do him a favor and I felt it was the least I could do after he made the effort to include me in his life. He could have left me on Pukapuka as an orphan, but he didn't."

Maina took another sip of water. "It didn't seem like such a big deal. The sailors would have some company during their stay here, and I thought the girls might enjoy the attention."

"So basically you used me to establish a home base," Jack said. "You lied to me about how you got to the island. You lied about your plans to move to New Zealand."

"I didn't mean to lie to you."

"So why did you?"

"It was just easier to tell everyone the same story."

"Was there anything you said that wasn't complete bullshit?"

"I told you that I loved you," Maina said softly. "That was true."

Jack sneered. "What would you know about love?"

"I know that my father—my *real* father—loves me."

"Which would explain why he had you tied to a bed in front of a camera with a fat, sweaty man between your legs."

Maina looked down. "He said that was my punishment for doing a runner, for trying to leave before my job was finished."

"And you just accepted that?"

Maina met his eyes again. "I've accepted a lot worse," she said. "Try being raped when you're six years old. That'll change your perspective on a lot of things."

It was shock tactics. It was meant to rock Jack. She'd have to do better than that.

He bulled forward. "And what was Teina being punished for?"

Maina's brow creased. She face-talked: *I don't know.*

"Tell me about Tor." Jack continued to push. "You were together on your father's yacht and then you see him again at Sparky's, but you didn't bother telling me that when you were complaining about Akimo perving you."

Maina nodded. "Yes," she said, "I did see Tor onboard. But he kept to himself and, like I said, I spent most of my time in my cabin. I hardly knew him, but I knew enough to mind my own business and not bother him when he was at the café."

Jack's eyes narrowed. Maina seemed to have all the answers.

"What else were you supposed to do for your father while he was here?"

She shook her head. "Nothing. Just help keep the crew entertained while they made arrangements to deliver the textbooks."

"The books were a diversion."

"Eh?"

"Your father used them as a tool to win his own form of trust on the island."

"What do you mean?"

"He was here to make movies," Jack said bluntly. "Movies of grown men having sex with teenage girls. Including you and Teina. Movies to be displayed and sold on the Internet. It's all part of a master plan that includes conducting sex tours of the South Pacific."

Maina's eyes distended. Her mouth gawped. "What are you talking about?"

Jack read her face. Saw the confusion. Saw that it was genuine. Saw that there was finally a grain of truth.

"Your father," Jack said, "is a pornographer. That's the real reason why he came to the Cook Islands. It had nothing to do with the books. It probably had very little to do with any great desire to meet you, his own daughter. He just wanted the brown girls. And he used you to help recruit them."

Her eyes blinked. Her chin quivered. She was going to cry. He squirmed. "Jack..."

Oh, shit.

He was out of his chair, leaning across the bed. They hugged awkwardly, mindful of the cast, of her wounds. Jack felt her sadness, wet on his shoulder.

"I was so excited about meeting my real father," she sobbed, suddenly looking younger, defenseless. "What am I supposed to do now, Jack? Tell me what to do."

Jack wanted to hate her for the lies, the deceit. For the way *he* was hurting. For the way Nile Ramsay and Ray Chimera and Jordan Baxter and everyone else had violated *him.*

He wanted to hate her. And found that he couldn't. Andre Larouche had used her. His own daughter was just another player whose only value was to help him further his schemes.

He hugged her again. He hugged her for a long time. He hugged her until the painkiller kicked in and she finally relaxed in his arms. Only when he knew that she was sleeping peacefully—when the fiends were no longer disturbing her—did he finally let her go.

Afterwards, he stood outside her door and looked in the tiny window for several minutes. He had no idea that someone was watching him just as intently.

FORTY-EIGHT

Jack was gone. Heather was gone. The hallway was empty. A door opened. A man stepped out, wearing an ill-fitting doctor's smock. He slipped into Maina's room.

Sleep beckoned. It enticed her with the promise of cool sheets. It offered sanctuary, a drifting chamber of calmness where her arm was whole again and she had the island to herself. The beach, the cobalt depths of the lagoon, a plate of chops sizzling at the marketplace. The birds, the rocks, the jagged jungle hues.

This is where she would sleep. This was her island. Her world. Her beauty. No one would ever—

"Girl!"

Fingers deep in the meat of her shoulder.

Go away.

"Wake up."

The sanctuary was fading: the sand, the water. The images shimmered. They quaked. They shattered into a million tiny shards of colored glass.

Maina opened her eyes.

The monsters were back.

"That was quite the night shift," said Elizabeth Katoa, scanning the patient list on the blackboard in the nurses' office. "I'm not sure if I want to start work this morning."

"Tell me about it," said Heather. She sat at one of the desks, her head propped wearily in her hands. "I actually made notes so I wouldn't forget anything in the verbal handover."

Elizabeth plopped down at another desk. "Let me see them," she said

Tor's hand was a slab over her mouth. His face filled her vision.

"No noise," he whispered.

Her head twitched a nod under his weight. He pulled his hand away. She licked mashed lips. She looked past him. The curtains were drawn around the bed. No one could see them.

"What do you want?" she said, careful to keep her voice low.

He went through the bedside locker. "Where are your clothes?"

"Don't know," she said, fighting to keep her eyes open.

He pointed to her pareu. "That will have to do."

He came around to the side of the bed. Slid one arm under her knees, the other under her shoulder blades.

"What are you doing?"

He breathed into her face. "He's not done with you yet."

"OK, I think I've got it all now," Elizabeth said, running her finger over the piece of paper Heather had given her.

"Good," Heather said, standing up. "Because if I don't get out of here soon, I'm going to crawl under this desk and fall asleep right here."

Elizabeth laughed without looking up from her reading.

Heather draped her sweater over one arm, and plucked up her bag from the counter. It was heavy. The kai she had packed for her tea break sat untouched in its depths, nestled beside her friend.

"I'm off then," she said, scooting between the desks.

"Do us a favor, eh?" Elizabeth said.

Heather stopped, hung her head. "What is it?" she intoned.

"You've left the blood pressure machine in one of the rooms," Elizabeth said. "Would you mind terribly fetching it for me while I go through the med book?"

"No worries," Heather said. She stood in the doorway to the office. To the right was the exit to the parking lot, where the nurses' transport waited to take her home. Waited to take her to the soothing confines of her bed.

She turned left.

Heather hesitated just inside Maina's room. She knew this was the last place she had used the blood pressure machine, but she couldn't recall closing the curtain around the bed. It really had been a right royal bitch of a night.

She heard the scuffle of shoe leather on lino. She grabbed the curtain and ripped it aside.

Tor spun to face her. Something sprawled in his arms. It took a second for Heather to register what the big man was holding: Maina. Head hanging. Cast dangling. Pareu gaping.

Heather's eyes were twin muzzles. They shot fire. "What the—"

Tor was quick. And Heather really did need to sleep. He'd released Maina and had his hand halfway to her face before her weary brain could flash the warning that she was in danger.

But Tor was maybe too quick. He'd underestimated the distance between them, how far he needed to stretch to connect. So, when the blow did thud into the edge of Heather's cheek, it wasn't packing his full power.

It was still enough to drop her. Her back slammed against the wall. Her knees accordioned. She collapsed. Her sweater flew. Her bag dumped. Its contents scattered.

Tor turned back to the bed. Heather lay numb on the floor, incapable of movement. She could only watch.

Watch as Tor reached for Maina. Watch as the girl scooted to the far side of the bed, her fear diluting the effects of the painkiller Heather had administered.

Maina squirmed, weighed down by her cast. Tor pawed at her, growling in angry frustration.

Heather's head was heavy. It drooped. Now all she could see was Tor's boots. They scrabbled for traction on the smooth flooring as he wrestled with Maina.

A buzzing. Was it in her head? Was she starting to black out? *Not now!* She had to help Maina.

Her bag was cloth roadkill on the floor beside her. It had divulged a diorama of her life: wallet, brush, hair elastics, surfboard keychain, a tube of lipstick, a package of mints, the emergency tampon, two plastic containers of food, now cold and clotted.

And her best friend: Roland.

Roland's tip moved in small, precise, carefully calibrated circles. Roland shimmied. *Roland buzzed.*

Heather stared at the vibrator. It was 11 inches of black rubber. It had a solid core. It had a hidden compartment where a pair of D batteries nested.

It was *heavy*.

Heather reached out her hand.

She used the wall for support as she struggled to her feet. The room spun as she took her first step. She needed to stop, she needed to regain her balance. But Maina's muffled screams kept her going.

Tor was struggling. He had one hand over Maina's face, the other around her waist, but his centre of balance was extended too far over the bed for him to straighten up.

Maina kicked. She flailed. She bit.

Heather teetered. She swayed. She was boneless. But somehow she made it across the room. She was behind Tor, Roland raised in an unsteady hand. He was too tall. She'd never be able to hit his head with any degree of force. Not with these useless legs holding her up.

She stepped back. She lowered Roland. She finally achieved a semblance of balance.

And then she drove the toe of her white nurse's shoe so deep into Tor's scrotum that she hit bone.

The breath roared out of Tor's mouth as he pulled away from Maina. He jackknifed, both hands jammed high between his legs, gasping. Gurgling. He crashed to his knees, poleaxed. Pivoted slightly, his eyes white platters as they sought the identity of his attacker. Heather saw the blood drain from his face, saw that the ragged scrap of skin on his cheek was now an albino blotch.

His lips moved. He gurgled, "Please."

Heather hefted Roland. Felt its density in her hands. Felt its capacity for damage.

"How tough do you feel now, arsehole?" she snarled into Tor's crumpling face.

She swung the vibrator.

LATER

"... *everyone here at Radio Raro and Teen Scene sends out a big kia orana to Teina McCrystal. We're wishing you a speedy recovery and a quick return to the show. This is the Great and Wonderful Johno bringing you all the—*"

Jack turned the radio off. He didn't need music today. What he needed were the native sounds of the island as he cruised through Avarua's downtown area.

He wanted to hear children playing. School kids calling out to each other as they made their way home. Tourists chattering over ice coffees in sidewalk cafes. Locals gathering outside shops to exchange goss. Even the traffic noise was a comfort to Jack.

These were the sounds of normalcy. The babble and hum and subtle vibrations that defined island life. A life that would never be disrupted by the League of Jackals.

It was mid-afternoon. Normally, Jack would still be at the newspaper office, working on the next edition. *Writing* for the next edition, now that he'd taken over Jordan Baxter's beat. Baxter would have no further need of it. Not for a very long time.

But a voice on the telephone had summoned Jack from his desk, had put him in the cab of his truck. Had afforded him yet another opportunity to soak up the sweet tropical juices of Rarotonga. Of his home.

The voice belonged to Jimmy Tauranga.

"Meet me at the taro patch behind Mii Nekelo's place," the constable said.

"I'm on my way."

"Oh, and Jack?"

"Eh?"

"You might want to leave your camera in your truck. This isn't pretty."

Jack understood. They had found Andre Larouche.

He was nearing the eastern end of town. The Rocket Bar was ahead to his left. A taxi idled in the parking lot. A man climbed out, retrieved a battered suitcase from the boot, and paid the driver.

Traffic was leisurely. A measured flow. It afforded Jack the opportunity to watch as the stranger made his way toward the bar's stairs. He had time to note the man's flash pareu shirt, the Ben Franklin sunglasses that provided shade from another broiler of a day in the South Pacific.

Jack smiled to himself. Roger Henderson would have more stories to tell his regulars.

And Jack would hear all of them. But that would come later. All in good time. In due time. In island time.

THE END

Printed in the United States
21494LVS00001B/532-558